WHAT
YOU SEE

FORGE BOOKS BY HANK PHILLIPPI RYAN

The Other Woman
The Wrong Girl
Truth Be Told
What You See

WHAT YOU SEE

HANK PHILLIPPI RYAN

A TOM DOHERTY ASSOCIATES BOOK
NEW YORK

WHAT YOU SEE

Copyright © 2015 by Hank Phillippi Ryan

A Forge Book
Published by Tom Doherty Associates, LLC
175 Fifth Avenue
New York, NY 10010

www.tor-forge.com

Forge® is a registered trademark of Tom Doherty Associates, LLC.

Library of Congress Cataloging-in-Publication Data

Ryan, Hank Phillippi.
    What you see / Hank Phillippi Ryan. — First edition.
        p. cm. — (Jane Ryland ; 4)
    ISBN 978-0-7653-7495-0 (hardcover)
    ISBN 978-0-7653-7498-1 (e-book)
    1. Women journalists—Fiction.   2. Police—Massachusetts—Boston—Fiction.
I. Title.
    PS3618.Y333W48 2015
    813'.6—dc23

                                                          2015023330

Our books may be purchased in bulk for promotional, educational, or business use. Please contact your local bookseller or the Macmillan Corporate and Premium Sales Department at (800) 221-7945, extension 5442, or by e-mail at MacmillanSpecialMarkets@macmillan.com.

First Edition: October 2015

Printed in the United States of America

0 9 8 7 6 5 4 3 2 1

To my father. For music and poetry, and everything, and especially this:

1971

HANK: *I have no idea what I'm doing, Dad. Every day, I'm just making it up as I go.*

DAD: *That's what everyone's doing, honey. Just making it up as they go.*

It's not what you look at that matters. It's what you see.
—Henry David Thoreau

What we see depends mainly on what we are looking for.
—John Lubbock

Things don't change. *You* change *your way of looking, that's all.*
—Carlos Castaneda

WHAT
YOU SEE

1

"*Some*body saw *some*thing. And most of them took pictures of it." Detective Jake Brogan watched the uniforms try to corral the chaos of tourists and brown-bag-toting Bostonians while two crime scene units unspooled parallel rolls of their yellow plastic tape. Sirens wailed, three EMTs leaped from a red-and-white ambulance, the beeping Walk signal ordered clustering pedestrians to cross Congress Street, and angry drivers honked disapproval as police cadets in orange bandoliers signaled all cars to stop.

Jake had heard screams through the plate-glass window of the Bell in Hand, abandoned his carry-out roast beef sub on the restaurant counter, ran half a block. Found this. Radioed his partner. Lunch hour, now put on hold by murder.

"Wall-to-wall spectators, the good news and the bad news." Paul DeLuca shaded his eyes with one hand. The two detectives had split up to grab lunch, D opting for the corner Dunkin's. DeLuca still held his iced coffee, third of the day. "Who called nine-one-one? Anybody run away?"

"That's what we're about to find out," Jake said. "Most cases, nobody saw anything. Here's the opposite. Too many witnesses. That's a new one."

In the center of the circular redbrick plaza, in the noontime shadow of the burnished bronze knee of the Mayor Curley statue, some poor soul in a once-white shirt lay facedown, his running shoes splayed, a navy blue Sox cap teetering on the concrete, the hilt of a knife protruding absurdly between his shoulder blades. Jake had immediately radioed the medical examiner, who was now only minutes away. They'd need to dispatch the cleanup team, too. With the Fourth of July a month from now, the mayor would go ballistic over the growing puddle of red staining this concrete pathway along the visitor-magnet Freedom Trail. So much for the beginning of tourist season.

Across the street, in the teeming marketplace behind Faneuil Hall, persistent vendors offered Sam Adams tricorns, BOSTON STRONG T-shirts, and plastic lobster souvenirs. Visitors unlucky enough to witness this noontime stabbing had already received a souvenir they'd likely want to forget. But not until Jake picked their brains. And cell phone histories.

"I want names. I want addresses," he told DeLuca. "I want their phones and I want their cameras."

From moment one, Jake knew this would be a mess. Some of these people would lie, some would make stuff up, some would see things that never existed, some would have something to hide. Some would run. Complicating it all, he and DeLuca technically needed individual warrants to seize property. If any onlooker knew the law and gave them grief about it, it'd be even more of a shit show.

He pointed his partner toward the cadets. "The supe sent the new kids to 'help.' *All* we need. Tell them not to let any witness leave without giving contact information."

"Where're we gonna put 'em all, though?" DeLuca sucked a hit of coffee through a clear straw. "The Garden? Maybe they can watch *Disney On Ice* while we get their deets."

DeLuca had a point. Even the bleachers of the nearby Boston Garden sports arena were no solution. How could Jake keep fifty or so witnesses, from little kids to one guy in a wheelchair, in semi-custody while a group of cadets practiced collecting personal information and asking for photos?

"If we'd gone to Santarpio's like I wanted, we'd be all the way in Eastie," Jake said. "Dispatch might have sent someone else to handle this mess."

"There is no someone else," DeLuca pointed out. "Vacation time, budget cuts, short staffing. We get the short straw."

"We get all the straws," Jake said.

A lanky blue-uniformed EMT wearing lavender latex gloves, black running shoes, and a pencil stabbed through her graying ponytail trotted up to the two of them. She gestured toward the two medics kneeling over the victim.

"Not a whole lot to tell, Detectives. White male, approximately forty-five years old, deceased. Stab wound to the back. Just the one. Happened, I'd say, pretty much instantly," she said. "We got here at twelve-oh-four. Called it at twelve-oh-five. Knife's still in, wouldn't have mattered. Thought the ME should see it as is. We'll let her look for ID."

"She's on the way. Thanks, Doc," Jake said. EMT Deborah Kratky wasn't actually a doctor, but she'd been on the job long enough to know as much as any medic. She'd even been there to see a rookie Jake handle his first homicide. It was up in the Blue Hills, a disturbingly arranged female corpse, turned out the victim of a Boston Strangler copycat. Ten years later, Jake no longer felt like throwing up at crime scenes. Not necessarily a good thing. Cops get bored, cops make mistakes. Jake never wanted to get used to murder.

"Anybody know anything?" he asked. "See anything? Say anything?"

"Not to me." Doc looked back at the crime scene, hands on hips, one eyebrow raised. "Crap. Would *you* stand there? With your little kid? Rubbernecking a dead person? Blood on the sidewalk? I sure wouldn't, if it wasn't my job."

A dusty yellow city bus, emblazoned GO BSO, wheezed up to the stop across from the bank. One of the cadets waved both arms at the driver, signaling him to move on. Faces peered from each square window, a puff of exhaust pluming to the curb as the bus pulled away.

"Whoever did it's gotta be big, lot of muscle. One blow like that?" Jake scanned the crowd for anyone who fit the bill. Would the killer be dumb or strange or crazy enough to hang around? Cadets were taking names, writing on clipboards. Couple of people tried to leave, didn't succeed. Most were texting, calling, taking photos. *Better not be erasing anything.* Evidence these days was ephemeral. One click of a button, it got zapped into nothing.

"Big? Maybe. Or maybe angry. Or full of adrenaline. Or drugged up. And spattered with blood," Doc Kratky said. "Maybe. Unless he—or she—has already dropped their clothing somewhere."

"In which case we're screwed," D said.

"One step at a time," Jake said. "Look at all those phones. Each one's got a possible photo."

Might as well try to stay positive. Maybe the days of relying on tiny specks of evidence in glassine bags, untrustworthy eyewitnesses, and fabricated alibis would fade into law enforcement history, as antiquated as a posse on horseback, wiped out by night-scope lenses and twenty-four-hour videos and satellite pings. They'd nailed the Marathon bombers using video from department store surveillance. All they needed to catch this bad guy was someone who'd clicked a cell phone camera at exactly the right time.

"Makes you understand how movie stars feel, right? Paparazzi?" Doc said. "Guess that's good for you guys, though. Reporters will be here soon, no doubt, trolling for tourist cam photos."

Ordinarily, Jake would be wondering whether "reporters" might mean Jane. This time he knew it wouldn't.

"What you see is what you get," DeLuca said. "Cameras don't lie."

"Witnesses do," Jake said.

Still, whatever was caught on camera could be their ace in the hole. Some of the bars that lined one side of Congress Street, not to mention the monolith City Hall itself on the other side, must have security systems. Those videos they could instantly seize.

"So we won't transport till the ME—" Jake heard two quick beeps of a horn, Kat's signal she was arriving. Jake knew she hated the siren. *No rush for me to get there,* she always said. *No need to announce another death.* "Speak of the devil."

The gawkers turned, each camera and cell phone now pointed toward North Street and the blocky white van, stenciled in black letters MEDI-CAL EXAMINER. The right-side wheels jumped the curb onto the side-walk. The driver's-side door clanged open, slammed closed. Jane always referred to Dr. Katharine McMahon as one of those Russian dolls in a doll, all dark hair and red lips and curves. Jane and Kat had taken a month or so to reach feminine détente, but they were okay now. Under her white medical jacket, Jake saw that Kat's hot pink T-shirt said LOVE IT LOCAL.

"See that?" DeLuca whispered. "You bet I will."

"Have some respect," Jake said.

"Why start now?" DeLuca said.

"So why'd you leave the *Register*?"

The very question, word for word, that Jane Ryland feared most. And the very question, word for word, that Jane had no idea how to answer.

Channel 2's news director, Marshall Tyson, all smiles and pinstripes, office strategically landscaped with award statues and celebrity photos and one duPont gold baton, had sprung it on her, but only after an excruciating half hour of niceties and journalism chitchat, followed by a play-by-play commentary on the A-block of the noon *Eyewitness News*, the broadcast still under way from the newsroom anchor desk outside his corner office.

"Well, it's complicated," Jane began.

Complicated wasn't even the word. It was a mess, from moment one, a mess.

Jane had walked the gauntlet of speculation, escorted by a chatty assignment desk intern, weaving through the newsroom's warren of cluttered desks and flickering computer monitors toward Tyson's office. Jane would be recognized, of course, from back when she was an on-air competitor. In the news business, which "talent" was "crossing the street" to a rival station was the most delicious topic of gossip, even better than who got fired for stealing promotional swag from the mail room, which reporters were getting sued, and why the noon anchor kept so many extra clothes in her office. No outsiders knew the scoop on what happened to Jane at the *Boston Register* last month. And how could she explain it?

In the midst of triumphant headlines at the *Register,* her investigation had uncovered a problem close to home. Jane proved a longtime reporter there had been fabricating stories. *For years.* Bad enough, but the clincher was worse. The newspaper decided to cover it up. Ignore it.

For Jane, that left only two choices.

She could be complicit. Or she could quit.

If she ratted out the paper for using fabricated stories, she'd argued, didn't it also put articles by *all* the reporters in question? If the public suspected some were partly fiction, would readers ever believe anything?

So here she was, once again a victim of her own damn ethics. Here she was, at the TV station that used to be her biggest competitor, discussing her third reporting job in five years. Not the most reliable-sounding résumé for a thirty-four-year-old, even in the nomadic climb-the-ladder world of journalism.

The intercom buzzed, and Tyson's cell phone *ping*ed with a text.

"Sorry, Jane." The news director tapped on his keyboard with one hand, used the other to grab his phone, tucking it under his chin. "Gotta take this."

At least this time she wasn't a supplicant. Marshall Tyson had called *her,* using a "heard you're no longer with the paper" opening ploy in his voice mail, followed by "come chat if you're interested in getting back on the air, if you're not too busy."

Busy? Jane had rolled her eyes as she listened to his message. Oh, she was busy. Busy being unemployed again. Busy facing her younger sister's wedding this coming weekend. Busy entertaining bride-to-be Lissa, arriving in Boston this afternoon. Busy prepping to meet her sister's fiancé, "Dan the man of mystery," Jane privately called him, who'd arrive whenever Daniel Fasullo's corporate jet landed from whatever exotic overseas location. Busy preparing for a trip home to the Chicago suburbs to play maid of honor.

The good news: Jake had promised to come with her to Chicago. This weekend.

Now that she was unemployed, and therefore no longer encumbered by the reporter/source prohibition against dating, she and Jake had been experimenting with going public with their . . . whatever it was. Relationship. Still being careful. But not always hiding.

Tyson was still deep in his phone conversation, looking out into the newsroom as he spoke. Jane followed his gaze, saw three young women at the assignment desk with two phones each plastered to their ears. Something was going on.

"When?" Tyson glanced at her, rolling his eyes in apology. She waved him off. She understood news came first. Anyway, it gave her time to think.

If Channel 2 offered her a job, did she want to go back to TV? Her bank account could certainly use the paycheck. And if the good guys quit, who'd be left? Maybe she could make a deal with Tyson to do only in-depth stories, groundbreaking investigative stuff.

Yes or no? Saying yes would mean she and Jake would have to return to the shadows. Right now, in this news director's office, she had to decide: Love or money? Seemed like she was doomed not to have both.

But wait.

She could simply say maybe. Consider it, talk to Jake. If Channel 2 wanted her, they would wait. She mentally acknowledged her own wisdom, patted herself on the emotional back. She had control of her life. She needed to remember that.

Tyson raised a palm to her, pantomiming *sorry, one moment,* as he stood. His door opened. The newcomer, horn-rims and oxford shirt, clipboard, looked at Jane, assessing.

"Sorry to interrupt, Marsh, but—"

"We got anyone who can go over there?" the news director asked. He'd hung up the phone without saying good-bye. "Jane, this is Derek Estabrooks, our assignment guy. Derek? Anyone?"

"Negative, that's the thing. Hey, Jane." He acknowledged her with a quick up and down. "We got the morning crews doing outta-town live shots for the noon, and the next shift is the two thirty people, so we're kinda screw—"

"You ever do freelance, Jane?" The news director, interrupting, pointed a forefinger at her. "We've got a big story we can send you on. Right now. You up for it? But we gotta have an answer. Right now. Yes or no?"

2

He'd gotten the shot. Totally what happened—well, not exactly totally, maybe. Bobby hadn't been at Curley Park from the exact moment one. But how cool was it that the bus was late, and he'd been running behind for class anyway, and he always had his camera ready just in case. And blam, he'd clicked off, like, twenty shots in a row.

Had he gotten a good one of the stabbing? Of the person running away? He thought so, even just the back of him. Or her. He couldn't wait to see, but he couldn't take the time to check yet. If he had? This'd be big.

Bobby Riaz tried to look small and inconspicuous, his RED SUX T-shirt, with, like, the same typeface as Red Sox, so people sometimes didn't get it, *morons,* was pretty much covered by his work shirt. Plus, nobody was looking at him right now. They were all looking at the dead guy under the Curley statue.

Television had that "Send it to 2" thing, where they'd show your photos or video or whatever. All he wanted was to be part of it. Get discovered. Move to LA and hit the big time. Photographer to the stars.

So far he'd been on "Send it" once, last winter, when that truck jack-knifed off the Longfellow Bridge, and he'd gotten that photo from underneath, some kind of hot liquid sizzling down into the snow from however the engine worked, and those two huge tires hanging off the edge into nowhere. They'd put his actual name on the screen, *photo credit Bobby R,* for about five seconds, maybe more, but then they'd put it on the website, too. So it was almost like having a published photo, right? All except for the money. And he bet he could get big money for today's. From someone. He just had to figure out who.

Luckily it wasn't as hot as it had been, even though the sun was a bitch today. He twisted his camo cap around so the bill was shading his eyes, then turned it the cool way again. Life was all about the image. The sun was making weird glares on everything, and the trees, totally leafy and totally in the way, didn't help. But he'd gotten something, he was sure. He had the eye. Even his mom said so.

His mom also said he'd get in trouble someday with his picture taking, but she was wrong, what did she know? The paparazzi were all over television, got big bucks and hung out with rock stars. Well, not exactly hung out, since they were always suing them and shit, but he was gonna be different. He figured that if you were nice to people, let them know you understood their fame, they'd let you take their pix.

And this moment, this very moment, might be the time his future would begin. But who would he be when that happened? He had to plan.

Who he was now? Bobby Riaz. What a sucky name. His mom's name was Jones, even suckier. Maybe he'd be Rob Something, maybe. Rob Avedon? Which was totally made up and didn't have anything to do with who he really was, but Avedon was a famous photographer, he'd learned that in class, and maybe people would think he was related. Who'd know? The guy was dead. Maybe he could be Bobby Arbus, after Diane. She was totally cool, and dead, too.

Kodak, that was too weird. Bobby Polaroid? He burst out laughing, then choked it back when some lady beside him took her eyes off the dead guy long enough to frown at him. Right, laughing at a murder, not cool. He coughed to cover it up. Pretended to talk into his Bluetooth earpiece. "Oh, so funny," he said to no one. "But can't talk now."

Oh. He had it! Bobby Land. Like Polaroid-Land, which he'd learned in class, too, a guy no one even knew about anymore. No one could argue about Bobby Land. He'd just let people think he was from a famous—and rich—family. Couldn't hurt, and might even help.

Bobby Land the famous photographer. What was the Boston thing?

One if by Land? He laughed again and got another glare from the stupid woman. He clicked off a shot of her when she wasn't looking. Take that, sweetheart. There's one by Land.

I'll help you, Tenley's mother had told her. *Get your foot in the door,* her father had told her. "You already love computers, honey," her mom had persisted, trying to brush her only daughter's bangs out of her eyes. "You'll love this, too."

But here she was. Far from loving it. *Dying.* Tenley Siskel's eyes were glazing over. Completely dying.

There was no way she could do this for much longer, none, let alone for the whole summer. She'd been literally *imprisoned* here in the City Hall traffic surveillance room a full solid three weeks now. She almost hadn't managed to drag herself in here this Monday morning. All she could think about was lunch, and then how forever it was until four thirty.

The clock was literally not even moving.

Tenley eyed the others in the monitoring center. Losers. Eyes on their screens. So intent on making sure not one little thing in their assigned sectors of Boston escaped their scrutiny. If she had a choice, she'd never set one foot in this place again.

Maybe, after she quit, she'd stand down there on the sidewalk and wave up at the surveillance cameras. She pictured it, could almost see it, her giving the finger to loser city. On video. That'd be hilarious. They didn't even save the digital fields, so they couldn't prove she'd ever done it. Hilarious.

She understood Mom thought she was doing a good thing by finagling this three-month job for her. You needed about zero brain level to do it, and she was only a fill-in while the zeros who worked here took turns having their pitiful summer vacations. And not too deep down, Tenley felt bad about complaining. Mom—and Dad, too—had enough to think about.

The green digital numbers on her monitor proved it had been one minute since she'd last looked. Her ears felt weirdly light, because her mother warned her City Hall "frowned on piercings." She adjusted her cardigan, buttoned carefully over her white T-shirt. As long as no one could see what was printed on it, they couldn't "frown" on that. She'd roll up the waistband of her skirt the second she got out of here. But this was, like, her disguise. She wore it during the part of her life she simply had to endure.

Tenley started her video scan again, beginning in the upper left, like her supervisor had shown her the first day. Ward Dahlstrom had explained, in his "boss" voice, that she had sector one, the perimeter of City Hall. Like that was some huge whoop. If her mother was such a big shot around here, why couldn't she get Tenley a more interesting job? But at least here she didn't have to talk to anyone. Sometimes she hated to actually speak to people. You had to face them, watch them looking at you. You'd know what they were thinking, all critical and worried and smothery. And curious. Just dying to ask you a question.

Camera one, pointed northwest, the pedestrians on Cambridge Street, going to lunch, which of course *she* couldn't do for another twenty-seven minutes, since Dahlstrom had given her the last lunch on the schedule, jerk that he was. She stared at the screen, at the boxy green "camera one" symbol blinking in the upper right corner, at the video pixels degrading around the edges, fluttering with its attempt to keep up with reality. But—nothing. The camera's eye saw nothing she was supposed to watch for, no traffic jams, no disabled cars, not even a jaywalker. A world where nothing happened. Like a metaphor for her life. These days, at least.

Surveillance fatigue, she'd read about it, and she could totally see how it happened. She was already sick of watching these screens, cars and traffic lights, buses and motorcycles. People on camera were mostly blurs. If the light was exactly right, a face might come into focus, but only for a fraction of a second, just long enough to be annoying.

Her stomach grumbled, the last of the morning's double-toasted-cut-in-half-and-then-half-again-the-other-way-with-extra-cream-cheese sesame bagel having long worn off. She could not believe she couldn't bring coffee to her computer console. How was she supposed to live without coffee? Dahlstrom had said all liquids were verboten, a fireable offense. She'd looked up "verboten." Fired over forbidden coffee. Might be worth it.

Camera two. She had to focus. Southwest, the brick expanse of City Hall Plaza, little makeshift stands selling cupcakes and bunches of flowers and home-grown vegetables. Blah blah blah. What if, like in one of her games, a huge flame-spewing dragon stomped its way across the—

She blew out a breath, willed herself not to look at the clock. Camera three. Nothing happening. Changed the screen.

Camera four, the monolith of the JFK Federal Building. Fuzzy pedestrians, nothing *ever* happened here. Why'd they have a camera? Worried some terrorists would rob the ancient basement coffee shop? Make off with a stash of expired candy bars? Ticktock, change the screen.

Camera five, northeast, she could actually see the Dunkin' Donuts, *thanks, universe* for once again pointing out what she couldn't have. A limousine sailed by, and Tenley imagined who might be inside, all leather and champagne.

Sometimes, just for grins, she looked for celebrities. Last Wednesday, she saw a guy who, for a second, she really thought was her fave singer Lachlan Zane, very underground and totally alt, and she'd considered maybe rocking a screen save, and maybe even selling it to one of the places that put cool or embarrassing stuff on TV, like that guy in the elevator, or that star who always destroyed hotel rooms.

It seemed like kind of a terrific idea until she'd realized how easy it would be to trace, and she'd be in deep trouble. Who knew what would have happened then, not to mention the level of grief she'd have to take from her parents.

Camera six. All fuzz. Pigeons nested in the little place above the screen and fritzed the heck out of it, pecking at the lens and perching on the connection. She'd report it. Soon.

Camera seven. Aimed at North Street and Faneuil Hall—Fan-You-Will, she called it, instead of Fan-yool, just to drive her mother crazy. She leaned forward, narrowing her eyes at the monitor. *Weird.* The shot was from high up, through the leafy trees, so it was like she was looking down from three stories onto the street. A row of touristy bars. The University Inn. The little alley by the wine store. The cameras were supposed to watch traffic and pedestrians on the streets, but—*weird.*

Funny that there were so many people in this shot and so few in cameras four and five.

Tenley clicked the silver mouse to bring in a closer shot. She'd been in Curley Park a million times, it was right across from her bus stop. She couldn't see much except trees, and tops of heads, and shadows. But there was sure an ambulance there.

Lacing her fingers under her chin, Tenley stared at the computer screen.

Would she get yelled at for missing whatever happened down here? She was following protocol, and she couldn't oversee every little place every little minute. She wasn't even supposed to. This was streaming video, live, and only archived if a viewer pushed the Record button to put twenty seconds into what they called the "video cache." But she hadn't pushed Record, because she hadn't seen anything. Not her fault.

The ambulance doors were open, and it was parked. She could see the dark outfits of the EMTs scurrying around. It had definitely been longer than twenty seconds since whatever happened began.

Her therapist promised that telling the truth could never hurt you. Was that really right? She'd only been following the rules, changing screens, it took a certain amount of time to look at seven cameras, the powers that be had to understand that. If she failed, at whatever, it was because the rules had made her fail. It seemed like she couldn't stop making the wrong decisions.

She leaned forward, narrowing her eyes. The shape of the crowd was changing. What was going on down there?

3

"Down that way—in the alley!" The cadet grabbed Jake's arm, and Jake followed the kid's pointing finger toward the narrow curved passage between the bank and the liquor store. "Some guy's apparently hiding in a Dumpster. Down there. Or put something in the Dumpster. Something like that." The cadet gulped for air, trying to get the words out. "A girl—I mean, a woman—told me. Anyway, what if it's the—"

"Who told you? Where'd she come from?" Jake needed specifics. "Where is she now? This girl-woman? What'd she say?"

"Ah, I don't know, she just said—what I said. The Dumpster. We were all taking names and addresses, see, they're still doing that, like you wanted, and she came up to me and—" The cadet's black plastic name tag said BRAD LONNERGAN. Lonnergan pointed again, jabbing the air. "Down *there*. What if it's the guy who—"

"You kidding me? Do you see her? Find her." This Lonnergan kid was not clear on the law enforcement concept. "Hold her. Do not let her leave. Understand? D!"

Jake signaled DeLuca with one finger. *Me. You. That way. Let's go.*

They couldn't afford to spook the crowd. All he needed, a mob following them into Franklin Alley, hooting like medieval peasants while they dragged some poor jerk from a Dumpster. Jake, checking to make sure D was behind him, snaked behind the spectators, dodging and weaving. Only one or two seemed to notice they were on the move. He and D didn't look like cops, after all. Just two guys wearing jeans and leather jackets. Walking fast.

Jake glanced over his shoulder again. Most eyes focused on Kat Mc-Mahon, the ME now kneeling over the victim. For once, better to keep it that way. Cadets—the ones with brains—were taking names and addresses. Asking if anyone saw anything. Asking spectators with cameras and cell phones to stand by. The whole thing was already verging on out of control. And now this.

But maybe this would solve the whole damn case and they all could go home.

Ahead of them, the alley. Cracked pavement, cobblestones scattered with gravel. Framed on the right by the bank's brand-new red brick, on the left by the pockmarked brownstone of Jodi's Liquors and the University Inn. With its twists and turns, only the first ten feet or so of Franklin were visible from the street. Jake knew it was a dead end. If someone was in there, like Lonnergan's "girl-woman" said, there'd be no way out except toward him and DeLuca. A bad guy who planned where he was going, or was at least familiar with this part of the city, would never have chosen this as an escape route. Unless he was panicking. Or hurt. Or trying to hide, waiting it out.

Or luring them in? Trapping them?

At the curb, Jake stopped, put up a hand, assessing. DeLuca skidded to a halt, almost slamming into Jake's back. Broad daylight, not like anyone could surprise them. The quiet hubbub of Curley Park softened into background.

One second, two.

Jake felt for his Glock, drew it, felt the sun on his face. A seagull squawked, swooping, headed for the harbor. *Lured into a dead-end alley?* Windows above. Rooftops. Where was the woman who'd sent them down here? Who was she? Whose side was she on? What if—well, there were too many what-ifs to consider right now.

"You ready?" he said.

"Ready," DeLuca said.

"On my three." Jake began, "One."

"Help!" A voice, from down the alley. "Help me!"

"Three," Jake said.

A dead body, a stabbing in Curley Park. And Jane was on the way.

It wasn't funny, not one bit of apparent murder was funny—Jane zoomed her Audi around the curve and onto Atlantic Ave.—but the fact that she, Jane Elizabeth Ryland, who two hours ago had been out of work was now on the way to cover a homicide, clearly proved the universe had a droll sense of humor.

She was simply to "gather facts," Marsh Tyson had instructed, and phone them in to the assignment desk. If it turned out to be big breaking news, she certainly *could* go on camera, since she'd dolled up in a black suit, black patent heels, and Gram's pearls for the non-job non-interview. She hadn't done a live shot for almost a year, but she had to admit the idea of live TV felt like home.

She shifted into third, open road ahead, past the Coast Guard building. Life was strange. She'd given the *Register* blockbuster stories—political corruption, an adoption scandal, mortgage fraud. And what did she get? Unemployment. But now, Jane Ryland was back. Freelance, sure, but with a lovely per diem. Take that, mortgage payment.

Only one snag. When Lissa arrived in Boston this afternoon, Jane might have to work. Lissa—who, Jane always forgot, demanded to be called "Melissa" after all these years—and her fiancé were coming to pick up their flower girl, Gracie Fasullo, Daniel's nine-year-old daughter who lived in Boston with his ex-wife and her new husband. Thanks to Daniel's previous marriage, Melissa was becoming Gracie's instant stepmother. The whole complicated thing sounded like the guilty-pleasure soap operas she and best friend Amy used to watch in college. In real life, what soap opera role was Jane playing? Older sister, living alone with a cat?

No, Jane decided. I'll be the successful reporter, determined and unstoppable, who breaks big stories and needs help from no one. I'll even call her Melissa.

"La-di-da," she said out loud. "Bring it on." *Jane Ryland, reporting for Channel 2,* she thought, trying it out. *Can do.*

She snapped the radio to all-news, listened through the crowd predictions for the Fourth of July concert on the Esplanade, the Chamber of Commerce estimate of tourist dollars for the summer, stories about the drunken antics of a state senator caught on a hotel surveillance camera, another runaway college girl, some kind of lobster shortage. Nothing about a stabbing.

Shortcut through the Greenway, into the glare of the noontime sun. Right turn on North Street. Definitely something going on. The red light from an ambulance flared over the cluster of onlookers, a zigzag backlit silhouette of heads and shoulders. Usually Jane would be able to see the tree-lined edge of Curley Park from this vantage point, but now the circle of grass and sculpture was blocked by the array of T-shirts and backpacks and shopping bags. A scowling cadet, too-big hat and orange webbed bandolier, was pointing oncoming traffic to turn left, away from the crime scene. So what? Jane was different. Jane was TV news. Jane was turning right.

She downshifted, touched her brakes, buzzed down her window, and leaned out, smiling. The sun hit her square in the face and glinted from the car's side mirror as the driver behind her honked, twice, then swerved to the left.

"Jane Ryland," she told the newbie cop. She'd done this a million times. She tried to stop herself from tossing her hair, because know what? This felt good.

"Channel 2 News," she added. Big smile.

The cop lifted his wire-rimmed Ray-Bans, narrowed his eyes at her.

Probably recognizing me, Jane decided. Next thing, he'll be waving me past the police lines and into the center of the action. She was back.

"Let's see some ID," the cop said.

4

"*Now* we're talking," Bobby Land whispered to himself, nodding, as he watched the woman in the black Audi argue with the cop. He recognized her, all right. That was Jane Ryland, the reporter, the one who had been fired or whatever, but she was still a hotshot, and hot, too, for someone her age. Was she his ticket to a new life?

He couldn't hear her, or the cop, but their bodies showed they were all about arguing. It was like watching one of those old silent movies, where you knew what was going on just from how they were acting. Jane had pulled up to the crime scene tape in front of the University Inn and was leaning out the driver's-side window, pointing toward the park. The cop was taking off his sunglasses, giving her grief, waving her off. She showed him something from her wallet, sticking it out the window. The guy shook his head again, pushed it away with both hands, turned to the other cars.

What was the big problem? Jane was a reporter, the real thing, every-fricking-body knew that. Obviously needed to get to the "scene of the crime." She called out to the cop, yelling at his back. Now she'd opened the door and got out, engine running, and walked up to the cop, still talking. Chick had balls.

"Let her through, moron." Bobby spoke out loud, since the cop couldn't possibly hear him. This could be Bobby's big break. He could see it now—Jane would go over to check out the dead guy. Bobby'd go up to her, tell her the deal. Say what he saw. See if she'd be interested in seeing his photos. Correction—in *buying* his photos. If they were any good.

His whole entire future might be contained in his little camera.

He must have gotten something. He didn't actually think about what was on the other side of the lens, not while he was shooting, he just click-click-clicked and checked later for the results. In this kind of on-the-spot breaking news, the action was so fast you couldn't take the time to think. Just point, shoot, and hope.

He watched Jane continue to negotiate with the cop. He felt like he could call her Jane, he used to see her on TV when he was still in high school, and they'd watched her online story about bad adoptions in his journalism class and—*hey*. From the corner of his eye. *Now what?*

He watched two obvious cops, leather jackets dead giveaways, sidle through the crowd, moving quickly and deliberately. Where were they going? Seemed headed toward that alley by the bank. Maybe better to follow them? What if they were on the way to a big takedown, and he could get the whole thing on camera? That'd make his career, right there. *Oh, yes, I got photos of it all,* he'd say to Jane. How much will you pay me for them? Two hundred dollars, maybe. Three.

He checked his battery, fine, plenty of juice. Now Jane was handing the guy a cell phone, maybe she'd called someone to convince the cadet to let her through. Maybe she didn't need his help and he should—where did the two plainclothes cops go? He eyed the crowd till he finally saw them, the skinny one and the preppy one, poised on the curb, focused down that alley. Someone, or some*thing,* was back there, no question. No one else seemed to care about those two, all the morbid onlookers still fascinated by the dead guy. But he, Bobby Land, had the eye. His mother always said so.

Cops? Or reporter? Which would be more useful to follow? Which would give him the faster claim to fame?

*   *   *

With the help of a credential-confirming phone call from the Channel 2 assignment desk, Jane finally negotiated her way to the perimeter of the crime scene. She'd left her car at the University Inn, given ten bucks to the hotel's valet guy to watch over it.

She paused, taking it all in. A nothing day, early June, lunchtime. That shockingly blue sky Boston sometimes lucked into. There was always the first moment at a murder scene, always having to juggle the stress of getting the story with the realization that someone's life was over. Her job was to report what she saw, what she heard, what she could discover. An odd career choice, really, to be the eyes and ears of the public. Observer, always, never a participant. And because it was "news," she had to do it as quickly as she could. A constant series of assessments, decisions, choices. Perceptions. So much of reality wasn't what it seemed at first glance.

Cadets had grouped spectators into packs of five or six, obviously taking names and info. That meant each and every one of those people was a potential eyewitness. A potential interview.

She'd record their sound on the Quik-Shot, the little video camera the station had given her. The size of a cigarette pack, unobtrusive, but wide format and surprising quality. The days of the hulking photogs lugging huge cameras were over—Jane could point and shoot and get it on the air, what they called a one-man band. The photographers' unions weren't happy about it. But it sometimes made things easier.

Jane pulled out the Quik-Shot, crossing mental fingers. Nothing like the first time using unfamiliar equipment. Nothing like trying it out with no practice. At a murder. If the red light was on, was that good, the universal signal for "camera rolling"? Or bad, the universal sign for "warning"? Jane would roll off a few shots, then check for audio and video quality.

They hadn't moved the victim yet, good thing. She got as close as she could, pushing through the looky-loos, then pointed the lens, rolling off thirty seconds as close up as appropriate—no blood allowed on Channel 2 News, so medium tight was all that would air. Then a wider shot, showing all the medics, then even wider, showing the crowd. Pan across to reveal the number of people. Tight shots of a few on their cells, a few others clicking off photos.

She was taking pictures of people taking pictures. Very twenty-first century.

The medical examiner was already there, meaning someone had died. Kat McMahon might slip her some inside info, if she could get to her. The two women still weren't sure of each other, still skittish about their conflicting responsibilities—Jane's to tell and Kat's not to—but Jake had let it slip that Kat and DeLuca were an item. So there was some solidarity in mutual professionally iffy behavior.

What had happened here? Jane would need to ask around, see if any of the onlookers saw anything revealing. She'd look for tweets, too, and Facebook posts. She could imagine the texts. *OMG, I'm at a murder!* The cops were certainly trolling for video, too. And they had dibs. Unless Jane got lucky.

Wide, medium, tight. Pan of the crowd. Establishing shots. She hit the double backward arrows—that *had* to mean rewind—hit Stop, then the one forward arrow, and after half a second of snow and a twist of color, saw the whole thing again on the tiny screen. Okay. It worked.

She stopped for a moment, the sun hot on her hair. An empty brown paper bag caught the breeze, fluttered, and flapped away. Someone had left a big phone book on the bench. Cops were everywhere. Was there anything she'd forgotten?

Across the street sat the grotesque gray stone façade of the monolithic Boston City Hall, a controversial and unattractive expanse of concrete and double-tall plate glass. She shot the exterior to illustrate the irony that this crime occurred right under the noses of the city officials. She zoomed in to one window in particular. The mayor's office.

Mayor Elihu Holbrooke—or someone in his office—could probably have seen what happened right from that window.

She tucked that thought away for later. This wasn't going to be her story, she reminded herself. She was a per diem. A freelance. A TV temp. Not that anything in TV wasn't temporary.

Now the interviews. She scouted the onlookers. Saw a possibility.

"I'm—" Jane began.

"Yes, I've watched you on TV, Jane," the woman said.

Bingo. Jane aimed the little camera.

"Could you tell me what you saw?" Jane had chosen the woman—khaki linen suit, possibly-diamond stud earrings, and leather briefcase—because she was reasonably well dressed, looked like she spoke English, didn't seem in a hurry. Profiling, sure, but the key was to get usable sound bites, articulate, containing actual information. Emotion, if you were lucky. Jane was also careful about diversity. It all mattered, requiring more judgment than simply sticking a mic at some random face. Unless that was your only option.

"I suppose so," the woman said.

To keep the context, Jane composed her shot so the circular park and the wide-open doors of the ambulance were in the background. This time of day, the sunlight was impossible. The only choices were squinty eyes or glary backlighting. Jane opted for sun on the woman's face.

The woman blinked at Jane a few times. Took a step away from the camera. Jane stayed put. No need to crowd her.

"Ma'am?" Jane said.

"I was getting lunch at the corner, at the counter," the woman began.

Cor-nah, coun-tah, Jane heard. So, a local. Good. "Then what?"

"I heard yelling. There's always commotion around here, with the traffic and tour buses and all, and my office is up there, on the third floor of the bank." She gestured behind her. "I'm used to it, so I got my takeout, as usual, assumed it was a . . ."

Jane let her talk, tried to keep her camera steady, hoping something usable was coming. The woman's back was to the murder scene—if it was a murder—so Jane could keep track of any changes while the woman talked and shift the camera if necessary. In the viewfinder, the video appeared black and white, which made it a pain to keep track of individuals. Still, the main attraction would easily recognizable: the one laid out on a stretcher. Jane had to get the money shots, the one of the victim getting loaded into the ambulance and of the ambulance driving away.

She supported her threatening-to-be-weary camera arm, holding her elbow with her left hand.

Nothing could stop her now.

5

As Tenley felt the touch on her shoulder, she flinched, spooked. She turned to see Ward Dahlstrom, boss man, big shot, *GQ* wannabe, who had all the other office girls swooning. Not her, of course, not ever. Ticktock, in four hours she'd be home.

"Miss Siskel? Are we ready for lunch in fifteen minutes?"

Dahlstrom smelled like peppermint and, she swore, scotch, even though it was barely lunchtime on a Monday. She hated his hands, his manicured fingernails. His preppy checked shirt. His show-offy watch. She and Lanna met him first when they came to visit with Mom, him and his stupid jokes, and even Lanna thought he was cool, "so much power" and "a real man" and "so handsome." Tenley never understood that. Plus, she completely loathed when he said "we" when he meant "you."

"I guess so," she said.

She felt Dahlstrom standing there, felt him walk away. He didn't like her. So what? Maybe at lunch she should head down to the park, see what was going on in real life, not sit here and watch the movie of it.

Tenley tugged her hair into a knot, looped the long strands twice, then stuck in a yellow pencil to hold it off her face. Blinked at the screen of Curley Park in front of her. Like a . . . movie? That made it, somehow, kind of different.

Watching her computer monitor was kind of like watching a movie. A movie of people's lives. Weird that it was her, a college student and the only remaining Siskel daughter, watching this Curley Park story—whatever it was—unfold.

The monitor was the only good thing about this job. It let her look for Lanna. Lanna, who she knew was gone, impossibly and unbearably gone. She watched for Lanna in crowds, in the audience at concerts, looked for her ponytail and shoulders at Starbucks. Sometimes thought she'd caught a glimpse of her just around a corner. She'd even—she was embarrassed to admit—run after a few girls, Lanna's name on her lips, but soon skidded to a halt, remembering her older sister would never return.

Lanna was dead. No one could bring her back.

But watching for Lanna was a way of keeping her alive. Thinking just the next moment, in the next screen, her darling sister would appear. She'd recognize her walk, or that way she stood, one foot on her knee like a stork, her ponytail bobbing outside her Newton North High School baseball cap.

It couldn't happen, of course. Dead, and buried, funeral and everything. She'd been there. There was no mystery, no suspense. Lanna, almost twenty-two, and cool, and beautiful, had "met" someone online. But one night she'd gone out late, no one knew why, and tripped, hitting her head on a log in Steading Woods, the expanse of pine trees and underbrush behind their house in Forest Hills. She was found the next day, just off the path. No trace yet of the "boyfriend," police said, after taking Lanna's computer. Looked like an accident, the police said. She'd had no suitcase, no purse.

Did Tenley know the boyfriend's name? Where her older sister might have been going? No, she'd said, and that was true.

But Tenley knew Lanna had been planning to run off with him. Someday, though. Not that night. She'd promised Lanna never to tell. And hadn't. Until it didn't matter anymore. She never forgot the way her mother had looked at her then, and her father, and even the cops. And everyone. *Everyone.* Could she have saved her?

Tenley had been eighteen. A kid. She'd loved her sister. Every cool sister has some cool boyfriend, and Tenley only wanted Lanna to love her. Sisters don't tell, Lanna insisted. There was nothing bad, Lanna promised.

How was Tenley supposed to know? Anyway, maybe it really was an accident.

Tenley had hidden in her room for . . . she didn't remember how long. Looking up "missing sister." Looking up "runaways." Maybe Lanna had simply gone for a late-night walk, wrong place, wrong time. Maybe, maybe, maybe.

How could she have—Tenley closed her eyes, imagined the Cape Cod beach where they all used go, imagined the seagulls swooping overhead, the whoosh of the waves. Tried to get calm, like her shrink Dr. Maddux tried to teach her.

How could Tenley explain she was just—looking for Lanna. Not expecting to see her. Not even, really, hoping. Just looking.

If Tenley ever had another sister, she'd never let her out of her sight.

Curley Park was still on her screen. She should click to the next one, but she had to admit things were getting a little interesting down there. She could kind of see, but not too well, there seemed to be someone lying on the ground, and they'd put up that yellow crime scene tape. Tenley was getting better at making things out in surveillance video, maybe her brain was getting used to it, but since this was a traffic room, the cams were focused on the street.

But there wasn't any traffic. Looked like the cops had stopped all the cars. Screens five and six were so empty, they were like still lifes. Seven, where the ambulance waited—she could see the doors open now—was getting more and more crowded. Now they were—*what was going on?* The shape of the crowd was changing. She poised her finger over the green button labeled RECORD TWENTY SECONDS.

Should she record?

Should she, um, talk to someone?

6

Jake felt DeLuca close behind him as they rounded the first bend in the alley. Flat out running now, the rhythm of their footsteps matching, the gravel spitting underfoot. The one stripe of sunlight between the buildings on each side layered a frustrating glare on whatever waited ahead.

Jake kept the Glock pointed at the pavement. Nothing they could do to stop the sound of their footsteps echoing off the graffiti-covered brick walls that tunneled them to the north. Whoever was back there, in the gloom, would know someone was coming.

Three pigeons, startled, flapped up in gray confusion. Maybe a rat scuttled away, or maybe it was only a shadow. Jake's eyes narrowed, listening as hard as he could with each step that brought them closer. They had no choice but to take the next two curves, see what the dead end had in store.

They'd arrive in thirty seconds. Less. A killer had stabbed someone in broad daylight in the midst of the lunch hour, in front of God knows how many people. Where had that killer gone? Down here? And if so, was he—or she—now hoping to kill again?

Was this another victim, calling for help? If so, were they about to see the Curley Park killer?

Or could this be the bad guy? Maybe holding his next victim?

"Help me!" The call came again, louder now, a man's voice, tight with fear. Or injury. Or play-acting.

Dammit, there was no way to see back there. Who'd told the cadet about this? Where was that woman? What did she know? What had she seen? Was she part of some plan?

They were headed into a dead end, with a stone killer on the loose. Sounded melodramatic. Until you were in it.

Jake managed one look over his shoulder as he ran, checking on his partner. "Set?"

D gave a thumbs-up with the hand that wasn't holding his weapon. "Set."

Jake had radioed they were going in, so backup would arrive if needed. Around the next bend, Jake knew, was a concrete wall and a Dumpster. No question whoever was back there had heard their footsteps, but could have no idea who was headed in their direction. Might declaring their identity spook whoever this was? Start a barrage of gunfire that would certainly end in disaster? Or would it reassure whoever it was, announcing help was on the way? Only one fricking way to be sure.

"Boston Police!" Jake yelled.

"Jane? It's Melissa." *Meliss—?* Oh, Melissa. At 12:46, when Jane's cell phone showed "blocked call," she'd hoped it was Channel 2. But Jane barely got out a "hello" when her sister started talking. The khaki-suit lady's interview was wrapped, and Jane was on the hunt for another likely candidate. Should be a man, since she already had a woman on camera. If she got two usable interviews, maybe three, that'd do it.

"Hey, Liss—Melissa," Jane said. "Are you here? Already? I'm so sorry, I'm right in the midst of someth—"

"Jane, look, I'm a little concerned," Melissa went on, as if Jane hadn't said a thing. So what else was new. Melissa probably wanted to change the color of the wedding flowers, or change the font on the place cards.

"If it's about the wedding, Liss, I do want to hear, and I don't mean to cut you off." A wedding was a once-in-a-lifetime occasion, and Jane had promised herself not to get in the way of Melissa's day. Even though Melissa thought all days were Melissa days. "But I'm out on a story, and the police are trying to keep me away, and it's—"

"A story? I thought you'd been fired again," Melissa said. "Anyway, this'll only take a second. You know Daniel and I were supposed to . . ."

Jane tried to listen and keep watch on the crime scene at the same time.

"I'm in Boston now," Melissa was saying, "but Daniel's flight from Switzerland got delayed. That means I have to stay at Robyn's house without him, which is way out of my comfort zone. Oh. Wait. Hang on."

Robyn, Jane knew, was Gracie's mother. Daniel's ex. Jane took a deep breath, asked the universe for patience and understanding.

And for at least thirty seconds in which nothing new happened.

Holding the phone between her cheek and shoulder, Jane pointed her little Quik-Shot at the crowd. While she waited, she'd get a few more wide shots of the scene, just in case.

Jake always complained about the lookies, not only their ghoulish curiosity but also how they contaminated a scene, sometimes even picking up evidence as souvenirs, and that the people who actually had information never wanted to tell it, while those who "didn't know shit," as Jake put it, tried to make the police believe they had the goods.

Wonder where Jake is now? She allowed herself to think while Melissa had her on hold. The EMTs still knelt by the victim. The ambulance doors remained open.

"Melissa? Are you there?" The onlookers' interest seemed to have moved from the body in the park to an alleyway across the street. Jane followed their attention with her camera. Something was going on back there, and she needed to find out what. She couldn't believe her sister was making her wait.

"Melissa?" She tried again.

She couldn't blow this very first—she hoped not "only"—assignment because of a phone call from her sister. She needed fifteen uninterrupted minutes, and there was nothing on the planet that could deter her.

"So here's the thing—" Melissa was back.

"I have to cut you off," Jane said, "because—"

"We can't find Gracie," Melissa said.

7

"No no no, wait!" The guy in the blue shirt, yelling, held up a hand, palm out, trying to stop Jake and D from coming any closer. "I'm not the bad guy!"

Forget that. This stranger in the dead-end alley was Jake's number one suspect.

The two detectives exchanged quick looks, Jake wondering if the expression on his own face was as baffled as D's. Both had instantly pointed their weapons straight at the man in the alley, the V of their arms aiming right at his center mass.

"Take him, D," Jake said. His Glock stayed rock steady. The man was big, tough looking—rugby player, maybe. Something in his eyes didn't seem like fear. "Now, sir? You get up, hands in the air, nice and slow. You budge, you bolt, you're done."

In the brick-walled cul-de-sac at the back of Franklin Alley, they'd found this guy, kneeling square on the back of another man, that one smaller, his sinewy arms sticking out from a white T-shirt. The guy underneath was face-planted in the concrete and gravel, arms splayed, not moving. His face was turned toward Jake, his eyes closed. Was he faking? Dead? How? Why? Who were these two?

"Listen, listen, it's all good. About time you cops got here." The man on top kept one bent knee on the middle of the man's back, the other on the pavement, balancing. Now he was gesturing Jake and D closer. "I'm

Calvin Hewlitt, I'm in security, and I heard the yelling, and saw this guy running—running. Not sure if I could have held this bozo when he comes to. He fought me like a—anyway."

His face bloomed red, red as his hair, his nose and ears flushed, sweat darkening his pale blue shirt. Breathing hard.

"I said *up.*" Jake kept the Glock aimed. What was this freaking guy doing? "Hands in the *air,* Hewlitt. Then freeze."

Hewlitt stood, one foot at a time, pushing himself up from the pavement, brushed a few pebbles from his hands and knees. Most rolled across the concrete, but one bounced onto the back of the "victim." The guy lay still. Not a fidget, not a twitch.

Jake's weapon was just as motionless.

Was that guy dead? The second victim of the Curley Park stabber? Or the stabber himself? Jake had to secure the scene ASAP, get this balance of power back for the good guys. Hewlitt looked like some average run-of-the-street moke—security guard, had he said? But who knew what a killer looked like.

"No blood on his shirt," D muttered as Hewlitt got to his feet.

"Maybe he ditched a jacket," Jake said.

No time for surprises now, no time for tricks, no time for seemingly dead guys to come back to life, maybe come back shooting.

Hewlitt eyed Jake, up then down, pointed to the guy. "Must have hit his head on the pavement when I brought him down. But as you can see, he's—"

"I. Said. Freeze," Jake repeated. "Right now. You do not move. You do not talk. And I said, hands in the air. Not in your pockets. *Now.*"

Jake had to keep his eyes on two people at the same time. Was one a killer? What if both of them were? Was this guy talking to distract him? D could cuff only one person at a time, and Jake couldn't afford to let down his guard. Or his weapon.

The redhead—thirtyish, Jake assessed, civilized haircut, okay shoes. Not a street thug. As he raised his left hand, Jake saw a gold band on his ring finger. Saw both knees of Hewlitt's slacks ripped, shredded, and his shirt twisted and smeared with dirt. In a struggle at Curley Park? Or here? And why? Damn. What *was* this?

"Hands behind your back," D said.

In one quick motion, D cuffed him, pulling first one, then the other brawny arm. D was a head taller, maybe, but the guy had him on muscles. The triangular shape of a body builder, or at least someone familiar with the gym.

Jake took in the whole scene, tried to envision what might have happened. Not that it mattered what *might* have happened. Conjecture and assumption, the two things that would kill a case. All that mattered was what *did* happen. And why. It was Jake's job to find out, and soon. On the brick wall behind them, some idiot had graffitied in puffy white letters: REGGIE IS AN ASSO. Below that, the guy on the ground, motionless.

Wait. Did his back lift? Guy was breathing. Jake crouched on the pavement, two fingers on the neck pulse point, closing his eyes, feeling for a heartbeat. It was there, barely. Held his palms flat on the guy's back. Breathing. Not dead. Good. He didn't want to move him, didn't want to turn him over.

"Get the EMTs over here," Jake told D.

"Hey," Hewlitt squirmed in the cuffs, protesting. "Listen, officers—"

"*Detectives*," DeLuca corrected. He grasped Hewlitt's arm with one hand, keyed his radio with the other. "This is Unit Two, requesting medical assistance for victim at Franklin Alley, top priority. Do you copy?"

"Copy," dispatch's voice crackled over the radio. "Unit is en route, ETA is in three, over."

Hewlitt shrugged, adjusted his manacled arms. "*Detectives*. Whatever. I'm sure you've noticed I'm not trying to run. And given the circumstances, I won't call my lawyer. Unless it becomes necessary. All I can say is, better make sure this man doesn't get away while you're taking me in custody. Like I keep trying to say, I'm not the bad guy."

"Bad guy? How do you know there's a bad guy?" Still holding his weapon, Jake carefully patted the back pockets of the man's jeans. Little guy, wiry, midthirties, maybe. No blood apparent, on this side, at least. Or on the ground, that he could see, at least. Jake always hesitated to move a victim—possible internal injuries, liability, making an injury worse—wished the damn EMTs would get here. Wasn't there someone back at the park Doc Kratky could spare?

"No wallet," Jake reported. "You happen to have that, Mr. Hewlitt?"

"We copy," DeLuca said into the radio. "Like Detective Brogan said, Mr. Hewlitt, you happen to have this man's wallet? You can hand it over, or I can search you. Your call."

"Oh, yes, *sir.*" Hewlitt widened his eyes, feigning confession. "You got me. Yes, I have it. Makes complete sense. I robbed this man, then held him down and called for help."

"*You* weren't the one who called for—" Jake began.

"What's with the attitude?" D interrupted. "You're lucky we didn't shoo—"

"I'm standing here, aren't I?" Hewlitt said. "You see me trying to get away? I were you, I'd be more interested in the bad guy."

"What happened here, Mr. Hewlitt?" All Jake needed, D and this mouthy possible suspect goading each other into some alpha-male pissing match. Where the hell was the EMT? "Do you know who this person is?"

"Know who he is?" Hewlitt rolled his eyes. "Are you *kidding* me?"

Jake slid a palm under the prone man's shoulder, scraping his hand against the gritty pavement. His skin was still warm under the jersey T-shirt. Should he turn him? Then, motion. A shudder. A cough. The man's nose wrinkled, his mouth twitched, his nervous system struggling into reality. The Bruins logo on his back rose, then fell, then rose again. Jake eased his hand away, wiped it on the leg of his jeans.

"He's coming to," Jake said. "Where's the—"

A siren keened in the near distance, the wail of the ambulance growing louder.

"You might want to get another set of handcuffs," Hewlitt said. "If this gentleman wakes up, he'll not be happy to see you, and five'll get you ten he makes a break for it. Like he tried to do when I grabbed him. You see where that got me. I'd figured on headlines. Instead I'm in a dead-end alley with two dumb cops."

"Detectives," DeLuca said. "With two dumb detectives."

Jake got to his feet, eyes on the fallen man, brushed the pebbles indenting the knees of his jeans. "You have something to say, Mr. Hewlitt?"

"Well, you might want to apologize," Hewlitt said.

"Jake," D said. Pointed. "Check it out."

The guy on the pavement was definitely moving. The fingers of his left hand lifted, paused, fell back to the concrete. Jake knew he should cuff him, just in case. He'd be damned, though, if this security guard asshole—asso, he thought, looking at the graffiti—could think he was telling him what to do. Jake was in charge here.

"Once again, you have something to tell us, Mr. Hewlitt?"

Hewlitt rolled his shoulders. He cleared his throat, all drama. "Like I said, I'm not the bad guy."

"Right," DeLuca said. They could hear tires crunching the gravel up the alley, a siren blurping. "So you keep telling us."

The siren came closer. Hewlitt pointed a scuffed cordovan toe at the figure on the concrete. Now clearly breathing, looking like he might come to at any second.

"*He's* the bad guy." Hewlitt raised his voice over the siren's wail. "I saw him stab the man in the park. Then I saw him run."

8

"You can't find Gracie?" Jane closed her eyes briefly, trying to blank out the crowd and the whirling red lights of the ambulance and the muttering undercurrent as gawking onlookers dissected the scene before them, voices dimmed in respect or horror. Melissa had finally gotten to the point, but that didn't mean Jane understood it.

"What do you mean, 'can't find' Gracie?"

"What part of 'can't find' do you not understand, Jane?" Melissa's voice, taut and demanding, grated through Jane's cell. Melissa was relentless when things didn't work her perfect way.

Jane poked an available finger into her nonphone ear, trying to block out the wail of an approaching siren. Failed. She looked up, frowning, scoping out the situation. The EMTs still knelt by the victim. *Why did they need another ambulance?* She couldn't shoot any video while she was talking on the phone. She turned her back on the whole thing. She'd give Melissa thirty seconds. Thirty charitable seconds.

"I understand 'can't find,' Melissa." Jane kept her voice careful, no need to add to her sister's distress. "You mean Gracie's late coming home for lunch or something? She's not where she's supposed to be?"

"Her mother—have you met her? Robyn with a *y*? Is going nuts," Melissa said. "She's the neediest person imaginable. But anyway, Gracie. She comes home from school for lunch. Thanks to Daniel's incredibly generous child support, they send her to Brookline Charter, close to their—well, anyway." Melissa was interrupting herself now, no need for Jane to try.

Jane kept her eyes closed and head down, the only way she could focus and not be distracted by little things like, say, her job and a murder. Both of which she was now, to her certain detriment, ignoring.

". . . but they haven't come home," Melissa was saying. "Robyn called the school, but she says they said Gracie left with her stepdad as usual, and that was that. We've called him, but he's not answering his cell."

Jane's call-waiting beeped in, an insistent little chirp that demanded her attention. Channel 2. No doubt wanting to know what she'd discovered. "I'm on the phone with my sister" was not a good answer.

"Hang on," Jane said.

"Ja—!"

Jane winced, frustrated with this whole juggling thing. If Gracie was really gone, truly gone, whatever "gone" meant, naturally that trumped anything. But Gracie was with her stepfather, right? And Melissa always overreacted.

"This is Jane," she said.

"Jane? You there? What's the scoop? Is there a suspect? Can you confirm a murder? This is Derek at the assignment desk, BTW. It's been more than fifteen mins since we got you past the rookie cop—you need any more help?"

"I, um—" *He was kidding, right?* Jane didn't need any help.

"You got video?" Derek kept talking. "Interviews?"

"Definitely," she said. She looked up, squinting. Noontime shadows made dark puddles at each onlooker's feet. Two of the EMTs were standing now, the other pointing the medical examiner to the man sprawled on the brick walkway. They clicked open the legs of a collapsible metal gurney. The crowd stepped back, as one, as if the medics needed additional room for this delicate procedure.

"Listen, Derek, no cops are talking yet. The ME is here. They're moving the victim now. Gotta get a shot of this, gotta go, I'll call you back." She hung up before the editor could give her more instructions. Or more criticism. Jane had this, no problem, she simply needed to do it her way. Back to Melissa.

"Lissa, it's me, I'm sorry, I had to—"

"She's fine." No more stress in Melissa's voice?

"What?" Jane tried to process what her sister said. "She's what?"

"Fine. She just called, she's fine. She's with her stepfather. Robyn's husband, Lewis. Evidently the left hand didn't know—anyway, I'll keep you posted on the drill for the rest of the day soon as I can."

"Great," Jane said, happy Melissa was not there in person to witness the massive eye roll. But Jane had been the good sister, on the outside, at least. Now she could go back to her real life without a guilty conscience. "Glad it all worked out, Liss."

"So we'll see you tonight, then? And finally get to meet your Jack?"

"Jake," Jane said. Counting to ten, backward, got to nine. "Jake Brogan."

"Jo-king," Melissa singsonged. "TTYL." And hung up.

The woman was a partner-track lawyer, for God's sake. Who would say TTYL out loud? But at least Gracie was fine. Another personal life disaster successfully solved.

Now to get her professional life back. She picked up the video camera and headed for the action. The ambulance doors were still open. She hadn't missed a thing.

Score one for Jane.

Finally, Jane was off the phone. Bobby Land sucked the inside of his cheek as he silently rehearsed his line. "*Hey, Jane Ryland? I'm . . .*" But she wouldn't care who he was. How about "*Jane Ryland? I've been a big fan of yours since—*" Well, since what? Since you were fired? That'd never fly.

Now she was getting away.

He watched her head toward the crime scene tape, saw the curve of her black suit jacket, her shoulder bag banging against her back, the way she ran over the cobblestones in those high heels. How did women do that?

He snapped off some photos of her. Stalling.

Come on, Bobby.

It was now or never, and he didn't have time for never. This was his career, his life, his one chance to grab the big time. The brass ring, his father used to say, whatever that meant.

Do it.

"Jane Ryland?" he called out, not too loud, just enough to get her attention.

She stopped, turned to him. Some of her hair had come out of her ponytail, and her black bag slid from her shoulder. She hoisted it back up.

"Yes?"

She looked like she was trying to be polite, he didn't blame her, some strange kid comes up to her, what's she supposed to think? He'd better get to the point.

"I'm, uh, Bobby Land? I'm, like, a photographer?" He paused, better make this sound as cool as possible. He handed her a card with his phone number. Smart that he'd just put "Photos by Bobby. Freelance photographer."

Jane narrowed her eyes at him, taking the card, then reached into an outside pocket of her tote bag. Awesome, she had the Quik-Shot, so she was up for getting video. But she wasn't here when the guy got stabbed. She might have locators, background stuff, aftermath, but she couldn't have the real thing.

She fiddled with her camera, flapped open the viewfinder, didn't point it at him.

"Were you here when it happened, Mr.—"

"Land," he said.

"Land. A photographer, huh?" She smiled at him for the first time. Suddenly she was all friendly. "When did you arrive? Did you get any pictures of what happened?"

He could tell, even though she was trying to be cool, that she was hoping he had something. He could also tell she was freaking a little, looking at the EMTs and the ambulance. He had to reel her in, convince her he had the goods. Even though he wasn't quite sure it was true. But he'd gotten pictures, action shots, of something, and more than she had, for sure.

"I was right here when it happened." That was true. "And I was shooting." Also true.

"Terrific. Great. Listen, can you do me a huge favor? Can you stand by a second, Mr. Land?" She reached out, as if to touch him, but didn't actually do it. "I've got to get shots of them putting the victim into the ambulance. You know the deal for TV. If it doesn't happen on video, it didn't happen, right?"

She smiled at him again, like she understood they were colleagues, like she understood he knew about getting video, and what was important, and what pictures could make or break someone's career. Or life.

"Sure, go for it," he said.

She lifted her camera, pointed it at the EMTs. They hoisted the guy onto the wheeled stretcher thing, then yanked up the yellow tubing of the metal legs even higher, bringing it to waist level. Everyone went silent, so silent he could hear the creak of the metal as the stretcher clicked into place.

He knew they couldn't talk while she was shooting, their voices would be recorded by the Quik-Shot's sensitive microphone. He put a finger to his lips, signaling to her that he knew how this shit worked. But she wasn't looking at him. That was okay. He could wait. He'd told her he had pictures. TV people lived for pictures.

He had her.

9

Tenley clicked the mouse to highlight the red Record arrow on the upper right of her screen. In a fraction of a second, it flashed to green, then a series of numbers appeared beside it. First the date stamp—month, day, and year—and then, in bigger numbers, a flashing countdown. Well, more like a count-*up*. The computers were programmed to retrieve and preserve the last twenty seconds of video, so the system was now in the process of recording digitized pictures, starting with what occurred twenty seconds ago. Pulling back the past. As if Tenley had the power to stop time, then start it again.

She couldn't help but wish she had that power with Lanna. She watched the clock tick off the time of the video cache. It recovered *three* seconds of the past, *four* seconds. If she could retrieve the past, knowing what she knew now, would she have told on her sister? Would she have broken that trust? But knowing what she knew now didn't matter. The past was over. *Nine, ten . . .*

"Miss Siskel?" Of course it was Ward Dahlstrom, hovering over her like a cloud of imminent criticism, but she guessed this was his job. They'd all been instructed to avoid "the twenty," since whatever was digitized and downloaded *existed*. No longer a fleeting unrecorded moment in time but a legally obtainable piece of reality. "Might there be something you'd like to tell me? I saw you hit the twenty. Is there something I should know?"

Tenley knew if you pushed Cancel before the counter hit twenty, the entire recording would disappear. *Thirteen, fourteen . . .*

The twenty-second cache was the compromise the city's big shots made with the civil liberties people, her mother had explained to her, after they got all pissed off, claiming the city's surveillance system was an invasion of privacy. As a result, though, every time a twenty was recorded, it had to be reported, entered into a video log, and never erased. Before the compromise, the city had digitized and stored everything, easy enough to do, but soon the lawyers for every driver who'd been accused of running a red light demanded the video as some kind of proof of their clients' innocence. She remembered her parents discussing it—"an evidentiary can of worms," her mother complained.

Fifteen. "Well, see that ambulance?" Tenley said. "And I think those are EMTs, see? I was thinking that if something happened down there, it might help someone if we—"

Sixteen.

"Help the police?" Dahlstrom did not look happy. "Why?"

Fine, she was only a peon and she was trying to help and Dr. Maddux had encouraged her to be more responsible. Assertive. Not afraid of people. So here she'd done that, done exactly that, and now her boss was frowning.

"In case . . ." she began, watching the count-up, knowing that in a few seconds, the past would be captured. This time, at least. There were no do-overs in life, her father always tried to tell her, as if she didn't know that. But. Maybe he was wrong. Maybe this was her moment to make it happen.

Dahlstrom reached out his right hand and clicked her mouse. She saw his hand had a bruise on the top of it, right in the center. She'd Purell the mouse, Purell everything, after he left. She wished she could Purell the air. He clicked on the green light just as it reached nineteen. The light went red. White letters popped up.

Cache TERMINATED.

"Can of worms," he said.

* * *

"You have the right to remain silent. Anything you say may be . . ." Jake aimed his Miranda warning at the poor schlub on the paramedics' portable gurney. Had he even heard it? They'd hoisted the guy—passive, drooling, and shuddering for breath—onto the thin flat mattress, then cuffed his left leg to the manacle bracket welded to the foot of the cot. The EMTs pulled three black straps across his trembling body and fastened the shoulder-to-waist webbing on each side.

Jake finished the rights as one paramedic checked the plastic strap couplings. The patient—victim?—wore running shoes, cheap, the soles worn and blackened. Both knees of his jeans were ripped, showing lacerations and scratches on his legs, scratches that would certainly correlate to the crumbling bricks of the walk beside the Curley statue.

"How is he?" Jake began. "You see his ID? I didn't want to look too hard."

"Good call. Possible internal injuries. Could have hurt." The older one hung the stethoscope back around his neck, shaking his head. "Heartbeat weak, pulse ox iffy. He's unconscious, and more than banged up, Jake. We'll get him to Mass General, check it out. Call you if we find ID. Okay, gang, let's get him inside."

They flapped open the rear doors of the orange-striped ambulance. The driver had pulled his vehicle nose-first into the alley's entrance. He'd have to make a tough U-ey to get out.

Jake and D had holstered their weapons, and D stood watch near Calvin Hewlitt, still cuffed, now silently watching.

"Sir?" Jake took a step closer to the gurney, smelled beer and sweat and fear. The patient—suspect?—had his eyes closed. Jake saw an ugly red welt on the right side of his neck. "Sir?"

Nothing. The guy's skin was pale, splotched with red. Could be drugs, or alcohol, or poverty, or panic. Why did people do what they did? But Jake didn't need a motive to convict this man. With any luck there'd also be bystander photos and surveillance videos of him in the act. *So talk or not, buddy,* Jake thought. *We got you.*

Jake stood, signaled to the paramedic. *Take him.* "Let's get him outta here."

The guy was going nowhere but the hospital, where he might recover, at least, and where, under armed guard, he'd get a doctor's attention. They'd find ID. With a clean bill of health, or cleanish, at least, his next stop would be the Suffolk County lockup. Match the fingerprints on the knife—if there were any—with this guy's? One and done. Shortest perp apprehension time ever. Even the hottest-shot defense attorney would have a tough time with that one. Case closed.

"Officers?" Calvin Hewlitt, still cuffed, had watched the whole thing, silent. "Might I remind you I exist?"

Shit. Problem was, although the mute suspect was most certainly— well, probably—the stabber, Jake had no way to determine whether this Hewlitt was the hero he claimed to be, or was involved in some way.

A witness? A good Samaritan? A partner in crime? Who was who in this deal? Sure seemed like—but "seemed" didn't matter.

"Just doing our jobs. Sir." Jake tried to balance the proper police procedure with the potential outcomes. Getting sued for false arrest always loomed. Police brutality, although there clearly wasn't any, would be a pain to handle. On the other hand, if this Hewlitt was part of the crime and Jake let him go, some theoretical lawsuit would be the least of Jake's problems. Plus, either he or D would have to ride with the injured guy in the ambulance. Even strapped down and cuffed, no telling what might happen. Or what he might decide to say.

"We have to bring you downtown, sir." Jake nodded at D, cocked his head toward the alley entrance.

"You're taking me out there, in front of everyone, in freaking handcuffs?" Hewlitt's face got even redder, the cords in his neck tightening, showing taut above his collar. "You don't think that's prejudicial? There'll be a raft of TV cameras, hell knows what else. I'm warning you, Officers—"

D opened his mouth to protest, Jake raised a palm to stop him. Guy might have a point.

"If my picture gets on television in these handcuffs?" Hewlitt tried to gesture, failed. "I'll own the damn police department. And I'll own *you*."

Bobby Land, totally psyched about his new name, had caught a flash of orange as the second ambulance made the sharp right into Franklin Alley, the same alley where the leather-jacketed cops had gone. An ambulance? With a suspect on the loose? Had to be connected. And where there was a connection, there was a good picture.

"Jane? I mean, Ms. Ryland?" Bobby touched her shoulder, just for an instant, didn't want to spook her.

The reporter turned around, took the viewfinder from her right eye, pointed the camera at him, then at the pavement. He could tell she was deciding what to do. His life hung in the balance. Well, not really, but this chance meeting felt momentous. His chest tightened. If she ignored him, he'd push harder.

"Hang on, okay?" she said. She'd already turned back to the crowd, aiming her little camera at City Hall.

Good. Bobby watched her back, saw her inching closer to the action, camera aimed steady, even in those high heels. He could tell she was kinda nervous about him, she'd retreated a little before, keeping her distance from him, but he couldn't worry about that. She'd understand soon enough. And accept him.

But he couldn't delay much longer. Whatever was going on in that alley was already under way. News would not wait for anyone, even Jane Ryland. Taking a chance, *seizing the moment,* like his professor always said, he took a few quick steps, got close enough to tap her on the shoulder again. He had the eye, and this was his chance to prove it to her. This would make his career.

10

Jane recoiled at the touch on her shoulder.

She'd told that annoying kid to wait. What was up with him? "Hang on," she called over her shoulder.

The ambulance with the ME riding along pulled away. Maybe this kid—Bobby? Robby?—actually had witnessed what happened, maybe gotten photographs of it, as he'd said. She reminded herself to be wary. Someone at a story often tried to latch on to her, to any reporter, something about the lure of fame or celebrity, as if being near a person who was "on TV" had some cachet. Everyone had an agenda, even if it was only proximity. Why did everyone hate TV but lust after celebrity?

But if he had actual crime pictures, that'd be big. And Jane needed big. She needed exclusive. She needed something that would clinch her a job at Channel 2.

It bugged her, though, that the groupie vibe coming from this kid was getting louder and louder. Reporters thrived on news tips, but sometimes tipsters got too invested, deciding they were part of the team. And once under way, an escalating fantasy relationship was tough to untangle. Jane still had people calling her years after they'd contributed to a story. Maybe it was the power of revealing a secret, of being the one in the know. The power of *telling*. But what if this kid knew something? Couldn't hurt to find out.

"Sorry," she said. "What's up?"

"I think it's going down in Franklin Alley." *Bobby*, she remembered.

Land. Like the camera. "I saw two cops, plainclothes, heading down there. And now an ambulance. It's, like, around the corner, so you can't see, but maybe you should—"

Jane glanced left, right, scanned the crime scene. Ambulance gone, cops still questioning clumps of possible witnesses. Traffic had started again, lunchtime returning to almost normal. Except for the bloodstain on the sidewalk. Two other TV stations had arrived, including her ex-employer, now competitor, Channel 11. *Ha.* With a bit of luck and a lot of fast driving, she'd beaten everyone on this story, and now they had to play news catch-up. *Little late,* she imagined the fun of telling them. *Excitement's over.* They'd get aftermath, that was all. Score two for Jane.

Was this kid about to provide score three? This day was not playing out as she'd imagined. Not anywhere near.

"Okay, Bobby," she said. She'd already started walking toward the alley, turning her back on her competitors. "Show me."

The moment her computer flipped to 1:00 P.M., the minute she saw the double zeros, Tenley clicked the mouse, putting her computer station to sleep and setting herself free. Forty-five glorious minutes. Outside, maybe in the sun. Where life happened for real, not on video.

She had to admit she was curious. Something was going on in Curley Park. Even though Dahlstrom stopped the recording, that didn't make it not exist. You couldn't erase reality. She was bummed about the deleted video, but it wasn't her fault. They better not blame her for it.

Out in the City Hall corridor, around the corner, she ducked into the ladies' room—four stalls, all empty—and rolled up the waistband of her skirt so at least she looked cool. She untucked the tail of her T-shirt, EFF-ING AWESOME it said, and tied her cardigan around her waist. She looked in the mirror, just long enough to remember her earrings were gone, but her hair would cover all those little holes. Now if she could get out of here without running into her mother. Mom's office was on a different floor, so all she had to do was pray to the elevator gods to protect her from coincidence. She hardly ever saw her mom at City Hall. It wasn't like bring-your-daughter-to-work time around here—*that'd be the day.* Tenley looked again at her mirror image, frowning. She was sorry she was such a disappointment.

But that's how the cookie crumbled, huh, family? One daughter dead, the other a disaster.

She pushed open the door, checked the time on her cell phone. Forty minutes to go. Down the zigzag staircase, out past floor three, no mother, past two, alone, past one, banging out the metal side door into the surprising glare of sunshine on Congress Street.

It was usually crowded at lunchtime, but today the swirl of cars and pedestrians had a feel of—*off.* Cops all over the place, some in uniforms directing traffic. Globs of bystanders milling around by the statues. She looked both ways on Congress, ignoring the crosswalk—pretty funny if someone upstairs was watching when she jaywalked, ha ha—and stepped onto the sidewalk by the park. A strip of yellow tape—CAUTION CAUTION CAUTION—prevented her from getting any closer to whatever she'd already missed. An empty brown paper bag caught the breeze, puffed up, and blew away.

She'd seen the ambulance arrive, but it was gone now. She was too late.

She was always too late.

How could she get the scoop on whatever happened? Seemed like some kind of law enforcement guys were interviewing people on the street. She sidled over to the back of one group, assimilated herself into the crowd. She'd stand there, try to blend in, see what she could pick up. No one cared about a college kid.

She looked up at City Hall across the street, counted two squares of plate glass down and three across. That was her mother's window. Right next to the mayor's. *Mom could look out here and see me in the park.*

She considered waving, thought better of it.

"I got here after I picked up my sushi." One poseur in a too-tight suit was holding up a glossy black paper bag, as if to prove his lunch to the woman taking notes on a little pad with a cheap-looking Bic. A cop, must be.

"Did you see anything?" the cop asked.

What was sushi guy going to say? Tenley took a tentative step closer, then another, so she could be sure to hear. No one noticed her, seemed like.

This time that was a good thing.

Jake cringed as the ambulance driver attempted to make the three-point turn to exit Franklin Alley. Fourth try now. Detective Angela Bartoneri, of all people, who'd been at the crime scene, would ride in the back, baby-sit the suspect. Thanks to the alphabet, Angie Bartoneri had always been seated next to Jake at the BPD's continuing education sessions. He and Angie also shared coffee, then dinner, and almost a hell of a lot more, but then he'd made detective before she did. Their relationship never recovered. Just as well, Jake told himself at the time—three years ago? four?—since the divorce rate for cops married to cops was probably about one hundred percent. Plus, if one person in a relationship couldn't be genuinely happy for the success of the other, it wasn't much of a rela-tionship. Angie'd moved on professionally and had recently been pro-moted to detective in the white-collar unit, assisting homicide when they needed backup. Working shoulder to shoulder with Angie again was—a trip. He'd also heard she'd now hooked up personally with some computer whiz. Very Angie. More power to her.

Jake had moved on, too. To Jane. And all that entailed. Now that Jane was no longer with the *Register,* the two of them had new decisions to make. Decisions that might be—Jake shook his head, clearing his thoughts of the mental tangent. Funny how fast your brain could plow ahead, even at the most unlikely time.

Before the rear ambulance doors closed, Jake had finished giving Angie the quick lowdown on the man she was chaperoning. "This guy didn't say a word, and no easily accessible ID," Jake added. "Maybe you'll have better luck. I read him his rights, so if he does decide to talk, you're covered."

"I'm clear on Miranda," Angie said. "Hope he heard you."

Jake ignored her sarcasm, outwardly, at least. "The guy in the cuffs—we'll check his ID now, see if we can get confirmation. Says he's a security guard."

"One phone call," Angie said. "I'll do it."

"Thanks," Jake said. Maybe he wasn't ignoring her as much as he imagined. "Anyway, Angie, the cadets are canvassing the eyewitnesses, getting cell phone photos. This guy should be a cinch to be ID'd, so once the photos come in, it's case closed."

"You know your stuff," Angie said. "I can see why you were promoted so early. Before *I* was, I mean."

"After all this time?" Jake couldn't stop himself. He looked around quickly. D, standing nearby, was focused on Hewlitt, the medics were moving their patient into the vehicle. "Are we really still gonna do this?"

"Do what?" Angie gave that smile. "I'm teasing, Jake."

Teasing? Not exactly the time for that. He'd go by the book.

"Bartoneri? You'll stay with him—whoever he is—at Mass General. Let me know the instant he says anything. I'll contact you when the witness photos come in. If they're potentially confirmatory, I'll bring them to the hospital. We'll get an arrest warrant, go from there. Questions?"

"No, sir," she said, eyes twinkling. "Yes, sir."

Angie's dark hair—Jake remembered it all too well—was twisted up under her navy patent-billed cap. If any woman could look good in a cop hat, Angie could. He watched her clamber into the back of the ambulance. She'd been a dancer, Jake remembered, until she'd gotten impatient with the food restrictions and turned to law enforcement instead. He'd felt twinges of jealousy over the other cadets lined up to spar with her in defense training. She'd been aware of their attention, too. Teased them, with that throaty voice of hers, then kicked their asses, every one, every time.

She stood, framed by one still-open white back door. Fluttered her fingers at him. "Detective? Hope our paths cross again."

She closed the metal door before he could answer.

Dammit. And dammit again. The back of his neck prickled, and it wasn't from the sun. He would not let Angela Bartoneri get under his skin. She was history.

The ambulance's piercing back-up beeps yanked him back to reality. Fifth try to turn around now. The driver stopped a fraction of an inch from the liquor store's redbrick wall, shifted into Drive, and crept toward the giant green Dumpster. The *Dumpster*. "A guy in a Dumpster"—that's what the cadet had relayed to him.

He and DeLuca had never looked in the Dumpster.

11

Cursing her too-tight skirt and too-high job interview heels, Jane finally caught up to Bobby. Running down a cobblestone and brick backstreet was the last thing she'd expected to do today.

"The ambulance is still in there, Ms. Ryland." Bobby had stopped at the entrance of Franklin Alley, pointing. "Hear the beeps? It's really narrow in there, so the driver's gotta turn round in the dead end. That'll give us time. You ready?"

"All set." She checked the viewfinder of the Quik-Shot, confirmed the stand-by light. She'd roll on everything, couldn't hurt. Bobby, now on the run, had his camera, too. Between them, they'd get whatever there was to get. *Go.*

Around the next curve, she saw Bobby's T-shirt disappear again. They had to be close to the end. She held a palm to her chest—the gym starting tomorrow, she promised—drew in a deep breath, and went for it. Then she heard the rev of an engine, and more back-up beeps. This ambulance was on the way out.

"Missed it," she whispered. "Damn." Now she'd never get to see who was inside. But at least she'd get—

A blast from a horn and a wail of the siren flattened her against the alleyway's brick wall. She watched the red from the whirling lights hit the side of the buildings. As the engine noise grew louder, she felt the red glare wash over her. There was barely room for her to stand if the ambulance was to pass. Bobby was nowhere to be seen. He'd clearly managed to reach the end.

The front of the white-and-orange van appeared. She held her ground, pointed her camera. *Rolling.*

"Move it, lady!" A voice from the open passenger-side window, elbow over the edge, one hand waving Jane away. A face peered at her, frowning, the sun glinting directly overhead on the medic's dark-tinted shades.

"Sorry, can you get by?" Jane grimaced, embarrassed. Kind of tacky trying to shoot video when you were part of the problem.

The medic in the front seat muttered something Jane couldn't hear, probably a good thing, buzzed up the window. Jane got as close as she could to the wall, plastering her black suit against the bricks as the ambulance edged by. She watched it gather speed, made sure her camera stayed steady, and the van disappeared from the viewfinder. *Got it.*

But what—or who—was still down there? Jane hurried toward the end of the alley, wincing less with each step now. She'd gone from one hundred percent skeptical of Bobby Land to joining his team in four minutes flat. Sure hoped her instincts were right. The black metal housing of an air-conditioning unit appeared, then, just around the next curve, and the dark green hulk of a Dumpster.

Almost there.

Death was all around her. It haunted her. Tenley sat on the curb in front of the bank, facing the park, seeing a forest of feet and legs, and looking up through the trees at City Hall, toward the blind-slatted window of her mother's office.

First her own sister dies. Now this. A man stabbed right here in Curley Park. She heard it from the sushi guy, then two others told the cop the exact same story. One man just standing by the statue, another man walking up to him, and next thing they knew there was yelling and one of the men lay on the ground with a knife in his back. And the other was gone. Could they recognize the assailant? the police had asked. No, they'd all said—white, male, that's about all. Had anyone taken photos? No, each had said. It all happened too fast. So now a murderer was out there. Maybe even standing near her. Pretending. Waiting for another chance to hurt an innocent person.

She hugged her knees, making herself small.

Was there any way to avoid it? Would death always follow her? Haunt her? It would have shown up on her traffic surveillance video if she'd been on that screen. She would have *seen* it.

Tenley wished she could run up to her mother's office, climb on that long pillowed couch like she used to when she was little, babysitter Lanna suggesting fort or voyage to Mars or princesses trapped by the scary evil monster.

But that was all play, and all gone, and her life would never be happy again. Yet the evil monsters existed, that was the scary part. *No.* The scary part was you didn't know who the monsters were. Or where.

She could just imagine the drama if she showed up in her mother's office now. Her mother probably couldn't stand the sight of her, probably still blamed her, deep down—or not so deep—for what happened to Lanna. Would Tenley ever stop thinking about that? She wouldn't. She couldn't even envision a time when she wouldn't think about Lanna every day.

What kind of life would that be? All those years, stretching out in front of her, all those years of just . . . loss?

The sun baked her back, and she knew her skirt would be dusty from sitting on the curb. She stuck her legs out into the street, one bare knee bruised from where she'd banged it on the side of her desk. She checked the lighted number of the big clock outside the bank—fifteen more minutes of her "lunch" hour. She should get something to eat, even though she was not hungry anymore.

"Hey!" A guy running by almost tripped over her, and she pulled her legs back, looked up in time to see him head away from the Curley statue. Right after him, a woman in a black suit, trying—ridiculously—to run in high heels.

Was the woman chasing the kid? Why? The woman carried a tote bag over her shoulder, so it wasn't like he'd stolen her purse or anything.

She hopped to her feet, patted the dust off her rear and adjusted her skirt, then watched the two figures disappear around the corner. Maybe she should go see?

Angie Bartoneri was the least of Jake's worries. The second she'd slammed herself into the back of the departing ambulance, he'd closed the door on thinking about her. Angie could hoard all the bitterness—or regret? or desire?—she wanted. *Teasing?* Jake had moved on.

Topping Jake's current worry list was the Dumpster, still unopened, and the still-handcuffed Calvin Hewlitt. The security guard, if that's what he really was, and self-professed hero, if that's what he really was, slouched with one shoulder leaning against the brick wall and was now trading muttered insults with DeLuca. The two of them, baiting each other with double entendres and smack talk, sounded like they belonged on some middle school playground. Now Jake had to decide whether he and D should bring this guy to headquarters. Or let him go.

Not an easy call. What if they were handcuffing a good guy? Hauling an innocent man to headquarters? On the other hand, what if they let a killer escape?

When in doubt, go by the book, Jake's grandfather always told him. They'd watch cop shows together on Gramma's flowered couch, back in the day. "The Commissioner," as Gramma had called her husband even after he retired from the force, constantly ridiculed the decision-making transgressions of whatever make-believe cop headlined the flickering black-and-white screen. "Not what a real cop would do," Grandpa would declare with scorn, clinking the ice cubes in the one-whiskey-per-day Gramma allowed. Then he'd proceed to tell a hero-worshipping ten-year-old Jake what a real cop *would* do. It was a master class in law enforcement, grown-up Jake realized all these years later. Going by the book was unfailingly the Commissioner's guiding principle. Now it was Jake's, too.

"Mr. Hewlitt?" Jake turned toward the handcuffed man, signaling De-Luca he'd take over. D retreated, but only a wary half step. "Thanks for your patience, but—"

"Thanks for my patience? My *patience*?" Hewlitt's dust-streaked oxford shirt was untucked on both sides. "How about 'thanks for catching the bad guy, sir,' and 'thank you for not suing the frigging hell out of the police department for unlawful imprisonment and illegal seizure'? And whatever the hell else breach of Fourth Amendment rights I can sue for. How about *that*, Officer?"

"Detective," DeLuca muttered.

Jake could see the smirk on D's face, Hewlitt couldn't.

Jake shot him a look. *Can you not resist?*

DeLuca shrugged.

"You were saying, Mr. Hewlitt," Jake went on. "You're an employee of a security firm at Faneuil Hall? Mind showing me your ID?"

"My ID?" Hewlitt furrowed his forehead, as if he were thinking intently. "The delight with which I'd show you my ID is immeasurable, except for one small item. Your colleague now has it, as you are no doubt aware, since he frisked me as if I were some potential terrorist at freaking Logan Airport, and took my wallet as well as my car keys and my phone. All of which I demand be returned. You'll note, however, he did not find a weapon or any other indication that—"

Shit, Jake thought as the man continued to complain. Hewlitt didn't talk like a security guard, though what did a security guard sound like? Or maybe some criminal defense attorney had coached Hewlitt about what to say if he was arrested.

"D?" Jake began.

DeLuca handed him the flap of cordovan leather.

"Sir?" Jake asked the guy. "Okay if I look inside?"

"Knock yourself out," Hewlitt said.

"I'll knock—" DeLuca began.

Jake ignored him, flipped open the wallet. Amex gold card, on the top. Calvin Hewlitt, member since 2000. Driver's license, Massachusetts, current, in the window. Jake quickly checked—the photo matched the face. Address in the South End, Jake memorized it. Bill slot thick with twenties. Lots of cash for a security guard. Or not. Jake pulled out a stack of credit cards and shuffled through them. Health insurance, AAA, Starbucks. Looking for a guard credential.

Nothing.

Ha. Got you, brother. And you're coming in. Jake heard the wail of the ambulance siren fading into the distance. Their suspect was on the way to Mass General, finally. The dead guy probably on the way to the morgue. Cadets had certainly gotten eyewitness accounts by now, and inevitably photos of some kind. And he hadn't even had to deal with any reporters, though Jane would demand the lowdown when they saw each other later. All in all, this episode was wrapping up pretty darn well.

"I'm not finding your security guard credentials," Jake said. Calm. Pleasant. Oddly, it would be a lot easier if Hewlitt was a reasonable suspect. They could take him downtown, do a full workup, and it wouldn't be Jake's final call whether to let him go. If his status was iffy, Jake could reasonably err on the side of caution.

"I'm not a security guard," Hewlitt said.

"You're—?" The last thing Jake expected him to say.

"What's more, I never said I was a security guard."

"Hell, you didn't—" DeLuca began.

"Sir?" Jake began to feel the confidence, the calming of the nerve endings that came with making the correct decision. He'd gone by the book, he'd looked for ID, he'd discovered a discrepancy in what the suspect had told him. Bang. That put the big guy in the back of the cruiser.

"I *said*—" Hewlitt's shoulders rose, then fell. Jake didn't like the look on his face. "I said I worked at a security company. As a matter of fact, I *own* the security company. Hewlitt Security. I'm out of business cards, but if you'd like to press speed dial one-one on my cell phone, feel free. That'll call my office. In fact, please do it. They're probably beginning to wonder where I am."

DeLuca pulled a black cell phone from his inside jacket pocket, offered it to Jake. Jake waved it away.

"However, *Detective*," Hewlitt went on. "If you'd like to call speed dial eight-eight?—which is what I'd prefer—you'll be calling my lawyer. Might as well. You'll be talking to her soon enough."

"Hey! Jake, shadow at your six o'clock!" DeLuca's stance changed, his eyes narrowed, his hand hovered over his weapon again.

Jake pivoted, followed his partner's instruction. Saw the shadow. Saw someone coming toward them. Holding something.

"Freeze!" DeLuca yelled. "Police!"

"What's going on?" Hewlitt backed against the wall, lowered himself to a crouch.

"Police!" Jake drew his Glock. Pointed it at the shadow. "Drop it!"

12

Jane steadied herself, trailing her fingers against the brick wall as she rounded what she figured must be the last curve in the alley. *Whose idea was this?* Hers, she had to admit. Bobby was already out of sight. If anyone were back in the dead end, waiting, she'd see them in about two seconds.

Voices. Yelling. *Police?* Someone yelled "Police!" Jake? Sounded—*did it?*—like Jake. Or was someone calling *for* the police? Calling for help?

She skidded to a stop, tucked her body behind a chugging black air-conditioning unit. One heel twisted in the rock shards between the bumpy cobbles, and she fell hard, yanked off balance, landing on her bare knee. Camera still rolling.

"Jane!" Bobby's voice. Calling for her.

Or warning her? She felt her stomach clench, felt the tension of the decision she needed to make, and make right now. Should she turn, run, get help? Or at least get away? Bobby had told her two plainclothes cops were down here, so it must be safe. Right? Unless he'd been wrong and they weren't two plainclothes cops, they were simply two guys. And with who knew what agenda.

She stared across the empty alley, trying to assess. A man had been stabbed to death not a block from here. The cops were clearly looking for the bad guy. But what if the cops had followed the bad guy down this alley, and now they were also dead, and Bobby had run right into their—

Go. She turned away, ready to head for the safety of the park and the multitude of police. But wait—leave Bobby? Who the hell was he, anyway? A street kid she'd instantly believed?

The yelling had stopped, but still there were voices, only lower. The air-conditioning unit kicked on, vibrating against her shoulder, making it impossible to make out words. Her scraped knee was bleeding, *lovely*, and she couldn't quiet her pounding heart.

"Jane! It's okay!" Bobby's voice again.

Footsteps. Coming toward her. They crunched in the gravel of the cobblestones, walking deliberately. Not running.

She closed her eyes. Just two choices now. She could run. Or she could wait. But she could no longer hide. She opened her eyes.

"Jane!"

Jake.

Jane?

Jane. In high heels and a black suit, hiding behind a rusting air conditioner in a filthy back alley a block away from a murder.

Jake attempted to keep the top of his head from blowing off. He'd left a still-complaining Hewlitt in the care of DeLuca. They ordered the paparazzi kid with the camera—what if they'd shot him?—to stay put. The kid had insisted that Jane Ryland, the reporter for Channel 2, was following him down the alley. But Jake knew Jane wasn't a reporter anymore, for Channel 2 or anyone else. So this kid was full of crap.

"Holy shit, Jane, what the hell're you doing?"

"Getting up," she said. "What're *you* doing?"

She hauled herself to her feet, one hand clutching a metal handle on the side of the air conditioner, the other holding some device. Her suit jacket flapped open, T-shirt grubby with dust and smeared with black stuff, her hair half out of its ponytail, her tote bag strapped across her body. One knee was bleeding, Jake saw, making a narrow red trickle down her bare leg.

"You okay?" He gestured toward her knee.

She looked down, licked a finger, and wiped away the blood. "Just a flesh wound," she said. "Cobblestone attack."

"Jane?"

"Yeah?" She was smiling as if this wasn't absurd.

"You realize this is ridiculous? Having this conversation? There's a paparazzi kid, showed up with a camera, insisted he's with you. I almost shot him, for God's sake. What the holy hell are you doing back here?"

Uh-oh. He knew that expression. Jane had something to tell him, and he wasn't going to like it.

"Jane? I'm serious. There's been a crime committed. We're looking for a suspect. I don't have time for—"

"I know, Jake. It's complicated." She paused, seemed to be considering again, then held up the device in her hand. "Detective Brogan? You're looking for a suspect? Can you tell us what happened in Curley Park?"

"Is that a camera, too? Are you fre—" Jake paused, trying to sort this out. She had a camera and was asking questions. Why? Whatever the reason, anything he said was about to be recorded, and that meant he needed to evaluate everything that came out of his mouth. He'd started to say, "Are you freaking kidding me?" then stopped. He narrowed his eyes, shading them from the sun with one hand. Jane still pointed that thing at him. "Ms. Ryland? Are you here in a capacity as a reporter?"

She lowered the camera. "Yeah, actually. I am. Listen, Jake? I have some pretty interesting news, but I promise I won't shoot what you say, okay? See? Camera's down? The paparazzi kid told me he'd seen two cops, I guess one of them was you, running after someone. So I figured I'd—I mean, *were* you running after someone? Was that the person in the ambulance? What happened?"

"Are you asking as you? Or as a reporter?"

Her face changed again. "I work for Channel 2. For now, at least."

"Jake!" his radio crackled in his back pocket. "Get back here!"

"Crap," Jake said. He turned toward the dead end, where he'd left DeLuca, Hewlitt, and the kid. If the kid was somehow in cahoots with

Hewlitt—could that be?—there'd be a damn three-ring circus about to go down.

Jake pointed at Jane. "Stay right here."

But no. She could not be here, this was potentially a disaster. He had no idea what DeLuca needed or why, but it was no place for Jane. He couldn't even process what she'd just told him—she worked at Channel 2? Since when? Right now, it made not one shred of difference.

He pointed the other way, toward the alley entrance. "No. Get out of here. Now. *Go!*"

"Jake!" DeLuca's voice again. "Hewlitt!"

He turned, drew his Glock again, and powered back into the dead end.

Hyoolit? What did DeLuca mean by Hyoolit? Like, haul it? Hurry? Had he wanted Jake to hurry? What was going on down there?

Jane watched Jake's back for about ten seconds. She contemplated his order to get out. Stay? Or go? Safer to go back to civilization, but safe didn't make headlines. She checked the camera. According to the digital read-out, it still had forty minutes of power.

Stay or go? She frowned as she leaned against the wall again, trying to hear, closing her eyes as if that would make her other senses more acute. Nothing. No noise from the dead end. No yelling. No gunshots. That had certainly been DeLuca's voice calling for Jake. So they *had* been the "two cops" Bobby had seen. But what—or who—led them into the alley? Whatever or whoever it was, seemed like someone had been carried away in an ambulance, and someone was still down there. If she stayed right here, behind her friendly neighborhood air conditioner, she could wait, keeping still, and see what happened. She nodded, agreeing with herself. Jake would have no way of knowing she'd ignored him until whatever happened was already over. And then it would be too late for him to care. Hiding was the answer.

Her phone rang.

Kidding me? She had turned the volume to the highest possible level to make sure she didn't miss a call. Now the stupid thing was giving her away. She pawed into her bag with both hands, managed to whap the thing to vibrate before it could ring again. So much for her plan to hide.

She paused, listening again. Voices, certainly, even raised. In anger? In fear? But nothing she could understand. Traffic rumbled from the surface road a block away, a few seagulls yelled at each other, the air conditioner's droning now familiar. She dropped back into her crouch, behind the black metal, seeing a swipe on the side where a coating of grime no longer existed. Grime most likely now on her suit jacket.

No sign of Jake. Either he hadn't heard her phone or was too busy to check it out.

She took a calming breath, then another, balancing one hand against the warm cobblestones. She was fine. At least she had a moment to collect—

Her phone now vibrated like an angry bee in the side pocket of her tote. She looked up, scanning the alley in both directions. She turned the phone off again. Whoever it was would have to wait. The newsroom, no doubt. Some journalism realities never changed, no matter where she worked. Those people, cocooned safely in their buildings all day, had no idea what it was like in the field. They'd call every ten minutes asking what's new. Well, if something were new, wouldn't she be calling them? And all the time spent answering the phone was time she couldn't spend getting the story.

Two hours ago she'd been discussing journalism theory with a pompous-ass news director. Now there was no more theory. Now there was reality. Baking sun, complaining thigh muscles, ruined suit, shredded heels, and a semi-twisted ankle. And a murder—maybe two—that was still a mystery.

DeLuca had told Jake to "haul it." Why?

Was something wrong? Or was something right?

Two of the people back there were good guys, that she knew for sure. But that was all she knew.

13

Tenley felt the air change around her. So dumb of her to think about going into that alley. She'd been sitting in the same spot on the curb for several minutes, elbows on knees and chin in hands, eyes closed, trying to decide how to handle her feelings. Trying to disperse the shadows, like her therapist always advised her to do. When Tenley felt herself spiraling down, Dr. Maddux always said to let the sunlight in. Feel the touch of the breeze, open your eyes to beauty and possibilities. Tenley didn't feel like opening her eyes to anything.

But the change in the air meant someone had sat down beside her. Part of Tenley's brain said, *Leap up, run, don't look back.* But that was silly. Figuring if she kept her eyes shut, no one could see her either? Like an ostrich? A million cops were here. She could open her eyes, and all would be normal and fine.

"Craziness, huh?" a voice said.

A female voice. A girl. Okay, then, not scary.

"What happened?" the girl was asking. "Did you see that ambulance come out of the alley? It was hauling ass."

Tenley turned her head a fraction, enough to see a smiling girl with tanned skin. A little older than her. *Lanna's age.* With short-short hair, a cascade of silver earrings, pretty cool, actually, cute, and a Nirvana T-shirt. Vintage. Her sister Lanna had one just like it, except this girl was half the size of Lanna. Lanna'd never fit into this one. *It wasn't Lanna's,* Tenley assured herself. Probably fifty million T-shirts like this one. And a million other cute girls Lanna's age. People who were not dead.

"If you don't want to talk, that's cool."

Tenley felt the girl shift her weight, as if she was going to stand.

"I know you, right? From school? No biggie. Sorry to bother." Her jeans were like the ones Tenley usually wore when she wasn't working, ripped knees and low-rise. Tenley saw a little of the girl's creamy skin above the waistband and a tiny tattooed star disappearing beneath.

"No, it's okay," Tenley said. Did she know her? She could pretend she did until she figured it out. So many kids at school, and she hardly ever connected. "But I just got here. Kind of."

"I've seen you on the bus in the mornings? Right? You work around here, too? I work over at . . ." She gestured across the street.

Quincy Market, Tenley guessed. Maybe at the Gap, or American Eagle. "Yeah, I work at—" Tenley began. The girl *did* look familiar. Kind of.

"I'm Brileen," the girl went on, rolling her dark eyes. "B-R-I-L-E-E-N. I know, huh? Why-Try-Bry they always used to say back in middle school. Drove me nuts."

She was sitting so close Tenley could see the glisten of her clear lip gloss, see the scattering of not-quite freckles across her cheeks.

"I'm named after an ice-skater," Tenley said. Why'd she say that to this girl? To make her feel better about her name, Tenley guessed. Although there was no reason to do that. Except to be nice, right?

"Skater? Is it Nancy?" The girl guessed. "Oh, I know. Tanya. Kristi?"

"Tenley," she said.

"Who?"

"Never mind." Tenley's mother had named her after some skater, now a doctor, who lived in Marblehead or wherever. "Tenley Albright was an ice-skater."

"You skate?" Brileen asked.

"As if."

"Looks like the cops are packing up. Did they talk to you?" Brileen stood, brushing off the seat of her jeans. "Hey. Wanna go get coffee? It's my lunch hour."

"Did they talk to *you*?" Tenley tried to keep up. Say what cool people would say. Did she? Want to go get coffee? "Coffee?"

Tenley looked up at City Hall, saw the white-globed camera just under the eaves, attached to the concrete below the mayor's office window. If someone inside were monitoring the right screen, screen number seven, they might be watching her. What if her mother was looking out the window and saw her and wondered who she was talking to. "Tenley has no friends." She'd heard her mom say those exact words to her father, not realizing Tenley, in the downstairs hallway, could hear every word.

Her father had said, "She's got to start participating, Catherine, living in the real world."

Like they agreed she was a loser.

She wasn't a loser. She was—she felt her shoulders drop, felt the girl looking at her. Sad. She was *sad*. But maybe she didn't have to be sad all the time.

"Yeah, coffee," the girl repeated, smiling. "We can go to the Purple."

"Sure," Tenley decided. The Purple Martin, Brileen must mean, the coffee-shop-ish pub by the alley. "The Purple is cool."

She had fifteen minutes—at least—before she had to return to the dungeon. And you know what? She would enjoy those fifteen minutes. She looked up at City Hall, even thought about waving.

See, Mom? She telegraphed her message to the second window from the left. *You were wrong. Again. I do have friends.*

"What the hell?" Jake barreled around the corner and into the dead end, alarmed by DeLuca's yelling, prepared for the worst but not really expecting it. If D were in real danger, he'd have radioed via dispatch for extra backup, not called only for Jake.

Maybe he was wrong.

DeLuca stood, his back to Jake. From the looks of it, trying to referee two unhappy campers. And, from the looks of it, failing. Good thing Jane was headed in the other direction.

Calvin Hewlitt had his back against the brick wall, his face twisting in anger, spitting out his words. "That'll teach you, you little—"

"You're the total *jerk.*"

The kid with the camera? More precisely, the kid who used to have the camera. When the kid had first surprised him and D in the alley, Jake had almost shot him, thinking the camera was a gun. No matter now— what used to be the camera lay on the ground, shattered into pieces. A lens rolled toward the left wall, then caught, wobbling briefly, between two cobblestones.

"Hey—both of you!" Jake approached the adversaries, arms outstretched, palms out, peacemaking. He hoped. "Back. The frick. Off. Both of you. Now."

Lucky for DeLuca, and for the kid, they hadn't uncuffed Hewlitt. Otherwise, these idiots would no doubt be deep in hand-to-hand combat by now. The kid would be toast.

The kid picked up a silver piece of what once was a camera, waved it in Hewlitt's direction. "It's all *his* fault! Look at this! That camera was my—"

Hewlitt strained at his handcuffs like a pit bull on a chain. "Then you should have kept it out of my face, you—"

"Calm down, the both of you," Jake ordered. Even with Hewlitt in restraints, his partner had been outnumbered. Good thing he'd called for Jake. Man-to-man defense was far more effective than zone.

"You have to be completely shitting me." The kid stomped a foot. "I have a perfect right to—that moron kicked my camera! Right out of my hand! And now look at it. That camera cost big bucks."

"You have no freaking right to take my picture, you punk." Hewlitt took a step, aggressive. "If one picture of me in cuffs ever gets—"

"But he *kicked*—" the kid was saying.

"I'm serious, Detective, I'm an upstanding, innocent—"

"Enough!" Jake yelled. He pointed at Hewlitt. "You. Hewlitt. Not another word."

"But—"

Jake looked at DeLuca, questioning. "He kicked the camera? Out of the kid's hands?"

"Before I could, it went straight up in the—" DeLuca demonstrated with the flip of a palm. "I mean, who'da thought—"

"What*ever*." Ridiculously, the damage made Jake's life easier. Take this guy in? Now he had a perfect by-the-book reason to do so. "Calvin Hewlitt? You're under arrest for malicious destruction of property, assault and battery."

"For not wanting my picture in handcuffs on the damn front page?" Hewlitt rolled his head back, incredulous. "*I'm* under arrest? *Me?*"

"See?" the kid sneered at Hewlitt, derisive.

"Shut *up*." DeLuca grabbed the kid by one arm, keeping him in place.

"See?" Hewlitt spat the word back at him, chin out.

There'd been a murder not two hours earlier, but now Jake was occupied in mediating a battle over a broken camera between a punk kid and a lawsuit-threatening potential suspect. This whole episode had totally gotten—

"But—" The kid was still trying to talk.

"And you, young man," Jake interrupted. He'd get this under control, return to some semblance of sanity, bring Hewlitt in for questioning, and then move on.

"But there's *pictures*. In that camera!" The kid kept talking, almost in tears, waving one hand at the shards of plastic and splinters of shattered glass strewn across the pavement. "Pictures of the *stabbing*! Now, because of *him*, they're totally wrecked, because of this—this—"

The kid stood, his chest heaving, one finger pointing at the molded silver halves of the camera, now split apart, revealing what looked like a tiny green circuit board, some sort of black plastic spool, slivers of plastic. The flat black view-screen, Jake recognized it from his own camera, lay in a dark shaft of shadow by the kid's foot.

And past that, the tiny green memory card, the postage-stamp-size heart of the camera, where all the digital information was stored. Keeping his eyes on the kid, Jake took a step toward it.

With any luck, and it was about time they had some, Jake's photo unit could still retrieve the photos recorded there. Holy shit. Were they all he'd need?

"Mr.—" Jake paused.

"Land," DeLuca said. "Bobby Land."

"Land." Jake kept his voice low, though his brain was in high gear. "You saw what happened? At the park?"

"The camera did, I think." Bobby bent down, picked up the silver metal piece that had obviously been the front of the camera. He turned it over, examining it, the sun hitting the shiny surface. "I look through the viewfinder, you know?"

Jake felt DeLuca take a step closer to Hewlitt. Hewlitt was cuffed, and finally quiet, but he could still try to run. A random security type who just happened to be in the alley at the right time? Jake had his doubts.

But the kid hadn't pegged Hewlitt as the stabber. And would have, right? If he'd seen him? Unless he was afraid.

Still, the kid was the key. They had a suspect—victim?—in custody, certainly now under armed guard at the hospital. They could get that suspect's photo, put it in an array, show it to the kid, all by the book, bingo.

So much for the hordes of probably unreliable bystanders at the crime scene. So much for fingerprints. Even the kid's testimony. That'd all be backup. The photos on this kid's camera would not lie. "Did you photograph the person who did it? Could you identify him?"

"And it wasn't me, right, punk?" Hewlitt called out.

"Was it?" Jake needed that answer, too.

"I've never seen that jerk before." Bobby wiped his mouth with the back of one hand, then the other. "But the guy who did it, um . . ."

Jake could tell he was trying to decide. That was good. "No" was an easy answer. "No" was adios, I can't help you, good-bye. "Yes" was more difficult. "Yes" meant maybe being branded a snitch, court appearances and cross-examination, the threatening possibility of retaliation and revenge. If Bobby Land was deciding, that meant the real answer was most likely yes, he could recognize the suspect. Yes was good.

Bobby felt the grit of street dust on the back of his hand, felt his mouth get drier and drier. Why had he told the cops he'd seen the person who did the stabbing?

The jerk bag against the wall, that's who'd put him over the edge. *I mean, like, he was allowed to break my freaking camera? And get away with it? Who the hell was he, anyway?* The guy would get into even more trouble if he, like, had wrecked valuable evidence of the crime. Which could, in fact, be there. Bobby wasn't totally sure.

Though now he was trapped. It was illegal to lie to the cops, everyone knew that, and if he couldn't recognize the "suspect," as this cop had called him, might he be in big trouble? And what happened to Jane Ryland, anyway? She'd been right behind him, she'd be able to help him explain, or get out of this. But Jane was gone. Crap. You couldn't trust anyone.

Bobby ran his tongue across his dry lips, wishing he were anywhere else, wishing he'd never opened his—but wait.

The memory card. Over there, in the middle of one square of gray cobblestone. If there was a picture of the stabber, if he had actually gotten it, they might be able to get it from the card. Not definitely, but maybe. Then he wouldn't have to identify the person at all. Would he? They could all go by what they saw in the photo.

The memory card was the key. All he had to do was get it.

Both cops were staring at him, waiting for an answer. The preppy one moved closer to him, Bobby saw that, watching him edge into his space, ready to nail him, probably, if he made a move. Which, he had to admit, had crossed his mind.

But if he tried to run for it they'd probably shoot him. And he'd look guilty as hell, of something, even though he wasn't.

Bobby took a deep, shuddering breath, the cop's eyes on him, the jerk's eyes on him, thinking about how this had all started because he thought he was in the right place at the right time. Now it might have been the wrong place.

"Mr. Land?" One cop came closer. The other one, the tall skinny one, had his hand right by his gun. The handcuffed guy, they'd called him Hewlitt, was staring daggers. They were all silent, waiting for Bobby. Waiting for Bobby to say something.

Why didn't he ever learn to keep his mouth shut?

But wait a minute. He had the eye. Right? And if there was a good photo in the camera, he'd be a hero, and it'd be all he'd need to make his career. Either it was there or it wasn't. If it wasn't—He mentally shrugged, imagining it. He could say he'd made a mistake. He was only a kid, after all. If it was? A good photo might, just *might,* change his life. Not exactly as he'd planned. But to be famous you had to be flexible. Open to possibilities. Someone had said that, he was sure.

"Well, I guess I . . ." he began, though he had not quite decided what to say next.

A yell, like the roar of a—?

Bobby, startled by the sound, tripped backward, losing his balance, stumbling over his own feet, landing on his ass as all the shadows moved and both cops were yelling, as Hewlitt, bellowing like a crazy person, charged toward him. Bobby raised his arms, ready to duck, ready to run, but wait, the guy couldn't punch him, he was in handcuffs, right?

With a sound that echoed through the cul-de-sac, Hewlitt stomped one heavy shoe on the memory card. "No pictures of me!" he shouted.

Bobby heard himself shouting too as the two cops grabbed Hewlitt's arms and yanked him away, twisting and pivoting even as they dragged him, his brown loafers scraping on the pavement.

It didn't matter. The memory card was useless, now tiny fragments of plastic and metal.

14

If Jane's phone didn't stop buzzing, she was going to crush it to tiny phone smithereens. Still crouched in the alley by the droning air conditioner, she tried to ignore her cell, the nasty little creature, the insistent piece of technology that connected her, relentlessly, to anyone who decided their life was more important than hers. She could hardly remember life before cell phones, when everyone on the planet couldn't electronically demand attention every minute of every day. Jane had understood she was over the edge on the phone thing the day she'd walked down the back hall of the *Register,* talking, gone into the bathroom, listening, and tried to figure out how to pull her tights down while she asked her source one more question. At that exact moment, she'd realized she was addicted, hooked, inalterably chained to it.

Was it Jake calling? Checking on her? Only three minutes ago, maybe less, he'd ordered her to leave the alley. She didn't want to admit she hadn't.

Jake was one of the city's top homicide cops, and this was a homicide. So where Jake was, that's where the story would be. Here she would stay until she discovered exactly what the story was. She couldn't hear a thing from way back there, but they had to come out sometime. She'd be ready.

The phone buzzed again. Maybe it was the assignment desk. Maybe they had updated information.

She dug out the phone, punched the button. *Private caller.* "Yes?" she whispered.

"Jane?"

Jane narrowed her eyes, trying to focus. The voice was familiar but off somehow.

"It's Melissa."

"Hey, Sis," Jane whispered. "You okay? I'm right in the midst of a—"

"I might need you," Melissa said. "Maybe. About the Gracie thing."

Jane took the phone away from her ear, looked at it in brief bewilderment, as if looking through it to her sister.

"But you said—" Jane began.

"I *know* what I *said*." Melissa sounded worried, her voice tight, cutting Jane off. "But I'm kind of freaking. How can I be a good mother if I can't even handle this? Daniel's not arriving until tonight—and . . . Anyway. That husband of Robyn's. He's—hang on a second."

Jane lifted her eyes skyward, pleading with the universe for one tiny break. Melissa was telling her to hang on? *Hang on?*

Jane peeked around the edge of the thrumming air conditioner. Saw shadows moving, the light changing, down where the turn began. Heard voices, then footsteps. Jake and DeLuca must be on the move. With Bobby. And whoever else was back there.

She had to get her camera. This story was about to break.

"Does your family live in Boston?"

Figures. Brileen was asking the one question Tenley hoped to avoid. Now she'd have to decide what to tell her. Reality was too complicated. Who her mother was. Who her father was. Who her sister was. Or wasn't.

The two girls had skirted the walkways of Curley Park, headed away toward the Purple, watching as bystanders, dismissed by the police, drifted back to wherever. Tenley had seen the first ambulance pull away, siren screaming, then another one come out of Franklin Alley. Now cars were being let through, as usual. Seemed like normal was back.

Tenley knew she had less than ten minutes more with this girl, this

Brileen. That would be barely long enough to grab a coffee. Not enough for the story of her family.

Maybe she should change the subject. Or find out more about Brileen, because in ten minutes, she'd have to say good-bye, and that would be too bad.

"Do *you*?" Tenley asked. "Have family in Boston?"

"Sure," Brileen said. "Doesn't mean I like 'em." She yanked the leather shoulder strap of a black laptop bag over her head, carried it cross-body.

"Tell me about it," Tenley said.

She looked down as they walked, watched how her steps matched Brileen's. Bri's feet in chunky Maddens, all thick laces and blocky soles. Tenley's were in black flats, which she used to love, just this morning she'd loved them. Now they looked like loser shoes. Why did everything always change?

"Hang on a second." Brileen tilted her head toward the alley. "Hear that? See that? Somebody's coming out," she whispered. She flattened herself against the bank's stone façade, gestured Tenley to do the same. "We should be careful. What if the bad guy is still—you know. Out there."

Tenley leaned out, just a fraction so she could see around Brileen.

"Hey!" Brileen whispered. "They've got someone in handcuffs? See him?"

"Whoa." Tenley edged away from the shelter of the building, wanting to get a better look. In about two minutes she was going to be late for work, which would be difficult to explain. If Dahlstrom even gave her a chance to explain.

But this was kind of like a movie. How could she leave now?

Jane was shooting the hell out of this, whatever this turned out to be. Jane's job now was to get everything on video. *Shoot first,* one journalism school professor had instructed, *ask questions later.* The whole class had lost it, laughing.

But that's exactly what she was doing.

Melissa had hung up on her—or maybe their cell phone connection had gotten dropped, Jane wasn't sure. But when Jane had heard voices, then seen shadows, then heard feet crunching across the grit of the alley cobblestones, she'd tucked herself behind the air conditioner again— seemed like she'd spent a lot of time there—knowing the next face she saw might be Jake's, and wondering how, exactly, she'd deal with that.

Jake would not be happy. And she did not have a good explanation for why she'd ignored his orders to leave. Not that she was obligated to do what he told her.

But it was a stranger's face she saw first, a blustering, muttering, muscle-bound guy in a sweat-soaked oxford shirt and ripped khakis, his hands cuffed behind him, being marched out of the alley by a scowling Paul DeLuca. Was this the killer?

Jane instantly pointed her Quik-Shot, checking that the camera was recording, making sure the sound was up, feeling the heart-swelling rise of news instinct, the hope that maybe, because she'd held her ground, she was now documenting the arrest of the guy she'd mentally headlined the Curley Park Killer. It was breaking news, it was exclusive, and it was a potentially career-clinching moment.

"Get her outta here," the man yelled. "I told you no photographs! I'm going to sue the hell out of . . ."

Jane let out a steadying spiral of breath. *Stay calm. Do this.* If the man didn't want his photo taken, Channel 2's legal people would decide whether to put it on the air. But in her book, a handcuffed man in police custody was a suspect and fair broadcast game.

She felt the warm flush of adrenaline as she panned the camera to fol- low DeLuca and the man out of the alley, the suspect's voice diminishing as DeLuca led him away.

Behind DeLuca was the kid, Bobby Land. His hands, not cuffed, were jammed into his pockets, his shoulders sagged, and a smear of dirt swiped across his face. The hipster-wannabe camo hat he'd worn so jauntily was jammed into the waistband of his jeans. He'd approached Jane all confident and conspiratorial. Now he was just an angry-looking kid, stomping down the alley in grimy scuffed sneakers, the untied laces dragging on the pavement.

And behind him was Jake. Jake had one hand on Bobby's shoulder, but didn't look as if he had the boy in custody. In his other hand, Jake carried what looked like a clear plastic bag of . . . Jane couldn't tell.

Just keep shooting, her reporter brain instructed. *Then follow them out.*

Through the viewfinder, Jane watched that plan go down the tubes. Jake stopped and turned back to look at her. She saw his face in the camera first, then looked past the viewfinder to see him in reality as well. She'd seen Jake laughing and crying, she'd seen him perplexed, amused, and concerned, and, a couple of times, irate. She wasn't quite sure how to label his current expression.

"Jane?" As if he didn't know who she was. Or couldn't believe it. "Why the hell are you—"

"Hey, Detective." She tried a conciliatory smile, all innocence and obedience. Two professional acquaintances meeting by chance. In an alley. After a murder. "Yeah, I was about to leave, just as you suggested, but then—"

"My camera is wrecked, Jane!" Bobby wrenched himself away from Jake, glowering, and took a step toward her. "Where'd you *go?* I had everything, like I told you, all the photographs of the stabbing, but then this moron—I can't even believe it. *Broke* it. All that's left is in that stupid plastic bag. Look!"

He pointed to the bag in Jake's hand with one accusatory finger. Jane backed up—partly to get a better shot of the bag, partly because she wasn't quite sure about the look on the kid's face. He was about nineteen or twenty, hadn't he told her he was in college? And though he obviously cultivated a kind of urban-hip streetwise vibe, he had a jittery quality, edgy as an abused pup trying to decide whether a newcomer was ally or enemy. A pup who had chosen incorrectly before.

"Wait, who broke it?" Jane asked. Had Jake smashed the kid's camera?

Why? The other perplexing thing was that Bobby had never told her he had photos of the murder. He'd only said he *might*. She pointed her Quik-Shot at Jake. "Ja—Detective Brogan?"

"*Enough.* From both of you." Jake clamped his free hand on the kid's right arm and yanked Bobby away from her. "Anything else you need, you get from headquarters, Ms. Ryland."

He pivoted, leading a still-complaining Bobby toward the sunlit street.

Two hours since she'd gotten this assignment, and now Jane had about three seconds before the only thing in her viewfinder would be an empty alley. DeLuca and whoever that was in handcuffs were already at the sidewalk. She had a camera full of something, but no idea what the video meant. She had to find out. And quickly.

"Detective Brogan? Can you at least identify the man in handcuffs?" she called after them. "Is he a person of interest in the Curley Park stabbing?"

Jake had turned his back on her and was leading Bobby out of the alley. He took another step, then stopped, and Jane saw the back of his leather jacket rise, then fall. Still holding Bobby's arm, Jake turned toward her, slowly. She saw his eyes narrow, his mouth in a taut line. She adored that mouth, knew every centimeter of it. She adored those dark eyes, and the laugh lines around them, had seen them as closely as anyone could see another human being.

" 'Person of interest'?" Jake drew out the words as he looked her up and down, making her feel as if he'd never seen her before. Sometimes he acted like a stranger. Did he think about her that way, too? "Where did you hear that phrase, Ms. Ryland? On the cops and robbers channel?"

And then her phone buzzed again.

15

Jane sat on Marsh Tyson's black leather couch, waiting for the news director to return. Thinking about her long journey to get here. A few years ago, a college journalism student had interviewed Jane for a school project. *You're my role model,* the girl had told her. Jane, still such a shining newbie that she'd believed that was reasonable, had answered the student thoughtfully, trying for passion and principle and optimism.

What would be the title of your autobiography? The girl promised Jane it would be the last question. And that was a toughie. At age—what was Jane then, thirty?—the story of her life as a journalist was still unfolding. How could she label it? How could she know?

The Best Is Yet to Come. She'd contemplated that title, but it seemed ungrateful. She'd been happy, and why dismiss what she'd already accomplished? *Just Do It* seemed derivative. *Never Give Up*? Just as clichéd. She'd felt compelled to give a good answer, an honest one. One that would give some insight into her soul. Even to herself.

Back then she'd just been assigned to the stress-inducing ratings-driven agenda of the investigative unit. She was negotiating the mortgage on her Corey Road condo. Her sister triumphantly finished law school. Mom got her terrible diagnosis. Her father was still chief of surgery at Oak Park Hospital. Jane still had her tortoiseshell cat Murrow, and she'd been almost engaged to a cerulean-eyed doctor, whose hours at Mass General had been equally unpredictable as her reporter hours but whose profession was the one thing in Jane's life her father couldn't criticize.

The Juggler. Jane had finally chosen that title, laughing and tossing imaginary balls in the air. The student paper had used it for the headline, much to her mother's delight and her father's disdain. Soon after, and then later, her dreams and plans had exploded and reassembled at light speed, altered with the whims of the universe. She'd begun to realize there was no use in planning and no percentage in predicting, and she'd learned that dreams sometimes had to change, even vanish.

Now Mom was dead. Murrow, too. After winning several investigative-reporter Emmys, Jane was fired from Channel 11 for protecting a source, though that's not how the bigwigs would have described it almost two years ago. The ex–almost fiancé was still lording it at the hospital, she guessed. She hadn't seen him since their fight. Her father, now emeritus, still asked her about him, but Jane would change the subject. Her Corey Road condo was still home, and new arrival Coda, now almost a year old, had expected Jane to adapt to her particular feline demands.

She'd met Jake. Not the best romantic choice, with her as rising star reporter and him as rising star detective. It created a clandestine relation-ship doomed from the start by police department and newsroom edicts prohibiting conflicts of interest. Last month, in one poignant moment at the end of a particularly emotional murder case, Jake had broached the idea of marriage and a future together. Over long dinners and longer after-dinners, they'd contemplated going for it, starting again, someone changing careers, maybe both of them. No pressure, plenty of time, just maybe. When, in a heart-pumping fit of indignation, Jane quit her job at the *Register,* with the *Register*'s lawyers warning her about the severe per-sonal and financial ramifications of even the hint of a leak about the fab-ricated news she'd uncovered, it appeared new doors might be opening.

Now she was juggling again.

Jake was not talking to her. He'd turned his back in the alley earlier, striding away, Bobby Land in tow. Nor was he answering her texts.

Lissa, oops, Melissa, wasn't answering her texts, either.

She was juggling Marsh Tyson, too. And the possibility of a freelance gig at Channel 2, especially if the Curley Park story panned out. They'd told her to hang on to the Quik-Shot, just in case, but they'd made a copy of her video, from the opening shots of the crime scene to the person-on-the-street interviews to the mysterious ambulance in the alley, ending with Jake walking away. Possibly the first time the potential end of a romance had been caught on camera. Talk about cinema verité.

Just keep swimming. She could hear her mother quoting one of their favorite hospital-bedside movies. *Miss you, Mom.* She'd try. She had no choice.

Marsh yanked open his glass door, letting in the chaos of the newsroom. Phones trilled, computers pinged, someone yelled "five minutes!" One wall of Tyson's office displayed a massive bank of flickering TV monitors, their audio clashing and incomprehensible, the volume of each set turned just loud enough to muffle the others. Jane looked at the white-lighted, six-digit readout above the door: 3:55:15. The four o'clock news was about to begin.

"Hey, Jane." Tyson closed the door, and it all went silent. He loosened his tie, rolled up his shirtsleeves. Jane had done her homework with a few Internet searches, knew a younger Tyson had once anchored weekends in Raleigh. Handsome local boy made semi-good, his mother the mayor of some North Carolina town, his father a big civil rights activist. Now he moved behind the scenes. More job security in management, Jane guessed, than being on-air talent. Almost anything was more secure than "talent."

"So. How'd you like it? Being out in the fray, tracking down clues, following leads?" Tyson still embraced his anchorman voice. Listing clichés was a skill he seemed to have perfected. "You rocked this one, Jane. Your video'll be all over the six. Exclusive."

Jane shrugged, accepting the compliment. "Thanks. I called the cop shop's new PR flack to get the deets on the victim and the guy in cuffs," she said. She almost laughed, hearing herself using that kind of phony jargon. She held up her cell. "But she hasn't called back."

If asked, Jane would have sworn she didn't miss TV. Didn't miss the relentless deadlines, the too-short video stories, the nature-of-the-beast shallow coverage. But all she could think about was how to break some new ground for the next show.

What's the most important newscast of the day? one journalism teacher had asked. *Trick question,* Professor Burke had said, holding up one finger, shushing them before the class could even guess. *The most important newscast is the next one.*

"I've got our desk people on it, too," Tyson said. "Plenty of time to write your story. Do a minute-thirty for the anchor. Beverly can voice it."

A knock on the glass door.

"Yo," Tyson said, gesturing the woman in. "Speak of the devil. What you got, Bev?"

Beverly Chorbajian, the station's new marquee anchor, her face on every billboard in Boston. Jane didn't remember when anchor clothes had become so revealing, but something was certainly working for glamorous and exotic Beverly. She had a steady job, at least. More than Jane did.

"Cop shop PR flack shot me a text, Marsh," Beverly said, waving her phone. "Oh, hi, Jane. Anyway, still no ID or fingerprints on the Curley Park vic. Still no ID or fingerprints on the Franklin Alley suspect."

"The police called him a suspect?" Jane asked. Would have been nice if the PR flack had returned *her* call, instead of Beverly's. Would have been helpful if *she* could have provided this fingerprint news. Such as it was.

"Nope, but that's what *I'd* call him." Beverly raised an eyebrow. "He was in handcuffs, right?"

"Whatever," Tyson said. "And?"

"That's it." Beverly tucked a strand of blonded hair behind one ear. "Flack said she'd ping when there was more."

"Let us know." Marsh pointed at her. "Now you better get ready."

"I'm always ready," Beverly said. She didn't exactly strut away, but she came close.

Maybe Jane didn't miss TV, after all. Her phone rang, buzzing and vibrating against the news director's glass coffee table.

"Cop shop, dollars to doughnuts," Tyson said. "Go ahead, Jane. Then give us the deets."

Jane crossed mental fingers it would be the police, providing her information to wrap this story. Better info than Bev got.

"Hello?"

"Jane, it's Lissa. Melissa. I had to hang up before because—well, listen. Seems like Lewis and Gracie have taken off. On an 'adventure.'" Melissa paused, took a deep breath. "Lewis apparently is 'impetuous.' Whatever Robyn means by that. Where are you, Janey? Because . . ."

Jane stood, hearing the uncertainty in her sister's voice.

"Cops? Something?" Tyson asked.

"Lissa?" Jane held up a hand, signaling Tyson *no,* not the cops. She was beginning to hate her phone even more. But for all their squabbles, she and Melissa were sisters. And that tone in Lissa's voice—one Jane had never heard. Melissa and Gracie had bonded, Jane knew. Even with Melissa's rigid view of the world, somehow the little girl had gotten through. Touched her heart, she'd said. But again, it was Lissa's—Melissa's— wedding. So, hard to tell.

"Melissa?" she said again.

Jane heard voices in the background, the hushed murmurs of someone else talking.

"She's nine years old," Melissa whispered. "Jane, I'm so worried, and Daniel's not here to help and—could you come? I need you. I really do. Please?"

"One second," Jane told her. *Please?* "Ah, Mr. Tyson? I—"

"So?" Tyson,was aiming his remote at the bank of TV monitors, goosing up the volume, one screen after the next. "Ready to write it up nice and juicy for the six? Lead story, sister."

Jane felt the warmth go out of her face, pressed her lips together.

"I can't," she said.

Tyson turned to her, his arm still pointed at the screens. It slowly lowered, and Jane's shoulders seemed to sink along with it.

"Can't." Tyson made it a statement. A bullet. He nodded, silently, considering. Then turned back to the monitors. "I see."

Jane waited a heartbeat. The day had started with an opening door. Now it was apparently slamming in her face.

"I have a family emergency," she said.

16

No way could he be in four places at once, so Jake had chosen the one that could clinch the case. Mass General. He jabbed the elevator button, waiting for the numbered lights above to make their agonizingly slow journey down to where he waited on L. Five o'clock. Shift change. Every elevator in the hospital would be stopping on every floor. It wouldn't help to be impatient, even though he was. He felt so close to *case closed* he could taste the celebratory beer.

Bobby Land would have to wait. Jake had stashed him in an office on the third level of Headquarters with a can of Sprite and a couple of sports magazines. Fortunately, the kid hadn't called for a lawyer or his parents, and, after admitting that he was over eighteen, thank you so much, had agreed to stand by until Jake got back. The memory card from Land's camera was a total loss, according to the techs in IT, so whatever photos he had taken were crushed out of existence. Jake had promised Bobby they'd investigate the shattered camera incident, so Land was probably happily planning his revenge—or lawsuit—against Calvin Hewlitt.

Hewlitt himself, not such a happy camper, was parked in interrogation room C with Paul DeLuca. In a cold blast of law enforcement irony, DeLuca had been partnered for the preliminary questioning with Angie Bartoneri, once Jake relieved her here at the hospital. Question one for Hewlitt: Why had he smashed that memory card? Just to keep his hand-cuffed picture out of the papers? Seemed more like an obvious move by a guilt-ridden person worried by something incriminating on it. Still, if

Bobby Land had seen whatever that something was, his eyewitness evidence was almost as probative as that caught on camera. Almost.

D had promised to let Jake know if Hewlitt said anything useful or instructive. Not likely, since the only word out of his mouth so far, according to D, was "lawyer." They couldn't hold him forever—eight hours, according to case law, until they had to cut bait. "Malicious destruction of property" would legally keep him at HQ for a while, but a good lawyer would get him sprung pretty damn fast. Hewlitt was trouble, Jake knew it. He just didn't know how. Yet.

John Doe No. 1 was in the morgue. Identification team was hot on his case, but so far, the stabbed guy—Caucasian male, middle-aged—was still nameless. Why wasn't he carrying ID? Everyone had ID. How'd he get to Curley Park? Victim and potential suspect both arrived at the park with no ID?

Jane would soon be pushing to get pictures of them both. She'd already texted him a few times, most likely about exactly that. He hadn't decided how to handle the Jane situation, so he was ignoring it for now. Jake hadn't seen a photo of the dead guy's face yet, so all in all, at this point, it was hard to come up with any theories. And maybe theorizing was a waste of time. This case might be solved in the next five minutes.

That's why Jake was headed to the guarded bedside of John Doe No. 2.

What was that guy doing in that alley? Why had Calvin Hewlitt jumped him? So far, according to the watch, John Doe No. 2 was so doped up he was out of it. Jake wanted to see for himself. Maybe hear for himself. Try to get some idea of what had gone down in Franklin Alley.

Jake texted himself a reminder—*Dumpster.*

On the way to HQ, he'd dispatched a crime scene team to check it out. They'd soon reported there was nothing inside, e-mailed him their photos of the empty bin. Jake used a thumb to scroll his cell phone through their wide shots and close-ups; grimy dented metal walls, peeling paint, streaks of black and bird shit, puddled floor.

Empty.

That's what worried Jake. Be a bad break if whatever had been in the Dumpster was now covered by layers of trash and detritus in the municipal landfill. He'd asked a cadet to get the pickup schedule. It was unlikely—Jake hoped this wasn't wishful thinking—there'd be a Waste Management pickup at noon on a Monday. Maybe the Dumpster was empty. Maybe the tipster had been wrong. Maybe it wouldn't matter.

He jabbed the elevator button again. Jane would have teased him about the futility of that. The alley. Who was the girl-woman who'd sent the cadet back there in the first place? He'd ordered him to find her.

Finally. Entering the elevator, he stepped to the side, getting out of the way as a frazzle-haired mom maneuvered a double-wide stroller into all the available space.

The good news, and the reason Jake was here? Though cadets were still looking through photos from bystanders' cameras and cells, they'd discovered one kick-ass lead. Jake pulled out the folded copy of the digital color snapshot DeLuca had handed him half an hour ago.

"Check it out," D had said. "Note the time stamp. Eleven fifty-nine A.M. Guy who took it's around if we need him."

They'd printed it out on letter-size paper. Not the best quality, but good enough. A medium close-up of someone's back, someone wearing a once-white shirt. Jake could tell it was a man, could tell he was facedown on the sidewalk, and could see a bit of Mayor Curley's bronze knee. Also in the photo was the clear image of the hilt of a knife, clutched in someone's hand. Someone plunging the blade into the man's back.

"Too bad you can't see the stabber's face," Jake had said to D.

"True," DeLuca said. "Thing is, we don't need to see it." He pointed to the stabber's forearm. The arm with the knife. "Look closer."

Jake looked. "Tattoo."

"Yup."

Jake had examined it again, close up, and then from farther away, holding it up to the light, as if that would reveal something. "Some fancy defense attorney'll probably try to argue the stabber was being a good Samaritan, trying to pull the knife *out*."

"Love to be there when he tries that," DeLuca said. "We'd hear the jury laughing all the way to the Cape."

"Yup," Jake said.

"So, my man. If our John Doe 2 at MGH has a tattoo? What you see is what you get. Another life drama successfully solved," DeLuca had said. "And in less than six hours. A new record, Harvard, even for us."

Jake put the photo back into his jacket pocket. Reaching past the stroller, he pushed the button for 6.

So that was cool. The afternoon had raced by, even though it usually seemed like time went by slower if you wanted the day to go fast, not today. Brileen had asked her if she wanted to get coffee after work, since lunch got too rushed.

Tenley had gone back to her desk, and time had completely flown.

She logged off, watched the screen dip to black, waved at the second shifters arriving to take the day team's place, and even smiled at the slobby red-haired guy who always took her spot. He looked kind of, like, surprised, so she guessed she'd never smiled at him before. Dahlstrom was nowhere to be seen, even better, as Tenley punched the ticking metal time clock. She usually hated that—who still had a punch clock?—but this time the little good-bye *ding* made her happy. She'd realized she'd seen Bri on the T in the mornings, must have, they just hadn't connected. And turned out Bri went to the same college. Now she was meeting a college friend for coffee. Cool.

Tenley made a quick pit stop, assessed herself in the ladies' room mirror as she rolled up her skirt's waistband. Once, twice, patted it into place. Wonder if Brileen knew Lanna? Brileen seemed a little older—but old enough to know Lanna?

Anyway. Dr. Maddux would be happy she was "getting out in the world," right? Should she text her mom, saying she was meeting a friend for coffee—wouldn't *that* be a surprise?—and not to worry, she'd be home? She *could* just go tell her in person.

Tenley stuck her earrings back in, felt the golden curves slip through the pierces in her ears. She felt like her old self, a feeling she hadn't had in however long she could remember. There was a Tenley she used to know, the one who laughed and read vampire books, who kind of liked math and computers and puzzles, who listened to music and secretly read movie star blogs. It had all soured, turned worthless, and gross and shallow, after Lanna. Died.

"After Lanna died," she whispered. She had to face it. And live with it.

She was only eighteen. And she was, she had to admit, kind of tired of feeling sad. Was it being unfaithful to be happy? She would never understand what happened to Lanna. She could never imagine forgiving herself for it. And she would always miss Lanna. Always, always, always.

But that didn't mean she had to give up her whole life. Lanna would want her to be happy.

She hardly remembered waiting for the elevator, hardly remembered waving to the snoozing security guard at the Congress Street side exit, hardly remembered poking the flat metal button to get the Walk sign. She'd started crossing before it even changed, because how could she wait? Because there was her friend Brileen Finnerty, across the street, sitting on the green bench. Exactly as she'd promised.

It was almost as if Lanna had given her a gift.

17

"My *fault*? *My* fault?" Catherine Siskel said it out loud to her empty kitchen, knew if she threw the framed photo of Lanna across the room it would serve only to shatter the glass, thereby destroying another part of their lives. Early this morning, her husband called to inform her that he'd "again" "unexpectedly" been "called" to meet with a client. And he "might be" "very delayed" coming home. So her photo-throwing drama would be wasted. What's more, she'd have to clean up all that broken glass.

Seemed she was always cleaning up something. The most internecine messes at City Hall were easier to manage than her own life.

It wasn't just Greg, she had to admit. Often she herself stayed late at the office, an explainable side effect of her job, but recently more an excuse to keep from having to go home to their daughter Lanna's forever-empty bedroom and her husband's empty eyes. What was he caring about these last months? Not her.

Now she was by herself, in their empty house. Tenley wasn't home yet, and if Greg found out, somehow he'd make even that her fault. In this morning's call, he'd insisted, as always, she make sure their daughter was home that night. Because of Lanna, he always said.

What else was new?

She was always concerned about Tenley. Greg hardly had to remind her of that. But Tenley had to live in the real world. She and her husband could not protect her from imaginary dangers. She'd be home soon.

"The girl is eighteen," she'd reminded Greg, unnecessarily, this morning. Now she shoved a bottle of sauvignon blanc into the fridge. At least it could be cold, even though she'd have to open it alone. She slammed the stainless steel door. *Taking her hostilities out on the fridge. Helpful.*

"She has a job at City Hall, a job *I* managed to finagle for her," Catherine had said. "Why is it my responsibility to make sure she's home at some random time you happen to select? No. Just, no. We need to let her have a life."

Catherine steadied herself against the countertop. Using the toe of her left black patent pump, she pried off the heel of her right shoe, then, with bare toes, slipped off the other. She left both shoes toppled over in the middle of the kitchen floor and paced by them, fuming. Taking off her heels was always such a relief, and the cool tile felt soothing under her feet. But this was no time to relax, she couldn't relax any part of her.

She replayed more of the morning's conversation—if you could call it "conversation"—in her head.

"I resent this, Greg," she'd said. "You go away, you call me from where the hell ever, you expect the world to work just the way you want and demand, and when it doesn't, it's everyone's fault but yours."

She leaned against the counter, the empty house deafening. She'd tried to be patient with her husband. He was still in mourning, still upset, relentlessly, viciously upset. Catherine knew the most effective way to handle an unhappy constituent was to listen, evaluate, and then design a solution. She did that every day at City Hall.

But finally she couldn't listen to one more word. "*You* lost a daughter?" Her scorn had pinged off the shiny windows of her City Hall office, and then against the framed photos on her office wall. "*I've* lost a daughter, too, Greg. We've both—I mean—not a day goes by that I—"

The kitchen floor tile no longer felt cool under her tired feet. She dropped her head back and closed her eyes, remembering, searching for new meaning in this impossibly recycled and reprocessed conversation.

How many times could they talk about the exact same thing in different ways? How long would the loop of sorrow and guilt continue before it destroyed them both? *All three of them,* she amended.

How her husband's brain worked she could no longer fathom. Twenty-seven years ago, was it now? when she was still Kate O'Connor, they'd met and married when they both attended the Kennedy School's public policy program. They'd cuddled in the common TV room watching the presidential elections and told each other "don't worry, be happy" every time they had a big paper due. She rebranded herself Catherine, took her husband's name in a fit of neofeminism, and went into local politics. He went into political consulting. They'd been the happy activist couple, making a difference in people's lives every day. Now they lived in a nice, but fringey, part of town, the mayor insisting it would prove that every part of the City of Boston welcomed everyone. The mayor lived in the welcome of Beacon Hill. But the woods nearby had been lovely. Until Lanna.

"How about this, Greg," she'd said, trying to use her calm-the-constituent voice though she knew he'd recognize that and be further annoyed. "How about if you come home tonight? For once?"

"I'll try," he'd said. "I will."

Catherine replayed those words, "I'll try," as clear as if her husband—*where was he?*—had just said them. She'd open that wine now and pretend nothing bad had happened, nothing bad had touched them, and nothing bad would ever touch them again.

She took a step toward the fridge and tripped over one of her shoes, stubbing a toe and almost falling against the drain board. *All* she needed. All! She paused, feeling her tears. Why did she always have to be the conciliatory one? She was hurting, too, and trying her best to cope. Huh. Maybe she'd even be better off without Greg. Let go of the past. Let go of *him.* Start over.

"Greg?" She'd finally interrupted whatever he'd been saying. "Forgive me here for the outrageous notion—but if you cannot manage to come home, how about if you pick up your phone and call Tenley yourself? Remind her you exist?"

A hang-up moment if Catherine had ever heard one, and it took every bit of her willpower not to do it.

"Tell Tenley I love her," Greg had said. And then he was gone.

"Never? *Never?*"

Jane tried to remember the last time she'd seen her sister like this. Over many years, Melissa had perfected annoyed-petulant and demonstrated it whenever she didn't get her way.

"You're saying this has never happened before?" Melissa stood next to a striped wing chair in Robyn and Lewis Wilhoite's living room, one hand on her navy silk hip and the other gesturing, underlining every time she said "never." Jane could picture the identical stance in a courtroom, Melissa as prosecutor, grilling some poor defendant on the witness stand.

Melissa's target now was suburban housewife Robyn Wilhoite, perched on the center cushion of her almost-gaudy chintz couch, alone, hands in her lap, fingers intertwined.

"Never happened that I don't know where they are?" Robyn pouted, fussed with the black cardigan draped around her shoulders. "Well, not really. I mean, lately Lewis is trying to be, well, he calls it *spontaneous*. He thinks Gracie should be more . . . flexible. Live for today, all that. They go on adventures."

Jane, standing by a multiwindowed mahogany breakfront, waited for her cue, not certain of her role. Melissa had asked her to come, her pleading voice on the phone making Jane's presence seem urgent, but after a brief two-cheek air kiss, Melissa'd essentially ignored her. Still, the best way to understand a story was to listen. Any good reporter knew that.

"Flexible?" Melissa was saying. "They go on '*adventures*'? My question was: Has it ever happened before? A fairly binary question. Yes or no?"

Robyn flattened herself against the couch, pressing into the flowered cushions as if she were trying to get farther away from her new—what was she about to become? Jane tried to parse the relationships. Robyn was little Gracie's mother, and Melissa would soon be Gracie's stepmother. So Robyn and Melissa were . . . there was no word for that, Jane realized.

"Gracie left her cell phone at home." Robyn's voice was a mix of whine and whisper. "Lewis isn't answering his, and I've left message after message. But he thinks the phone is silly. He says it's a 'technological noose.' Strangling real life."

Lewis sounded like quite the piece of work.

Jane tried to catch Melissa's eye, but her sister focused on Robyn.

"I see. I suppose. Still." Melissa slapped the back of one hand into the palm of the other, like a politician making a point. "Daniel arrives from Geneva tomorrow now, if all goes as planned, and we're all supposed to fly back to Chicago. What if they're not back in time for that? It's the wedding!"

"Why is *she* here?" Robyn pointed to Jane.

Jane saw Melissa shake her head, quickly, as if to clear it, change the tone. She stopped her rapid-fire interrogation and lowered herself onto the wing chair, tucked her silk skirt under her, then reached out a conciliatory hand. Not quite touching Robyn but coming close.

"I'm *so* sorry, Robyn," Melissa said. "I tend to accelerate right into lawyer mode. It's the wedding. I'm a little on edge. Jane's here simply in case we need to call someone. We're family, right? She's family. But the easiest solution is most often the correct one. That's why I'm asking—before we make any major decisions—if it's possible your husband just forgot to call to update you? That his cell battery is dead? That he and Gracie are, I don't know, getting pizza?"

A tiny jagged streak of black mascara blotched one of Robyn's cheeks, and she yanked her pale hair behind her ears, twisted it up on the back, let it fall. "Pizza?"

"Robyn?" Jane took a few steps closer. "You're saying Lewis and Gracie have never been off your radar? He picks her up at school for lunch?"

"Well, not totally. Of course I don't *always* know where they are," Robyn said. "Why would I?"

Well, Jane thought, I *would know where* my *daughter was.* So any suspicious mind—and Jane was proud of hers, a necessary quality in a reporter—would wonder if the reportedly manipulative and clingy Robyn was truly upset over Gracie's whereabouts, or simply trying to screw with the woman about to keep her daughter from her for three months a year. A suspicious mind would also speculate whether obviously skeptical Melissa was upset over Gracie, or over Robyn's center-ring disruption of her own prenuptial plans.

Jane had a glimmer of the wrenching dominoes of divorce. Melissa had confided to her that Daniel missed his daughter. The little girl wrote him loopy-lettered postcards about kittens and school and being the flower girl.

Daniel's impending marriage to Melissa, who Gracie thought was "awesome," Melissa had confided, was a chance for father and daughter to reconnect. But reconnecting with her father—while living with stepmother Melissa—meant being yanked from her mother, leaving the stepfather she seemed to love, moving to another city every summer, and being made to live a semi-schizophrenic life. Not uncommon, but maybe not the best for a nine-year-old. Maybe not the best for anyone. But the couple, bolstered by Melissa's know-how of the legal system, had pled their case to a probate court, a judge had ruled, and so it was.

Jane watched the mother and bride-to-be as they continued their familial tug-of-war. How did anyone know what was overreacting and what was a real emergency?

"Lewis didn't want Gracie to go, you know? That's what's beginning to worry me." Robyn took out a cell phone, tapped some numbers with manicured thumbs. "He was bulls—I mean, so upset about it. 'She's my daughter, too,' he kept saying. And I know he was upsetting Gracie. Talking about how she'd miss school and her friends and her cat. I didn't know how to handle it, but I truly thought he'd get over it. I mean, if it has to be, it has to be. We made our beds, I guess."

"Was he ever . . . inappropriate with her?"

Had to give Melissa credit for asking that, flat out. Jane had been wondering the same thing, puzzling over how to phrase it. Lawyer Melissa had probably phrased it many times, in and out of court.

"*What?* No, oh, absolutely no." Robyn was shaking her head, even while Melissa was talking, waving the question away. "Are you serious? No. He was never, *never* . . . he's been wonderful, until the judge—anyway. He's just sad, I guess. You know accountants, they're all about logic and planning and making things turn out the way you want. But Lewis recently decided to break out of the mold. Show his emotions. Try new things. Experiment. 'Live to the fullest,' he started saying. 'Life is short.' Anyway. I'm texting him, again."

Jane watched these players inhabit their roles, trying to analyze whether what she was seeing and hearing was blanketing some complicated emotional subtext. But theoretical motives and familial chess games aside, where was Gracie? If Lewis Wilhoite was a manipulative emotion-hiding planner, those were not reassuring attributes. Was Robyn protesting too much? Hiding from reality?

A nine-year-old and her stepfather were not where they were supposed to be. The stepfather didn't answer his phone. Not a good thing. If they were out getting ice cream, fine, they'd all have a good laugh, someone would get yelled at, and it would all be happily ever after.

If not?

"Ah, Melissa?" Jane wasn't sure of the protocol here, but she was sure their focus should be on Gracie. "Robyn? Do you think we should call the police?"

18

"He say anything?" Jake whispered his question to the cadet stationed by the bed in room 610. Although if John Doe No. 2 was going to be awakened by sound, the bings of the IVs, the hiss of the oxygen, and the beeps of the monitors would have roused the patient—suspect—long before Jake arrived.

"No, sir." The cadet shrugged, stashed his cell phone in a jacket pocket. His name tag said RONALD VERRIO. *Young*, Jake thought with a pang. When did Jake himself become not-young?

"He's out, you know, sedated, and with that oxygen mask on," Verrio said. "Been out like this since I got here."

Verrio wasn't supposed to be using his personal cell on watch, Jake knew, but he'd let it go this time. Nothing more boring than babysitting a potential suspect. Unless and until, of course, said suspect woke up and spilled the beans.

"Where's Bartoneri?" Jake knew Angie was supposed to be guarding the suspect—victim—but she was not in the room.

Verrio pointed to his watch. "I replaced her," he said. "She got called back to HQ."

"Gotcha." Jake was just as happy not to see her. No need for any more personal complications in a—well, that was an understatement. No matter what Angie might want, their relationship was a thing of the past.

The man's eyes remained closed, his ashy face pocked with stubble, his salt-and-pepper hair matted against a pink scalp. He lay motionless, propped on two white pillows. A translucent plastic oxygen mask covered his mouth and lower face. So much for getting a cell phone photo to help with ID, Jake thought. Maybe a doctor could move the mask just long enough to let him get the shot.

The guy looked grim. Gray. Frail. Much worse than he had in the alley. Someone had tucked a thin white blanket around him, pulled the thick binding up to his chin and secured the lower edge under his feet, making him a white lump in the center of the flat metal-tubed bed. So. The tattoo. Right upper arm. Now under the blanket.

Jake reached a hand toward the cover, ready to pull it down to check for the red rose intertwined in the shield, a playing-card-size design he knew from the bystander's photo was inside the crook of the stabber's right elbow.

Then he stopped, hand poised in midair. If Jake yanked away the blanket, would some defense attorney insist it was an illegal search?

"Shit," Jake said.

"Sir?"

"Did you see a—anything on this man's right arm?" If the man's arm had been exposed, in plain sight, all well and good and by the book, and this case could proceed to arrest. Or at least a discussion with the brass. But by the random ridiculousness of the universe, that crucial patch of skin had been hidden by a solicitous nurse.

"Anything like what?" Verrio examined his own right arm, as if to check what might be there.

"The guy we're looking for has a tattoo. On his right arm. Did you see his arm?" Jake thought for a moment, considering. It might be something that would wash off. "Or what looks like a tattoo."

Verrio squinted his eyes, maybe trying to picture it. "I don't think so, Detective."

Jake's gut twisted. No? If this guy didn't have a tattoo, it made for a whole different story. It meant Hewlitt had attacked him in Franklin Alley and accused him of being the stabber, maybe in a last-ditch attempt to throw Jake and D off the track. If this guy died, the ruse might have worked. But Hewlitt couldn't have known about the tattoo in the bystander's photograph. He'd have to call D, instantly, and let him know this latest wrinkle.

"Really? No tattoo?" Jake said, peering at Verrio.

"No. I mean, not no there's no tattoo." The newbie's face reddened. He yanked at his earlobe. "I mean, no I don't think I ever saw his arm. It was covered up when I got here."

The puzzle pieces reassembled again. Now Jake had a dilemma. The man's medical records, flapped in an aluminum folder, dangled from a twisty chain of flat metal links attached to the white plastic tubing that formed the foot of the bed. Certainly the doctors would have noted distinguishing marks. But medical records were legally private.

He blew out a breath, impatient with well-meant but time-consuming rules. Cops didn't need to break those rules to close their cases, he didn't, at least. And once the legal bullshit started, it was difficult to stop. To pull down that damn blanket or to look at the records, Jake reluctantly decided, he needed a warrant.

But wait. Had he seen the tattoo during the Franklin Alley altercation? If he had, that would be enough probable cause. He closed his eyes, briefly, picturing it. Trying to. Nothing. Still, Jake could simply wait for a nurse or someone to come in, wait until the blanket was pulled down, and voilà, the answer.

"Oh, I get it." Verrio nodded, gesturing at the covered-up arm. "You think you'd need a warrant?"

"Yeah," Jake said.

The cadet looked at the floor, then back at Jake. Shifted his weight. "Okay if I go take a leak, since you're here?"

"Sure." Jake smiled, shook his head. "Thanks, buddy. But even if you leave, I'm not gonna look."

The door closed behind Verrio with a click of the sleek metal latch. Jake was alone with the man—suspect—and the beeping machines, and the invisible maybe-tattoo. If he had a tattoo? That was probable cause to arrest him for murder. If he didn't? He was a victim of something.

Jake simply couldn't be sure of what.

Could he have misunderstood? Bobby Land stared at his silent cell phone. Or had Jane Ryland lied to him?

He'd chosen the chair closest to the door of the little office the cop had parked him in. Put the unread magazines on the seat beside him, balancing the almost-empty Sprite can on top of them. He was super alone and having a hard time sitting still, waiting. Dee Something, the skinny cop, promised to come back, but that was, like, an hour ago.

Bobby swallowed the last sugary slug of tepid soda and put the can back on the magazines, balancing it right in the center of a basketball hoop.

At least the cops had allowed him to keep his phone. Which, he guessed, meant they weren't thinking he had anything to do with anything but were honestly trying to make up for the dumb-ass way they'd let the dirtbag in the alley kick his camera to shit. He'd thought about just letting it all go, especially since he'd kind of led the cops to believe he'd actually seen the stabbing, but the outrage over the busted camera was too much. Someone had to pay for it, and it wasn't going to be him.

Incredible bummer.

Could have been so cool, having the big evidence, getting his photos everywhere, like the beginning of his career. He mourned those photos, longing for them with the certain knowledge of a vanished opportunity. Scuffing the brown carpeting beneath his running shoes, he imagined what might have been—his photos on TV and in the paper, everyone clamoring for the rights, limos and lawyers and famous people, and his mother finally realizing . . . well, screw it. Reality. Someone had to pay.

He would take his chances on what he said he'd seen. Go with the flow. Maybe his memory could get a little worse as time went on. Or. He paused, imagining it. Maybe his memory could get better.

Huh.

He had been there, after all, when the stabbing took place. Maybe if he really concentrated he could reconstruct the scene a little, remember it better. If they, like, showed him pictures of suspects, the way they did on TV? He'd know who it *wasn't,* at least. Not a black guy, not a big guy, that narrowed it down. He *had* seen something, right? Through the lens. All he had to do was put himself back in the moment. He couldn't be the only witness, that was for sure.

And they weren't gonna crucify some guy only based on what *he* said. He was a kid, after all. Plus, no one could prove what he did or didn't remember.

First the stabbing, then the photos, then meeting Jane Ryland and all that, then the guy in the alley. And his smashed camera and the pulverized memory card. All he ever wanted was to get his photos on TV. He'd been totally in the right place at the right time, and it should have worked out. Now, through no fault of his own, he was in the cop shop, his camera busted, and trying to decide whether to continue to lie to the police. Plus, he was going to be marked absent from class.

A loud knock on the office door surprised him. Bobby flinched, almost knocking over the teetering soda can as he stood. There was silence for a fraction of a second, then the door swung open.

19

Jane heard phones ring in three places, a trill from the Wilhoites' red wall-mounted kitchen landline she could barely glimpse from her living room vantage point, a jangle from the portable on the antique desk, and the three-chime alert of the cell phone clutched in Robyn Wilhoite's unsteady right hand.

"Call from . . ." The disembodied techno-voice floated over the living room. Robyn stood, her cardigan falling from her shoulders, staring at the screen of her cell.

"Who is it?" Melissa whispered.

". . . Lewis Wil—" the voice continued. Jane had never met Lewis or Gracie, but a silver-framed five-by-seven of what must be the two of them was displayed near the desk phone. Gracie mugged for the camera in front of a pink-blossoming tree, her curly almost-blond pigtails held up with Hello Kitty barrettes and her flowered overalls spilling over her sneakers. One hand clutched a stuffed hippo. The other clutched the hand of a smiling middle-aged man. Lewis?

He wore owlish glasses and a Patriots cap. An accountant, Jane remembered. He hardly looked physically equipped to defend an abducted daughter, though Jane knew people summoned surprising strength when necessary. Her reporter brain concocted a vision: Lewis bleeding in some parking lot, Gracie now who knows where with who knew who. Exactly why Jane had pushed to call the police. But before that discussion even got under way, here was Lewis on the phone. Maybe everything was okay. Maybe.

Lucky she hadn't called Jake about this. She guessed.

Robyn picked up the desk phone and punched a button on her cell. The ringing stopped.

"Lew?" Robyn almost whispered. "Are you there?"

"Is he there?" Melissa, frowning now, looked like she was struggling not to grab the phone from Robyn's hand. Robyn stared at the thick creamy pile of the carpeted floor, holding the phone so tightly Jane could see the blue-tinged veins on her hand.

"Lewis?" Again, Robyn's voice came out in a breathy tremble, half inquiry, half plea.

Jane narrowed her eyes. Was Lewis Wilhoite calling for help? Or with an embarrassed explanation? It would be a relief to be angry, she thought. Everyone home, everyone happy, after a marital spat or even a misunderstanding.

"Lewis," Robyn implored.

Why was Wilhoite apparently not saying anything?

"Is it him?" Melissa asked again. She leaned forward, maybe trying to get as close as possible to the phone. Jane realized she was doing the same thing, straining to hear, but Robyn had the phone so close to her face not a sound escaped.

Another problem. Simply because the phone voice announced it came from Lewis didn't mean it *was* Lewis. What if someone else was using Lewis Wilhoite's phone? A white cat appeared at the archway to the kitchen, blinked at them, waved its tail, and slunk away.

"Robyn, put it on speaker," Melissa said.

"So they never found out what exactly happened to your sister?"

Another of the questions Tenley hoped Bri wouldn't ask. But if she was going to live in the world, and have friends, questions about Lanna were inevitable. Now, sitting in this booth at the Purple, she'd have to answer.

"I mean . . ." Brileen Finnerty's voice dropped to a dramatic whisper, and she pointed to the sugar container as she talked. Tenley handed it to her across the yellow-speckled laminate of their table, felt the sticky grit hardened on the outside of the faceted glass.

"I mean . . . That's kind of strange, isn't it?"

Where was Bri going with this question? She couldn't read her new friend's face and didn't want to look like she was staring at her. She stirred her own coffee, considering. Maybe "What happened?" was a normal question. Polite, even. "What happened" was what life is about.

Plus, no matter what Tenley did or didn't tell her, Brileen could pull out her cell phone and Google the whole thing.

She and Bri had dodged elbows and trays of spilly drinks to claim the last empty booth, but the place, fragrant with beer and fried stuff, was so wall-to-wall crowded it was somehow easy to feel alone. The kids from Emerson and Suffolk and Boston City congregated at the Purple for free popcorn and multiscreen sports and eddying swirls of conversation. A couple of times some guys—one, Tenley thought, pretty cute—had stopped by the table. Tenley felt a little flutter of interest from their attention. But one dismissive look from Brileen had sent them packing.

So chitchat, and school stuff, they both went to Boston City College, both on summer vacay, Tenley a sophomore and Bri in grad school, so they both knew the downtown campus and the brownstone dorms over by the Public Garden. And, yes, it was the graphic arts building, Bri agreed, where she'd seen Tenley. That made sense. Tenley told about her City Hall job, describing the cameras and what she could see down on the street from her vantage point above. But then Bri brought up family, and what was Tenley supposed to do? Pretend Lanna had never existed?

She told the short version, short as she could. Omitting the part about keeping Lanna's secret. She could barely face that herself. And now Bri was asking what happened.

Her new friend picked up her mug, a coffee-colored ring on the white paper napkin beneath it showing as Bri took an experimental sip, then looked at Tenley from under her lashes.

Bri waited. Tenley was supposed to answer. Say what happened.

"No, they never really found out," Tenley said, trying to sound like a normal person having a normal conversation. "The police investigated, you know? Took her computer, all that. Interviewed us. But there was just no real . . . evidence, whatever. They decided she tripped on a branch. The case is closed now."

Bri dumped more sugar into her mug, a tumbling cascade of white grains. "Police lie, you know. They do it all the time."

Why would Bri say that? Tenley took a little sip of her water, the nubby plastic glass slick with condensation, stalling.

"Lie?" Tenley said. Her voice came out as a little croak, and she cleared her throat to hide it. *Try, Lie, Bri,* she thought. Silly.

"Sure." Brileen leaned across the table, closer to Tenley, her elbows on the slick surface, chin on her hands, revealing another little pink star tattooed just under her left wristbone. "Let me ask you this. Are your parents, like, extra careful of you? Always wanting you to be home at a certain time?"

"Well, sure." Tenley frowned, a little, couldn't help it, couldn't figure out where this was going.

"Your mom and dad know where you are now?" Bri looked at Tenley.

A pang of unease prickled Tenley's neck and behind her eyes. Her mom did and didn't know, a little of each. She hadn't told her exactly, why would she? Come to think of it, yes, her mother was maybe overinterested recently with her whereabouts. Her father, too, the times he was home, at least, which was less and less, which made it all worse and even more impossible.

Brileen's soft laughter floated across to her. "I'm sorry," she said. "I didn't mean anything, I was just, you know. Asking."

Tenley felt the flush come up over her cheeks. Brileen had just been making conversation, of course she had.

"Oh, it's okay." Tenley mustered all the bravado she could. Maybe change the subject? "My mother works at City Hall, too," she said. Brileen had asked about her family, after all. Maybe that would impress her.

"Cool. It's just that . . ." Brileen sat back, rested her shoulder blades against the booth's black leather padding, the tips of her fingers splayed on the table, nails on both forefingers bitten to the nubs but polished, shiny, the color of eggplants. "You know. If the police don't really know what happened to your sister, how do they know the same thing, whatever it was, won't happen to you?"

20

For a case that started out with too many witnesses, how come there suddenly weren't enough? Jake ignored the elevator, yanked open the stairway door, and raced down the five flights to the hospital lobby.

"Can you hear me? I'm in the stairs," he told DeLuca. He'd left a swaddled John Doe No. 2 under the care of Ronald Verrio, instructing him to use that contraband cell phone to snap a few legal photos of the guy's right arm the second it came into view. One picture could clinch that evidence, no need for Jake to take the time now to see it in person. Though after what DeLuca was now telling him, hurrying back to Headquarters seemed pointless. Before he could get there, everyone he cared about would be gone.

"Freaking lawyers," DeLuca was saying. "Hewlitt called some bigwig chick, who showed up all briefcase and fast talk, and somehow made a deal to pay off Bobby Land and spring the both of them."

"Somehow?" Jake was at the third floor, a gloomy mustard-painted expanse of concrete blocks and taped-up laminated No Smoking posters. He grabbed the slick banister, swung himself around to the next level. Looked at his watch. Pushing seven. "Somehow how? Courts are closed."

"Not if you have the cash, my guess." DeLuca's voice was ripe with disdain. "Hewlitt's convinced a judge to make it all go away. A hundred bucks, released on condition he show up for arraignment 'at some later date.' The judge also ordered Hewlitt to 'make it right' with Land."

Jake, now on the second-floor landing, tried to make sense of it. Now they had no cause to hold Hewlitt. Lawyers, story of his life. "What does 'make it right' mean?"

"What do *you* think, Harvard?" DeLuca said. "Bucks, I'd say."

Right. "So, Land? Where is he now?"

"Hang on, lemme check. You wanna hold?"

"Will do." Jake would drive to HQ, try to whip this case back under control before it all went to hell. He knew DeLuca was following up with the on-scene officers about other images they'd taken from cell phones, and scouring witness reports. Angie Bartoneri had requested the surveillance video from surrounding buildings. She'd let them know as soon as she got it. And Calvin Hewlitt's background.

Hewlitt. His story was bullshit, bet the ranch. How did he and John Doe No. 2 get into the alley? The camera thing? Lawyer or no, that guy was guilty. Now Jake would have to fight through a battalion of legal gatekeepers if he wanted to get anywhere near him.

Crap. Too much to do.

Through the middle revolving door—why were they all so damn slow?—out to the curb. Cruiser door open, ignition, liftoff.

He had a dead John Doe in the morgue. A possible suspect swaddled in the hospital. If Jake could uncover a solid connection between the two of them, the rest would fall into place.

Hewlitt was involved. Or—not.

Land was a potential eyewitness.

As for John Doe 2? If he had a tattoo, pizza for everyone and justice prevails, because that meant the killer was safely in custody at Mass General Hospital. If there was no tattoo? Back to square one.

The light at Congress turned red. Of course. He watched out the cruiser's broad windshield, seeing his future instead of the pedestrians.

He was supposed to meet Jane and her family an hour from now. Crappy timing. He was angry with her. But, whatever. They'd argued before. She was still Jane. He hoped, for everything's sake, he could still make it.

All he could do was keep the show on the road. Police work was all about step by step, solving one element at a time. *You can't reach the end of the road until you begin the journey,* his grandfather used to say. It was all good.

And the light turned green.

The scene in Robyn and Lewis Wilhoite's living room was now a full-fledged drama. Robyn, sobbing, sat on the couch. Melissa was barricaded behind the wing chair. Jane stood by the desk. All stared at the black mesh of the speakerphone, hearing the buzzing dial tone. Whoever had called had hung up.

"I'm calling Ja—a police detective I know," Jane said. "Right now."

Time to bring in the big guns. Big gun Jake, or whoever Jake told her to call. Jake, who she'd last seen, fuming, in Franklin Alley. Jake, who they were all supposed to meet in about an hour. Ridiculous timing, but he was still her Jake. He'd find out about this tonight anyway. Why not now?

No one had heard from Gracie or Lewis since the first phone call three hours earlier. Back then, Lewis assured Robyn they were on an adventure, and they'd believed him. Now, at almost seven o'clock, no one was sure. Robyn said she'd called friends and hospitals. Nothing. The longer the daughter and stepfather were whereabouts unknown, the more the potential for disaster.

Melissa stopped the dial tone, then picked up the receiver. "I'm dialing star six-nine," she said. "That'll connect us with whoever called."

Robyn took her hands from her eyes. "But we *know* who called," she whispered. "Lewis."

"Or someone using Lewis's phone," Jane said.

At that, Robyn's sobs grew louder. Jane hadn't meant to upset her, but the truth was the truth. The sooner they faced it, the sooner they could resolve this.

For the first time, maybe ever, Melissa seemed flustered. She shook her head, adjusted her pearls. "Oh, right," she said. "Just trying to hel— never mind."

"That's why we have to call the police." Jane punched up her own phone's Internet as she talked. She typed in AMBE. The AMBER Alert website appeared. "Okay, so," Jane went on, scanning, figuring the family and ex-family and family-to-be dynamics would be sorted out as soon as Gracie was safely home. And Lewis, too. "The site says an AMBER Alert may be issued if . . . let me see . . . okay, a couple of other things, but mainly, if an abduction has taken place, or the child is at risk of serious injury or death."

Jane stopped, all eyes now on her. The implied question wasn't pleasant, but neither was Gracie's situation. Jane looked at Melissa, hoping for an alliance. Melissa dealt with cases like this as a prosecutor, at least from time to time. When a potential abduction—*if* that's what it was, she kept reminding herself—was this close to home, would it cloud her judgment?

"Jane's right." Melissa stood a little taller, Jane noticed, straightened her shoulders. "Robyn, do you think Lewis has taken Gracie?"

"Certainly not," Robyn said. "I mean—"

"Wait," Jane interrupted. She'd been replaying the day in her mind, realized what they'd forgotten. "Lewis's phone is obviously working again. He called you. Try calling him now, see what happens."

Robyn clicked numbers, using both thumbs. She stopped, deleted, started over. "I'm too nervous to dial," she whispered.

"Even if the cops *traced* the call," Melissa said, "it would only tell us where the *phone* is, not where Lewis is. That might not be the same place."

Robyn made a whimpering sound, then sighed, then started dialing again.

"Leave a message if no one answers," Jane said.

"But why would he call"—Robyn clamped the phone to her cheek, looked at Melissa with pleading eyes—"and not say anything?"

"It could have been a—" Melissa seemed to be searching for a word. "You know, he sat on the phone, it hit speed dial. Could be they're fine. Maybe he didn't say anything because he didn't even know he had called."

Possibly, Jane had to admit. But it didn't explain where the two were.

"I'm calling the police." Jane hit 22, Jake's speed dial. Forget about asking permission. If she was wrong, Jane thought, fine. Happy to be wrong.

"Jake?" Hurray, no voice mail beep. Imagine, a phone call actually going through. "It's me."

Jane.

"Hey." Jake turned off the ignition and opened his cruiser door, holding the phone against his shoulder. He'd parked in the police garage, a dankly crowded basement full of cruisers and memories. Just a few months ago, a bad guy had held a cadet hostage here. Another cop shot and killed him as Jake tried to defuse the standoff. The supe had called it a success, but to Jake, death never felt like success. He couldn't step onto the oil-soaked concrete without thinking of it, wondering what he might have done differently.

"Hang on, just parking," he said. Stalling.

Jane. He was supposed to meet her, and her family, at the restaurant in forty-five minutes.

He slammed the cruiser door. "One more second," he said.

He hadn't answered her texts. *Here it comes.* He grimaced as he walked toward the stairs. He *had* been kind of a jerk.

"What's up?" he asked, trying to erase the past with a conciliatory tone. Might as well let bygones be. He and Jane would figure it out. "We still on for tonight?"

His frown deepened as he heard the story. Jane's calls from her sister, and the distraught mother Robyn Fasullo Wilhoite, and the nine-year-old Gracie Fasullo, potentially missing, along with, perhaps, her stepfather Lewis Wilhoite. Or not.

None of the names pinged. Jake had the city's "most wanteds" in his head, and a top twenty list of local sex offenders, as well as a roster of usual suspects, the gang members and losers and ex-cons and low-life local scumbags considered bad pennies at HQ and in the district courts. There was no Lewis Wilhoite.

He started climbing the stairs from the basement garage, rounded the landing to the lobby floor, still listening. Jane's voice was guarded, he could tell. Stating the facts, without her usual appraising commentary or revealing inflection.

"Am I on speaker?" he asked. "Everyone in the room?"

"Nope." She cleared her throat. "But yes, they're here."

"There has to be a potential abduction for an AMBER Alert," Jake said. "Or a—"

Jane interrupted. "Yeah, I know. But no one is, uh . . ." She paused, as if choosing her words carefully. "No one is exactly saying that's what happened. Apparently he takes her on 'adventures.'"

"Well, yeah. So, problem. Although we don't need a formal alert to be on the lookout for a missing kid, you know? We just like to be pretty sure the kid is actually missing," he said. "Has—what's her name, Robyn? Has she called everyone she knows?"

"She said so," Jane said. "Hang on for a sec."

Jake tapped his wallet against the flat black security pad designed to keep the stairwell free of intruders and opened the door in to the lobby of police headquarters. Built twenty years ago, it was still dismissed by the veterans as "new." The marble-floored great room, which was designed to be intimidating and welcoming at the same time, failed at both. The ceilings were too high, the chairs too uncomfortable. Two-story windows let in all the light, so much that in summer it was glaring orange and hot, in winter freezing and gloomy gray.

"Jake," Jane said. "They're okay."

He could hear hesitation in her voice. She didn't sound quite right.

"Who's okay? Wilhoite and the little girl? Are they there? With you?" If she was seeing them, case closed. Another family emergency resolved. Happened all the time. Panicked parents, missed connections, mixed signals, easy explanations.

"No," Jane said. "Robyn has the stepfather—Lewis—on the phone, though. They—hang on. Sorry to keep doing this, Jake. Just hearing this now."

"Sure." Jake waited, watching the beams from the illuminating street-lights outside HQ on Schroeder Place create bands of light and shadow on the dust-streaked marble floor. Every passing footfall echoed in the cavernous lobby, whether the clack of high heels or the thud of the cops' regulation black boots. The squeak of a rubber-soled running shoe distracted him. Jake looked up to follow the sound.

Bobby Land. Head down, walking fast. Almost to the revolving door.

"Hey, Bobby. Land." Jake took a step toward him, then another. Jane was still away from the phone. At least now he could find out the latest. Calvin Hewlitt had been ordered to make it right with this kid. Jake still wondered what "make it right" entailed.

Land looked up, registered Jake. Stopped. And gave him a thumbs-up.

"Copa-cetic," Land said.

He'd put his camo hat on, bill to the back. Jake tried to unsee his phony-rebellious Red Sux T-shirt. The kid had probably shelled out forty bucks for that get-up, all to prove his antipathy to "the man." Did he ever consider who profited from the forty bucks?

"All cool, all set," Bobby was saying. "You guys rock."

Jake knew the cops didn't "rock." If this kid was happy, it probably had something to do with money. Calvin Hewlitt's money, presumably. Jake was eager for details. Calvin Hewlitt's hush money might pay for the camera, but it wouldn't quiet Jake's questions.

"Jake?" Jane's voice in his ear now. "Here's the scoop."

"Hang on, Jane." If the girl and her father were okay, Jane could wait a second while he corralled Bobby Land and set up a time for an interview.

"Is that Jane Ryland?" Bobby took a step closer, pointed to the phone.

Okay, that was interesting. The boy knew Jane? Oh, right. Land talked with Jane as Jake led him out of the alley, so the kid knew they were connected. Land might think she was calling as a reporter. Jake's thoughts stopped, turned a corner. *Was* she a reporter? Not for the *Register* anymore, that was for sure. But Jake remembered she'd mentioned Channel 2, a reference he still hadn't grasped.

"Excuse me?" Not answering the question was sometimes successful.

"Yeah, Jane Ryland," Bobby said. "You know. The one you were talk-ing to in the alley today. Wondered, because I was trying to call her, and she wasn't where she said she'd be."

"Which is where?" Jake asked.

"Who are you talking to?" Jane was saying.

"Channel 2." Land held up two fingers. "She told me she was a re-porter for Channel 2, but when I called there, they were, like, I have no idea what you're talking about."

"Really?" Jake said. She'd told him she was at the station, too. Why would she say that unless it was true? But he didn't want to discuss it in front of Bobby.

"Jake?" Jane made his name into two syllables, inquiring. "You hear-ing me?"

"You want to give me your phone number, I can have her call you," Jake said.

"So that *is* her? Is she at Channel 2? Or not?"

Persistent kid.

"Jake? Are you hearing me? I guess everything is okay with Lewis and Gracie," Jane was saying. "They went out to the mall to buy clothes for Gracie's trip to Chicago, had a flat tire, then a broken jack. Phone battery died. But it's all good. They're at the repair place, and the guy there had a phone charger."

"So our previous plans are still in effect?" Jake tried to sound like they were talking business.

"Is someone there with you?" Jane said. "You're so funny. I can always tell. I guess that's a good thing. Anyway, yeah, so far so fine. Melissa is freaking, but what else is new? So. We pushed the dinner reservations to eight-thirty, Brookline Taverna. Jerry's on duty, he's holding a table. Daniel's still stuck in Geneva. Lewis and Gracie will get there when they can. Apparently Gracie's jazzed about getting to stay up late. All's well that ends well."

"Hey. Tell her to call me," Bobby said, pointing at the phone. "I know she's gotta still be a reporter. She was covering the story, right? Tell her I know the whole picture. I'll tell her everything."

"Great," Jake said. That one-word answer would work for Jane and Bobby, too. Clicking off the phone, he waved to Sergeant Thomason, the veteran desk clerk who'd just arrived at her longtime post behind the shoulder-high intake booth. Monday nights were always a parade of human drama: fallout from weekend domestic squabbles, battles over reneged sports bets, complaints about unfairly towed cars. "Fill out the form," Shelley Thomason would instruct one unfortunate after another, her cigarette voice both sympathetic and dismissive. "I know, life isn't fair."

"You'll tell Jane everything, huh?" Jake shook his head. Life isn't fair, he thought. "Your call, Mr. Land. But here's the deal. You're gonna have to tell *me* everything, too. And you're gonna have to tell me first."

21

"Mom? I'm home."

Catherine Siskel opened her eyes, slowly, processing the voice, remembering. Tenley. Home. *Good.* She closed her eyes again, tight, trying to unstick her contacts—she must have fallen asleep here on the couch still wearing them. *What a pain.* Opened her eyes, tried to focus. *What time is it?* Dark in the living room now, even with the shades up and curtains tucked back, so hard to tell. She must have slept awhile. Didn't really matter, though, and in truth, might be a somewhat reassuring sign. She hadn't been sleeping well at night for—well, since Lanna, if she had to honestly calculate. *Greg,* she thought. He hadn't slept well, either. With her, at least.

"Hey, honey." Her voice came out a little croaky. She cleared her throat, tried again. "In here."

Tenley appeared in the archway to the living room, her canvas messenger bag strapped diagonally across the buttoned cardigan. Catherine knew Tenley had probably unrolled her skirt on the way home, trying to fool her mom. Lanna had never been a problem when it came to clothes. She was always impeccable, more fashion conscious even than Catherine, who prided herself on dressing for success. What could Tenley be dressing for?

All Lanna's clothes were still in her bedroom closet, still arranged by color and season, just the way Lanna had left them. Tenley's clothes were arranged by last use, hangers optional. All of that ran through her brain after one look at her one remaining daughter. *Will I ever see just Tenley? And not the empty space where Lanna used to be?*

"Hi, Mom."

Catherine saw Tenley's eyes light on the empty wineglass. "Hey, honey." Catherine ignored the girl's silent rebuke. "Did you have fun? Where were you?"

"Why do you always have to know that?" Tenley frowned, adjusted the strap on her bag. "I'm in college. I have a job, thanks to you, right? If you want me to be self-sufficient, *in the world,* like Dr. Maddux says, why are you always bugging me about, like, where I am?"

"You know why, Tenley." Catherine's head felt like a dark fog was circling, muffling her thoughts. She knew her reaction was too harsh, heard her own unfairness, and yet couldn't figure out how to soften it.

"You think the same thing that happened to Lanna will happen to me." Tenley's voice, a sarcastic singsong, mocked the reality. She ran her tongue across her front teeth, her nervous habit. "Don't you?"

Catherine remembered Tenley's baby teeth. When the very first one came out, tooth fairy Greg had tucked a dollar under the little girl's pillow. Catherine remembered the braces, too, and the "braces-off" celebration. Lanna had showed Tenley how to use lipstick, her reward for making it through orthodontia. And now Lanna was gone.

"Honey, of course I don't. That was, you know, an accident." Of course, that was not a good answer. Accidents could happen to anyone. That's why they were accidents. Catherine struggled to remember what a good mother would say. She used to know, but it all seemed far away. Work, that was easy. Running a city, easy. But having a daughter—two daughters, once—there was no Kennedy School for that.

"I love you, Tenner, but as long as you live here, which I hope is a long time, I simply feel more comfortable knowing where you are. When you have a daughter, you'll understand."

"Yeah. About that," Tenley said.

"About what?" Catherine's mind floundered, trying to keep up with this conversation. *When you have a daughter,* that was the last thing Catherine had said. "Are you—?"

"OMG, Mom." Tenley rolled her eyes heavenward. "That's disgusting."

Catherine watched her blow out a breath, as if deciding whether it was worth it to continue the conversation with such an idiotic adult.

"Forgive me, dear, if I've ruined your life by being so dense." Catherine had meant to gently tease, but her words came out derisive. Why were they fighting? How could she stop it? "Why don't you just tell me what you mean?"

"I *mean,*" Tenley said, "I'm thinking of moving out."

"Don't. Even. Move."

Bobby Land heard the words, felt them, soft and whispery in his ear. Someone—one person?—had clamped two strong hands around his, yanked them behind his back. And now he couldn't move.

He'd been walking from the police station to the Ruggles T stop, ready to take the subway home, enjoying the last of the evening light, noticing how the shadows fell across the Vernon Street pavement, seeing a couple of seagulls, off course, he guessed, silhouetted against the twilight. Calculating f-stops in his head, thinking about how he could get a good shot of them. With the new camera he was about to buy.

He touched his jeans pocket, reassuring himself that the big fat check from that woman lawyer was still there. He could deposit it first thing in the A.M., then hustle downtown to Bromfield Camera and pick out a prime piece of camera real estate. They'd have to respect him then, right?

He stopped, staring at the random pieces of grass stabbing up through cracks in the sidewalk. He was still in mourning, deeply in mourning, for those pictures Hewlitt had destroyed.

But hey.

He started walking again, shaking it off. Funny how a little dough could help erase all the bad. There'd be other good shots, right?

"Right," he said out loud.

And it was kind of a cool story, actually, the fight, and the destroyed memory card. Exciting and dramatic. He'd talk to Jane Ryland, she'd call, for sure, after the cop gave her his number. Maybe he'd even get on TV. He could just see it, him on TV and that blue line with his name under it: *Bobby Land, eyewitness.* He'd witnessed something, that was for sure.

He pictured it again, the noontime image forming in his brain. Tourists. The statue.

Yeah, he might have to testify. He planned it as he walked. That detective said he'd be showing him photos of some suspects when he came in tomorrow. So, fine, he might actually recognize someone. And if he didn't, he'd cross that bridge when he came to it. He still hadn't quite decided how much he remembered.

But then, that voice in his ear.

And now he was almost shitting his pants. Who the holy crap had come up behind him?

He could feel the person's chest against him, actually feel them breathing. There was only one, and not that huge, but they must be doing some kind of martial arts hold or something, Bobby couldn't fight back. How could some asshole rob him, like, not two blocks from the police station? Why would they think he had anything to rob?

He was gonna be so screwed. He couldn't even comprehend how—

"Listen to me," the voice was saying, all whispery and hissing. Bobby could smell cigarettes, and leather? And something else. What? But no time to think about smells. There was only time to, like, pray to whatever, that he come out of this alive.

"And listen to me good."

And now he felt something at his side, sharp—like a . . . like a knife. At his side. *Like the one that stabbed the guy in Curley Park.* His knees buckled and the night went white and then black and his eyes were, like, on fire. What if he never saw anything again, not ever, and his mother would wonder where he was, and the cops would call and he would never—he slammed his eyes closed, kept them closed.

"I could kill you right now," the voice went on. "I could stab your freaking eyes out, too, and then what would happen to your little career as a photographer?"

This person knew him?

"Have you talked to anyone about what you saw? Have you?"

"No." Bobby managed to get the word out, it was true, thank crap. He hadn't told the reporter anything. The lawyer woman hadn't asked. He didn't say anything to the cops either. That detective Brogan seemed, like, in a hurry to get out, and they'd set up the interview time for tomorrow morning. Would there even be a tomorrow? He opened his eyes, wide, looking for a way out. "No, nothing, no one, I promise, I haven't talked to—"

"Lucky for you, little man," the voice said.

Bobby opened his eyes, desperately trying to wrench himself away. They were right in the gloom, right where the streetlights didn't reach. No one in sight. If he yelled, called for help, he could get stabbed in one second. He twisted again, frantic, then felt the threat of the blade through his thin T-shirt.

Good-bye. The thought floated into his consciousness, then settled in to stay. *Good-bye.*

22

Jane looked at her watch, calculating. The maître d' at the Brookline Taverna had asked her when the other two guests would arrive. And no one knew the answer.

It was now nine P.M. They'd been here thirty minutes. It felt like three hundred. The not-missing stepfather and not-missing daughter had not appeared. Robyn clutched her cell phone, checking it periodically. The phone stayed silent.

How long could it take to fix a tire? What was taking them so long? Where were they?

Laughter from other tables of happy diners only underscored the gloom cloud looming over theirs. Jane was starving. She craved a glass of wine. And a fork to stab herself in the throat. First meetings were often awkward, but this one was Emmy-winning awful.

Melissa had told Jane that Daniel's plane was still delayed, that she hadn't told her fiancé anything about Gracie, and that she was freaking out. Not the most auspicious mental state for her sister to meet Jane's boyfriend. Now Melissa's "conversation" with Jake sounded more like a prosecutorial grilling. Jake was clearly distracted, his answers almost brusque. *Lucky Daniel,* Jane thought. More fun to be stranded in an airport than be sitting at this table.

There must be some kind of Heisenberg effect for families, Jane thought, some force that mutates a perfect beau into a perfect stranger.

Real Jake, intelligent and thoughtful and warm, was nothing like this icily argumentative table Jake. She wondered if she had changed in Jake's eyes, too.

They had to talk. Without family. She and Jake were sitting so close they could touch each other—but they couldn't say an important word. Not about each other. And not about the dead man in Curley Park.

Robyn, red-eyed and fidgeting, was regaling Jake with a nostalgic anecdote about Gracie. Robyn's cardigan, now unbuttoned, revealed an ice-blue silk blouse underneath. Also unbuttoned. Farther than Jane might have recommended.

"I mean, Jake, she's the cutest!" Robyn had the fingers of one hand curled around Jake's forearm, leaning in. Her other hand still clutched that phone.

Jake cleared his throat. Took an impossible sip from his empty water glass. Melissa looked as if she'd like to stab someone, anyone, even herself.

Stab. That was the second time she'd mentally used that word. Jane allowed herself to think, briefly, about Channel 2 and the Curley Park incident. What had been on the six o'clock news? She yearned to call Marsh Tyson, somehow make amends. She'd left four hours ago explaining her defection as a family emergency. At least what she'd thought then was an emergency. Tyson had seemed to be understanding, and they'd parted with the agreement that she'd talk to him tomorrow. Their new relationship had started auspiciously. Now it felt like a loose end.

"And then, I remember one time . . ." Robyn's reedy voice, relentless and persistent, carried to Jane's end of the table. Melissa escaped toward the ladies' room. Jane escaped into her own thoughts, making sure her face was pointed, politely, in Robyn's direction.

Loose ends. One, she should inform Marsh Tyson that Gracie was okay. He'd want to know, if only because a missing nine-year-old and her stepfather were a potentially headlining news story. Now, thank goodness, it wouldn't come to that.

Two, what had happened in Curley Park?

And three, if Jane did start working at Channel 2, should she be having dinner with Jake in public?

She looked at him, now tête-à-tête with the just-returned Melissa, immersed in a verging-on-argument about a Supreme Court decision on life sentences for juvenile offenders. *Lovely,* Jane thought. *This is a bad Lifetime movie.*

She felt a touch on her thigh. Jake's hand, hidden under the edge of the white tablecloth, gave her leg a surreptitious squeeze. She put a secret hand over his, silently reassuring, connecting. Okay, then, she almost smiled, they'd make it through this together. A wretched family dinner was almost a rite of passage.

Everything would be fine. As soon as Gracie and Lewis arrived.

The waiter appeared with a dripping pitcher of ice water, hovering behind Melissa. Jake's cell phone vibrated on the table, moving, in infinitesimal jumps, across the tablecloth.

Robyn stopped talking. Her phone was ringing, too.

"You come back here, right now!"

Tenley heard her mother yelling behind her as she raced up the stairs to the second floor. She'd ignore her, she didn't have to do what her mother said, she was eighteen and—

"Right now!" Her mother's voice came closer, and Tenley could hear her bare feet slapping on the hardwood steps. Tenley could run faster than her mom, especially since she was fueled on coffee and not sauvignon blanc.

Tenley yanked open the door of her room, stared at the unmade bed. Her suitcase was in the closet.

"What on earth are you talking about, Tenley Rebecca Siskel? Moving out? You are not moving out, not as long as—"

Tenley whirled to see her mom, hands planted on hips, in the hall behind her. Mom's blouse had come untucked from her skirt, a white silk tail hanging over the gray linen. Her hair had come out of its ponytail. One strand now straggled, limp, over one cheek. She looked all off balance, one-sided, and Tenley figured that was a pretty great metaphor for their entire lives.

"As long as what?" Tenley shot back. "You can't make me do *anything.*"

"Oh, yes I can, missy."

Her mother's face was getting red. Seriously, Tenley wished this whole thing had never happened, but her mother had started it, and now it seemed like it was impossible to undo. And maybe it was time for the shit to hit the fan. They'd all tiptoed around the whole thing for so long, maybe they all needed to face reality. Whatever reality was now.

Tenley stepped into the hall, slammed her bedroom door closed with one yank of her arm, and in another swift motion, opened the door to Lanna's room. Sacred, sacred Lanna's room. There the pristine white bedspread lay unwrinkled over a float of pillows, lacy and lacier, and a smiling teddy bear perched, reclining, on top of them, endlessly grinning at the emptiness.

"She's gone," Tenley said. Her voice sounded different than it ever had. She picked up Teddy, held it at her mother, accusing. "This is a stuffed bear, an old stuffed nothing bear that used to be hers, and you keep it. Why?"

Tenley hurled the bear across the room. It bounced off the silver-and-white wallpaper and landed on a tufted stool, then toppled to the pale blue carpet. She couldn't believe she was doing it, it was kind of a tantrum, but the pretending should be over. Over! She wanted a life, her old life, her real life. When she mattered.

Her mom leaped across the room, grabbed Teddy, clutched the stupid stuffed thing to her chest. Shouldn't she have clutched her daughter? Comforted *her*? Wouldn't *that* have been the right thing to do?

"See, you care about the bear more than you care about me. It's still all about Lanna, right? Your dear Lanna. Why did you even *have* me?"

Tenley found the knob of the closet door, pulled it open. A puff of lavender and cedar scented the room.

"What are you doing? Don't—" Mom, still clutching the smiling bear, held out the other hand as if to stop her.

Hell, *nothing* was going to stop her. Tenley felt her chest get tight. The way it did when the police came to tell them about Lanna. The way it did at the funeral.

She could barely see now. Her mind was short-circuiting as she stared blindly at the rainbow of Lanna's clothes, all lined up like that in the closet, all the whites at one end, blacks at the other, colors in the middle. She reached in, grabbing, wild, not caring, yanked out hanger after hanger, using both hands, crazy upset, she was *crazy* upset, but whatever, whatever, whatever.

She threw the hangers to the floor, the curved metal tangling the silk and cotton and knits. She knew she should stop. But the space behind her eyes was white, and all she could see was the past, and how it had killed her future. Unless she just—stomped it all out. Talked about it. Until her mother faced it.

"Give this stuff *away*," she yelled, or whispered, she didn't really know. And all she could hear was her mother sobbing, having sunk to the floor, her hands clawing through the chaos of fabric and hangers, trying to unscramble it. "Make room in *our* lives!"

23

"Where? When?" Jake knew it was bad form to answer his cell at the dinner table, but he was a cop, and sometimes these things were life and death. People understood that. He'd reluctantly taken his hand from Jane's leg—touching her had been the only good moment of this entire evening so far—when he saw the caller ID: *DeLuca*. He hunched his shoulders, shielding the conversation.

"What's his condition?" Jake asked. This was the last thing he'd expected. "Wait—he was on the street? Walking? Walking where? Hang on, okay? I can barely hear you."

Jane touched his shoulder, head tilted, eyes narrowed, inquiring. *Hang on,* he lifted a finger at her. She'd been with Bobby Land in the alley. Did she know anything about him? From what DeLuca was now saying, that kid had been mugged only a couple blocks from police HQ.

"But I just saw him—" Jake stopped midsentence, calculating. He'd raced out of HQ to get to the restaurant, not exactly lights and sirens, but fast enough. Jake stood, putting a contrite expression on his face.

"Sorry, you all, excuse me, one moment," he said, and headed to the restaurant's back corridor, away from the bustling waiters and the buzz of conversation.

"So he was walking?" Jake covered one ear with a hand, and DeLuca's voice finally came through.

"Yeah, on Vernon Street, looks like, possibly on the way to the T, ya know?" D said. "He's in bad shape, gotta say. Iffy, I gotta say. Transported to MGH. I'm almost to his room. How long till you get here?"

"Fourteen minutes. Twelve, maybe." Jake estimated the time, the Beacon Street traffic. He thought about what must have happened to Bobby Land, whose day, Jake was certain, had not in any way turned out as the young man expected. "Next of kin?"

"Yeah, we're looking, but so far nada. There's a blue billion Lands in Boston, not to mention the burbs and Cambridge, and he's got no ID on him now. We'd have gotten it when we interviewed him, but that never happened. Remember? Hewlitt's legal stooge got there first, and it was adios."

"What the crap is up with the ID thing?" Jake said. John Doe No. 1, the dead guy, and John Doe No. 2, maybe-tattooed guy, hadn't had IDs either. He eyed the dinner table across the crowded restaurant, saw Jane now leaning toward Robyn, who had her cell phone up to her ear. Gracie and Lewis must be close by now, and though he'd regret—in a parallel universe—missing the dinner, this was duty calling, and undeniably socially acceptable .

"I know, but if the kid was robbed, they'd take his wallet and ID, right? Kinda SOP for a bad guy, Harvard," DeLuca said. He'd never let up on the Harvard thing, like Jake was the only cop who'd ever graduated from there. "They probably tossed it, they always do. We'll find it, no sweat. You on the way?"

Jake stared at the wall, envisioning what might have happened. Bobby Land at the cop shop, waiting, he has a phone, maybe. Okay. Hewlitt and lawyer, whoever, meet with him and "make it right." Do they give him money? They both leave HQ, where do they go? Land then leaves HQ, Jake encounters him in the lobby. Jake leaves, gets in his cruiser. Land leaves, walking. And then—

"Jake? Earth to Jake." DeLuca's voice in his ear.

"Here's my thing," Jake said. "How'd anyone know Land would be there? On that street, at that time?"

The sounds of the restaurant swirled around him, DeLuca silent, as Jake walked toward the table, pausing to let tray-balancing waiters go by, then stepping aside to let a harried-looking young woman carry a fussing pinafored toddler toward the bathrooms. He'd need to say his good-byes and make it right with Jane. And everyone. There'd be other times. He hoped.

"Maybe they didn't know," DeLuca finally said. "Maybe it was random."

"Yeah." Possible. But unlikely. "Two–three blocks, you said, from HQ? A ratty-looking kid in a stupid T-shirt? Why would anyone jump him? There? And then? Hey, is there surveillance video?"

"Yeah, I—hang on," DeLuca said.

Jake arrived at the table. All eyes were on Robyn, talking into her cell, then frowning, then talking again.

"Jane?" he whispered, leaning close to her. She turned, looking up at him. She'd shredded the white cocktail napkin that had been under her water glass. A nest of damp paper crumbles littered the place mat in front of her. "I've got to—"

"Better hurry, Jake," DeLuca interrupted. "I'm here. And the doc is saying it looks bad."

Jane turned, feeling Jake's hand on her shoulder. He was still on the phone. Why wasn't he sitting down? *Wonder if it's about Curley Park?* Could she ask him?

"You've got to—what?" she replied. He hadn't finished his sentence, but now Jake was listening to someone on the phone again, a concerned look on his face, eyeing the door, clearly looking for a way out of here. Well, who wasn't?

And with what she'd been overhearing from Robyn, the evening was not even close to over. Maybe someday they'd laugh about this. At Gracie's wedding, maybe, they could all swap teasing stories about the night she'd brought Jake to meet Melissa, and how Gracie and Lewis had kept a table full of grown-ups waiting. *The night Gracie wasn't missing,* they could call it. The stuff of family lore.

"Sorry, Jane, I have to go." Jake was talking to her again, his voice almost a whisper. He bent low, his face touching hers, his hair against her cheek, a moment that made her eyes involuntarily close with the intimacy.

She turned to face him, her back to Robyn, and for a moment covering Jake's hand with hers.

"Everything all right?" she murmured. Though obviously it wasn't.

"Yeah. I'll call you," he said, matching her tone. "As soon as I can. Sorry to leave you with this." He kept his hand on her shoulder, squeezed, briefly. Gently. "Whatever it is. Is the Gracie situation okay?"

"Seems like it, from what I heard Robyn say," Jane said. "See? She's smiling. And she's off the phone."

"Love you," he whispered.

"You, too," she said. And everything would be fine. It would. Somehow. *The night Gracie wasn't missing.*

"Sorry, Robyn. Sorry, Melissa," Jake was saying. Jane felt his hand leave her shoulder, felt him straighten up. He raised his cell phone in explanation. "Got a call from HQ. I'm going to have to miss dinner. I hope we can do it again before—"

At that moment, Melissa had nudged an elbow into Jane's side. Jane turned to her sister, frowning. *What?*

Melissa rolled her eyes for a fraction of a second, an expression Jane recognized from more than thirty years of interpreting Lissa's silent communications.

"So please give my best to Gracie and Lewis when they—" Jake continued.

Melissa shot a brief but withering glance at Robyn and her phone. *Listen to this.*

"They're not coming," Robyn said. "That's what I've been trying to tell you. Lewis is such an idiot."

*　*　*

There's a portrait of a happy marriage, Jake thought. He paused, his mind already out the door, knowing DeLuca and the unconscious Bobby Land waited for him at MGH but unable to think of a way to leave after Robyn's surprising statement. If she called her husband an idiot, that meant he and Gracie weren't in danger. Jake had handled enough family squabbles, mediated enough he said/she saids to gauge when things were going bad. From what he saw right now, this one seemed low level. A flat tire, a missed communication, an unpredictable and self-centered mother who wanted attention. He did not envy this Lewis guy, who had to live with that and a preadolescent stepdaughter about to be relocated halfway across the country. Tough for any family to handle. But even the most complicated families often worked out their own issues. And he had to get to MGH and Bobby Land.

"Everything okay?" Jake directed his question at Robyn. "I need to—"

"Yes, I suppose." Robyn smoothed one darkened eyebrow, then gave him a weak smile, fussing with her sweater. "I'm sorry, I'm just frazzled, I don't mean Lewis is actually an *idiot*—" She shrugged. "The tire's still not fixed. They said we should just go on with dinner. Make the best of it."

"So . . ." Jake took a step closer to the door. Good news, have fun, adios?

"Duty calls, Jake, I understand. Now, wine for everyone." Robyn waggled her fingers in the air, gesturing for the waiter. "Girls' night out."

Jake hesitated, eyeing Jane, but she waved him away, shaking her head, then mimed for him to call her. Okay, then. He was excused.

"Bye," he said. "Again, sorry. Call me if you need anything." And he was outta there. Poor Jane. He was semi leaving her in the lurch, with the mercurial Robyn and the officious Melissa. Not the most successful introduction to Jane's sister. But duty *did* call. And he felt guilty for welcoming it.

24

Lewis is such an idiot? Jane winced at the disrespectful and inappropriate statement. Robyn probably meant it to be funny, but it wasn't, especially not after what she'd put them through with this on-again, off-again ordeal. It wasn't a loving remark in any way. She wished Jake were still there, but he clearly needed to go. Was there some breaking news she was missing?

Now there were four empty places at the table, and three women who sat silent, watching the waiter pour a California red.

Robyn raised her glass, toasting. "To parenthood," she said. "Never a dull moment. Now, where's my menu? I'm starving."

Ow. Melissa had kicked her under the table. Jane could see she was trying to hide her disdain as she raised her glass as well. Jane nudged her in return, sisterly solidarity.

Jane swallowed her first sip of wine. Thinking. First, Melissa had called her, somewhat upset, saying Gracie was missing. Then she wasn't. Then she was. Then she wasn't, she was with Lewis and the flat tire. Now she still wasn't, although the flat was complicated by some car problem and they wouldn't arrive for dinner. Jane scratched her cheek with one finger. What would she do in the same situation?

"So, Robyn?" Jane didn't want to overstep any boundaries, but they were almost family. "Would you like me to go pick up Gracie and Lewis? They could leave the car, and someone could take Lewis to get it in the morning."

"I was thinking the same thing," Melissa said. "Why should they have to wait in some bleak garage? Poor Gracie must be—"

"Oh, thank you, Jane, but they're fine. Lewis is always making ridiculous decisions. Probably why he's out of a job now, right?" Robyn ignored Melissa, directed her words to Jane. "In fact, he says Gracie's scarfed down a package of Twizzlers and an orange soda, and she's zonked out, sleeping off her sugar high on the waiting room couch. She adores Twizzlers. She'll do anything for them."

She laughed. "Lewis says they're fine. He's probably worrying now, stalling, because he knows how unhappy I'll be." She took another sip, bigger, and Jane saw a frown cross her face. "And he's right. My daughter was gone for, what, four hours? Five? I was completely—well, anyway. You can imagine. Should we order?"

Jane moved her fork back and forth across the tablecloth, twisting it between two fingers. This was the woman who'd been so upset a few hours ago. Now she sipped wine while her husband and daughter ate candy in a local garage at nine at night. Probably a good thing Melissa and Daniel would soon have Gracie for part of the year. Give the kid a little normal.

One way, then the other. Jane watched the fork make disappearing grooves on the little patch of tablecloth. Robyn was holding forth about some problem Lewis was having, chatty and blithe, as if the episode of the "missing" daughter and husband never occurred.

Something was not right about all this.

The waiter arrived, interrupting Robyn's monologue, to take their orders. The woman was a talker. As any reporter knew, sometimes that was a good thing.

"Robyn?" Jane returned the puffy leatherette menu, then smiled, attentive and oh so friendly. "How did you and Lewis meet?"

Robyn leaned forward, eyes sparkling, taking center stage. "Well," she began, "long story short. After the divorce . . ."

Long story short always meant the opposite, but Jane kept a smile on her face, as with much fluffing of hair and gesturing of hands Robyn spilled her entire history as a divorcee.

"Daniel and I just fell out of love, I guess," she said. Then a year or so of regrouping, "a single mother doesn't have the easiest time, but we made do." And her foray into online dating—"Can you believe it?"—ending up with the "steady and reliable" Lewis Wilhoite. Who she'd known "for years" and reconnected with online.

"It was love at first—" Robyn paused. "How would you put it? Click!" She laughed again, a laugh Jane was relieved she didn't have to hear every day. "We clicked, right? We clicked, get it?" she said again.

Robyn made a joke, and apparently had to repeat it.

"So funny." Jane stabbed at her swordfish. It was no doubt delectable, but her mind was elsewhere and her appetite had vanished. She'd never met Lewis Wilhoite, but she pictured a henpecked schlub. Which probably was uncharitable. He'd been fired, apparently, for some reason, and was now unemployed. Jane could relate to that, at least. She almost laughed, which made her realize how long it had been since she laughed. Robyn was still talking.

"And we got married almost immediately, you know? He went to Wharton School of Business—you know Wharton, right, Jane? Soon he'll find a new job, I'm sure of it. So no hard feelings, right, Melissa? And you and Danny are happy now, right?"

"Yes." Melissa's first comment in fifteen minutes.

This dinner was one for the advice columns. *Dear Miss Manners,* Jane mentally composed the letter. *My sister and her fiancé invited me to dinner with his ex and her new husband and their daughter, and to meet my boyfriend, but then . . .*

"And Daniel is wonderful, of course." Robyn pointed to Melissa with her fork. "For you."

"Of course." Melissa's voice was colder than Jane's fish.

By the time dinner was over, with Robyn insisting on banana cream pie and espresso, there had still been no word from Lewis and Gracie.

"If she's not worried, I *guess* I'm not worried," Jane whispered to Melissa as they walked to the parking lot, Robyn trotting ahead.

"Nutcase," Melissa said. "Can you believe she called her husband an idiot? I can't believe Daniel was married to her."

Jane held her tongue. *He obviously can pick 'em,* she had started to say, then thought better of it.

"Did Gracie ever mention—anything bad about him? To you?"

"Never," Melissa said. "She told me she 'adores' him. She calls him Daddy, that's a good sign. I met him once, he seemed, I don't know, fine. I'm just—"

"You'll get Gracie tomorrow," Jane said. "You'll shop, Daniel will arrive, you'll go from there. All good."

"I'll call you." Melissa gave her sister a peck on the cheek.

Robyn had opened the car door, and was waving at Melissa to hurry.

"Whack," Melissa said, shaking her head. "Poor Gracie. A ditz of a mother and a dolt for a stepdad. Gracie may adore Lewis, but she'll be much better off when she's with us."

"I'm calling your father. Right this minute." Catherine Siskel sat on the floor of Lanna's bedroom—it would always be Lanna's bedroom—surrounded by a multicolored flood of her dead daughter's clothing.

Tenley, her chest heaving and her eyes rimming red, stood over her, dangling the battered Teddy by one plush paw, the silly bear blue-eyed and oblivious, as if a full-blown mother-daughter combat was not under way.

I'm calling your father. How often had she said that, to both girls, back when things were right? Greg had been the arbiter of all battles, the negotiator, the fixer, the Band-Aid, the confessor and absolver. It was one reason she—*she did*—loved him. When had he ceded the role of peacemaker? Given up on his family?

"Oh, right." Tenley's voice went up and down the scale, drawing out the word in a sneer. "Like he's gonna care about me."

"Of course he cares, you—" What word could she use to describe her own daughter? They were all hurting, still hurting, and they'd all gone to therapy, but Catherine was not sure if any of it was doing any good. Tenley seemed to become angrier and more rebellious, and Greg, well, Greg had become more and more distant. He avoided Tenley, even Catherine could see that, although whenever she could, just to keep the peace, she'd pretend everything was fine. She'd turned to her job at City Hall for solace. At least when things went wrong there, she could analyze them and fix them. It didn't always work at home. Lately, it never worked.

"Of course he cares." Catherine started again. "That's exactly why I'm calling him. If you don't want to listen to me, okay, but you are *not* moving out. That's—"

"He's not in charge of me. I'm eighteen and I can do what I want."

Catherine tried to stand, maybe hug her daughter and make this all better, but her heel caught in a swirl of knit—*Lanna's long-sleeved black sweater*—and she tripped, tumbling back to the carpeted floor.

By that time, Tenley had stormed out. Catherine heard the bedroom door slam.

She got to her knees, reached into her skirt pocket, pulled out her cell phone. Dialed.

Greg's phone rang once, twice, where was he? She waited two more rings, only to hear the computer voice of the phone system: "The customer you have called is not available."

Catherine stared at the cell phone in her hand. It was pushing ten at night. Where was Greg? And why was his phone off? Even if he were with some—*other woman*, her brain said the words she'd been dreading before she could stop it—he'd still get voice messages, wouldn't he?

She tried to untangle her emotions, like her doctor suggested. Anger, definitely. Tenley was behaving like a child. Frustration, yes. She didn't seem able to handle the situation.

But also, also, also. Worry. Catherine was worried.

25

"Anything in his pockets?" Jake stood at the opening of Bobby Land's curtained emergency room cubicle. The kid's face was a pale moon above the thin blue blanket. Jake had spent more than his share of this day at Mass General, and it looked like he'd be staying into tomorrow. DeLuca had gone for coffee. It was just 9:47. They'd need a lot of it.

The two patients they needed to question were still unconscious, D had told him, doped up and sedated while doctors waited for test results. At least John Doe No. 2 and Bobby Land were both alive, which was one good thing. Young Officer Verrio was still with John Doe 2. He'd check soon for the update on that tattoo.

Bobby Land was now under the watchful eye of a frowning and fretful Detective Angie Bartoneri. She'd been sprung from HQ after the truncated Hewlitt questioning only to be reassigned here as babysitter. Apparently she'd taken her sweet time getting here. Jake recognized her current expression from countless quarrels and ridiculous spats. She was feeling "pissed and dismissed," as she always put it.

"Did I find anything in his pockets?" Angie didn't even rise from her folding chair as she repeated Jake's question. She'd propped her not-exactly-regulation black boots on the metal tubing lining one side of Land's portable bed. Swung the boots down as Jake entered, not quite in time to hide the attitude. She crossed her legs, tossed her hair. "Like what?"

"Like whatever is in his pockets," Jake said. When Angie was annoyed, it was like talking to a five-year-old. The more they realized they'd gotten under your skin, the more manipulative they'd be. Now was she also trying to be . . . sexy? Jake had to stay professional.

Angie didn't answer. *Screw it.* He'd treated her like an adult. She'd have to get over it.

"That his stuff?" Jake pointed to a pair of Levi's folded over the back of a chair in the corner, the Red Sux T-shirt folded on the chair. The kid's stupid camo hat was nowhere to be seen. "This looks like what he was wearing when I last saw him. Did he have a wallet in his jeans?"

"I just got here," Angie said. "Perhaps DeLuca knows. Perhaps he'll tell you when he shows up with that coffee. You're lucky to have him for a partner. Instead of me."

"Detective Bartoneri. Angie. Give me a freaking—" Jake said. "It's not my fault."

The boy on the bed stirred. Jake heard a tiny plaintive sound, almost a sigh. Land's eyes fluttered, then went still. Jake checked the square black screen of the wall-mounted monitor. Heartbeat, fine. No alarm beeps or flatline, just the steady, jagged digital rhythms of sedated sleep. An IV drip was taped inside the crook of his left arm. No tattoos, Jake noticed. That would have been interesting, if Land and John Doe upstairs had matching tattoos. But real life wasn't like *Law & Order.* TV cops solved their crimes in fifty-two minutes.

Jake waited until Land's breathing calmed, then took four steps to the Levi's on the chair. Picked them up, started to check the pockets.

"Ahem." Angie stood, twisted her hair onto the top of her head, then let it fall back over her shoulders.

"Ahem?" Jake stopped, midsearch.

"Aren't you worried about the legality of that search, Detective? You have a warrant to go through Mr. Land's apparel?"

"Mr. Land is not a suspect," Jake said. "As you well know. Or perhaps you don't. Nevertheless." *Nevertheless?* Jake couldn't believe he'd said that.

"Mr. Land is a victim of a violent assault," he went on. "If we can ascertain a motive for such an assault, then—" *Ascertain a motive?* Why did she persist in baiting him? "Anyway, Ang, you know this is by the book."

"Knock yourself out," Angie said.

Jake held back from rolling his eyes. This whole night was a disaster. He felt inside the left front pocket of Land's Levi's, nothing. Right front pocket, nothing. Back left pocket, nothing. Back right pocket, nothing.

He picked up the T-shirt. And underneath, on the chair, was a wallet.

"Hey," he said.

"They found it in the bushes," Angie said. "But who knows if it's his, right? You sure you don't need a warrant?"

Jake gritted back his inappropriately nasty response, dumped the pants on the chair, and pulled apart the wallet's black strip of Velcro, opening a flap of silver-and-white Tyvek. Angie raised an eyebrow at the ripping sounds, then stared at the wall again, actively ignoring him. Three slots for credit cards and ID. All empty. Jake knew the kid's name was Bobby Land, but that was all. DeLuca had HQ tracking down the next of kin. No T passes, though, no college ID. Nothing. He opened the long pocket where bills should be. No money.

"Empty," he said.

"Surprise surprise," Angie said.

Then he noticed what seemed like another compartment, secured by another bit of Velcro. Angie turned her head toward him at the sound as he opened it. Inside, a piece of paper, folded in thirds. Jake tucked the empty wallet under his arm and opened the paper. A cashier's check, from Bay State Bank. The name "Bobby Land" was written in felt-tip pen, on the "pay to" line. Today's date. And the signature was—Jake squinted at the name. No matter how he looked at it, an illegible scrawl.

But the amount was easy enough to read. A five, then three zeros, a decimal point, two more zeros. Someone—clearly Hewlitt and his lawyer—had paid off Bobby Land with this five thousand bucks. The check they'd prepared—in advance—to "make it right." Seemed like they hadn't planned any negotiating.

Why was that the only thing left in the wallet? Muggers didn't take checks? Or maybe the check was so well-hidden they didn't find it. Identity thieves were only interested in cash and IDs—was that the motive? Or maybe they were tracking down where the kid lived.

"Find something?" Angie deigned to look at him.

"Maybe," Jake said. "Maybe a fat check to Bobby Land from Calvin Hewlitt."

"Ca—Who?" she said.

"Who what?" DeLuca stood at the doorway, holding a tray with two coffees.

Jane deposited her tote bag on her dining room table. Ridiculous name, since no one ever dined there. The walnut expanse served as a handy extension of Jane's filing system, holding her research, stacks of usually meaningless mail, and accumulating magazines.

"Hey, cat." Jane grabbed the tiny calico, who had padded into the room and hopped on the table. Another reason why no one ate there. Coda loved to curl up on the magazines. It all worked.

Coda writhed out of Jane's arms and scampered into the kitchen, hoping for food. Jane was starving, too. She should have brought the uneaten swordfish home for the cat. It was almost eleven o'clock. Time for the news.

She took a few quick steps down the hall to the study, grabbed the remote and clicked to Channel 2. Beverly Chorbajian, fashionably tousled and dressed more for cocktails than news, faced the camera with practiced grim concern. Behind her, a hard-edged red-and-black graphic warned of "Curley Park Chaos." "And at this hour," Beverly was saying, "police have not yet released his identity. Let's go now live to the scene, where Roberta Gibson has the latest . . ."

Curley Park was dark at this hour—the reporter illuminated by a portable Klieg, dim streetlamps, and the occasional flare of car headlights. A few windows glowed, yellow rectangles in the monolithic City Hall.

Remote in hand, Jane watched the story go by. They'd used her video of the first ambulance, then the second ambulance, then a couple of the eyewitness sound bites. "I was getting lunch at the cor-nah," the woman said. Still no photo or drawing of the victim. And no explanation of the second ambulance, or what had happened in that alleyway. That kid. Bobby Land? He had given her a card, right? She should call him. See what had happened at the police station.

Jane shrugged, staring at the shifting colors on her TV screen. Did it matter? She wasn't covering the story. She quickly scanned through the other stations to see if anyone had any new info. Far as she could tell, they didn't. And no victim pictures, either.

Why did she care about this? After today's crazy freelance afternoon, she wasn't even a reporter anymore. She should leave the crimes to Jake, be relieved about Gracie, and think about making a new life for herself. And feed the cat.

Laser focus on the bright side, Jane. Okay. She was no longer required to stand in front of an empty building or in a deserted park after eleven at night to illustrate where an event had taken place twelve hours earlier. Right? She didn't miss TV, not really, not at all. If Marsh Tyson never called her again, good riddance. She could get a job as a—well, she'd figure that out.

"This is all about Calvin Hewlitt. Gotta be." Jake kept his voice low as he talked with D, though Bobby Land was still dead to the world. They'd released Angie Bartoneri to HQ, even though she'd insisted she wanted to stay here with Land at the hospital. Probably trying to convince DeLuca she was a team player. But Jake didn't need her attitude.

Bobby Land hadn't moved. His breathing was shallow but steady. A couple of nurses in flowery scrubs had stopped by, checking and rearranging and tucking, then left, promising to return. A real hospital room was allegedly in the works, but with no next of kin and no insurance, things were not moving very quickly.

Jake showed D the wallet and the check. "This has gotta be from Hewlitt. You think it's authentic?"

DeLuca tilted his head back and forth, examining the check, rubbing it between his fingers, then handed it to Jake. He leaned against the wall, took a slug of his coffee. Winced. "Six of one," he said. "Who knows what a bad guy would do."

The pulsing of the monitor, a series of steady soft beeps, underscored their conversation. Bobby Land, eyes closed, was motionless, resting on two white-cased pillows.

"Maybe the check isn't the point." Jake pictured that Vernon Street crime scene, not far from HQ. A crumbling curb, scraggly trees and battered chain-link fence surrounding a vacant lot, a trash-littered expanse soon to be cleaned up for additional police parking. It was just out of HQ's surveillance camera range and not quite to the cameras of the nearby Ruggles T stop. Who could have known that?

"Hewlitt's a surveillance guy, remember?" Jake answered his own question, keeping his eyes on Bobby Land.

"He could have known the camera's scope," Jake went on. "Picked that very spot on purpose. Waited there. He knew the kid was leaving HQ, might have even asked if he was taking the T. The kid is . . . a kid, after all. He's not going to be suspicious. Plus, they'd just handed him five thousand bucks. And who else would have known Bobby was even there?"

DeLuca shrugged. "Maybe he called someone."

"From what phone?" Jake thought back. Had he seen Land with a phone at Curley Park? When he'd brought him in? Shit. No idea. Land wasn't a suspect, so no one had searched him or inventoried property. Now he appeared to be a robbery victim, but they had no idea if anything was missing.

The beeps continued, punctuating Jake's thoughts. The incident might have been random, sure. Some mugger, seeing a skinny white kid alone after dark, decides to take advantage of a vulnerable victim and just see what he—or she, fine, but most likely not—could get.

"But why?" DeLuca said. "Why would Hewlitt give him a check, then beat him up?"

"Think about it, D. True or not, Hewlitt thinks Bobby Land saw what happened in Curley Park. And does not want him to tell. That's the key to this whole thing. Hewlitt crushed the camera's memory card, but he couldn't wipe out Bobby Land's real memory. See where I'm going with this?"

DeLuca shook his head, disagreeing. "Land'll be able to ID his attacker. Narrow it down, at least. If it was Hewlitt? He'd have *some* idea. Maybe it was someone Hewlitt called in?"

"You watch too much TV," Jake said. TV. *Jane.* He needed to—*they* needed to—

A series of high-pitched demanding beeps. An alarm. Jake stood, turned to the stack of monitors, three beige metal boxes scaffolded to the wall on a floor-to-ceiling aluminum rod. Each had wires and tubes connecting to the body on the bed.

"Damn," Jake said. "Go get a doc—"

"On it," D said.

The beeps stopped, their sound coalescing into a piercing one-note tone. Jake, now alone with the victim in his curtained cubicle, watched the jagged electronic line of Bobby Land's heartbeat plummet to the bottom of the screen.

26

Tenley shoved one more gray T-shirt into her nylon gym bag, a black shoulder-strapped tote with mesh pockets on the sides and zippered pouches at each end. *If you don't have time to take everything,* the thought had crossed her mind, *it's almost better to take nothing.* She had to move ahead. Start over. Maybe Brileen could help. She closed her eyes, regrouping, shaking off the residual anger from the fight with her mom. Her stupid mother would be happier with her gone, no freaking question about that. She was a little bummed she wouldn't be seeing Dr. Maddux anymore, he'd done his best to help. He never told her what to do, or criticized her, or even brought up Lanna, unless she did it on her own. She was also pretty much burning her bridges with the work thing, but she wouldn't miss Ward Dahlstrom. And it wasn't like that was her life ambition, to sit in front of a computer. So.

She paused. Hearing the silence. Feeling like—*good-bye.*

So many memories in this room. She'd grown up here, sleeping in this twin bed, which once had a flouncy pink princess bedspread and ruffled pillows. She'd dumped the fluff for plain white sheets when she turned fifteen, since her mom wouldn't let her get black ones. Her once-treasured collection of stuffed animals was relegated to plastic bags on the upper shelf of the closet, the latest incarnations of music and movie posters thumb-tacked to the blue speckled wallpaper. Kurt, for vintage. Katy, for power. Keanu in the old *Matrix.* She'd gotten in big trouble for the thumb tacks, but then her father realized it was easier to leave the posters up than to rip them down and repair the wallpaper. Now her parents could do whatever they wanted with the room. She was done with it.

A knock at her bedroom door startled her. Tenley lifted her chin and turned away. She'd locked her door, of course. Locking her mother out of her room, locking her mother out of everything, locking herself in until she wanted to get out. That would be soon. Very very soon.

Another knock. Louder. "Tenley?"

Tenley pictured her mom, all freaking out. Upset. Too much wine made her face all puffy, though she was always fine by morning. Now she probably wanted to say she was sorry. But Tenley wasn't sorry, and she wasn't about to let her mother off the hook. Her mother wanted her gone. Her dad did, too. She only reminded them of their darling Lanna.

Now they could avoid all that complicated stuff. Forget about her. Starting now.

She didn't answer.

"Tenley? I know you're in there. Listen, honey?" her mother said. "I know we need to talk, I really do. But I have to go out. It's a work thing."

Tenley frowned. That was the last thing she expected to hear. Her mother had to go out? At this hour? It was, like, midnight. Or later. What work thing? Why? But if she asked, she'd have to talk. And she refused to have a conversation. She didn't care about it that much. Her mother could go wherever she wanted.

I hope she's not driving, Tenley thought.

She pressed her lips together, reminding herself not to care, and not to answer. It didn't matter where her mother was going. And, all in all, it might make Tenley's life a lot easier. Things were finally working out.

Catherine stood in the hallway, shoulders sagging, tears welling. The phone in her hand almost felt hot from the call she'd just received. It was well after midnight. *Could it not wait?* It was all too much. How much could she be expected to handle?

She'd try one more time to connect with her daughter. Then she had to go. If her husband was so concerned about Tenley, where the hell was he now? She'd feel better about leaving if Greg were home. If Greg were *anywhere* she could find.

"Tenley, it's important. I know you're angry, I now you're upset and . . ." *I'm sorry.* The words stuck in her throat, but an adult had to make the first move. This was her daughter. Her only remaining daughter. "I'm sorry, Tenner. I don't want us to be upset with each other. I know it's horribly late, but I have to go. Okay?"

Silence.

She paused, flattening one palm against the white-painted wood of the bedroom door. Geographically, her daughter was inches away. Emotionally? Across an endless universe of misunderstanding and sorrow. Right now, Catherine didn't have time to fix it.

"I know you hear me, honey," she said. "I'll be at my office, okay? If you need me? Come see me when you get in tomorrow. Okay?"

Silence.

Tenley waited. Waited. Waited. Listened for footsteps. Heard her mother walking away.

That was, like, ironic, right? That her mother was leaving? She imagined herself telling the story to Brileen with lots of clever inflection and just the right cool words. They'd be sharing an apartment. It wouldn't matter that Brileen was a little older. They'd compare notes on classes and guys and real life, without any dumb parents hovering over them like prison guards. Brileen and her roommate were looking for a third, she'd said. Their old roommate had moved out, but the girl's parents had paid the rent for the rest of the year. How cool was that?

The thick metal zipper sounded extra loud, extra final as Tenley closed the bag. She slid her computer into the outside padded flap. She slung the bag over her shoulder, feeling the weight of all her possessions, all that she was taking with her from her past. Heavy, and light at the same time. She could come back, right? Someday? If she needed anything? Now, she needed her freedom.

She felt the corners of her mouth turn down, felt, somehow, like she was about to cry. Suddenly the poor stuffed animals crammed into the plastic bags seemed so sad, shelved and unloved. She'd never hear her big sister's laughter again—Lanna was dead. What were all those years for, anyway? Eighteen years of breakfasts and vacations and graduations and pictures on the fridge? Lanna got beautiful, her mother got powerful, and her father, *Daddy,* who'd always protected them and provided for them and made them feel safe, seemed to have faded from their lives along with his doomed daughter.

That left her, Tenley. On her own.

One last look around the room. Tenley had always loved how the streetlights made little speckles on the ceiling through the fluttering lace curtains. Long after she gave up the princess bedspread, she would fall asleep pretending the tiny lights were dancing fairies, protecting her and coming to wish her sweet dreams.

She lifted one curtain to peer outside. One story below, her mother's car was backing out between the budding white rosebushes lining the Siskels' paved driveway. Her mother was leaving.

Fine. Tenley was leaving, too.

27

Jane coughed, blinking, trying to get her bearings in the half-light of her bedroom. The air conditioner hummed, chilling with a white noise that made sleeping under the downy white comforter a delicious luxury. Her cell phone was rumbling across her glass-topped nightstand. She squinted at her alarm clock. Middle of the night. *Uh-oh.* Coda muttered a protest meow, her sleep also disturbed by the ringing phone.

"She's fine, Sis," Melissa's whisper hissed in her ear.

"She's fine? Gracie? Great." Jane was glad to be awakened, this was good news. "Lewis, too? Melissa, why are you whispering?"

"I don't know," Melissa said. "But see, if Gracie were *my* daughter, I'd have gone right out to pick her up. I mean, she's nine! And I'm calling you because—Janey, how am I supposed to know what to do? I can't make a big deal out of nothing, but it doesn't feel like nothing. Daniel is relying on me. I can't *lose* his daughter, for God's sake. We're about to get *married,* and—"

"But they're not lost, right? They're fine." Jane wiped the sleep out of one eye. "So where are they?"

"I. Don't. Know." Melissa paused, either sighed or yawned. "Robyn went to sleep, but I'd been sitting in the living room, watching out the front window. But no one came home."

"So Lewis called, or what?" Jane sat up, plumping the pillows behind her so she wouldn't doze off. Coda, a dark silhouette, jumped onto the comforter, turned a circle, did it again, then nestled in the curve of Jane's knee. *The night Gracie wasn't missing,* Jane had called it. Seemed like she was right. Hurray.

The long and complicated day seemed distant now. Marsh Tyson. Gracie. The murder at Curley Park. The altercation in the alley. Two ambulances. Two victims? Unfinished stories.

Where was Jake? Did he already know how the stories ended?

"Jane?"

Jane started at the voice in her ear. She must have been half asleep. Missed something. "I'm here. What again?"

"Like I *said,* they're at a motel," Melissa whispered. "Robyn came to the kitchen, got a drink of water or something. She saw me in the living room and got all flustered. She said they'd called, and she was sorry she didn't tell me, but she 'thought I was asleep'—what an *idiot*—and they told her they were 'zonked' and would be home in the morning. Lewis told Gracie they were having 'an adventure,' and she was thrilled with the little motel soaps and all the pillows, and they'd be fine."

"A motel?" Jane tried to decide if that was reasonable. Nothing was reasonable in the middle of the night.

"Yeah, they'll be home in the morning. Turned out it's better that I'm here." Melissa's voice was so low Jane could barely hear it. "Oh, Janey, I'm so sorry to bother you. I just needed someone to—maybe I'm silly to worry. But the woman is so unreliable. Seems like her husband is, too."

"No, I hear you, I'm glad you called. I agree it's—unusual," Jane said. "And you'll be a good stepmom, Lissie. Daniel knows that."

Silence. Jane could hear Melissa yawn again, or sigh. "Thanks, Sis," she said. "I hope so."

At the employee garage, Catherine Siskel punched in her code—L-A-T-E—on the flat black pad. LA-TE stood for Lanna and Tenley. Now it was also about the time of night. *Or, morning.* Almost two thirty. She waved at the blinking security camera above her, the all-seeing eye that recorded everyone who entered. The yellow-and-black-striped barrier arm lifted, allowing her into the basement shadows, the murk of the parking area pin-spotted with dim orange lights. An array of empty spaces stretched in front of her, white stripes with stenciled names spray-painted at the edge of each one.

SISKEL COS, hers read. The chief of staff got the slot right next to Mayor Elihu Holbrooke, who, in all likelihood, was home with his wife and beagle, asleep in their overdecorated Beacon Hill brownstone. If she had to wake him up, it wouldn't be pretty.

It was her job to make sure the mayor was *not* called, unless there was a dire emergency or an arriving celebrity. Or contributor. Tonight was none of the above, which made it Catherine territory. She shifted into Park, took a swig of tepid water from her plastic bottle, checked her face in the car's pull-down mirror. She'd slapped on a little makeup every time she'd stopped at a red light. It would have to do.

Ward Dahlstrom would be there already, probably still seething that Catherine had kept the job—and parking spot—he wanted. So would Kelli White Riordan, the veteran city attorney who insisted on her middle name to amplify her old-Boston political genealogy. As if anyone cared.

Catherine tapped her fingers on the chrome railing as the elevator lifted her to the executive level. They'd read the subpoena, then see if there actually *was* any surveillance video for this afternoon. The traffic cams, where Tenley worked, recorded only if someone hit the cache button. If they had video, they'd hand it over.

It was all part of her job—the bad news as well as the glory. The e-mails had flown all afternoon, and she'd expected the subpoena, just not in the middle of the night. Still, a man had died in a city park, right across from City Hall. They had a victim in the morgue and a John Doe under police watch in the hospital. When crimes were solved quickly, the cops looked good and the mayor looked good. Which made Catherine look good. And she knew that when they identified the victim, someone's family would be in mourning. So if Catherine was a little tired, hey, she'd get over it. She knew what mourning felt like.

The Fourth of July was imminent. Boston's biggest tourist attraction.

The pressure was on to close the case before the Esplanade fireworks. If it wasn't, there'd be fireworks of another kind.

Who would kill in broad daylight? she wondered as the elevator doors opened. A killer on the loose was bad enough. One operating in the middle of a million holiday picnickers would be like a bad thriller movie. And a murder right outside City Hall? Probably the first time in history. She might have seen it herself if she'd been looking out the window at the right time.

Be disturbing if Tenley had seen anything. Her daughter hadn't mentioned it, but then Tenley never mentioned anything about anything.

Catherine pushed open the glass doors into the reception area. A wide-windowed foyer designed to accommodate favor seekers and job hunters, it had been outfitted with lumpy low-slung couches and old magazines to discourage supplicants from hanging around. The receptionist, a dire wolf in cardigans who'd been around since the Flynn years, ruled the place with stabbing fingernails and a practiced glare.

Her reception desk was vacant at this hour. The corridors had been darkened by the city's vaunted automatic energy-saving program, the air conditioners barely humming. For an off-hours meeting like this, that made the atmosphere close and gloomy and stuffy. Like being inside a submarine. *Or a sinking ship.*

Dahlstrom stood in the middle of the room, holding a flat plastic CD holder, waving it at her as she entered. "It's all here," he said.

"What's all here?" Catherine nodded at Kelli Riordan. Even in her trademark pencil skirt and starched white blouse—at this hour!—the woman looked disheveled and sleep deprived.

"You mean the CD?" Catherine asked.

"The murder," Dahlstrom said.

28

"He's in a coma?" Jake rubbed a hand over his face, staring at the ICU doctor. Bobby Land, beaten and bleeding internally, was on the verge of death. Hard to grasp that this poor kid, now wired with tubes and monitors, was the same one who'd assured Jake everything was copa-cetic. All smiles, hiding five grand in his pocket.

One thing was sure. If he died, the mugging of Bobby Land would no longer be simple assault and maybe robbery. If he died, it'd be murder.

Either way, cops' point of view, now two victims from the Curley Park episode. Connected, had to be. Should he send someone to watch Calvin Hewlitt?

"You're sure?" Jake instantly regretted the words. Of course the doctor was sure. But it was three A.M., and Jake's brain was running on empty.

Black embroidered script on a white lab coat identified him as Antonio Piva, MD. "I'm sorry." The doctor quickly surveyed the empty waiting room. "Are you calling the next of kin?"

"We don't know who that is," Jake said. This night had crashed and burned. Bobby Land on a ventilator. All they'd gotten from him was a wallet and a cashier's check. *Calvin Hewlitt,* Jake thought again. He and his lawyer certainly must have asked where the kid lived. That alone would give Jake a reason to go knock on Hewlitt's door. But first Jake needed to finish with the doctor. "We're looking."

"We'll wait to hear from you, then." Dr. Piva flapped his aluminum folder closed, took a step toward the double doors of the ICU. "I'll let you work."

"You, too," Jake said as he left. "Thanks."

Land's family must be missing him, whoever they were. Maybe they'd be smart, and lucky, and call the cops. Lucky, in this case, meant they'd learn their son was in a coma. If they weren't so lucky, no one would ever know who this kid was, and if he died he'd be buried by the next funeral home in the city's charity rotation. Jake wiped one eye, from fatigue and frustration. *If* he died.

His phone vibrated in his jacket pocket. He pulled it out, looked at the caller ID. DeLuca, who was upstairs in maybe-tattooed guy's room.

If that guy was dead, Jake was quitting and going to law school, like his mother always wanted. Lawyers got to sleep. And their wives could be reporters.

Back to reality. "Yeah?"

"Developments," D said.

Jake dropped his head back, closed his eyes for a defeated second. He knew it. "Yeah, developments here, too."

"You go first," D said.

"Bobby Land's in a coma." Jake was still wrapping his brain around it. "Shit."

"Yeah. So tell me maybe-tattooed guy is hanging in."

"Who?"

"Room 606," Jake explained. D didn't call him tattoo guy, of course. "The stabber."

"Oh, him. He's, yeah, hanging in. Worse than they'd thought, though. Medically, it's iffy," D said. "Legally, he's screwed. Cuz here's my news. You know we subpoenaed City Hall surveillance. That's still pending, but Supe knows a guy who knows a guy who says City Hall might have gotten the whole thing. *Might* have. Pre-show, stabbing, and aftermath. We're supposed to confirm. Wouldn't that be a slam dunk?"

"They . . ." Jake pictured it. The whole crime caught on camera. Not from some random tourist snapshot, the hoped-for bonanza that so far produced nada. But from a flat-out kick-ass freaking videotape of the entire freaking thing. Good-bye to speculation, good-bye to conjecture, good-bye to interviews and court procedure and warrants and neighborhood canvasses and story-changing vision-impaired witnesses.

Good-bye to doubt.

"So it's possible we could—"

"Yup," D said. "Get some popcorn, bro. We might be going to the movies."

For the five millionth time, Tenley put her hand on her bedroom doorknob. This time, for sure, she was ready. Her bag slung over her shoulder, good-byes said, decisions made. Hours ago. Her whole new life waiting. This time, *for sure,* she was ready. She put the bag down. But now it was, like, middle of the night.

She pictured what she'd have to do. Though thinking about it now, when did the buses stop running? Or start? She could check that on her cell. She should have done that first. Maybe . . .

She took her hand off the doorknob. Stared at the closed door. She could take one more minute to figure stuff out.

Okay. Her mother wouldn't be home anytime soon. She'd told Ten to come to her office tomorrow.

And her dad sure wasn't going to show up. He'd obviously dumped both her and Mom. Gotten tired of them, or too upset. Always acting strange. Always gone. Actually, if she allowed herself to think about it, he was weird even before Lanna had—*anyway.*

She sighed, still creeped out over this afternoon. Someone had gotten killed, somehow, right where she kind of was. *Oh.* That's probably why her mother had to leave. Called in to—what did Mom call it? Spin. Put spin on it. A murder outside City Hall was gonna need a lot of spinning.

Tenley lowered herself to the floor and rested her head on her tote bag, using it like a big lumpy pillow. Crossed one ankle over a knee, stared at the ceiling. Flapped one black flat against her foot.

Thought about it all.

What if she waited? Went to work, like always, but took her bag of possessions. Her mom would never notice, and if she did, she could say it was for . . . she'd make something up when the time came.

And really, why hadn't she and Bri planned it that way in the first place? She'd been so excited about getting out of here and starting over that she'd—

She took out her cell phone, went to messages, punched in Brileen's number. Still lying on her back on the pale blue bedroom carpet, she held the phone up in front of her.

RTG. She typed. So Brileen would know she was ready to go. Then: *Woot.* So Bri would understand she was excited. And then: *Sorry so late, tho. Mom at work thing. How abt CU in AM?*

She hit Send.

The cell phone transmitted, and she imagined her words flying toward Brileen. She watched, her eyes blearing with exhaustion and kind of fear and kind of, whatever the word was for wondering if this was the right thing to do.

2nite! The message popped up, with its little trill of arrival.

Tenley stared at it. Tonight? Tonight what?

Should she respond? Or did Brileen have more to say? She typed *2nite what?* and a new message appeared.

We come get u! U home?

We? Tenley thought.

Yes. Tenley typed, because what else would she say? But Brileen didn't know where she lived, so she'd still push for tomorrow. Tomorrow would be much easier.

But another message from Brileen appeared before Tenley could formulate her new plan, let alone type it.

K! On way. C U in 5 mins, k?

Tenley stared at the words. Was it okay? Was it?

* * *

"The murder? Is on the DVD? Did you see it? Who else has seen it?" Catherine yanked open the door to her inner office, waved Kelli Riordan to the guest chair.

Ward Dahlstrom was pacing, wiping his glasses with a white handkerchief. She noted how disheveled he looked, his checked shirt for once not starched to perfection, a lock of hair for once come loose.

Catherine punched the green button on her coffeemaker. Four A.M. She'd need a lot of damn coffee. Absolutely no way she was going to call Mayor Holbrooke, not until she heard the whole story. Her brain revved, questions piling on top of each other.

"The traffic room, right? So who pushed the twenty? When?"

She paused. No one had answered her yet. "So?"

Dahlstrom cleared his throat and waved toward the city attorney. "You want to take this, Kelli?"

"Take what?" Catherine selected an ultra dark roast from the spinning pod holder. Might as well go big. "Anyone else want coffee?"

"No thanks," Riordan said. "Here's the situation. You know how the traffic video works."

Riordan always had to communicate step by agonizing step, as if listeners could not keep up with her agile legal brain. Faster to let her explain it her way. Even though Catherine simply wanted to see the video. In about one second, she was going to play it, explanation or not.

She worried, since it was a traffic cam, that Tenley might be involved. She was probably asleep now, shoes probably still on and arms splayed over her plaid bedspread. They'd solve the family issues in the morning. They were still family, after all.

"Sure, I know how it works." Catherine poured sugar into her coffee. Maybe she could hurry this along. "It's all what you see, live surveillance, not taped, unless someone hits the cache button. That was our compromise with the ACLU types. We don't keep any traffic cam video. So like I said, who pushed the twenty? When?"

Catherine saw Riordan and Dahlstrom exchange glances. Clearly she wasn't up to speed.

"What?" she said. "You're scaring me here."

"No, no, it's fine," Riordan said.

"It's fine." Dahlstrom had moved a pile of files from Catherine's wide windowsill, making room for him to lean against the wooden ledge.

"You want to fill me in?" Catherine's patience evaporated. It was too late—or early—to screw around. "Kelli? Now?"

The lawyer shifted in her chair, uncrossed her legs, crossed them again. Moved her briefcase to the other side. "Bottom line," she said, "we actually *do* tape."

Catherine tilted her head, blinked, trying to understand. "Do tape what?"

"The traffic cam. There is no 'cache,' you know? It's all—well, the bleeding hearts made such a stink over it, we had to agree not to tape. But according to the mayor, it was essentially a public safety issue. He decided public safety trumped the right to privacy—"

"If there is such a thing in this day and age," Dahlstrom interrupted.

Riordan ignored him. "So the mayor made an executive decision that all traffic cam video would be recorded and stored."

Catherine stared at the lawyer, hearing the buzz of the coffeepot, smelling the first fragrant note of dark roast. No matter what was said next, they were doomed. Their own miniversion of Watergate, Iran-Contra, Abscam.

Politics, lies, and videotape.

"Did you know this, Dahlstrom?" Catherine tried to calculate their exposure. Like trying to measure the temperature of the sun. Why even bother? Screwed was screwed. "Who else knows?" Catherine had to ask, even though she knew it was even too late for that. There were no secrets in politics, not unless everyone was dead. And these days, even that didn't help. Because video never dies.

"No one knew, pretty much," Riordan said. "Except me and Ward and the mayor. It's all digital, transmitted to an off-site cloud storage company. The company has no idea what it's getting, of course. And we can access it if need be."

Riordan shrugged. "So that was our predicament today, as you can now understand. When the police subpoena said—" She clicked open her leather briefcase, took out a folded piece of paper. Scanned it, then read. "'Any and all video surveillance footage of Curley Park on . . . blah blah today's date, yesterday, actually, and blah blah a time span of ten in the morning until three in the afternoon,' then we had to decide whether to hand it over. Or lie."

"Why didn't you tell me this? Why didn't the mayor tell me?" Catherine's brain churned with the possibilities, the conflicts, the legality. She almost wished she could talk to Greg about it. They used to discuss things like this, political dilemmas, and destiny, and the role of the truth. The goals of being a public servant. Who were you serving, really? But Greg was gone, who knew where, and she was on her own. With an epic can of worms.

"That's a topic for discussion," Riordan said, "but hardly the point right now, correct? We can't admit, publicly, that we have video of anything that happened in Curley Park—or on any of our traffic cams. That'd be political suicide for Mayor Holbrooke."

"It would show he's a liar," Catherine said.

Riordan didn't answer.

"Which would be true," Catherine said.

Riordan didn't answer.

"So what's your suggestion?" Catherine asked.

Riordan didn't answer.

Catherine sank into her swivel chair, barricading herself behind her wooden desk, looking at the lawyer who was about to ruin the mayor's relationship with just about everyone in the city. Constituents, cops—hell, who knew what other evidence those tapes might contain. Catherine shook her head as the choking possibilities unspooled. Lawyers. Crap. They'd start issuing subpoenas for every bit of video that existed. Reopen court cases, criticizing the city for withholding evidence. Which, if she was understanding correctly now, would be completely and devastatingly true. And the press. Double crap. The press would go completely nuts.

This was one of those moments where careers were made or broken. They'd taught her Pythagoras at the Kennedy School. "Choices are the hinges of destiny." Which, okay, seemed a bit portentous for this occasion, but nevertheless, her choice right now would be massively important. It could even bring down the city government.

The mayor was an idiot. Even a fifth grader knew the cover-up was always worse than the crime. Not that there was a crime. Was there?

"What's our legal exposure?" Catherine asked. "Can we claim some kind of public safety exemption?"

Riordan took a deep breath, blew it out in a long sigh. "Here's how I envision—" she began.

"Wait," Catherine said. No more explanations or rationalizations. Time for the main attraction. "That DVD. Before we decide anything. Let's see it."

29

Jane knocked the rumbling phone onto the floor. 6:04 A.M. Lovely. She scooped it up just in time to prevent the voice mail from kicking in. *Private number,* it said. It had better not be a sales call.

"Hello?"

"Janey."

Melissa. "What? Are they home? Lewis and Gracie?"

"No. And it's kind of—a mess," Melissa said, her voice low. "I'm trying to stay calm. Someone has to. Robyn is in her room, sobbing. Lewis isn't answering his phone. I'm in the hall, about to call the police. Do you have an inside number?"

Jane sat up, shaking off sleep. A litany of horribles paraded through her brain, but no reason to mention them. She'd wait to hear reality.

"What kind of a mess?" Jane said. Coda opened one eye, inquiring, went back to sleep. "Melissa? I didn't dream it, right? Last night you said they were fine."

"No. Yes, but—here's the deal. Remember yesterday Lewis was supposed to pick Gracie up at school. At lunch?"

"And they had a flat tire, and then it had to be fixed, and then they stayed at a motel."

"Well, turns out Gracie never got to school," Melissa said. "She was never there yesterday. The school just sent some automated e-mail to Robyn, asking if Gracie was going to be sick again today—"

"Sick?" Jane threw off the comforter, rolled her shoulders, tried to focus. The room was still dim, the early-morning sun edging through the slatted blinds. "Again?"

"Yeah. Apparently Lewis called her in sick yesterday. But she wasn't sick. What if he took Gracie *yesterday*, hours before anyone even would miss her? And now they're who knows where? What if all those phone calls were—"

"To give them time to get farther away? *Whoa*. Didn't Robyn even wonder? I mean, didn't you think it was strange, from moment one? The whole thing?" Jane stood up, her white T-shirt, one of Jake's BPD hockey team jerseys, hanging almost down to her knees.

"Completely! Like I told you last night," Melissa said. "But what was I supposed to do, right? I'm the—" She paused, and Jane could hear the frustration in her silence. "The new girl. The interloper. She's Daniel's *daughter*, after all, and that woman is her mother, and now Gracie's out there, with some nut of a stepfather, and—"

"Hey. Hey. Sweetheart, I know its seems . . . ungood." Jane couldn't think of a word that conveyed "potentially hideous and alarming" without terrifying her sister any more than she was already. "But Lewis *did* call last night, right? Saying they were fine?" *Which might not have been true,* Jane didn't say.

"Whatever. I think Robyn should call the police." Melissa's voice, harsh and bitter, still had a soft edge of sorrow. "I mean, why not? But she won't. So Jane? Could you—"

"Call Jake? Or give you his number?" Jane finished the sentence. Just like she'd done all the years growing up together. Jane babysat her little sister when Jane was fifteen and Melissa nine. Before that, she'd shared her stuffed animals, let her little sister win at Candyland, taught her to play War and Spit and how to do a French braid. "The girls," their father had called them, as though they didn't have separate personalities. Then Jane went off to college, and Melissa gloried her way through high school. When Jane came home, it was as if they didn't know each other anymore. Melissa continued to exceed expectations. Their mother died. Their dad favored Melissa. Jane was outgrown. Unnecessary. Third wheel. Childhood's end.

And now all of that was in the past. Jane was the older sister again. Protective and in control.

"Yes, would you, Janey?" Melissa asked. "I mean, it might all be fine. But I can't help but worry Gracie's in trouble. Don't you?"

Catherine heard the whir of the computer mechanism as her disc drive opened, felt the hesitation as she settled the DVD into place, pushed it in carefully, delicately, the way she'd done so many times, until the door clicked closed. She heard the spin of the player as the disc engaged, watched the first screen of the illicit video pop up in the center of her screen.

"Hit the green triangle to make it play," Riordan said. "There's no sound."

Catherine held her tongue. She knew how to make it play.

She clicked the mouse.

The time code said 11:55:42. First, a tree-lined Curley Park, bustling with tourists and businesspeople, an ordinary June day. It was sunny, she could tell by the shadows, the majority of faces with sunglasses.

Surveillance tapes used to be impossible to watch. She'd seen endless clips of unrecognizable bank robbers, no mask necessary, identities blurred incognito by the primitive recording capabilities. The action in Curley Park was several stories down and a block away from the camera. This was clearly a new-generation video, not fuzzy or jumpy, but still not as sharp as a movie or TV. The faraway faces were tiny. Featureless.

"You can't recognize anyone," Catherine said, hoping she was right, as she watched the tourist parade, balloons and shopping bags, lots of little kids. She put the action on pause, turned to Riordan and Dahlstrom. "It's leaves and tops of heads. This is just a blur, far as I can see."

Her colleagues stood behind her, one leaning over each shoulder, peering into the monitor. Kelli Riordan smelled green and summery, like she had showered in citrus rainwater. Ward Dahlstrom smelled like coffee and musk, thick with tension. Catherine wished they would back off, let her see it, let her think, but there was no way to say that. The video clip was brief, they'd told her. Fifteen minutes.

"Well, watch," Dahlstrom said. "Yeah, there's trees, but see how the park itself is in the open?"

"Ward." Riordan raised a palm. "Shut up."

They watched in silence as the secret movie of a Boston noontime unspooled. These people had no idea they were being watched, let alone taped, Catherine thought, no idea their actions would later be scrutinized by three nervous staffers trying to decide whether to launch a full-scale cover-up to protect their big-time boss. Whether to hide evidence from the police.

Catherine saw a few people sitting on the various park benches, hats and feet, shopping bags. A kid touched Mayor Curley's bronze knees, supposed to be lucky. She'd done that a few times herself. It was all she could do not to fast-forward. *Let's see it,* she thought. *Get this damn thing over with.*

When the time code hit 11:56:42, one of the people on the bench stood up, a guy, it looked like, in a T-shirt, maybe. The others on the bench moved farther away from each other, reallocating the space. The man moved toward the center of the park.

"That's him," Dahlstrom said.

"Shush," Riordan said. "Let her watch."

"Watch what?" Catherine said. The time code read 11:58:59. Then 11:59:00. The man didn't move. "What?"

Fifteen seconds later, a man carrying a shopping bag walked into the park, then stopped next to the man in the T-shirt. His back was to her, but she could see he was wearing a baseball cap, white shirt, and tan pants. There was something about his stance that seemed—

Catherine leaned forward, as if getting closer would make the out-of-focus images more distinct. It didn't help. Squinted. That didn't help, either. The image nagged at her.

And then it happened, so quickly Catherine almost didn't see it. When she hit Rewind, moved the white dot backward along the video line to re-play the scene, she still could not grasp what she witnessed.

"My God," she whispered.

She heard Kelli Riordan puff out a breath, felt her stand. Heard her brushing down her skirt, moving away. "I know. Hard to watch. They ex-change the bag, he dumps out the—I don't know. Phone book? Then he just turns and stabs the person. Then whoever it is, cannot see his face for shit, just runs. Dammit. It's right there."

The screen had gone to black. And so did Catherine's brain. She wres-tled herself to the present moment with every ounce of human resolve she could muster.

"I need to think," she said, surprised that she recognized her own voice. Surprised she could even speak. She looked at her watch. "Give me an hour. We don't have to do anything this second. This is a lot to digest."

She had to get them out of her office. Had to, had to, *had to.* She qui-eted her mind, willed her heart to be still, willed her hands not to shake. "Ward? Kelli? Go home. In the morning, we'll brainstorm. Decide what to do."

"Do we have to admit we have this?" Ward asked. "I mean, what if we simply, ah, pretended—"

"It's a subpoena," Riordan interrupted, her voice tinged with sarcasm. "If we actively fail to provide materials we are aware are in existence, any judge would rule that's an illegal—"

Catherine didn't care what these two thought. Not now.

She held up a hand, calling on every bit of her self-restraint. Their speculation and bickering had to stop. "Kelli, I need you to check the pre-cedents for something like this. Local option executive privilege, extraor-dinary powers potentially granted to the mayor, public safety exemptions. I mean—anything. And we'll reconvene at seven thirty."

"Eight," Kelli said. "Or, say, eight fifteen."

Had Tenley seen this? *Oh, my God.* Her daughter. Her daughter who she'd fought with, and yelled at, and left alone. Her daughter who, according to Dr. Maddux, thought she'd never be understood, never be happy, never have a real family again. Maybe she was right.

"Fine," Catherine said. Let Kelli micromanage. "Eight fifteen."

Her office door slowly clicked shut, sealing out the rest of the world and leaving Catherine alone with the video. She stared at the freeze-frame on the screen. This was life, and it was real, and by the ridiculous vagaries of the universe and technology, it was all caught by the uncaring eye of the surveillance camera.

Did they have to tell the police they had it? What if there was a way for the police to solve this crime without knowing about the video? If the point was to catch the bad guy, wouldn't any method of coming to that conclusion be satisfactory? And then the mayor's pompous and arrogant decision wouldn't destroy them all. Politically, at least.

She should call Tenley. But she couldn't do it. She'd let her sleep. Let the poor child have one more hour of her world. And maybe—Catherine was wrong. Maybe she was mistaken about what she'd seen.

Catherine's hand felt odd, heavy and uncooperative as she lifted it to her white plastic mouse. Her engagement ring shimmered under the halogen desk light. Her wedding band, a thin platinum circle that matched her husband's, reminded her of the day they were married, a gorgeous July afternoon, blue skies, puffy clouds, she and Greg, smiling, surrounded by friends and possibilities. Two weeks from now, she realized, was their anniversary.

She clicked again on the little green triangle, dragged the dot to 11:59:00.

And watched, once again, the videotaped murder of her husband.

30

"Can you talk?"

Jake heard the tension in Jane's voice. If she was up now, calling his cell phone at just after six, it was important. He hoped she'd gotten some sleep, at least. He sure as hell hadn't, dozing all night in an uncomfortable chair, waiting for maybe-tattooed guy to show his arm or wake up. The man might be a killer, and Jake still had no idea who he was.

"Sure, I can talk," he said. "Are you okay, Jane? Where are you?"

"Home," she said. "Trying to get dressed. You're on speaker. And yeah, I'm okay. But—"

"Gracie? And Wilhoite? They home?" That awkward dinner at the Taverna seemed decades ago. He needed food. Jake frowned. He had to check on Bobby Land, too, hadn't heard from upstairs for three hours now. It had been less than twenty-four hours since the Curley Park murder. Was he any closer to the solution?

His frown deepened as Jane spun out the story. Gracie had never been at school? And now Jane was telling him Wilhoite was not answering his phone.

"Does Robyn think—" He stopped. Better not to put words in someone's mouth. "What does Robyn think?"

"Who knows?" Jane said. "I'm getting it all by way of Melissa. She wanted me to call you and find out what to do. She can contact you, right? I gave her your number."

"Jane?" Damn. His call-waiting had clicked in, interfering with what

Jane was saying. He'd been trying not to picture her getting dressed, since that wasn't the point, but she'd mentioned it, and after that it was hard to resist. He'd rather think of her getting *un*dressed, rather see it in person. Now someone was interrupting. Maybe word on Land? Or maybe D with the video? Jake could happily stay awake long enough to see that. "Hang on," he said.

"Jake?"

"One second." He clicked away to the new call. "Brogan."

"Detective Brogan?"

"Yes?" A familiar voice, but he couldn't quite—

"It's Angie Bartoneri," she said. "How quickly they forget. Anyway, Detective. I have a call you might want to take. I called Missing, but they insisted I give it to you. Transferring now."

"Who?" Jake started to ask for details, then realized, after the click and change in tone, that Angie had already transferred the caller. Always a game with her. "This is Detective Brogan," he said.

"My name is Catherine Siskel," the voice said. "And I'd like to report a missing person."

"Jake? Jake?" Jane, one arm in her black T-shirt and the other one out, glared at the phone, annoyed. Stupid speakerphone was incredibly unreliable. She pushed the other arm through the short sleeve. Taking two quick steps, she punched the phone to regular talk. So much for multitasking. And she needed coffee. "Jake?" she said into the phone. "You there?"

Nothing. Jane grimaced, yanked down her T, wondered if she should hang up and try again. She hadn't accomplished a thing with this phone call. Robyn was counting on her. Or at least Melissa was. Where the hell was Gracie? This was a job for the police, no question. She'd hang up, call Jake again, get her cop on the case. She clicked the reset, ready to start over.

"Hello?" The connection sounded funny. Maybe she was still on hold. "Jake?"

"Jane?" Not Jake.

She tucked the phone between her check and shoulder, zipped up her black jeans. She could throw on a scarf and blazer if she needed to look presentable, or stick with the simple jeans and T if she was only going to be at Robyn's. Impossible to predict what the day would bring.

"This is Marsh Tyson," the voice said. "At Channel 2?"

"Hi, Marsh." Jane frowned, getting her bearings. It was six thirty in the morning. This was not a social call. "What's—"

"Glad you're up," he said. "Listen. Our sources at the cop shop say there was some kind of assault near the police station late yesterday. Headquarters, by the Ruggles T stop, you know where that is?"

Of course she did. "Yes, I—"

"Apparently, this is somehow connected to the Curley Park stabbing. So says our source."

"Your source?" This was a new one. When her boss told her something was based on a source, was she supposed to ask who it was? Or take him at his word and go from there? That was the thing about journalism, especially these days. Always a new ethical dilemma, without any new rules to resolve it.

"Trust me on this, Jane. The identity of the source—it's a nurse, okay? But you'll find the info for yourself, right? You'll dig, fill in the blanks, get confirmation. So, Jane? How about another freelance gig? You covered Curley Park, you know the players. You shot the video. I assume your— sister was she, or niece?—is not really missing, or we'd have heard about it by now. So, what say you? Your personal life calmed down enough to sign on?"

Jane paused, staring at the toes of her black flats, trying to assess who she was and what was important. Telling the truth was always the best option. Right now, however, she didn't know what the truth was. Had her life calmed down?

"It has and it hasn't, Mr. Tyson," she said. "Calmed down."

"Marsh."

"Marsh. My sister's fiancé's daughter—" She stopped midsentence.

Too much information. But Melissa and Robyn—and the police—could handle the possibly missing Gracie. They didn't need Jane in person, right now, at least. If they did, she'd be available. Plus, she needed the money. Quitting her newspaper job had been a glorious and unregretted moment of honor and principle. But that did not pay the rent. Or make car payments. And she didn't even want to think about health insurance. She was unemployed, for the second time in two years, depressingly, and with her savings evaporating, that was not good. Melissa had Jake's number. Jane could stay fully involved with them *and* handle the freelance gig. Let the juggling continue.

"Anyway. Sure," she said, not feeling sure at all. "What's the plan? Want me to come into the station, or meet a photog somewhere? And do you have any info on the victim? Name, next of kin? Why do they think he's connected to Curley Park? Is he—it's a he, right?—in the hospital?"

"That's the thing, Jane. No, he's not in the hospital. Not as of half an hour ago. He's probably on the way to the morgue. And no next of kin, that's why we called you. Call the cops. See what happened. Find the victim's family."

Shoot. Exactly why she didn't miss television. She'd done vulture patrol duty way too many times. She did not want to be in a position—not ever again, thank you—to tell a grieving family they'd lost someone. But she could at least look into this, see what developed. The police would have to inform the family of their loss, anyway. Police. *Jake.* Where had he gone?

"Okay," she said. "Can do." She'd tell Melissa where she was, keep them all looped in. It'd work. "Can you tell me the victim's name? Age? Anything?"

Jane listened to the sound of rustling paper on Marsh's end of the line. Weird to be in television again. Wondered if she'd remember how to do it. She smiled. Not weird. It was her job. Getting the answers, making them public. Kind of like Jake, but without the badge and gun. *It's your calling, honey,* her mother had told her.

Channel 2 better have kept all her video from Curley Park. Soon as she could, she'd look at every frame. Be interesting if the victim was in it. More than interesting.

"Jane?"

"I'm here." She went to her closet, selected a muted gray-and-black scarf from the too-full hooks, used one hand to twirl it around her neck. Add a blazer, she'd be good for TV, if need be.

"According to the source, the dead guy's name is Land," Marsh said. "Bobby Land."

31

Tenley tried to bury her face in her fluffy pillow, the same one she'd used forever. Somehow it didn't feel the same, didn't smell like that flowery stuff her mother used on the laundry. She sniffed, turned over, tried to get comfortable. Felt, somehow, a shadow over her.

"It's too early, Mom," she muttered. "Five more minutes."

Then she remembered. Not her pillow. Not home. Not Mom. She sat bolt upright.

Brileen stood over her, hands on hips. Smiling. "Wake up, kiddo."

Tenley put both hands over her eyes, rubbed, trying to get her bearings. Brileen and her girlfriend, Valerie, cute like Brileen was, older, colleg-y, had come to pick her up in a car. Tenley tried to remember the car, but she was not good at cars. They'd driven, like, toward Fenway Park—she was not good at directions—and then to this house in . . . somewhere. Why was she so tired?

They'd all had wine, she remembered. And chatted for, like, hours. Valerie was cool. And now she had a headache.

"Now you're remembering," Brileen said. "Never have four glasses of wine, sister." She wore a little flowered skirt and a striped tank top, Levi's jacket, strappy flat sandals. Laptop bag over one shoulder. "I've got to go. Val's already at work. Go back to sleep."

Tenley's neck hurt, not bad, though, like a crick. She looked around the little room, trying to assess. She spread her arms, noticing she was still in the T and jeans she'd worn the night before. Twin bed, the only one in the room. Windows on one wall, filmy curtains, revealing an about-to-be sunny day outside. Open door to a cheerily wallpapered corridor. Her backpack lay in the corner, zipped closed. Nothing threatening, nothing unpleasant. There was something, though, about last night—*right*.

"How did you know where I lived?"

"Huh?" Brileen was digging into her bag.

"When you and your . . . friend picked me up."

"Valerie."

"Right. You never answered me about that last night. Did you?" It was all a little fuzzy. "How'd you know my address?"

Brileen had her cell phone out now and looked at Tenley, made a goofy face. "You told me, Miss Wine-for-brains. At the Purple."

Had she told her? Her *exact* address? She didn't remember doing that, but she guessed she might have. Must have.

"Really?"

"You're losing it," Brileen said. "You were freaking over the—thing. In Curley Park."

"Oh, crap. What time is it?" Reality came washing over her. She had to go to work. Of course she'd go to work, it wasn't like she was giving up everything in her life, she just wasn't going to live at home anymore, like every other college kid decides at some point. Her point was now. She still needed an income. Even more.

"It's only, like, seven." Brileen punched some buttons on her cell. "I've gotta go. Val and I will see you later?"

Tenley thought about her own cell phone zipped into her backpack. Should she call her mother, let her know where she was, at least? Wherever that was. She'd find the address, easy enough, and then make it to City Hall by eight thirty. It'd be like a regular workday. Mom would never know.

She thought about her phone again, her *silent* phone. Her mom obviously hadn't come home last night, didn't even know Tenley had gone. Because Mom would have called, right, if she had missed her?

Or not. And see, that proved it. Proved no one cared about her. They'd rather she be gone. It was her fault about Lanna, and every time they saw her, they remembered what she'd known but hadn't told, and blamed her again. Now she'd left home, and no one even noticed. Problem solved. She'd done them a favor by leaving.

"Tenley?" Brileen said. "Tonight?"

"Yup." Tenley'd decided. "See you tonight."

Jake recognized the name, impossible not to. Catherine Siskel. The mayor's chief of staff. A tough, smart, political lifer. At City Hall through two administrations. Now part of a third, always moving higher up the political ladder.

Jake glanced at the man in the hospital bed. Maybe-tattoo guy was still motionless, monitors beeping, oxygen hissing. He moved toward the door, opened it, and stood in the hall, keeping the door open and his voice low.

"Of course I know you, Ms. Siskel." Also because of the daughter. The one who had died, out in Steading Woods. A year ago? Less. Angie Bartoneri had worked on it, he remembered. Made sense that's why the woman had called Angie. The old ME's office had ruled that death an accident. "You said—someone missing."

"Yes," she said. "My husband."

Her husband? Her *husband*? A VIP with a dead daughter, and now a missing husband? Missing Persons had made the right decision giving him this call. Even though it would have been more by the book for Angie to fill him in on the background, not make him rely on his memory.

"Detective—?"

"Brogan." Jake took out a spiral notebook. He'd transfer the notes to his new phone when he could, if need be. "I often handle—special cases. Let's take it one step at a time. Your husband. His name is? When did you last see him? Forgive me, but why do you think he's missing?"

"Greg Siskel," the woman said. "Gregory Atkins Siskel. I last saw him, um . . ."

Silence. Clearly she was calculating the last time she saw her husband, which did not seem like it should be that tough a question. The last time he saw Jane? Eight thirty-five last night. Boom, easy.

"Yesterday morning," Catherine Siskel finally said. "He was on his way to work at the—he was a—is a—" Her voice caught, Jake could hear it over the phone. "He didn't come home last night."

"Ma'am?" This was all wrong. Tired or not, he knew it. It was more difficult to make up a story than people expected. Cops knew how to listen. And they knew the sound of a lie. "Do you have a recent photo of him? Maybe a video?"

Catherine steadied herself, one palm on her desk. Why would he ask for a video? What did he know? Or maybe, no—home movies. People had family videos.

Why wasn't this easier? Lying was simplest if you pretended it was true. It was a trick she'd learned at news conferences. Now she felt as if big heat lamps were focused on her, like in the old gangster movies when they sweated a confession out of the bad guy. But she wasn't the bad guy; she was the victim.

Problem was, there was no way to reveal how she knew it.

"Ma'am?"

She needed to sound worried but not hysterical. Because in her created story, all she knew was that Greg was missing. Not dead. She cleared her throat, pretending. "Sorry, I'm upset. I'm sure it's all fine. I hope it's all fine. Certainly I have a photo. May I e-mail that to you? Is that the most efficient way? I already described him to Detective Bartoneri."

"Yes," the detective said. "Sooner the better."

Catherine wrote down the e-mail address he dictated. "Doing it now. Hang on."

She clicked on the camera icon, found a photo of Greg—*oh, God, Greg*—in her pictures. Recent enough. The four of them—*the four of them*—up in the White Mountains on their last ski vacation, red faced and bundled in parkas. Arms draped over each other's shoulders, Lanna's long auburn hair curling out from under her knit cap, Tenley looking at her with that mixture of jealousy and affection only a little sister can have. Greg and Catherine were bookending their girls, squinting in the glare of the sun, looking straight at the ski patrol camera. She hadn't taken a photo of the family, or Greg, since Lanna died, she realized.

Now, two people in the photo were dead. And the other two were fighting. Soon as she was finished with this charade, she had to call Tenley. There was no way out of it. Tenley would have to be told, and then it would be awful. Catherine had no poker face for that, and no idea how to handle it. The extent of her mothering skills had already been reached, already been sucked dry. The future—no Lanna, no Greg—was uncharted territory. Treacherous and fearsome. And lonely.

But for now, step one. She'd send the photo. This cop would realize, pretty damn quickly, she hoped, that he'd discovered the identity of the victim in the city morgue. She'd probably have to go identify Greg—*oh, my God*—her knees went to jelly, and she balanced herself on the desk again, woozy. She'd get through it.

And then, since they had the assailant in the hospital, done and done. Case closed. No video necessary. She'd tell Kelli and Ward that the cops identified the dead man and didn't need the video. She'd save the mayor's ass. Again.

Who would save *hers*? And who killed her husband? Why? There was so much she didn't know about Greg. Maybe it was simple, though. His wife worked at City Hall. His daughter, too. He might have been mugged, left with no ID when the thief took his wallet. That was a perfectly reasonable explanation. Horrible, but reasonable.

It would be a firestorm. But at least she could try to keep it personal and not have it detonate a career-destroying political scandal.

"Sent," Catherine said. The sound of the mouse click echoed through her office, seemed to ricochet off the windows and the framed diplomas on her walls, ricochet off the political photos lining her bookshelf, ricochet off the wall she'd built around her feelings. "I'll wait to make sure you get it. Are you a missing persons detective, is that why I was transferred to you?"

"Great," the detective said. "While we're waiting, though, fill me in a bit more. First the basics. When was the last time you talked to your husband? Did he say anything that might lead you to believe something was wrong? Sorry for being personal, but were the two of you having any problems? Had he threatened to leave? Had *you*? Why did you decide to report this? Why did you decide not to wait any longer? Do you have any indication that he may have met with, ah, an accident?"

Oh, my God, just look at the photo, Catherine thought. Show it to one of your colleagues working the Curley Park case. Show it to the medical examiner. She sat at her desk, stretched out her fingers, willing herself to stay calm. Breathe. There was nothing untoward about his questions. They were exactly what anyone would ask. These were Missing Persons 101 questions, no subtext, no hidden motive. She was hearing double entendres and accusations that weren't there.

She didn't have to try to sound weary and sad. She could feel her nerve endings, every one of them, edging closer to the surface. She'd been spinning stories so fast, she'd forgotten this was about her husband. Her *husband*. Who had annoyed her and baffled her, who'd been distant and dismissive and aloof since Lanna died. No, since before Lanna died.

How could she possibly battle through that barrage of questions? Maybe she should tell the police the truth. It wasn't her fault, after all, that the mayor had set up this web of lies. Not her responsibility, really, to protect it. It would be such a relief to let go. To go home. To be with her poor daughter.

"Ma'am?" the detective was saying. "I know that's quite a list of questions for you, but I know you can appreciate we'll need the answers. I'll need to come talk with you in person. Are you at City Hall?"

32

Jane handed the business card across Marsh Tyson's desk. "Oh, my gosh, Marsh. Bobby Land? Look, he gave me his card. At Curley Park. He was—I don't know. A crime scene groupie. A wannabe. He latched on to me, and then—"

Marsh's desk phone rang. He took the card, centered it on the blotter in front of him, took the call, raising a finger. "One minute, Jane," he said.

She stepped away, giving him a little privacy. Needing some for herself, too. The last time she'd seen Bobby Land was with Jake. Jake had taken him away, had him in custody. Jake had put the kid in his cruiser at the Curley Park crime scene, the alley next to the crime scene, at least. And now Bobby Land was dead. How? Why?

She'd called Jake three times, no response—*where the heck had he gone?*—then left an urgent message for him. And one for Melissa. Neither had answered their phones, or their texts. If they needed her, or if they figured out the Gracie situation, they'd call.

Bobby Land was dead. Had anyone, maybe Bobby Land's mother, reported him missing? She could call the cop shop, that'd be public information.

She dug in her tote bag for a spiral notebook, flipped it over so the recognizable *Register* logo printed on its cover didn't show, clicked open her pen. First thing, call the number on Bobby Land's card. Well, no. She shook her head, pen poised over the notepad. No use in calling a dead person.

Jane grimaced, embarrassed at how she'd forgotten what this was actually about. Compassion fatigue, they called it. She was so fearful of it, the emotional carapace that hardened journalists, caused them to compartmentalize disaster, make grim jokes about reality. A college student, a boy, really, she'd met yesterday was now dead, under suspicious circumstances. Should she have paid more attention to him? Was there anything she could have done?

Jane shifted her weight to the other foot, flapped the notebook against her palm, fidgeted in the open doorway of Tyson's office, pretending to watch the video monitors lined up on the opposite wall.

She pursed her lips, frowning. Why didn't the police know Land's next of kin? Hadn't Jake taken him to the station? But Land hadn't been a suspect, he'd been a victim. Maybe he'd lied?

Marsh hung up the receiver, picked up Land's business card. Waved it at her.

"No use calling this, I suppose," he said, giving it back. "But we've got to regroup. Our source who's tight with the cop shop just told me they've got a lead on the Curley Park victim. The stabbed guy? Might be the husband of a City Hall bigwig."

"Really?" Jane said. In the relentless hierarchy of TV journalism, this was an interesting call. Was the murder of the husband of a city official bigger news than a mugging victim killed steps away from the police station? They'd have to decide in time for the six o'clock news. "Who?"

She raced through her mental Rolodex, trying to recollect the names of women who held high positions at City Hall. The city corporation counsel, Kelli Riordan. The new press secretary, Wadelle Tran. The mayor's chief of staff, Catherine Siskel. There must be more. Marsh Tyson had quite the source. But someone was always ready to spill a secret. Jane's own career relied on it.

"They didn't say." Marsh focused on the flickering TV screens.

Jane heard Marsh selecting his words, pluralizing the pronoun. That usually meant it was a woman. She didn't change her expression, as if she hadn't noticed.

"Forget the Land story, Jane. We'll give it to another reporter." Marsh gestured at the monitors. "See? Unit three's at the cop shop already. You take the City Hall lead. You have sources there, right? And we'll get Mary in HR to handle your per diem. We don't expect you to work free."

"Deal." And there it was. When the time came, she hadn't even hesitated. She was back in TV. With all its faults. *Forget Bobby Land,* Marsh had said. Easier to say than do. She tried to yank her brain away from regret and sorrow. Land was no longer her story. Still, she couldn't help thinking about him.

"Great," Marsh said. "Welcome aboard."

"Thanks." *Onward.* She checked her watch. Seven thirty. "So, City Hall's still closed, but that doesn't mean no one's inside. I'll head over and see who's there. Plus, the mayor's going to have to face the cameras at some point, right?" She smiled. "Once someone tells him what to say."

Marsh pointed a forefinger at her. "Right. Make sure the desk has your cell number."

"Got it." Jane flipped her notebook closed, ready to head out, then stopped. She should have thought of this before. "Marsh. Surveillance video of Curley Park. Think City Hall has any?"

There was no way this could get worse. Jake had been about to call for backup so he could head to City Hall, but then the white-coated Dr. Piva emerged from the hospital elevator. He'd told Piva to alert him if Bobby Land's condition changed. Looking at the doc's grim expression, Jake didn't have to ask what happened.

You sure? The words almost came out of Jake's mouth again. But of course Piva was sure. Bobby Land was dead. *Damn.* Land might have been a crucial witness.

Jake leaned against the tiles of the hospital wall, regrouping. Times like this, being a cop sucked. When you almost forgot you were supposed to be a human being first. Jake took a moment, remembering Land had been a real person, a kid, not simply a cog in the justice system.

The photo from Siskel pinged onto his phone.

And now Catherine Siskel—alive and powerful—was demanding attention. There was no by-the-book here.

He tapped the photo, enlarging. Catherine, two young girls—he recognized Lanna—and a man. Which answered one question. He glanced into the hospital room, confirming. The missing Greg Siskel was not the comatose maybe-tattooed stabber in the hospital bed. No way. Greg was big, taller than his wife, not exactly a hulk but certainly not the graying mug now wired and tubed to the medical devices.

Nor could Greg Siskel be the John Doe in the morgue. Catherine Siskel had described her husband to Angie. Bartoneri had seen the victim at Curley Park and would have snagged that solve for herself.

Siskel had probably called Angie because she'd known her from the Lanna Siskel investigation. Missing Persons clearly made Angie transfer the case to him because Catherine Siskel was a VIP.

But he'd transfer it right back. Missing could handle this just fine. He had two dead people.

Two dead people killed in public places. And if the chief of staff's husband was really missing, marital misunderstanding or not, that would amp up the news coverage volume considerably, even if no connection existed. A total public relations debacle. The supe would probably have already called Mayor Holbrooke to coordinate the public response to the Curley Park incident. Cases connected to City Hall always had their own procedures and sensitivities.

He should get DeLuca, hit City Hall together. D would still be asleep at this hour, since their usual shift didn't start till ten. Jake himself was pretty damn tired right now. Been a long time since he'd pulled an all-nighter, but he'd get coffee, power through it, visit the disturbingly double-talking Catherine Siskel, then take a nap—somehow—this afternoon.

Jake rubbed his eyes, then flipped the Siskel photo back to normal size, but his phone defaulted to the camera roll and all his saved pictures. *Damn.* He scrolled through, trying to retrieve the Greg photo. Then he stopped, pausing, even though he was in a hurry. He'd looked at this one photo so many times it would be tattered and flimsy by now if it had been printed on paper. Jane had called it a Diva-dog photo bomb. She'd been trying to get a selfie of her and Jake, and his golden retriever Diva had shoved her nose in between them. Jake could have sworn the darn dog had a grin on her face.

Jane. He hadn't returned her call.

33

Jane weighed her options as she trotted down the concrete steps of Channel 2's employee exit.

Jake hadn't returned her call. Good news? He was on to something and she'd soon find out. Or bad news? He was on to something and she'd soon find out. Should she call Melissa? But Melissa hadn't called again either, so obviously there was no news on that front.

She passed the edit booths and the always mysterious engineering department with its coils of cords and byzantine contraptions, and then pushed open the station's heavy rear door, blasting the interior air-conditioned gloom with morning sunlight. Only Boston had June days like this, flat blue sky, briny wind off the harbor carrying the scent of salt and seaweed, the skirl of cranky shore birds arguing over the shards of garbage left behind by Haymarket fruit and vegetable vendors. Jane could walk the two blocks to City Hall. She took a deep breath, centering herself in the day.

Gracie, Jake, Bobby Land, and a mysterious City Hall employee. A whole list of unanswered questions. At some point, maybe soon, she'd know something. She'd learned to be challenged by uncertainty, not daunted by it. You never knew the end of the story until you got there.

Passing the JFK Federal Building and trotting down the expanse of steps, Jane crossed the concrete tundra in front of City Hall. They called the building's architecture Brutalist. Not just a description of the exterior, with its massive concrete teeth and stacked narrow windows, Jane thought. It was brutally difficult to find your way around inside the illogical structure. Boston City Hall was a pain, an inconvenient marble-floored disaster for anyone in heels. Maybe it was designed deliberately to keep people out.

Not her, not today. She yanked at the glass side door on the plaza level. Locked. She checked her watch. Seven fifty-eight. She'd try another entrance.

Down a set of steep steps, up Congress Street, toward the ground-level door. Maybe a guard would be there, let her in. She had no press credentials, she realized. Hoped that wouldn't put a snag in her plans.

Pausing a beat, she stared across the street at Curley Park. Crime scene tape still garlanded the circular bricked area where the stabbing occurred. No police officers were on duty guarding it. Did they think there was still evidence there? Or had no one bothered to take the yellow plastic down?

She'd forgotten to ask Marsh Tyson about her Quik-Shot video from yesterday. Bobby Land might be on the tape, which could be helpful for the story. Would they broadcast his picture, asking if anyone recognized him? She shook her head, answering herself. No. They'd have to wait until police confirmed an identification. Or asked for help.

She bracketed her face with her hands, peering through the smoky glass of the door. Inside she could see the guard's desk and chair, empty. Lights on, but no one home. Eight o'clock now. Where was everyone?

Footsteps behind her. A haggard middle-aged man in a checkered shirt who looked like he hadn't slept much tapped a white pass card against a metal box attached to the door. With a mechanical click, the door unlocked.

She smiled, as if she and the guy were best friends. "Hi," she said. "Gorgeous day, huh?"

He looked at her, semi-quizzical, then adjusted the sheaf of papers under his arm, juggled a Starbucks venti with foam oozing from the plastic lid. Pulled open the door. Paused. And that was all she needed. It was a public building, after all. And she was the public.

"Thanks," she said. Big smile.

And she was inside.

Catherine stared at the photo of her husband, her dead husband, wondering how long it would take the police to figure it all out. Wondering how long it would take *her* to figure it out. Wondering why her life had crashed and toppled off the cliff into sorrow and tragedy. She pressed her fingers to her temples, tried to hold back her tears.

Although the cop would be expecting her to be sad, right? Her husband was missing? Was it suspicious if she was *too* sad? Was it ridiculous to be protecting the mayor, and the city, instead of running to the police, screaming, *Someone killed my husband*?

How do you know? They'd ask.

"What the hell," she whispered, and dropped her forehead onto her crossed arms. Maybe if she just went to sleep, this whole thing would disappear, evaporate into the past. Or have never happened. Maybe it wasn't Greg.

But what she saw was all on tape, right here, right in front of her eyes. She could watch it again and again. Had she been nasty to Greg, the last time they talked? Had it mattered? Had they been arguing over something meaningful? It was over Tenley, she remembered. Whether Tenley could stay out. Mundane. Ordinary. What if she had known that was the very last time they'd ever talk? Would she have handled it differently, forgiven him, forgiven everything, decided not to sweat the small stuff?

Now there was no small stuff. All the stuff was huge and hulking and relentless. What had Greg been doing at Curley Park? It must have been just after they'd talked on the phone. Had he been on the way to see her, maybe to apologize? Had he been in the wrong place at the wrong time? Who had killed him, for God's sake? And why?

And that cop was on the way.

She punched the intercom to Ward's extension. He and Kelli Riordan were supposed to meet with her at eight fifteen so they could strategize.
So much for that idea. Now she had strategy of her own to handle first.
She'd have to stall them. She should have arranged to meet the cop somewhere else. She wasn't thinking straight. How could she?

A knock at the door disoriented her even more. Ward? Kelli? The cop?
He couldn't have gotten there by now. Could he? *Dammit*. She was
panicking, and this was not the time for that. It was certainly Kelli and
Ward, just as planned. But she wasn't ready for them, not yet. She'd make
some excuse, send them away.

Another knock. "Catherine?"

"Come in," she called. She touched her hair, her cheeks, tried to pull
herself together. She'd take Kelli's research and say she had to study it,
which was true. The mayor wouldn't arrive for an hour, probably two.
At this point, it was all about stalling, as long as she could. If the police
identified the victim—*Greg*—in Curley Park, they wouldn't need to tell
anyone about the video.

Would they?

The door opened.

"Hi," a voice said.

A woman took two steps into her office. Not Kelli. Younger, pretty-
ish, with a black T-shirt, black jeans, a gray scarf around her neck.

"Mrs. Siskel? I'm Jane Ryland. From Channel 2? You have a moment?"

"Do you have an appointment?" Jane Ryland. A reporter. No wonder
she looked familiar. What the holy hell she was doing here? To show up
unannounced at Catherine's office was a surprising breach of protocol.
And security.

"Jane? All press inquiries must go through public relations."

She looked at her watch. It was eight o'clock, maybe three minutes
after. That cop was supposed to be here any second. If Jane saw that police officer coming into her office, she'd put two and two together. No
matter what answer she came up with, the result would be disaster. Cath-

erine knew about Jane Ryland, knew her reputation perfectly well. If this tragedy magnet so much as smelled a story, she'd never let go. "You know the rules."

The reporter took another step into the room. Then another.

Catherine stood. This had gone far enough.

"I can't help you," she said.

"But you don't even know what—" The reporter stopped, midsentence. Turned to look in the hall behind her.

Catherine leaned forward across the desk, trying to see what Ryland was seeing. Maybe her secretary had finally arrived? But Siobhan never got here before nine.

Jane stepped aside, revealing the newcomer. Leather jacket, Levi's, black T-shirt, sandy hair, needing a shave. Holding out a badge.

"Catherine Siskel?" The cop seemed nervous. Eyeing Jane Ryland. Well, of course he was. He'd shown up at her office and a reporter was already there. He probably thought Catherine had called her. How would she ever explain any of this? *And her husband was dead.*

Catherine felt her stomach lurch, felt the floor move under her, felt the earth twirl off its axis and spin her into outer space.

"Excuse me," she said. She clamped a hand to her mouth, horrified at what was about to happen. Looked at her open office door. Embarrassed, overwhelmed, defeated. "I have to throw up."

34

"Did you get any sleep?"

It was a ridiculous thing to say. Jane was so flummoxed to see Jake in Catherine Siskel's office that she blurted the first thought that popped into her mind. Her second thought was that if Jake was here, she was on the right track. That, she did not blurt.

"Ms. Siskel seems to be in extremis," Jake said. "Hope she makes it to the bathroom."

"Yeah." Jane blinked, trying to decide what to do. Jake needed a shave. The black T-shirt and Levi's were the same ones he'd worn yesterday. The exact same ones, she decided, not just another from Jake's collection of identical work clothes. Jake had not been home since they'd last seen each other twelve hours ago at the Taverna. Where had he been? And why?

She shifted to the other foot. They were alone in the chief of staff's inner office. The wooden door to the outer reception area had slammed closed behind Catherine. Ten after eight. Back to the question. "So, uh, what're you doing here, Officer?"

"Detective," Jake said.

It was one of their routines, an inside joke because people always called him officer. It would be followed by him saying the one phrase that especially annoyed *her*: "And you are *who*?" She'd reply "your worst nightmare" and ask him to "speak into the microphone," usually a beer bottle or wineglass. Then they'd laugh, and kiss. And go from there.

This time no one laughed. They each paused. If Marsh's source was correct, Catherine Siskel's husband might be a murder victim. That's why she was here. Jake, too, probably. Jane put a hand on his arm, felt the familiar leather of his jacket. They were alone, after all. "You okay?" she asked, still holding on. "You look tired."

Jake rolled his eyes, got a funny look on his face. "Lots going on. How about you? When last we saw each other—"

He paused, his eyes softening, put his hand over hers. She could tell he almost smiled.

Love you, that was the last thing they'd said to each other. *Love you, too.* But this was not the time to discuss that, though Jane could not repress her own desire to smile at the memory. It was all she could do not to move even closer, stand nearer to him. Who would know? What was the protocol for this?

"Anyway." Jake cleared his throat, squared his shoulders.

Jane knew he was going into cop mode. Probably a good decision. She stepped away, changing the moment, silently agreeing to keep it business.

"What's the latest with Gracie?" he asked. "Any news?"

Jake was scanning Catherine Siskel's office as he talked to her, hands now linked behind his back, peering at the framed photos on the bookshelves, checking the top of the wooden desk. *Plain sight,* she knew he'd say. *Anything I can see is evidence.*

"Didn't Melissa contact you?" Jane frowned. A little niggle of uncertainty crept up her spine. "When I didn't hear from her again, I thought the two of you had connected. Really? No? Hang on. I better call her."

Jane grabbed her cell, dialed Melissa. Voice mail. *Really?* Waited, left a message. Maybe it was good that Melissa hadn't called her, or called Jake. Maybe all was well. She mentally crossed her fingers. No need to panic herself over imaginary disaster. Melissa was a lawyer, an adult, and fully capable of handling this.

"So, seriously." She stashed her phone, saw Jake looking out the window. "What *are* you doing here?"

"I could ask you the same thing."

"Yup," Jane said.

"So? I'm asking." Jake turned to her, focused on her.

She knew that look. He thought she'd tell him anything when he gave her that look. Sometimes, under the right circumstances, she would. This was not one of them. She glanced at the door, paused. Nothing. No one. "Good luck with the 'cute' look," Jane said. "Seriously—"

"You said that," Jake said. "I get it. You're serious."

"C'mon, Jake," she said. Might as well tell him the truth, since they were always off the record anyway. The moment he'd shown up at Siskel's office, she knew the tip had been accurate. Plus Catherine had run off to throw up, a sure sign of crushing distress and grief. On the other hand, maybe it was a colleague's husband who'd been stabbed, and Siskel was simply upset. Jane narrowed her eyes, considering.

She poked him in the arm, then leaned on the edge of Siskel's desk, crossing her arms in front of her. "Okay, fine. Two questions. Does anyone have surveillance video of what happened at Curley Park? And is Catherine Siskel's husband the victim of that stabbing?"

Jake stared at her, trying furiously to decide how to answer. Where the hell had *that* question come from? If he paused too long, Jane would know he was calculating what to say. She could read him way too well. Times like this, that put her at an advantage. And half the time, she got him to say more than he planned. Still, his only real dilemma was how to tell Jane she'd gotten a bogus lead without seeming to feed her inside information. Clearly she'd heard something was up with Catherine Siskel's husband. She simply had the facts wrong.

The identity of the man in the morgue, John Doe No. 1, was still unknown.

"That's some chase you're cutting to." Jake tried to look concerned and unconcerned at the same time. He wasn't worried about the video question. DeLuca was on that. They'd get whatever they could, though he knew the City Hall traffic cams were only live feeds, ever since the mayor had

caved to political pressure, deciding so-called privacy was a bigger priority than law and order.

"Catherine Siskel's husband?" he repeated her question. "Who told
you that?"

"Oh, right," Jane said.

It killed him when she did that, stuck out her tongue at him. It sent
his brain off in another direction entirely.

"Like I'm going to tell you my source," she was saying. "Besides, I
know you, *Detective*. Answering a question with a question means you
don't want to answer me. Which means I'm right."

"But you're not!" Damn it. She'd done it again. But she *wasn't* right.

"Jane," he said, starting over. He eyed the still-closed office door. The
digital clock showed 8:14. How long should he wait for Catherine to return? "Do you think you should check to see if Catherine Siskel is okay?
Or I'll do it if you want."

He saw the change in her expression.

"Oh, yikes," she said. "I'm a terrible person. Of course, I'll go look." She
started away, then turned back. "Except, ah, I don't really know her, you
know? She was about to order me to leave. You think she'd want me to—"

A knock at the door. "Catherine?"

A woman's voice.

He and Jane exchanged glances. Viewed through a stranger's eyes,
they were two uninvited, unwelcome guests alone in the empty office of
a top-level city official.

"You're the cop," Jane whispered. "More acceptable for you to be here
than for me. Although Catherine never actually told us to leave."

"Yeah, because she could barely talk," Jake said.

Another knock. Then the door opened.

"Who're you? And where is Ms. Siskel?" A black-cardiganed lioness
with a mess of gray hair and red-framed eyeglasses took up all the room
in the open door. Brandishing a lethal-looking metal clipboard, she
looked them up and down as if she couldn't decide whether to make

them stand in the corner or throw them overboard. "Does Ms. Siskel know you're here? How did you get in here? I'm one second away from calling the police."

"He *is*—" Jane began, then stopped as he caught her eye.

Call the police, huh? Jake loved this part. "I'm Detective Jake Brogan, Boston PD." Jake did the badge thing, which stopped the woman's rat-a-tat questioning.

She stared at the badge, coming closer to inspect it.

"Is something wrong?" she asked. "With Ms. Siskel? Or what? I'm Siobhan Hult, her EA. What are you doing here? Do you have an appointment? I know you don't have an appointment. Did someone call you?"

She pointed to Jane. "And who is she? Why is *she* here? Are you a police officer, too? Let's see your badge."

Okay, so it didn't stop the questioning. An EA? Oh, executive assistant. *Geez.*

"Ma'am? Ma'am?" Jake tried to interrupt her. And now Jane's phone was ringing. He glared at her, couldn't help it, and she clicked it off.

The outer office door opened again. Jake relaxed. It had to be Catherine Siskel. She was the one who had called *him* to report her husband missing. He'd been here a total of fifteen minutes and made zero progress, except to almost get thrown up on, encounter his secret girlfriend, and be interrogated by a crazy person.

But it wasn't Catherine at the door. A sleek-haired blonde, tight black skirt and impossible heels, carrying a sheaf of legal-looking papers, swept toward them, almost elbowing the secretary—the EA—out of the way.

"Siobhan?" The newcomer stopped at the threshold of Siskel's office. "What's going on? Where's Catherine? We have an eight fifteen. And will someone please explain to me why there's a reporter here?"

35

Darn it. Tenley hated when someone came into the office bathroom when she was there. And this early in the morning? She'd left Brileen's as soon as she could, so she could get to work on time. Weird that she wanted to get to City Hall. Never thought *that* would happen. But getting whisked away from home and waking up in an unfamiliar place—even though she'd agreed to go and all—now seemed a little less like a cool adventure and a little more like a dumb idea. She could always go home again, though, no biggie.

Since she'd brought her backpack to work, all her stuff, it was like she'd never been in that house. She'd seen the metal numbers on the wall beside the front door and the name on the street sign—798 Cadogan Street—before she headed to the bus stop, which she'd looked up, easy peasy, on her phone.

Her phone. Her mom still hadn't called. That was kind of good news, since now, with any luck, she'd never know Tenley'd sneaked out. Later, Tenley would explain to Brileen. It wasn't like she would never see her again, she'd say, they were pals, after all, she'd say, but she didn't think the time was exactly right to—

Anyway now, though, someone else was in here, in an out-of-the-way bathroom nobody *ever* used this early. Hiding in the stall, Tenley pulled her feet up, crossed them yoga style, balancing herself on the toilet so her feet wouldn't show under the door. Silly, and totally uncomfortable, but if she came out while someone was in the bathroom, she'd have to talk to them, and she didn't feel like it. She didn't even start work till nine, almost an hour from now, but she was allowed to use her City Hall ID to get in whatever the time. The guard guy downstairs at the lobby desk had been dozing at his post. She'd waved and walked right by him.

She heard someone turn on the water, full blast, in one of the metal sinks that lined the back wall. She tried to peer under the stall's door to see if she could recognize feet, but, tilting, almost fell over. It didn't matter who it was, anyway. She'd wait her out. No one could be in the bathroom forever.

That was weird, though, the person had now gone into the stall next to hers but left the water running, *moron*. The person coughed, like she was puking, which was incredibly gross, and if that person actually threw up, Tenley didn't care what happened, she was so out of here.

Her rear was killing her now. All she needed, to be trapped in the john with a hangover-throwing-up person. Could life get any weirder?

The person didn't throw up, thank God. Although sounded like she was trying hard enough. The toilet flushed, the stall door opened, the water turned off. Okay, final-fricking-ly. She was almost out of here.

She adjusted herself, trying to keep her balance, trying to imagine what the person was doing. A wisp of color went by the crack in the doorjamb of Tenley's stall, but not enough to recognize anyone. *Come on,* Tenley thought. *I want to leave.*

Silence. But not quite silence. Now the woman was making a phone call. What was this, her office? Tenley tried to lean against the tiled stall wall, felt the metal flusher thing instead, and succeeded only in making a wet spot on the back of her T-shirt.

"Tenley?" the voice out in the bathroom said. She almost fell off her perch on the toilet. She knew that voice. Her *mother*. Her freaking mother. But how had Mom known she was in here? And her mother had been trying to throw up? Why?

All this raced through Tenley's mind the second she heard her own name. She almost opened her mouth to answer, even though she was one hundred percent baffled. Impossible for her mother to have seen her in here, right? But then Mom kept talking, and Tenley realized she wasn't talking to her. Not in person. On the *phone*. She was leaving her a message, on her cell! Which right now was under her desk in the surveillance room.

"Honey? I'm at the office," her mother was saying, "and just checking on you, but you must be on your way in. I'll find you as soon as I can."

Tenley rolled her eyes. Her mother was about to come looking for her. What if she'd discovered Tenley'd sneaked out? And now was totally pissed? But Mom didn't sound mad.

"And, um, Tenley? I'm sorry about last night."

Okay. She was apologizing. And not mad. Whew. Her mother paused. Tenley strained to hear what would come next.

"I need to talk to you, honey," her mother finally said. "It's important."

Tenley waited, heard her mother click off the phone. And then—was her mother crying?

She waited, not sure what to do. Part of her felt like hiding here, like, forever, pretending, trying to erase the whole thing from her memory. The other part of her felt like crying, too, but she couldn't quite pinpoint why.

Silently placing one sneaker onto the aqua-tiled floor, then the other, Tenley stood. Smoothed down her skirt. Unrolled the waist to make the skirt a little longer.

Paused, listening to the quiet sobs.

"We're checking on a story," Jane said, crossing the city attorney off her mental victims list. This Kelli Riordan, in her patent-heeled power outfit, did not look like a person whose husband had been killed. No grieving wife would still have on that much mascara if she'd gotten such devastating news. Jane's money was still on Catherine Siskel. Plus, Jake hadn't gone to Kelli Riordan's office. He'd come here.

"Nevertheless, my questions still stand," Riordan said. "What are you doing here? What 'story'? And where is Catherine Siskel? Detective? Ms. Ryland, isn't it?"

"She's in the bathroom, I think," Jane said. "She wasn't feeling well. I was about to go check on her."

"Not feeling well? Why didn't you tell me?" Siobhan Hult picked up a black desk phone, punched a few numbers with one demanding finger. "I'm calling her. Then *I'll* go check on her."

"Check on who?"

A man strode into Catherine's office, looking at each of them in turn. *Uh-oh.* The checked shirt guy with the coffee. The one Jane bamboozled into letting her into the building.

"I'm here for the eight fifteen." He narrowed his eyes at her. "Hey. Aren't you—"

"She's a reporter," Riordan said.

Jane could have sworn the woman was trying to send telepathic signals of some kind to this newcomer. An odd emphasis on "reporter." Widening eyes. A barely perceptible flash of distress. But she could be wrong. Everyone at City Hall hated reporters. Riordan was probably the president of the Hate Reporters Society.

Jane smiled to prove she was a nice person, not there to cause trouble.

"Call the cops," the man said. "This woman *sneaked* by me into City Hall when I walked in—how was I supposed to know—"

"He *is* the cops," Kelli said, pointing.

"I *am* the police," Jake said at the same moment.

Now there were five people in the same office. Pretty interesting. And possibly suspicious. Meantime, Catherine Siskel was probably still cleaning herself up in the bathroom and wondering why no one had gone in to make sure she hadn't passed out on the floor.

At least they seemed to have forgotten Jane's "sneaking" episode.

The EA hung up the desk phone. "No answer from Ms. Siskel," she said. "I'll try to see if she's—"

"No," Kelli Riordan interrupted. "*I'll* go. Listen, Ward. Is her daughter here?"

"Not until nine," Ward said. "Supposedly."

Daughter here? Jane looked at Jake, trying her own telepathy. *Did you know about a daughter here? I didn't.*

No. Jake used a fraction of an expression to convey his surprise. *Me either.*

Time to take back the morning, Jake thought.

"Ladies and gentlemen," he interrupted the three staffers. "We're all busy, and I understand you're concerned about your colleague. But I'm here to talk with Ms. Siskel privately. I'm sure any meeting she had arranged with you two can be postponed. Ms. Hult, will you go check on Ms. Siskel? Thank you."

The EA opened her mouth, closed it, and flounced from the room.

Jake waited until the door closed behind her. "I need your names and contact information, please," he went on. "And you mentioned a daughter. Does Ms. Siskel have a daughter who works at City Hall?"

Jane's phone rang again. She made a face, like, *sorry.* And went out into the hall.

"I'm Kelli White Riordan, city attorney." The woman flapped open a leather portfolio, presented him an embossed business card. "You'll understand why I'm concerned with your tactics. Might I ask, once again, why you're here? As the city attorney, I have every right—in fact, it's my responsibility to know."

"It's a private matter, between me and Ms. Siskel. I'm sure she'll contact you if she deems it necessary." Jake put the card in his pocket and turned to the man—Ward? He'd tossed his Starbucks paper cup into an empty wastebasket and now seemed at a loss for what to do with his hands. He'd already yanked his shirt collar, scratched his nose, smoothed his hair.

"And you are . . . ?" Jake asked.

Checked shirt and Riordan exchanged glances. Times like these Jake wished for telepathy. Clearly these two had some agenda.

"Ward—" He stopped, frowning. The office door had opened again.

Jane.

"Dahlstrom," the man went on.

"Title?" Jake prompted. It was nothing Jane couldn't hear.

Dahlstrom looked at Riordan as if needing some guidance from the lawyer. She waved a weary hand. *Go ahead.*

"Director of external communications."

"I see." Jake almost laughed. Politicians rivaled only cops for unmitigated jargon. "Communications?" Maybe public relations? Did it have to do with spinning the Curley Park murder? "And that means . . . ?"

"Detective?" Riordan answered instead. "He handles our surveillance cameras."

36

Catherine yanked a length of towel from the automatic dispenser, doused it with cold water, and held the soggy paper to one cheek, then the other, cooling her flushed face while trying not to wet the escaping tendrils of her hair. Every muscle in her body ached. She realized she'd been clenching everything, trying to prevent fifty land mines from blowing up in everyone's face.

And who was taking care of *her*? No one ever took care of her. Maybe it was her own fault. Every time Lanna talked about leaving, she'd ignored it instead of talking about it. She was a terrible mother. And look what happened.

Her husband started being distracted and distant and silent. Instead of trying to understand him, she'd ignored it, focused on work, figured he'd get over whatever it was. She was a terrible wife. And look what happened.

Now she was a terrible chief of staff, too, crying in the bathroom while the mayor's political career was about to fall apart. To keep that from happening, she had to lie. And cover up what she knew about her own husband. Her career—and Tenley—were all she had left. Yes. It was her own fault.

She soaked the towel again, listening to the water gush from the faucet, wishing she could jump into the sink and swirl down the drain, lost and forgotten and swept away by the tides of Boston Harbor.

But *Tenley*. She still had Tenley. She would do everything in her power, starting now, everything, not to blow that. She'd be a good mother. Make up for her failings. She'd go to Tenley's office, right now. Leave her a note. Arrange lunch. She looked at her face in the mirror, all blotches and red-rimmed eyes. *Oh. Greg.* Another sob escaped her. Poor Tenley.

"Mrs. Siskel?" Someone was pounding on the bathroom door. "Mrs. Siskel! Are you in there?"

Siobhan. What was she doing here this early? How'd she find her in *this* bathroom?

"I'm fine," she called out, attempting to remove any trace of sorrow from her voice. She felt like grief was strangling her. But she could not let anyone know. She raised her voice over the sound of the running water. "Two minutes, okay?"

The meeting. Shit. She moved closer to the door but didn't open it.

"Are Kelli and Ward waiting?"

"In their offices," Siobhan said. "Are you *sure* you're fine?"

"I'll call them, thanks so much, all good." Catherine tried to sound cheery and normal. Exactly what she wasn't. "All good," she whispered.

Another lie.

Surveillance cameras? If Jane hadn't been so distracted, she'd have pounced on that admission and moved into high reporter gear. Did they have the Curley Park murder on tape? Jane knew about the whole traffic cam controversy and the hullabaloo over the decision. Did City Hall have other cameras that recorded? There couldn't be sound, because it was illegal in Massachusetts to record voices without permission. But you could record silent video. And if there was a person in charge of surveillance, there had to be surveillance.

But the call she'd just taken from Melissa had changed Jane's entire day. She'd had to call Marsh Tyson, once again, explain she had family issues. He seemed understanding, said he'd assign someone else to the City Hall story, but who knew what he really thought.

She also had to tell Jake about Melissa's call. Somehow. He'd just heard about this surveillance guy, and that was potentially critical. This was, too.

Standing on the threshold to Siskel's office, Jane cleared her throat, needing to get his attention. All three turned to her. Ward annoyed, Kelli disdainful, and Jake concerned.

"Ah, Detective?" she said. "Sorry to interrupt, but ah, I've got to, uh, go." Incredibly inarticulate, but her mind was racing so fast her voice couldn't keep up with it. She hitched her tote bag over her shoulder, locking eyes with Jake. She had to let him know it was important, but she didn't want the two pols to think he had anything but a professional connection with her. "Regarding the story we were discussing earlier. I do need to follow up with you about that as soon as you have a moment."

"You'll need to call the public relations department, Ms. Ryland," Jake said. "Maybe in about ten minutes? I think the special duty officer will be there by then."

Great. He understood. She'd call him on his cell in ten minutes. She tried to keep the fear and anxiety out of her voice and knew she was failing. How was she supposed to handle this? Melissa was waiting for her, and it seemed like—*dammit*. She looked at her watch.

"Eight thirty-five, then?" She tried to signal with her eyes, *Please, Jake, we need to talk.* "Right?"

"Everything okay, Ms. Ryland?" Jake asked.

"Sure." She tried to make that sound like a lie. To him.

Jake looked at Riordan and Dahlstrom. "Excuse me," he said. "I'll just show Ms. Ryland to the elevator."

A wave of gratitude washed over her, almost tears, as she turned away from the office. She felt Jake behind her.

"Jane, what?" he whispered.

"Gracie," Jane said. "Melissa called and—"

Jake reached for his radio. She put out a hand, stopping him. "No," she said. "That's the thing. Melissa called to say that Lewis had called Robyn—you following this?"

Jake nodded.

"It seems like there's some sort of ridiculous battle over Gracie, between Robyn and Lewis, which Lewis decided to solve by taking her. Problem is, Melissa had no idea there was a battle. And now—"

"Is she okay? Is Gracie okay? Where are they?"

"Yeah, apparently she's okay. Lewis took her—" Jane shook her head. "I don't know. According to Melissa, he told Robyn he was 'taking Gracie far, far away,' and she'd 'never see her daughter again.' It's all about the wedding and Daniel, and then she said he said—ah."

She jabbed the elevator's Down button, jabbed it again. She'd get out of here, grab her car, head for Melissa. "Hate this," she said. "Why do elevators never work?"

"Honey," Jake whispered, "tell me what happened."

"Okay. Apparently Robyn talked him off the ledge. I have no idea where they are, but now he's promised to give Gracie back."

"Great."

"To me," Jane said. The elevator was finally arriving. Forget the chance to land a job at Channel 2. Gracie came first. The rest would work out. It was not about her. It was about Gracie. If she was part of the solution, so be it.

"To you what?" Jake said.

"Melissa said that Robyn told her—" She paused, reading his expression. "I know, but that's all there is. Robyn said Lewis told her at first Gracie'd never see Robyn or Melissa or Daniel again. Even threatened to leave the country and take Gracie with him. But when Robyn said she was calling the police, he gave in and agreed to give Gracie back. But only to me."

"That's ridiculous," Jake said. "Or insane."

"That's what I'm worried about," Jane said.

Jake could see the fear in her eyes, as well as the determination. Being a reporter was kind of like being a cop, but without the badge or gun. Or training. Or backup. Jane always asked the right questions, always listened to the answers, and never made snap judgments. Had a good instinct. But—just like some cops—she sometimes wanted to be a hero. And this was no time for that.

"No way, Jane," he said. "I don't care what some crazy-ass moron is demanding. If he's taken Gracie without parental permission, that's—shit. Let me think about this."

Jake could hear the elevator laboring toward them. "What are you supposed to do now?"

"I don't know, exactly. Go to Robyn's. He's supposed to call at ten with instructions."

"Do you know where they are? Lewis and Gracie?"

"I know nothing," Jane said. "At all."

The elevator doors slid open. Her expression changed. "But what can I do?" she said. "I have to help. I'd never forgive myself if . . . and you know? Maybe they're just having a ridiculous argument. Maybe the guy is scared. Trying to come up with a way to save face. Who knows why anyone does anything."

Jake had a murder to solve, maybe two, and two still-unidentified victims. Was Jane right? Who knew why anyone did anything? Fear was a powerful motivator. Revenge, greed. Jealousy. Sorrow. Love.

Jane entered the elevator, turned to him. When the doors closed, she'd be gone. The hallway was empty, office doors along the corridor closed, and dark.

He slammed a hand against the thick rubber edging of the elevator door. Leaned close to her.

"Jane, I'm serious." He saw a flicker of a smile cross her face, the first he'd seen in the last fifteen minutes. "Okay, fine. But I mean it."

The doors struggled to close, thumping and insistent. He held them open. Leaned in even closer, supported by his arms against the demanding doors, his body in the hallway, his head close to hers. He couldn't control her. It was part of the reason he loved her. But he could try to keep her safe. He would kiss her, he would, damn the hallway and damn City Hall.

Two young women approached, coffees in hand, chatting. They looked at him inquisitively, as he stood holding the door. He smiled at them—*nothing to see here, move along*—to indicate all was well. But the moment had passed. It was probably for the best.

"Do not," he said, straightening up, now holding the door with just one foot, "do anything without calling me. Somehow, I'll come with you."

"Will you?" she said. Her smile got bigger. She reached out, touched his cheek. "Promise?"

He burst out laughing, wondering if she'd done that on purpose. The doors closed and she was gone.

37

"Mom, Mom, it's okay." Tenley'd waited until Siobhan went away, trying to think of a way she might come out from the bathroom stall without scaring her mother, but no matter how she did it, her mom was still gonna be surprised.

Catherine's almost silent little scream of shock made Tenley scream, too, a copycat reflex. Tenley stood, the beige metal door clanking against the toggle lock behind her.

Her mom was staring at her, pushed a curling wet strand of hair from her tear-streaked face.

"Mom? What's wrong?" Tenley took a step closer. Man, she looked awful. Worse than when Lanna—She should hug her mother, she guessed, but somehow couldn't bring herself to do it. "Are you sick?"

"Were you hiding from me? Why?"

Tenley couldn't read her mother's expression. Like she was sad *and* mad, and trying to get her balance.

"No, really, Mom. I didn't know it was you." All true. She would have stayed in the stall until whoever it was left. "But when I heard Siobhan talk, then you talked, then I knew. But what's wrong? What're you doing here—and so early?"

"It's not really early," her mother began. Correcting her, as usual. But then she stopped midsentence. Her shoulders dropped. "Oh, Tenner," she said.

Then silence. Her mom turned the water off, and then it was really quiet.

"What?" Tenley said. This was incredibly awkward, and Tenley didn't know how to handle it. What was making her mother so upset? Unhappy? Was it something to do with her? Had she found out about last night? "What?"

Her mother leaned against the fake marble counter, then stood up straight, patting the rear of her skirt. She tested the counter's surface with one finger, sighed, then wiped it dry with a bunch of paper towels. She sniffed, dabbing her red nose with another wad of towels, and leaned back again. Like she was trying to think of how to say something. Well, if she was mad about last night, she'd have no trouble coming up with what to say. She'd said plenty of mean stuff to Tenley in the past. Well, maybe not exactly *mean,* but critical, at least. So maybe she didn't know Tenley had sneaked out. Good. Anything else she could handle.

Tenley looked at the floor, away from her mother's face. Unless this was about the video. She felt her stomach tense, like it always did when she was anxious. But it wasn't her fault the video got erased. It was Dahlstrom's.

"You remember yesterday—the, ah, situation in Curley Park?" Her mother's voice did not sound mad. But it did sound like something bad was about to come next.

Crap. It was about the video. Her stomach was killing her. "Mom, that wasn't my fault." Time to stand up for herself, for once. That guy Dahlstrom, no matter how cool Lanna had thought he was, probably blamed everything on her, like, ratted her out to her own mother, and now he probably told her mom she had to fire her own daughter, which would be humiliating and awful. And that's why her mother was crying. Because she thought Tenley had been a failure, yet again, the pitiful misfit daughter of the big-shot chief of staff. Maybe it would be better if she *had* stayed away, stayed at Brileen's. But, hey. No way. She wouldn't take the blame for something she didn't do.

"Not your fault?"

Her mom was scowling. She knew that expression, knew it perfectly. Double crap. Her mother didn't believe her.

"Mom, I'm not kidding. This sucks. I saw what happened. I tried to—"

"You—saw?"

"Yes, like I said." Why was Mom acting like Tenley was lying? "I did everything right. I saw something was going on, whatever it was, I pushed Save. But that Ward Dahlstrom, you know? Saw me and came over and pushed Cancel. So we *would* have had it, you know? But *he* did it, *he* pushed Cancel."

She'd already said that, but now she was really pissed. Like that guy was going to get her in trouble? Screw it. Let them fire her. She was so out of here.

Her mom's face had gone all white, or gray, and her eyes got so big.

"You saw—" her mom said again.

What was the big deal? Yes, she'd said that, a million times, yes, she'd seen—well, it was all a blur, and she guessed not from moment one, but still.

"Yes, Mom, like I said. But—"

The bathroom door pushed open. They both turned to see who was invading their private territory, interrupting.

"Go away!" Her mom actually yelled at the person. The door slammed closed.

And it was all quiet again. Her mother tossed a soggy wad of paper towels into the silver bin along the wall. It landed on the edge, teetered, then fell to the floor. Her mother made no move to pick it up.

"Tenley," her mother said, "I have terrible news."

Jane dropped her tote bag by the table at Robyn's front door and followed Melissa into the living room. Her sister looked crazy-disheveled, hair yanked back, jeans, bare feet. Robyn was in a bathrobe, ice blue chenille, belt knotted at the waist, her pale hair tousled over her shoulders. Lipstick, Jane saw.

"Robyn?" Jane stopped at the edge of the jewel-toned Oriental rug, scanned the room. Just the three of them. "He hasn't called yet, has he? Have you heard anything new?"

"Jane." Robyn sipped something from a china cup on table in front of her, replaced it in the saucer. In her other hand, she clutched a cell phone, gestured with it. "Thank you so much. Melissa's been lovely, and I'm not quite sure exactly how to handle this, and now I'm so grateful you're going to . . ."

Jane knew that look on Melissa's face. *For better or for worse,* she'd be promising a few days from now. Well, here was a possible worst. She watched her sister pull it together, arrange her face in a semblance of patience and professionalism.

"Legally, this is a mess, Jane." Melissa crossed her arms over her chest. "It's not kidnapping. Gracie's not adopted, but Lewis has partial custody, as guardian, and as such"—she glanced at Robyn—"legally it creates a quagmire, because we cannot report Gracie as lost or missing or abducted. In the eyes of the law, she's legally with her stepfather."

"But now he says—" Robyn stopped, dabbing at her eyes with a white tissue.

Melissa shook her head. "Look. Legally you and Lewis are having a marital disagreement. In the eyes of the law, that's something you'll have to work out for yourselves. Unless. Has Lewis—again, forgive me—threatened you or Gracie? It's a question that needs to be asked. And answered."

Robyn took another sip from her cup. "No, no. Really. *No.* Like I *keep* saying. Of course not."

"Do you think Gracie's in danger? At all?" Melissa persisted. "If so, that provides us a way in. We call the police, explain that Lewis threatened Gracie, explain we are in fear for her life. They take over. I mean, Daniel's plane is supposed to be here. In *two hours.* If his daughter is still gone—I mean, if I haven't—"

"Melissa?" Jane had to interrupt. Robyn was on edge, Melissa verging on frantic. Two women who shared so much—and had so little in common. But it wasn't doing any good for them to snipe like this at each other. And no one had ever intimated Lewis was dangerous, or was going to hurt Gracie. Had they?

"It's nine forty-five. Lewis is supposed to call at ten, right?" Jane looked at Robyn, confirming. "Is that what he said? He'll tell me where to pick up Gracie. And I'll bring her to you both. And Daniel." She sighed, mulling it over. "I mean . . . is it possible Lewis is simply acting out his anger that Melissa and Daniel are taking Gracie away?"

Robyn made a little sound, like a gasp, or a whimper.

"I'm sorry, Robyn," Jane said. Now her own words were sounding harsh. She shouldn't have said "taking Gracie away." "I only meant—for the summer. I know *you* are willing to accept that, right?"

"Of course," Robyn said.

"But maybe Lewis is upset? He's been a good stepfather, loving and . . . appropriate. That's all Melissa is really trying to confirm. I'm thinking maybe he's embarrassed at his behavior. Maybe he, I don't know, loves her so much he can't bear to lose her. And now he doesn't want to deal with, you know, Melissa and Daniel. The ones—in his view, at least—who are ruining his life."

"We—" Melissa protested.

"He—" Robyn's voice was stone.

"I'm only saying." Jane held up a palm. "I'm a safe option. I pick her up; he doesn't have to face you. Gracie doesn't even know there was a controversy, right? So she's not traumatized in any way. As far as she knows, she was on a spontaneous fun jaunt with her dad. Melissa and Daniel bring Gracie to the wedding, you and Lewis get your lives back."

She paused, gauging the reaction. "Right?" She nodded at each in turn, as if that would encourage them to agree. It sounded semi-plausible, and Jane had almost convinced herself to believe it. She pictured herself holding Gracie's hand, walking into this living room, happily ever after. "Right?"

Silence.

"I don't know," Robyn wailed. "I don't." She stood, then threw herself onto the couch, head in hands, blonded hair tumbling across her shoulders. When she looked up again, her face had paled to ice, her eyes wide. "She's my *daughter*. I'm terrified. Lewis sounds completely crazy. And I don't believe a word he says anymore."

"Then we're calling the police," Jane said. "End of story."

"No!" Robyn stood again, hand on hips.

The phone rang.

38

Had Catherine Siskel been crying? Maybe. Still, Jake figured, no one looked too hot after they threw up. Her face was red, and her blouse, now rumpled and askew, had come out of her skirt. Throwing up sucked. It meant you were either sick—which this woman wasn't—or upset. Which she clearly was. Or feeling very guilty.

"You okay, ma'am?" Jake continued to assess as the chief of staff headed to her desk. The secretary had retreated to her own territory. Riordan and Dahlstrom were dispatched to wait for a call summoning them. Now he and Siskel were alone. Now she'd have to explain. Her husband was missing, she'd told him. He'd finally find out why she thought so.

He'd already texted DeLuca to get over here. With a missing husband and two dead guys, counting Bobby Land, the day was—*duh*—out of control. Turned out D had not been sleeping, as Jake had predicted, but was staking out Calvin Hewlitt's condo. So far, though, he reported no activity. DeLuca had requested a backup to take over Hewlitt watch. Who caught it? Angie Bartoneri. Jake shook his head. *Figures.* With luck, though, Hewlitt would never know the occupants of the beat-up gray van parked opposite his South End brownstone were employees of Boston PD and not Paul Revere Landscaping.

Not even twenty-four hours since the Curley Park murder. Jake had been awake the whole time.

"Coffee?" Catherine Siskel was asking him, gesturing to one of those pod coffee machines.

"Thanks," he said, grateful for as much coffee as anyone could provide. "Appreciate it. Black is fine."

Still, luck of the Irish, because he'd been called here, he'd also gotten a damn good lead about City Hall surveillance video. Which, despite her loss, the enigmatic Ms. Siskel would have to explain. The coffeemaker hissed and gurgled, and hot water spat into a white mug. Jake smelled dark roast.

"So your husband?" he asked. "I take it he hasn't called."

Siskel handed him the steaming mug. Her hand trembled, the slightest bit.

"No," she said. "He's a consultant, so there's no office he uses. Just home. He didn't come home last night. He's not there now. And not answering his cell. Mind if I sit?" She gestured to the black leather swivel chair behind her desk. "I'm not feeling that well."

"Of course." Jake took a less-comfortable guest chair opposite. "Has your husband been gone for twenty-four hours?"

Siskel blinked, looked at her watch. "Ah, I guess not," she said. "I mean, technically? No. I talked to him on the phone around eleven yesterday morning. It's almost ten now. So fine, twenty-three hours. Is there some—"

"Technically," Jake said. Funny word to use. He took a sip of coffee, then looked at Siskel. She slid a little notepad across her desk, and he put the hot mug on it like a coaster. "Technically," he repeated, "we can't move into missing-persons mode until an adult—especially one we have no indication is in danger, or—"

He stopped, reading her expression. "What?"

She shook her head, barely. "Nothing," she said.

"Ma'am? Do you think your husband *is* in danger?" This is exactly what he sensed. The woman was not being straight with him. If she'd murdered the guy herself, or hired someone, this is how he'd imagine her behavior. Half sentences. Distractions. Evasions. All the elements of a cover-up. "Has he been threatened, does he have enemies? Is he driving? Is there a car we should look for?"

"No, he—I have the car."

Again, subtext. Omissions.

"Ma'am?" Shifting in his chair, Jake took out his spiral notebook. De-Luca had teased him mercilessly about his BlackBerry note taking. It wasn't that Jake was backing down. The notebook method simply turned out to be easier.

Tolja, D had said. Whatever.

Jake flipped the notebook open.

"You know, I've handled many missing person cases, Ms. Siskel. And there's a pattern we see, even though each case is unique. The family is—worried, sure, but there's always a theory about what *might* have happened. Abducted on the way home from school. Drunk again. Incipient Alzheimer's. Ran off with the other woman."

Jake paused, checking Siskel's expression for a response. Poker face.

Jake went on. "Gambling debts? Fired from work? Deep into drugs? Leading a double life with a new family?"

Still nothing. Okay, then.

"And ma'am, I've got to tell you, in my book? You're behaving as if you, in fact, know what happened. And maybe you somehow want me to find out about it, so you can act surprised."

Jake remembered when his mother always seemed to know what he was doing. "I have eyes in the back of my head," she'd say whenever he'd stashed candy or contraband comic books. Or sometimes—especially during Jake's lurching adolescent encounters with girls—she'd say, "I have ESP, my dear, don't try to lie to me." Jake still didn't understand exactly how his mom could have known he'd invited high school senior classmate Olivia Magnussen to their house that Saturday night while his parents were at the symphony.

Now, twenty years later, he knew "intuition" was a mixture of training and experience, and he appreciated how he could use it to perceive beyond the exterior. "A good cop will know if it passes the sniff test," his grandfather used to say. Jake wished Commissioner Brogan had lived long enough to see him in action. Or even better, to give him advice. Although sometimes it felt like he still did.

Jake recognized the look on Catherine Siskel's face. He bet it was exactly the one Jake used when his mom caught him lying about Olivia Magnussen.

"Know what happened?" she replied. "Surprised?"

Had it been less than an hour ago that Jane accused him of ulterior motives when answering a question with a question? She'd been right. And here it was again.

Jake stood, elaborately flapped his notebook closed. "If you're not going to be cooperative," he said, "might I ask why you called the police? Let me put it this way, ma'am. What did you expect we would do?"

Catherine fussed with her coffee. Her eyes shifted toward a side door in the room, looked at it so purposefully that Jake turned to see who she was looking at. No one.

"I expected," she drew out the words, looking at Jake again, "to give you a photograph of my husband. And then you would look for him."

"Look where?" Jake said. His question came out more sarcastically and a little louder than he'd planned. But he had too much going on to parry her transparent attempts to manipulate him. No one had heard from Greg Siskel since yesterday's phone call, she'd insisted. He wasn't at home, hadn't come home last night, didn't have an office, wasn't answering his cell. But his wife was not giving the police one bit of useful information to help them find him. In truth, not offering any information at all.

"Can you give us *any* idea where we might look? Or are you thinking—simply out there in Boston?" Impatient and frustrated and exhausted, he waved toward the office window, a double-tall pane of plate glass, topped with a strip of slatted blind, that looked out over Curley Park. "Maybe out someplace on Congress Street? Or maybe in Curley Park?"

Jane was using every bit of her hearing ability to figure out what was being said on the other end of Robyn's "conversation." Even so, even scooting to the edge of the big armchair, she could hear only Robyn's terse responses. Robyn, cell phone clamped to her ear, sat in the corner of the Wilhoites' living room couch, one leg tucked under her, the edge of her blue chenille robe touching the fringe of the figured carpet. The phone had rung just before ten. Lewis was supposed to call at ten.

Jane looked at Melissa, mouthed a question. *Lewis?* Melissa, standing by the desk, shrugged her answer. *No idea.*

"I understand," Robyn was saying. "Okay." She clicked off.

"Lewis?" Melissa took a step toward her, palms out, inquiring.

"No." Robyn looked at Jane, then at Melissa. Put down the phone. "My lawyer."

Melissa planted her fists on her hips. "What?"

"What?" Jane echoed her sister's incredulous tone. *Robyn had called her lawyer about Lewis and Gracie?* Lewis had clearly instructed her to tell no one.

"Are you kidding? A lawyer? Why?" Melissa's voice went up in pitch and volume with every question. "What if the lawyer calls the police, Robyn?"

"Oh, Melissa, I'm not a *complete* fool." Robyn stood, tossed her hair, brandished the phone at Melissa. "Of course I didn't *tell* him. And *I* didn't call *anyone*. He called *me*. It's none of your business, anyway. Obviously privacy's one more thing in my life that's going out of control."

"It *is* our business," Melissa protested. "Because—"

"Fine." Robyn cut her off. "Lewis and I are—"

She flipped a hand in frustration, then plopped down on the couch again, the flowered cushions plumping beside her as she sat. "Unhappy. Okay? We're un-freaking-happy. *I* was doing my best. *I* was trying to stay sane. *You* try living with the Mr. Midlife Crisis. Suddenly he's Mr. Impetuous. Mr. Spontaneous. *I* was the only one trying to make it work. As I told him in no uncertain terms."

Robyn made a dismissive sound, *whatever.* "We didn't argue in front of Gracie, of course. Poor thing has no idea her stepfather's a nutcase."

"Nutcase?" Melissa's eyebrows hit the ceiling. "Does he *know* you're talking to a lawyer? Are you getting a divorce?"

This development put the situation in a different light, Jane thought. Two parents, one a "nutcase," playing marital chess with a little girl as their pawn. Melissa in the middle of it, too. What could Lewis's endgame be?

"Divorce? That's *also* none of your—" Robyn began.

Jane's cell phone beeped. She'd set the alarm for ten. She waved a hand, hoping to quiet the escalating tension. She was glad there was a coffee table between the two women.

"Melissa, listen. Robyn. I don't know what's going on with you, but Lewis asked for me, he drew me into this." She paused. "We have to think about Gracie now. If you have any inkling she's in danger, we need to call the police."

"No police," Robyn insisted. "Lewis *will* call. It's not that there's danger, it's only—"

"Only what?" Jane said. "It's after ten."

"He can be, well, careless," Robyn said.

"Careless?" Melissa narrowed her eyes at Robyn. "What does that mean?"

Jane thought back. This woman's story was somehow—evolving. "Robyn? Did you ever ask to talk to *Gracie* on the phone?"

"No." Robyn shook her head. "But look, he'd never harm Gracie. It's only me he wants to hurt."

"Hurt?" Melissa interrupted.

"Oh, no, not hurt physically." Robyn waved her off. "But he's always been jealous. When I married Danny instead. He called him a big-shot asshole."

"Police," Jane said. *Yeesh*. She took out her cell. "Right now."

"Jane. Listen." Melissa put her a hand on Jane's arm, stopping her, pulled her aside. "I'm really trying to stay calm here. That's what Daniel would want, I know it. What if I'm—overreacting? What if I look like the crazy one?"

"Really?" Jane tried to read her sister's face.

Melissa pressed her lips together, nodded. "Look. Lewis has already said he'd return Gracie. If he doesn't call soon, then fine, all bets are off, we call the cops. But if Lewis is simply upset and jealous, and late because he's careless, as Robyn seems to be saying, we'll just do what he says. Until we get Gracie."

"You certain?" Jane wasn't. "Really?"

"Really. You're right. Lewis is remorseful. He'll call, and you'll go pick up Gracie, Jane," Melissa instructed, turning back to include Robyn. "Daniel's plane gets in at one. His driver's bringing him here. It'll be fine. Not everything is a big drama. Agreed? Robyn?"

Robyn nodded. "Agreed."

Jane did not agree. Not at all. But no one seemed to care. It was already a drama, far as she was concerned. Who was this Lewis Wilhoite, anyway? She tried to remember what Robyn had told them in the restaurant last night.

"You guys? It's five past ten," Jane said. "How long are we going to wait for the call? Meanwhile, Robyn? Can I use your computer?"

39

Tenley wanted to go home. Just go home. Home where all her stuff was, and where even Lanna's goneness was better than living somewhere Lanna had never existed. It wasn't yet time for her to leave. It wasn't. There was only one *home*, no matter what she'd told Brileen, or how she had felt, or the anger she'd stored away over her parents, poisonous as nuclear waste. Her mother needed her now. They needed to be together.

A minute ago, her mother had called Ward Dahlstrom, made some excuse so at least Tenley wouldn't get in trouble for missing work. Now Tenley curled up in the big chair in the greenroom off her mother's office. She and Lanna hid out here when they were younger, with Lanna as babysitter and, later, companion. They'd painted each other's toenails. Read comics. Lanna had even taught her to text. All in the little room with no entrance from the hallway, a room the size of a super-big walk-in closet that was connected to their mom's office, where dignitaries and emissaries and deal makers could hide from paparazzi and nosy reporters. There was even a private bathroom. Five minutes ago her mom had stashed her here, ordered her not to come out, not to make any noise, until she returned. A police officer waited in Mom's office. What was she telling him? What she'd told her daughter?

Tenley could almost replay the tape in her head. How absurd to be told of her own father's death—his *murder*—in a tile-walled public bathroom at City Hall.

"We should go someplace private," Mom had said.

"This is private," Tenley'd replied, still on edge, still suspicious, still worried, by seeing her mother so upset. Still a little nervous she might get in trouble over the nonexistent video.

Mom had put a hand on each of Tenley's shoulders, looked straight into her eyes. When had she become as tall as her mom? She remembered so clearly being little, her mother—and her father!—scooching down to come to eye level with her. Not anymore. She met her mother's gaze on an equal level.

"Tenner, honey." She'd heard the tremor in her mother's voice. "It's difficult, it's awful, and I know you've—we've—already been through . . . through hell."

Tenley's eyes widened, remembering. She heard the rumble of the plumbing, the buzz of the fluorescent lights, the clack of footsteps in the hall. She tilted her head as if listening, mentally reenacting the scene, living it as if for the first time.

"What?" she'd asked. Was her mother sick? A whole scenario of potential disasters flooded Tenley's imagination as fast as her brain could concoct them: cancer, hospitals, death, abandonment. Maybe divorce? Okay, right, that wouldn't surprise her. Her father had ignored Tenley, ignored Mom, too, since Lanna. Divorce would end in abandonment, too. Everything did.

"It's your father," her mother began. She took one of Tenley's hands, palm up, traced the lines on her skin as if she were a fortune teller. "I remember when you were so tiny, you couldn't wrap your hand around one of my fingers," her mother whispered.

Okay, this was scary.

"What, Mom? What about Dad?"

Her mother pressed Tenley's hand to her own cheek. Tenley felt the clammy skin, damp from tears, felt the clutch of her mother's grasp.

"He's dead, honey," her mom said.

The word didn't even make sense. Tenley tried to capture it, think about it, remember what it meant. Her father? Her father who—was dead?

"Why?" It was the first thing that came out of her mouth. It didn't make sense, she realized that as soon as she said it, so she thought of what else. "When?" Which also wasn't exactly the right question, but somehow her brain wasn't working, not at all. They were in the bathroom, a stupid bathroom of City Hall, and her mother was telling her an impossible thing. "How?" she asked. And then, "Are you sure?"

And her mother was sure.

What she could not handle, could *not* handle to the point of almost screaming, was that she had seen it. Seen it on the video monitor.

"Tenley Rebecca Siskel," she whispered to herself. She pounded a fist on each of the chair's padded armrests to punctuate her own stupidness. "Shut up."

Because she hadn't seen it, not really. The world was so dumb. She'd worried that she might get in trouble because she wasn't looking at the screen when it—the *murderofmyfather*—happened. As it turned out that was a good thing. The universe spared her that, at least. Even though her brain insisted on remembering what she *had* seen, everything was kind of fuzzy, and you couldn't really recognize faces.

Would she have recognized her father anyway? His stance, the funny way he held his arms, something about his walk? Had he been coming to see her? Or Mom? Why had he been in Curley Park? She hadn't gotten to ask her mother about that.

She replayed yesterday morning. Her brain was a video game, starting and stopping, fast-forwarding and rewinding. She sighed, crossed her legs under her, burrowed herself into the curve of her chair. She was so tired. She closed her eyes and envisioned the scene yet again. She'd pushed Save on her computer. And then Ward Dahlstrom said something about the police.

Why would he mention the police?

She thought about Lanna, and what had happened to her in Steading Woods. And her father, and what her mom said happened to him in Curley Park.

Did that make any sense? Two violent deaths in the same family? Was that the random act of an uncaring universe, like she'd read about in school?

Or was there something else? Something that maybe meant she wasn't safe either? Or her mother?

She wrapped her arms around her chest, leaned her head against the soft side of the chair, felt the nubby thick upholstery press against her cheek, and without making a sound, cried and cried and cried. And somehow, like the smoke from a tiny forgotten fire, Tenley felt her childhood vanish, vanish just like Lanna did, vanish like her father did, leaving her alone.

"Our man's on the move." DeLuca's voice crackled through Jake's two-way, interrupting Jake's questioning of Catherine Siskel. Probably for the best. He was impatient with her evasions. His annoyance was about to escalate farther than was wise.

Jake heard motion, engine noises, acceleration.

"I'm in the van," D's voice came through again. "We're on him. Can you move into second position? Everyone else is out of pocket."

D paused again. Jake knew he was trying to talk on the radio and drive at the same time. Exactly what traffic cops gave civilians tickets for.

"Copy," Jake said. But why did they need him? Wasn't Angie on the way? "But Bartoneri?"

"Doctor's appointment, she says."

Give me a break. "I've gotta get the cruiser, so it'll be five at least till I'm on the road."

"Copy," D said. "Stand by, let me get in position."

There was no way Catherine Siskel hadn't heard every word, but no matter. It wouldn't mean anything to her. The amount of juggling Jake was about to pull off was ridiculous. The mayor had promised to beef up the BPD budget, but so far their staffing was still frustratingly tight. Everyone from cop to admin was exhausted, short-tempered, and bitter. And law enforcement certainly would suffer. Jake wanted to look on the bright side, but there wasn't a bright side. He'd been without sleep for a solid twenty-eight hours now. That was supposed to keep the city safe?

"Looks like he might be headed toward the Pike now," DeLuca said over the radio. "He goes west, he's out of jurisdiction, so we'd have to call the staties or forget it. He goes east, we'll nail him."

There was no backup car for DeLuca. The motor pool was also gutted by budget cuts. Now Jake had to put aside the City Hall investigation to focus on whether Calvin Hewlitt was up to no good. Which left John Doe No. 2—maybe-tattooed guy—guarded only by a cadet outside his hospital door. If they'd had a budget for it, and a warrant, D could have tapped Hewlitt's car with a tracking gizmo, see if he left town, see who he visited. But they barely had enough resources to follow the guy, let alone convince a judge to bug him. It was the old-fashioned way or nothing. But he'd be easy to trail on the eight lanes of straight-arrow Massachusetts Turnpike.

"Copy," Jake said. "I'll go with lights till I get in earshot."

What if Calvin Hewlitt was the Curley Park killer, not the guy claiming to have captured him? Who did that make tattoo guy? What role, if any, had he played in Bobby Land's death? A video would be one easy way to answer two of those questions. If there was video of the incident, Catherine Siskel had to know.

"I've got to leave," Jake told her. He pulled a card from his wallet, placed it on her desk. The thick paper made a little tap on her leather-cornered blotter. "Two things, quickly. One, call me if you want to tell me more about your, ah, missing husband. And in approximately thirty minutes, call the Boston Police Department's Missing Persons division, ask for Sergeant Naka. Kiyoko Naka." He spelled it. "She's the one who had you call me. You tell her I sent you. Tell her it's been twenty-four hours. Got that?"

Catherine Siskel took the card, smoothed it between two fingers. She pressed her lips together, seemed to be considering. She nodded, looking at the card, without a word.

Was she crying? What was she not telling him?

"Two." Jake checked his notebook. "Ward Dahlstrom, the surveillance supervisor. Does he have video of what happened in Curley Park? If he does, that's our top priority. We need that. Right now."

"Video?"

Jake strode toward the door, radio crackling, on his way to help track Hewlitt. Great. A potential fugitive on one end, a potential liar on the other.

Enough with her bullshit. "You already have a subpoena demanding it." And even though this was *his* bullshit, he couldn't resist. "And ma'am? Don't leave town."

40

And there it was.

"You know Wharton, don't you Jane?" Robyn had said it last night, at dinner, as a waiter hovered.

Now Jane had found Lewis Wilhoite. On the Wharton School alumni roster. Lewis Delano Wilhoite, class of '91. A photo, too.

Jane rolled the padded chair closer to the desk in the Wilhoites' study and clicked the white mouse on their computer. Twenty-some years ago, Lewis wasn't the pudgy accountant milquetoast Jane had imagined but a normal-looking sandy-haired guy in a preppy shirt. One of a row of mostly white-male thumbnail photos taken by a commercial photographer.

Rats. She'd half expected not to see his name. She would have easily believed it if Lewis had been some kind of impostor. But there it was, as described. Lewis Delano Wilhoite, summa cum laude. The online yearbook listed all kinds of community good works. Big Brother. Boy Scout.

When she was a little girl, Jane's father had told her to ask the universe if she really wanted something. Eight-year-old Jane had decided that was simply another way for him to say no. Now she was asking. *Let Gracie be safe.*

She put her chin in her hands, elbows on the desk, thinking, looking around the little study. Maybe a third bedroom, with a desk, printer, pencil holder. One wall bookshelves. On another, an array of black-framed photographs. Lots of Robyn. A baby—Gracie?—cradled in masculine arms. Toddler Gracie clutching a stuffed rabbit, hand in hand with an unidentifiable man. Lewis? Robyn and someone in wedding attire. Lewis? Older Gracie with the same man, glasses and sandy hair. *Lewis.*

So far, Jane had not heard the phone ring. The computer clock slid to 10:30 A.M. She eyed her cell phone. Time to call Jake.

The Wharton website faded, and a screen saver—the family's white cat—appeared. Jane closed her eyes, clamped down the cover. Splayed her fingers on the smooth silver of the laptop, then, with one quick motion, flapped it open again. Went to the Wharton page, clicked on the photo of Lewis Wilhoite. Blinked at it, trying to memorize it.

Then she looked up at the wedding photos on the wall. Compared. Looked at the computer again.

Fifteen years, maybe more, separated college Lewis from wedding Lewis. Of course, Jane herself looked significantly different from her college photos. Thank God. But.

She tapped one finger to her lips, considering, then shrugged. Picking up the laptop, she lifted the computer next to the wedding photo, bringing the two pictures of Lewis as close together as she could.

"What are you doing?" Robyn asked. She stood in the open doorway. Jane jumped.

"Jane?" Melissa stood behind Robyn.

"Did he call?" Jane asked.

"Not yet," Robyn said.

"Did you call *him*?" Jane asked.

"No answer," Melissa said. "But yeah, what're you doing?"

"Here's the thing." Jane turned the laptop screen so the women in the doorway could see it. "This is Lewis Wilhoite's Wharton photo. But look. I think—I think it's not the same Lewis who's on the wall."

Ignoring the elevator, Jake had raced down the back stairs at City Hall and slammed himself into his cruiser. The yellow crime scene tape was still up at Curley Park, but otherwise it was midmorning Boston as usual, buses and straggling commuters, tourists with backpacks and foot-dragging kids. Frustratingly, cadets were coming up with zero in their search of all those bystanders' cell phone photos—so far they'd viewed a repeatedly useless collection of blurry bodies, backlit silhouettes, out-of-focus trees, and an occasional shoe. Surveillance tapes from local businesses were nonexistent, deleted, erased, or fuzzy as hell. So much for the new technology. A couple of Facebook and Twitter posts, all capital letters and italics, but nothing helpful. No leads. And still no next of kin on Bobby Land. He'd call Kiyoko Naka in Missing, see if anyone had reported a young family member who'd disappeared. Someone must be wondering where this kid was.

So far, they were nowhere on Curley Park. Not a good thing.

Boston had more than three hundred cold cases, a pitiful record for unsolved murders. Jake vowed that the number wouldn't rise on his watch. Before he could crank the ignition, DeLuca radioed in.

"The good guys win, Harvard. Sit tight. Hewlitt's eastbound on the Pike, headed right for downtown, looks like."

"Or the airport," Jake said.

"Shit," DeLuca said.

"In which case, the good guys lose," Jake said. "Since we have no way to stop him if he's bolting."

"Shit." DeLuca's radio clicked off.

Did Hewlitt know Bobby Land was dead? Had he participated, somehow, in that murder? Without any hard evidence, much less a warrant, they had to find out what Hewlitt was up to. He'd done a fast Google, found "Hewlitt Security" at Faneuil Hall. Had to be him, but hadn't Angie—*at the doctor's, for crap sake*—even done a web search? He'd do his own, soon as he got half a second. Hunches, intuition, and logic did not make a case.

"He's semi-speeding." DeLuca's voice again. "Past Prudential. So there's only two more exits. The Ted, and then the split. Want me to pull him over?"

"Why? Just to show him we're on his tail? He'd recognize you."

"Shit." The radio static seemed to underscore D's annoyance. "You got any better ideas?"

What DeLuca called "the split" would take Hewlitt either down Exit 24A to the twisty narrow one-way streets of the financial district where he'd be a huge pain in the ass to follow, or Exit 24C, to the south shore. Also a pain, since he'd be out of jurisdiction. But if he chose Exit 24B, he'd be headed right into Jake's waiting arms. At HQ, Hewlitt had told DeLuca he "worked security" at Faneuil Hall. Had Angie Bartoneri confirmed even that? Could be Hewlitt was simply going to work. They'd see.

"Jake. There is a God," D's voice came over the radio. "He's passed the Ted. Not using the airport tunnel, not going to the airport. One down. You set?"

"Standing by," Jake said. "He goes to the south shore, we're screwed."

"Well aware," DeLuca said.

Had to be the first time Jake participated in an undercover in a car chase without moving. He didn't close his eyes—times like this that was too risky—but he pictured DeLuca on the road, hanging back a few car lengths, different lane, monitoring his quarry's every move. D loved a good chase, but this one would employ no flashing lights or screaming sirens. The whole point was to remain unobtrusive. The only possible snag? Hewlitt had seen DeLuca in Franklin Alley. Hell, more than seen, DeLuca'd held a gun on him. If they made eye contact, Hewlitt might recognize him. Even so, it'd be no biggie for Hewlitt to see a cop car on the Pike. If anything, it'd just make him stay under the speed limit, probably the only driver who did.

"Bingo." DeLuca's voice crackled the radio into life.

Jake bolted upright. He must have fallen asleep, just for a fraction of a second. Not good. He should have brought some of Catherine Siskel's dark roast with him.

"Bingo what?" Jake said, making sure his voice sounded normal.

"Hewlitt and his jockmobile are headed right to ya. Getting off at

Government Center." DeLuca's voice was triumphant. "Black Isuzu Trooper, ski rack on top. And listen to this. His plate is GUILTY1."

"No way." Jake cranked the ignition, shifted into reverse, backed out of the spot and onto Congress Street. "You're bullshitting me."

"Yeah, I am," D said.

"You're an asshole," Jake said.

"So I hear," D said.

41

"Not the same Lewis Wilhoite?"

Jane watched her sister's face change as she realized what Jane had discovered, saw Melissa's expression morph from questioning to suspicious to accusatory to frightened. Jane was holding up the laptop like a tiny electronic billboard. Melissa and Robyn examined the thumbnail-size snapshot, then the photos on the wall, comparing.

The three of them stayed silent for a beat, each processing what Jane revealed. If the Lewis Wilhoite in the photo was not the Lewis Wilhoite who married Robyn, then who was the man who had Gracie? Who had Robyn actually married?

"That's terrifying," Melissa said.

"That's ridiculous." Robyn waved at the computer screen dismissively, turned her back for an instant, then whirled to face them. "My husband might be a bit"—she looked at the ceiling, as if searching for exactly the right word—"quirky. But he is who he is. I mean, I married him four years ago. I know him. He's got a passport, a birth certificate, I've seen them. I'm not a compete fool."

She stopped, put her hands over her face, then wiped underneath each eye with one finger. She straightened her shoulders, almost challenging them. "You *think* I'm a complete fool?"

Melissa and Jane exchanged worried glances. Jane felt silly, standing there holding the computer, and placed it on the desk, still open to the archived photo.

"You want to call the police now?" Melissa said.

Jane winced at the venom in her sister's voice, though she understood it. If Robyn had been duped by this guy from the start, the situation was far more dire than it had seemed at first. Her mind raced, playing out the scenarios. A grieving father making a misguided play to keep his stepdaughter was one thing. A masquerading con artist with a phony background who'd stolen someone else's resume and lured Robyn into marrying him was a whole other story.

"Did you never look at the Wharton photos, Robyn?" Jane asked. "Was there anything about his past that seemed off or out of whack? Did his history ever seem to change?"

"I don't know." Robyn paused, tilted her head as if reflecting. "I mean, I accepted what he told me, there was no reason to check on anything, you know? We never looked up *my* college photos, either, come to think of it." She peered at the computer screen and reached forward to click the mouse, zooming in on the photo. Clicked it even closer.

"Huh," she said. "And now I'm going over everything he ever said, everything he ever told me." She stared at the screen again, the photo now blown up to an extreme tight shot. "And now, looking closer? At everything? In a different way? I have to wonder. I do. What if none of it is true?"

"The only explanation is that Lewis Wilhoite lied about his own background," Melissa interrupted, shaking her head. "And that means—and I'm sorry to say this, Robyn, but there's a little girl involved—it means we have no idea who we're dealing with."

"*My* little girl," Robyn's voice twisted into a wail.

"And Daniel's," Melissa said. "And mine." She pointed to the computer. "Jane, did you look him up anywhere else?"

"Not yet. But that's a job for the police now, don't you think?"

"Absolutely," Melissa said.

Jane eyed the landline on the desk. "I'll call—"

"No. No police." Robyn crossed her arms over her chest, her Rapunzel hair curling over them. Jane saw Melissa meet her gaze, then take a step toward her.

"Robyn—" she said.

"No!" Robyn faced Melissa as if there were no one else in the room. "Lewis specifically said no police!"

She grabbed the phone from the desk, waved the handset at them in one all-encompassing accusatory arc.

"And who knows what he'll do now. Right? Right? Or even where they are! Oh, my God. It was all made up. All that flat tire and garage and Twizzlers and I just believed it, it was so Lewis, but I never thought—but I see it now. I *do*! He'll hide her forever. He'd never hurt her, ever, but he'll, he'll, change her hair, and change *her* name, just like he must have changed *his* name!"

"Robyn," Jane began, wondering how to stop her from spiraling into hysteria. "I think we'll be better off if we contact the police."

But Robyn was crying now, ignoring Jane, full-on sobs racking her body, her shoulders shaking with the effort. Her breath came in gulps. "Because I *am* a fool, I'm so incredibly gullible, and I was so unhappy after Danny and I split up." She looked at Melissa, then touched the phone pad, tracing the numbers with one finger, caressing, as if remembering something, a long-ago call, or a lost connection. "I never should have married him."

Jane heard the anguish in the woman's voice, felt her escalating grief, and knew she was powerless to help her. Crusading Jane, big-shot reporter, investigator extraordinaire. Well, she'd investigated, all right. And discovered the lie that made this family fall apart. It was better to know, she supposed. But the question was: What did they do now?

"It's ten forty-five." Robyn's quavering voice was now barely a whisper. "Gracie's gone."

The greenroom was supposed to be private. And it was. Mostly. If you sat on the couch or in the big chair, like most people did, you only heard murmurs from the adjacent Chief of Staff's office. But Tenley stood, her ear pressed to the door. If you got into the spot she and Lanna discovered through a series of increasingly successful experiments, you could hear just about every word that was said. Usually, it was pretty boring stuff, political arguments or street cleaning. She'd heard her mother swear, which she used to think was pretty funny. And she learned her mom was always in charge, even telling the mayor what to do. *No wonder she and Dad had fought sometimes,* now she thought about it. Dad was the dad, but Mom had the power. Or thought she did.

Tenley's eyes welled. Guess Mom didn't have enough power to stop what happened to Dad. Or to Lanna.

Maybe that's why she seemed mad all the time.

Tenley tuned out, thinking about Dad, and Mom, and Lanna, and herself, and her life, and how a lot of things sucked. A man's voice, kind of yelling, brought her back. Her mother's voice was still unintelligible.

Who was her mom talking to, anyway? She listened as hard as she could.

"You have a subpoena for the video," the man's voice said, kind of angry. Video? "Don't leave town," she heard him say.

Tenley leaned against the dark green wall and stared up at the checkerboard of white acoustical tiles on the ceiling. That's what the cops on TV told people when they were in trouble. Like if they were a suspect.

Like in a crime.

So that was weird.

42

"Don't move." DeLuca's commanding voice cut through the radio static, louder than the city bus wheezing by on Congress Street, louder than the kid on the sidewalk wailing his little-kid complaint as a frowning parent yanked at his hand. Surprised, Jake shifted his cruiser into Park, clicked the handset to reply.

"DeLuca? You talking to me?"

"I'm right behind this guy now," DeLuca said. "He's stopped at the light, headed for North Street. Stand by, Harvard—Hewlitt's coming right to you. Five mins, maybe four. Copy?"

"Copy."

Jake buzzed his window up. He'd stuck his head out into the briny summer breeze freshening off the harbor, trying to stay awake. Hewlitt would be here in less than five minutes. No time to hit the Dunkin' on the corner. Jake was running on fumes, relying on adrenaline instead of caffeine. This whole thing had started almost exactly twenty-four hours ago.

The Isuzu. Jake saw it turning right onto Union Street.

"Duck!" DeLuca ordered. "He's coming right at you. If he sees you, we're screwed."

Jake snaked himself down behind the steering wheel, unclicking his seat belt, his T-shirt catching on the nubby upholstery. Raking his chest against the plastic wheel, he scooted down until his chin hit the rounded bottom. This was gonna hurt, but he wouldn't be like this for long.

Reaching up with his right hand, he tried to angle the rearview mirror so it faced in the general direction of the—*got it.*

The black car pulled forward at one of the meters, stopped, and in one motion eased into the white-lined spot. Jake watched the mirror image, grateful his cruiser was unmarked. If his back held out, this'd work.

"Got 'im?" DeLuca's voice was a whisper.

"Got him," Jake said.

"I'll park at Area A," D said.

The neighborhood police station up the block would be the perfect hiding place for DeLuca's cruiser, lined up with other marked cars.

Squinting now as the noonday sun bounced off his side mirror and into his eyes, Jake realized that Hewlitt hadn't gotten out of his van. He remained sitting in the front seat. On his phone? Jake couldn't tell.

"He's still in the car," Jake said to the radio. "What's he waiting for? Or who?"

"You'll soon find out," DeLuca said. "That's why you're Boston's finest."

Jake didn't feel so fine. His back already ached, his knees were bent in an impossible way, and the glare of the sun interfered with his line of sight. Ducking had initially seemed a good idea, a way to protect Jake's identity in a crucial moment, but for the long haul, there'd have to be a plan B.

An uncomfortable stakeout was an unavoidable part of the job. He'd sat in this unmarked cruiser in front of a suspect's home for hours, eating red Swedish fish, wondering how much coffee his body could hold without a bathroom break. He'd huddled in dark corners of vacant buildings in the dead of Boston winters, and nursed phony cocktails in the impossible lighting of hotel bars. Watching for the library wallet bandit, he'd stationed himself by the copier at the Boston Public Library for so long an irate reader reported him for "hogging" it.

Stakeouts were not supposed to be fun. If Jake got the bad guy, it all would be worth it.

The dark shadow of City Hall edged across the front seat as time ticked by, a giant sundial reminding Jake of how long he'd been hiding. Hewlitt had returned to the scene of the crime. Or perhaps simply to his place of business. Getting the scoop on Hewlitt's CV was on Angie Bartoneri's list of assignments, Jake thought again. Was she actively trying to sabotage him? For dumping her? Incompetence or petulance. No place for either in Jake's life.

He kept his eyes on the rearview mirror. Hewlitt's silhouette was a statue. There were too many damn places Hewlitt could go, and he could choose faster than Jake could follow him. Jake could only watch, best he could, then notify D and leap out of the car to follow as soon as Hewlitt was under way. Fifty-fifty, he thought. *Fifty-freaking-fifty.*

To stay awake, Jake ran down his to-do list. Check with Evidence and Kiyoko Naka in Missing Persons. He needed to nail down Catherine Siskel and those security cameras, and get hold of Ward Dahlstrom, the man supposedly in charge of surveillance. From what they'd explained, the city's traffic cams could be looking at this same scene right now.

Jake stared at the mirror, then reached for his radio. "D," he said.

"Copy."

"Can you take over for a couple minutes?" Jake slid across the front seat, never taking his eyes off the mirror, and reached for the handle of the passenger-side door. The one nearest the entrance to City Hall.

"Got your six," DeLuca said.

"That mean yes?" Jake watched the mirror. Still nothing.

"You're breaking up," D lied. "Gotcha. I'm under way. Corner of Sudbury and Congress. I see him. Front seat."

"Great." Jake said. Still nothing. "Over to you. Radio me when he's on the move."

"Why?" DeLuca said. "Too much coffee? You hitting the head?"

"Nope," Jake said. "I have an idea."

A harsh jangle from the black desk phone cut across the Wilhoites' study. Jane felt her heart beat faster. "Is that him?"

Robyn let out a yelp.

The phone rang again.

"For God's sake, answer it," Melissa ordered.

"He's always called my cell before." Robyn seemed verging on tears, all nerve endings, exposed and raw, holding her silent cell. "Lewis can be so—manipulative, you know?"

"Answer it," Jane said. "Manipulative"? Another word Robyn hadn't used before, like "careless," and "jealous," and "nutcase." "It might not be Lewis. It might be someone with information about Gracie."

When the phone rang a third time, Melissa took a step closer, reaching out as if to snatch the phone herself. Robyn stepped away from them, one pace, then another. Clutching her cell phone to her chest.

"I'm afraid," she whispered.

"Afraid?" Melissa's voice went up, incredulous. "Afraid?"

"Robyn." Jane kept her voice calm. Being part of the story was unnervingly different. "We're all afraid. But answer the phone."

The room went silent as Robyn picked up the landline handset.

"Hello?" Her voice quavered, barely audible.

Jane and Melissa leaned toward her, eyes narrowing. Jane tried to gauge Robyn's reactions as interminable seconds ticked by. Then a full minute.

"Jane." Robyn, wide-eyed, handed her the phone. "It's Lewis. He told me what he wants. Now he wants to talk to you. Tell you in person."

"Thank God," Melissa said.

Jane grabbed the handset from Robyn, put it to her ear. Said, "Lewis? It's Jane" almost before she had it in place. Waited.

Nothing.

She tried again. Nothing. "Lewis? It's Jane Ryland," she said, louder. She pressed the receiver closer to her ear. Maybe there was a bad connection, or she'd been put on hold? She turned to Robyn. "Was the call breaking up? Could you hear him?" And then into the phone. "Lewis?"

Nothing.

"Robyn?"

"Isn't he talking?" Robyn asked. "He asked for you. See? I told you he was manipulative. Did he hang up? Or—did *you* disconnect somehow? Oh, no, Jane, did you cut him off?"

"Of course she didn't," Melissa said. "Did you?"

Of course she hadn't. Jane put the handset back to her ear; she could hear that the line was open, so she was connected to someone, somewhere.

"The line is still open," she said, "but there's no one there."

"I can't believe it." Robyn plopped down in the desk chair and dropped her head into her outstretched arms, a mass of blond hair and trembling chenille.

"Can you hear *anything*?" Melissa took three quick steps to stand next to Jane, holding out her hand. "Give me that. Let me see."

Jane looked at the phone again, baffled. She held it up to her sister.

In green letters, the display showed CALL ENDED.

43

She knew this guy somehow. Tenley raised her eyes over her computer monitor, surreptitiously examining him as he came into the surveillance room. Where had she seen him? He was pretty cute, in jeans and a battered leather jacket, kind of cool in an older-guy kind of way. Not someone who worked at City Hall, she was pretty sure.

She checked him out again, couldn't resist. He looked intense, eyes darting from desk to desk, scanning, like he was looking for something. Or someone. Ward Dahlstrom, maybe? Usually he'd be here to make sure no one sneaked out early for lunch, hovering and bossy like they were little kids. *The less the scope of someone's power, the more they'll try to inflict it on you,* her dad used to say.

Dad. She let out a jaggedy sigh. She'd wanted to go *home,* Mom did, too, but her mother had hugged her, hard, asked her to be brave and not to say a word to anyone about her father. They had to wait, Mom said. So Tenley *would* wait, and try to be brave. And she wouldn't say a word, not one. Like, who was even gonna ask? If her mother could do it, she could do it. They were the only two left.

It was hard to concentrate, though. Sorrow and confusion had pretty much blotted out everything else. It was difficult to decide what was important.

The leather-jacket guy had stopped by the desk closest to the door. Nancie Alvarez, the department's assistant manager, sat there, skinny and skittish as a baby spider. He was talking to her, his voice too low to overhear. Tenley saw him point at the bank of real-time video monitors displayed across the wall.

She pressed her lips together, holding back tears, trying to focus on her screen and not the guy. Mom had promised to come get her at lunchtime. They'd talk, she promised. Right now Tenley was drained. She'd cried and cried in the greenroom, so hard her whole face hurt. Now there were almost no tears left. Weirdly, she also felt—how would Dr. Maddux put it?—remorseful, maybe. Because she was so self-absorbed. She'd been so focused on herself, she hadn't thought enough about how her mom must feel.

She was totally relieved her mother didn't know about last night, her sneaking out to Brileen's, and she would never tell her. *That* secret it was okay for Tenley to keep.

The atmosphere of the room changed. Tenley looked up.

Nancie Alvarez was standing. She turned toward the back of the room and pointed. Not at the screens, but at Tenley. *At her!* Now the guy was coming her way. Holy frigging crap, was she in trouble now?

"I'm Detective Jake Brogan," the man said, stopping in front of her.

OMG. *OMG.* A detective. A detective! Was he here about her father? Her mother told her not to say anything. Tenley's throat closed, her voice disappeared. What if he asked about the video from yesterday? She flinched as the detective flapped open one of those police things at her, like a wallet, with a gold badge inside.

"Miss Alvarez says your computer monitor is set to observe the Curley Park area," he said. "Can you show me that, please? Show me what's happening right now?"

Could she? His voice was really calm, not like she'd done anything wrong, and he didn't look mean, but she still felt her eyes widen and a clench of fear and uncertainty twist her stomach. Of all the stupid times for stupid Dahlstrom not to be here. Why did *she* have to decide this? She was only a kid.

"I'm not sure I'm allowed," she said. This guy was a cop, though, and for sure he hadn't gotten up to the surveillance room without some kind of permission. She looked across the room, hoping for help, or guidance, or advice. Nothing. Everyone else was at their own computers, pretending not to look at her at all. They probably thought she was in trouble for not being here on time this morning. Even though she'd been with her mother. Should she call her mom now?

"Boston Police, miss," the detective said, like reminding her. Like she could forget.

If she said no to the police, would she get in even more trouble? Or would she be a hero? Crap. When was the last time refusing to do what the police said made you a hero?

She gave up. She simply, totally, gave up.

"Here." Tenley stood and gestured to her chair, letting him take her place at the monitor. *Fine.* Let them yell at her. Nancie had sent this police officer her way. She was in charge when Dahlstrom was gone, so Tenley was only following orders. Her life was already ruined, anyway. One more mistake wouldn't make one bit of difference. Whatever. Nothing mattered. She leaned forward and clicked her mouse so he could see the Curley Park screen.

"Is this what you wanted?" Tenley said.

Jake hadn't wanted to push this girl. If she balked, or if the woman at the front decided to call security, this surveillance opportunity would vanish, obliterated by a shit pile of bureaucracy. It wasn't exactly kosher. He guessed he should have gotten a warrant, but he wasn't taping or looking at private documents or removing any paperwork.

He was simply getting a better vantage point.

It would be legal to look out a City Hall window, no question. This was exactly the same thing, except he was now sitting in front of an exceptionally well-placed window. Couldn't argue with that. And there wasn't much time.

There was *no* time, in fact. It had been risky to leave his lookout and race up here. The plan was simple. D would raise his arm if there was action, or give a radio call. So far no updates, which meant Hewlitt wasn't on the move. Strange. Lucky, but strange.

Did Tenley—maybe eighteen? nineteen?—know her father was "missing"? She had the same haunted look around her eyes as her mother. The same sleek dark hair, the same angular jaw. A sad life, that family. Be interesting to find out what, if anything, Catherine had told her. He'd add that to the to-do list.

There it was.

Hewlitt's black Isuzu. The roof, part of the hood, and the clearest possible shot of the passenger-side door. The driver's side was partly obscured by trees, but once Hewlitt emerged, he'd be in clear view.

Jake even saw the unmistakable shape of DeLuca, now leaning against the Union Oyster House building a scant half block from Hewlitt's car. Jake clicked his radio twice, the "I'm in place" signal. D one-clicked as reply. *Received.*

"Were you here yesterday, Miss, uh, Siskel?" He pretended to stumble on her name. No reason for her to know it meant anything to him, much less that he suspected her mother of lying to him. Whatever Catherine Siskel was hiding wasn't about the Curley Park stabbing, which was his top priority. "During the incident?"

He risked a quick glance away from the monitor. The girl was frowning, looked distressed, her face pale and dark eyes widening. She had a bunch of holes in her earlobes. *Kids.*

Back to the screen. No movement at Hewlitt's car yet, only the ebb and flow of lunchtime traffic, a scatter of jaywalkers, people strolling with shopping bags and dogs on leashes. Couldn't see faces, not well, at least, but no matter. Jake only needed to see which direction Hewlitt walked.

"Miss? Were you here?" Not a tough question. Either she was or she wasn't.

"Yeah," she finally said, "I was here yesterday. But I didn't see anything."

"Nothing?" he asked, his eyes still on the screen.

"Um, ambulances, I guess," she said. "I was on a different camera at first."

He couldn't afford the time to look at her. But she was hiding something, too, her tone was an open book. The Siskel family had a lot of secrets.

"The incident get taped?"

"Not by me," she said.

Interesting answer. And then he saw DeLuca's shadow change. Did his arm go up? So much for the signal idea.

Jake leaned in closer to the screen, squinting, trying to bring the video into better focus. The quality was good, clear and in color, but just far enough away to be frustrating. "Can you make this zoom in?" he asked.

"Yeah, you can." The girl leaned toward the screen, her shoulder briefly touching his, clicked the white plastic mouse and dragged it. The scene expanded into a million blocks of unidentifiable pixels.

Shit. "Put it back, please." Jake tried to keep his voice calm.

She clicked and dragged again. Back in focus. D still by the building. The car door still closed. There was movement, pedestrians on the sidewalks making jagged blurs of color. Then one figure stopped near the passenger side of Hewlitt's car. The person stood in the lee of the maple tree, only half in sun, striped by shadow.

Jake put a fist to his chin, watching. D hadn't moved.

The figure on the sidewalk—*female?* female—took two steps toward the car. Her head turned and she looked up. If she had known the camera was there, she couldn't have looked more directly into the lens.

Jake still couldn't see her features, but could make out her bare arms, and bare legs under what must be a short skirt.

"Oh!" The girl next to him made a sound, a strangling gasp.

Jake turned, caught a glimpse of her face. Three words came to his mind.

Seen a ghost?

44

Outside the Wilhoites' house, it was a quiet June early afternoon in a comfortable suburban neighborhood. The breeze whispered through the blossoming crabapples, the sun shimmered rainbows in the water from the irrigation systems hidden under pristine green lawns. But inside the Wilhoites' otherwise unremarkable Cape Cod, it was crazy town. Lewis and Robyn, and Gracie, and Melissa, even the absent Daniel were all embroiled in a family drama worthy of daytime TV.

Now Jane was part of it.

As she backed her Audi away from the house and onto the narrow street, Jane could only hope she was about to play a role in the final scene. As soon as the curtains closed, with Gracie safe and the Wilhoites out of her life, she would make a grateful exit. Except for the wedding. Jane winced as the car bumped over the curb. She shifted into first, then turned toward Boston. This story better have a happy ending. She couldn't call Jake for help, because Robyn had insisted—*implored*—no police.

"The University Inn," Robyn had told her. A boutiquey hotel near Faneuil Hall, "the U," everyone called it. The place where Lewis and Gracie were now supposedly swimming in the rooftop pool. Gracie, who had no idea this ugly dispute was swirling around her, was simply a little girl on a summertime adventure with her stepfather.

"He always forgets to charge his cell," Robyn had explained. "That's what must have happened. He didn't hang up on you, his phone went dead. Lucky he'd told me all of it."

Robyn had also explained that Lewis wanted Jane to come to the hotel and wait in the lobby. At some point in the afternoon, he would bring Gracie to her, introduce them, and leave. Lewis would call Jane's cell to tell her when.

Surely this was the dumbest idea anyone had ever concocted. Even though Jane was kind of a public figure, and almost a family member, and, as a result, safe, it was still dumb. Jane had almost said that out loud. But then Robyn had dissolved in tears and run upstairs, leaving Jane and Melissa staring at each other. Jane had no choice but to go as instructed.

She stopped for gas at the station just before the entrance to the Mass Turnpike, grabbed a cello-wrapped pre-fab turkey sandwich and a Diet Coke, then added some Twizzlers for Gracie, just in case. In midday traffic like this, Jane calculated it would take half an hour to get to the University Inn.

Dumb, dumb, *dumb,* she thought, as she pulled onto the Pike. And good-bye to her TV career. Marsh Tyson at Channel 2 would be crossing her off the employment list, that was for sure. Maybe she should turn this whole thing into a Lifetime TV script, get a million dollars, and run off with Jake.

She shifted into third, passed a rickety landscaping truck, then a yellow bus full of kids, goofily smiling faces plastered to the square windows. A mop-topped little girl waved at her as she passed. Jane waved back, then the bus was behind her.

She couldn't understand it, using a child in a battle for parental power. Seemed like that's what Lewis was doing. And who knew about Robyn, who seemed to be letting him off the hook while helping perpetuate all this. Why didn't Lewis simply bring Gracie home?

The crime scene tape was down from Curley Park, Jane noticed. She pulled to a stop, ready to hand her car over to the maroon-jacketed valet guy at the U. She got out of her car, brushing the turkey sandwich crumbs off her black jeans and onto the potholed pavement of North Street.

"Nice to see you again, Ms. Ryland," the valet said.

Again? Oh. The same guy who'd parked her car when she worked the Curley Park story. Just yesterday! The name above his shirt pocket read *Tim*.

"Thanks," she said. "Seems to have calmed down, huh? They arrest anyone?"

"I was about to ask *you*," Tim said.

"No idea," she said, thereby admitting to both of them how out of it she was.

She gave him her keys, then hitched her tote bag up over her shoulder, remembering yesterday. Remembering the distasteful reality that disaster made good television, and that she'd understood good television might mean a job for her. How could all that yesterday seem so far away?

Now she was about to camp out in a hotel lobby with a pack of Twizzlers, waiting for the delivery of a—what would TV news call it? The hostage in a custody drama? Or simply a little girl caught between two selfishly unreliable parents?

Tim held out a rubber-banded stack of pale blue numbered tickets, poised a ballpoint pen over one. "How long will you be this time?" he asked.

"Good question," she said.

Not sixty seconds ago, Catherine Siskel's in-house intercom had buzzed. She'd raced down the stairs as soon as Nancie Alvarez alerted her. That *cop*? Now with *Tenley*? Damn cops. Their lies and their pretense. He'd pretended he had someplace to be. And where the hell was it? Downstairs, interrogating her daughter? Why?

Now every head turned toward her as she entered the surveillance room. Workers popped up like frightened prairie dogs, then plunked down in their seats at her glowering reaction. Tenley and that detective turned to acknowledge her arrival. Nancie approached her, but Catherine held up a palm. *I'll handle this.*

"Detective Brogan? Tenley?" She waved the others back to work. "Might I ask what's going on here?"

Her head throbbed. If the public learned that contrary to what their mayor had specifically promised, every bit of surveillance video for City Hall was being taped and stored, that'd be the end of his tenure as mayor, the end of his career, and the end of the careers of every single person who knew about it. For a moment, though, she had the advantage. The cop looked like he'd been caught with a hand in the cookie jar. Which he most assuredly had.

Catherine pressed her lips together, struggling to calm her raging blood pressure. *Politics and power run best on a need-to-know basis,* she'd learned at the Kennedy School. Sometimes, even usually, that kind of compartmentalization worked. But the unavoidable reality was right here, right now. And there were no more degrees of separation.

She'd told this cop a lie—that her husband Greg was missing, whereabouts unknown.

She'd told her daughter the truth—that Greg was dead.

And now they were here, together, side by side, looking at the surveillance screen of the very place where Tenley knew the "missing" Greg had been killed. If they had shared information about that, Catherine was doomed.

"If you're looking at the city's proprietary surveillance system, you certainly have a search warrant," Catherine said. "May I see that please? Now?"

"Ms. Siskel," the detective began, "don't misunderstand. The reason I'm here is that—"

Tenley was looking at her, Catherine realized with a pang, exactly the same way she had twelve or so years ago, standing with her little toes curled over the edge, right before the first time she dived into the deep end of the neighborhood pool. Catherine had yelled at her, *Do it!* And she had.

Now Tenley was in another precarious position. This time, Catherine had already instructed her about what to do, and Tenley seemed to understand. But who knew how the girl would react, faced with a cop asking questions? Again? Poor Tenley. A dead sister, and a murdered father, and a miserable failure of a mother.

"Just a moment, Detective." Catherine signaled across the desks. Nancie Alvarez came to her side. "Give us the room, please, Nancie."

In fifteen seconds, the three of them were alone. To face whatever the hell this cop was trying to pull.

"Now, Detective." Catherine knew the best way to control the conversation was to be the only one talking. She smiled, barely, to indicate she had the power but she would be reasonably pleasant about it as long as he didn't try to argue. "I can assure you that you need a warrant for this, whatever you're doing. Come with me to my office now. I'm sure we can work it out."

"Not gonna happen," the detective said. "And feel free to call headquarters. But right now," he turned, gesturing at the screen, "I'm essentially doing nothing more than looking out a City Hall window. There's certainly nothing prohibited or illegal about that. In fact—"

He stopped. Placed both palms on her daughter's desk and, elbows splayed, leaned toward the computer screen. He muttered something, clearly irritated. Unclicked a radio from his belt, pressed a button. "D? Anything?" he said.

Catherine heard the tension in his voice.

"Door's still closed. No ignition." A voice came from the other end.

Catherine took a step toward the computer, trying to see what the cop had reacted to with such seeming dismay. What were they talking about? All she could see were trees, pedestrians, and the rooftops of the buildings across Congress Street. Cars. More pedestrians. Storefronts. She looked at Tenley, raised her eyebrows, questioning. *What?*

Her daughter shrugged, pleading, eyes wide.

She's on the deep end of something, Catherine thought again. *But what?*

The detective had turned to Tenley, pointed his cigarette-pack-size black radio at her.

"You know who was standing by that vehicle, Miss Siskel," he said, saying her name correctly. "And you need to tell me. Now."

"What vehicle?" Catherine stepped between Tenley and the cop, barricading her daughter behind her. Reaching out a hand, she touched Tenley's thigh. *Be quiet.* "What are you talking about?"

45

Jane had commandeered the only accessible wall plug in the inn's lobby and hooked up her cell phone to keep it charged. Checked that the volume was on, the ringer up. Sat on the cordovan leather couch, the cord draped over the padded armrest. A navy-jacketed concierge had inquired whether she needed help. Even though the answer was yes, she shook her head. There was nothing the concierge could do.

"I'm waiting for friends. They'll be down any minute," she'd said. She hoped that was true.

There was one bank of elevators. From her carefully selected couch position she could monitor whoever got on and off. Only one car served the pool/skyview level. Already, she'd seen a few kids wrapped in hotel towels flip-flopping out that elevator door, crossing the lobby to the snack shop, then returning to the rooftop sunshine. Maybe Gracie and Lewis were there right now. Jane pictured Gracie, splashing and happy, oblivious to the drama her stepfather was creating. Still, he'd promised to send the little girl home today. End of story.

Jane had never met Lewis or Gracie. But she'd seen enough photos to recognize them, apart or together. Besides, unlike the setup of a usual stakeout, they'd be looking for *her*. Lewis would, at least.

Jane fidgeted. Couldn't get comfortable. Tourists milled at a display rack of multicolored pamphlets, a bored-looking clerk at the registration desk talked on her cell phone, and canned music competed with the splashing water from a stone fountain in the center of the area.

Waiting was frustrating, no matter what. Stakeouts were relentlessly and irretrievably terrible. No food, no bathroom, shivering or broiling, hours of waiting for something that might never happen, and when it did, managing the blast of surprise, panic, and chaos. Truth be told, watching for a kid in a cushy hotel lobby wasn't as bad as foot-freezing snowstorm duty, or that time she'd been assigned to Humarock Beach in a hurricane, pelted by sand and drenched to her core, simply to tell viewers it was windy and raining.

Even though she wouldn't get wet or ice-coated on this stakeout, the apprehension and nerves were exactly the same. She picked up her phone from the chrome-and-glass side table, turned it over and over, twisting the power cord.

When the phone vibrated, it startled her so completely she dropped it onto the soft leather. Snatched it up, hit the green button. She'd been here only fifteen minutes. Mentally she'd prepared herself to wait much longer.

Good.

"Jane Ryland," she said. She scanned the elevator doors. All closed. Was this about to be over?

"Marsh Tyson, Channel 2," the voice said. "Checking in. You anywhere near City Hall? You were going to call me when you were available. All hell's breaking loose over there."

"Hell? Breaking loose? At City Hall?" Jane was echoing, stalling, trying to think and keep her eyes on the elevator doors at the same time. She had call-waiting, so that'd beep if Lewis called, but unlikely he'd do so now, right? Robyn had told her "later in the afternoon." She could stay in place, give Marsh Tyson a few minutes, and try to regain her claim on the reporting job. Four hours ago she'd been tracking down a potential scoop in Catherine Siskel's office. With Jake. Had the Curley Park murder been solved? Had she missed the whole story?

"Well, manner of speaking," Tyson said. "We're still trying to track whether the Curley Park murder victim was connected to a City Hall big shot. So we've got the live truck parked there now, finally, Congress Street side. But there's no reporter to staff it. Our next big newscast isn't until five, and we could always go voice-over from the studio. But checking on your availability."

Jane stood, then got yanked down onto the couch as the length of the cord ran out. "Ah, yeah," she said, regaining her balance. Okay, she hadn't missed anything. "I'm near City Hall. But I'm right in the midst of—"

The elevator doors opened, the sun glaring on the silhouettes emerging. A kid. A kid who was exactly the right size. And a man.

"Marsh?" Jane pulled the plug from the wall, took a few steps closer to the elevators, out of the glare. Every hair on her head had turned gray, she was sure. "Hang on. I've got to . . ."

A little boy in a too-big Power Rangers T-shirt and huge running shoes scampered toward the center of the lobby, his father trotting after him. The father swooped up the kid and briefly held him high, their peals of laugher echoing across the marble-and-glass lobby as they twirled through the revolving front door and out into the sunshine.

Jane sat, her knees unsteady. The elevator doors had closed again. "Listen, Marsh?" She tried to infuse her voice with some semblance of confidence and composure. "I'm very interested in working with you, and eager to get back on the air. But I'm so sorry, probably not today. Again, and it's incredibly unusual, but this family thing has got to come first."

And with that, it did. She knew it did. And she wondered where Jake was and why the whole thing was so complicated. And why everything exploded at the same time. And why every time she tried to gain control of her own life, something happened to prevent it.

"Let me know," Marsh said. A pause. "If you're interested."

"I will." And she would, certainly, because the whole Gracie thing was about to be over. "And I am."

"That's *good* news," Tyson said. "And that's—"

The elevator doors opened again. And there was Gracie. Unmistakably. Unquestionably. A tumble of sandy curls, wire-rimmed glasses. Yellow sundress with fluttery ruffles on the shoulders.

Alone.

"Talk soon," Jane said. And hung up.

* * *

So. Mama bear was protecting her cub. Jake had seen this before, so many times, the parents trying to keep the cops away from their precious ones, not even knowing or caring what their kids were up to. But this girl, this Tenley, still barricaded behind her mother, had recognized someone on the surveillance shot. Her spontaneous "Oh!" proved it. That car could pull out at any second. If it did, he and DeLuca were screwed. Why would Hewlitt drive to that spot, then drive away?

"We saw a person who seemed to walk up to the black Isuzu." Jake kept his voice calm. "The car belongs to a person of interest." Jake chose a phrase the police never used, but television—and Jane—did. "I'm pretty sure your daughter could tell us who she was. And that would be important."

"My daughter?" Catherine Siskel's previously confident demeanor seemed to deflate a bit. Obviously she was choosing her words carefully, clearing her throat before she spoke. "My daughter is mourning the death of her sister," she said. "I can tell you, Detective, even so, she sometimes 'sees' her sister in crowds. I'm sure she only—"

The woman turned, linked her arm through her daughter's, pulled her close. "It's okay, honey," she whispered. "Did you think you saw Lanna again?"

Jake's phone vibrated in his pocket, a text. He checked its screen. From MP, it said. Missing Persons. "GOT ID 4 BOBBY LAND. ACTUAL L-N RIAZ. COLLEGE STUDENT. CALL HQ."

Before he could respond, he saw Tenley twist away from her mother.

"Not *Lanna*, Mom. Give me a break. It was just—someone I thought I knew," the girl said. "No biggie."

Jake could tell she, too, was choosing her words carefully. Whatever agenda these two had, they were not doing a very good job of hiding their distress. Were they in it together, whatever it was?

"Miss Siskel? Someone you 'thought you knew'? *Thought* you knew? Whoever got into that car might be headed for trouble," Jake said. He wasn't sure if that were true. They didn't even know if the young woman had gotten in the car, but why was the daughter being so hesitant? What was so difficult about saying, *Yeah, it's my pal Sally Shmoe, she knows I'm in here, and always looks up*? Instead, this girl was covering up.

Her mother was, too.

Jake's radio crackled. "Door still closed," DeLuca reported. "Ignition on. Stand by." On the surveillance monitor, the taillights of the Isuzu flickered red, then white. A group of pedestrians sauntered by, briefly blocking Jake's view. The car didn't move. Was the girl inside? D hadn't said.

"Miss Siskel?" Jake said again. "Who did you see?"

Tenley's mind raced ahead. If she told this detective who had walked up to the car, she'd also have to say how she knew her. What if her mother started digging? Like she always did? What if she found out Tenley'd bolted last night?

On the other hand, what if Brileen was in trouble? *Even in danger?* If Tenley just let her be driven off by who knows who, then she'd be doing exactly the same thing she'd done with Lanna. She'd kept a secret, and as a result, her sister got killed. That's how she saw it, at least.

How many times had she beaten herself up over that, given herself do-overs in her head, making a different decision? How often had she imagined the outcome totally different, with Lanna still alive and gorgeous and happy and their family all together?

Now the universe offered her exactly the same decision. Whether to keep another secret, or tell the truth to the police about what she saw and what she knew. How could she possibly consider making the same mistake again?

"Her name is Brileen Finnerty," Tenley said. "I met her yesterday afternoon, lunchtime. Down in Curley Park. After all that was—going on, you know? I don't really know her, but she goes to my same school. I mean, she's older, in grad school. I think."

She heard a little noise from beside her. Her mother had moved closer to the computer monitor. Peered at the square box of video on the screen.

"Brileen—how do you spell that?" The detective pulled out a little notebook.

"I—" Tenley frowned. "I don't exactly know," she said. "We just met yester—"

"Finnerty?" the detective said. "Have you ever seen that black Isuzu before?"

"Finnerty." Her mother said the name, then spelled it. She reached out, touched the image of the black car with one finger. Took her hand away.

How would Mom know how to spell it? Maybe she was guessing. But her mother had a weird look on her face.

"Brileen. Finnerty." Her mother dropped each word like it was heavy. Like she was tired of holding it.

"Yeah," Tenley said. That was strange. "How do—"

"Do you have her contact information? Address? Cell phone?" The detective kept talking, seemed really concerned about this. Maybe Bri *was* in danger? So good thing she told. He watched the screen the whole time.

"You met yesterday, down there in Curley Park? Like I said, have you seen that car before?"

"How did you two meet?" Her mother asked. "You and Brileen?"

"Ms. Siskel? Mind if I ask the questions here? Tenley? The car?"

"I'm not good at cars," Tenley said.

She heard a noise, a knocking, and they all looked toward the front of the office. Nancie Alvarez opened the door, leaning in, only her head and shoulders crossing the threshold. The hall was empty. Everyone must have scattered. The luckies.

"Is it okay if we—" Nancie began.

"Not yet!" her mother called out. The door closed again with a metallic click. "When did you *really* meet, Tenner? How long have you *really* known this girl?"

Tenley felt her stomach curl and her brain start to fry. She remembered how she felt when the police had questioned her about Lanna. Her skin had gone all cold, and her insides no longer fit into her body. It was that way now.

At least the detective wasn't asking about her father. She had no idea what she would say then.

Why did everything always seem to depend on what she knew? Or did? Or saw?

46

Gracie's white sling-back flats clacked across the dark marble floor. She carried a strappy white patent backpack over one shoulder. Tanned and coltishly lanky, bare arms and legs, she had the awkward gait of a preteen girl in shoes that didn't quite fit. Jane stood, but didn't rush toward her, waiting to see what would happen. Where was Lewis? Hadn't the plan been for him to deliver Gracie to her?

The girl strolled across the lobby, dipped her fingers in the fountain, moved on. She didn't appear to be looking for anyone. If she'd been instructed—*Find Jane Ryland, she's a woman, younger than your mom, brown hair, and she'll be waiting for you*—wouldn't she be scanning the room? But Gracie seemed headed for the snack bar. Or the front door.

Should Jane go get her? Stop her? At least ask? No one else in the lobby seemed to pay much attention to the girl in yellow. The concierge lifted his head as she walked by his broad wooden desk, gave her a fleeting vacant smile. The valet guy hung another jangling ring of keys in his storage cabinet and ambled outside. A pack of rollerbag-toting tourists heading for the waist-high registration desk partly blocked Jane's view of Gracie for a few seconds, only her curls and ruffles peeking between the adult bodies and black wheeled suitcases.

Gracie's eyes were on the front door. Was she going to leave?

Jane took a step in her direction. She didn't want to scare the girl, and if this was not the moment Lewis was—handing her off? Giving her up? Making the exchange? Whatever it was, Jane didn't want to ruin it.

Maybe Gracie hadn't seen her. Or recognized her. Jane hadn't bothered to refresh her makeup and her hair was not very carefully pulled back, so if Gracie was looking for someone all TV glam and polished, Jane was pretty much incognito. Gracie might be too young to remember Jane from Channel 11, her last on-air story more than a year ago. But her stepfather, or someone, would have described her, and pointed the girl in the right direction. If that's what the plan was.

Gracie stopped at a grouping of massive terra-cotta-potted fake palm trees near a rack of flapped-over newspapers. She plopped her white backpack onto the floor, then perched on the curved edge of one of the pots, legs sticking out in front of her. She seemed to be staring at her white-patent toes, moving her feet side to side, back and forth, moving her head in unison. Certainly not looking for anyone. But waiting? For what?

Maybe Gracie had misunderstood her stepfather's instructions, thinking Jane would come find her. Jane twisted the cell phone in her hand, flipping it over and over, considering. That actually made more sense. Gracie would be told that Jane would find *her*, right? Jane was the adult.

She spooled out a breath, trying to decide what to do. Keeping one eye on the girl, she checked her cell, on the unlikely chance someone had texted or called, explaining exactly what the plan was. They hadn't. *Imagine that.*

Could anything go wrong if Jane simply approached her? After all, Jane was family, almost, kind of, soon to be. Certainly someone had mentioned her name in connection with the wedding as well as this afternoon's plan. Jane pursed her lips, never taking her eyes off Gracie.

Should she call Robyn? Melissa? Try Lewis's number?

If Jane weren't standing in the middle of a hotel lobby, in public, she would have yelled in frustration. But there was no one to yell at. She closed her eyes, briefly, semi-defeated.

Okay.

It couldn't hurt if she approached Gracie, still perched by the potted palm. Obviously waiting. This wasn't some spy movie or TV drama; it was the lame-brained scheme of a stupid stepfather trying to avoid embarrassment. Too darn late for *that,* Jane thought.

She took a deep breath, slung her tote bag over her shoulder, plastered a non-threatening expression on her face, and headed across the lobby. Muzak played some tinkly-mushy background music, soothing and summery, the fountain splashed, and the elevator doors opened, closed, and then Jane was facing the little girl. She stopped, keeping a reasonably non-intimidating distance, a step away.

Gracie looked up at her. Then down. As if she had no idea who Jane was.

"Gracie?" Jane leaned closer, touched her on the shoulder for an instant. "I'm Jane, okay?"

Gracie looked at her again, then stood, grabbing the strap of her backpack with her right hand.

Good.

"Ready to go?" Jane asked. Or maybe, she should make sure. "Your stepfather told you to come with me, right? Didn't he?"

Gracie took a step back, stumbled against the pot, sat down again. Stood up. "How do you know my name?" she whispered. Her eyebrows drew together, and the corners of her mouth turned down.

Uh-oh.

"Oh, I didn't mean to alarm you, honey," Jane said. "I'm Jane. Didn't your stepfather tell you I was going to take you home? To your mother? And I have Twizzlers, just for you."

"DADDY!" Gracie screamed, the force of her entire body straining behind her little voice. "HELP! Stranger!"

Gracie turned and ran, skittering and sliding across the marble floor, racing toward the elevators, her backpack abandoned, arms flailing, yelling at the top of her lungs the whole way.

Every head in the lobby came up. Every person in the place stared at Jane. The concierge leaped from his desk. The clerk bounded from behind her registration counter. Every uniform in the room now beelined toward Jane. Two security guards, in starched steel gray and running shoes, banged through an unmarked metal door she hadn't even noticed.

"We saw the whole thing on surveillance," one yelled at her. "Stop right there, ma'am. Now."

"No, no." Jane put out her hands, smiling, blushing, embarrassed. What must that have looked like on surveillance? Her in the lobby, alone, compulsively checking her cell, black T-shirt and jeans. Waiting? Stalking? Approaching a little kid? She'd actually touched her! Offered her *candy*!

"No, no," she said again. "It's all a misunderstanding."

"I bet," the taller guard said. He conferred with the muscle-bound one by rolling his eyes.

"I'm Jane Ryland," she began. This was going to be funny. Someday. Not right now, when these guys thought she was a child molester. "I'm a reporter, from Channel . . ." Her voice trailed off. She wasn't anyone from anywhere now, and if this guy didn't recognize her from TV, which she hadn't been on for more than a year come to think of it, she sure didn't look like a TV reporter. What's more, she didn't have any press credentials. Nor was she actually covering a story.

She started to unzip her tote bag. She'd show them her driver's license, they'd call Robyn, and all would be well. These rent-a-brutes were only doing their jobs. There were bad people in the world, and they didn't always look bad on the outside. It would take one phone call to prove she wasn't one of them.

"Listen, listen," she said, trying to look innocent as well as make the explanation as simple as possible. "That little girl is my sister's fiancé's daughter. Her stepfather asked me to come and—"

"Ma'am? Keep your hands out of that bag, please." The guard took a step closer. The other one was behind her, sandwiching her between them. She smelled their bubble gum and acrid aftershave, the leather of their belts. The stupid Muzak was still tinkling along, the world's most inappropriate sound track. Every single face in the lobby openly gawked. "You'll have to come with me."

"No, I don't, I really don't, it's all fine." She felt her heart twist a little, a prickle of sweat across the back of her neck. This was solvable, but it wasn't going well. Not at all. And the harder she argued, the harder these guys dug in. "I don't, because this it just a big misunderstanding. If you'll listen, for one second, my sister's fiancé's ex-wife is—"

"Like you keep saying. But you can tell that to the cops, miss. They'll be here any second."

Jake saw Catherine Siskel's eyes dart to the surveillance monitor. She leaned toward it, moving her daughter aside, frowning. What was she looking at?

"What are all these cop cars?" Catherine narrowed her eyes, peering closer at the screen.

"Whoa," Tenley whispered. "Do we need to start the ta—"

"Hang on," Jake interrupted. His radio had crackled to life again.

"Jake?" Behind DeLuca's voice, behind the static, rose a flaring high-pitched wail. Sirens.

"Copy," Jake said. "D?"

Static.

As they watched, two BPD Crown Vics, blue wig-wag lights flashing through the sunshine, careened down Congress Street. They tore past the surveillance cameras and skidded to a halt in front of the University Inn. Weird to see all the action but not hear the sirens or the squeal of the tires. The cruisers pulled up to the sidewalk, bumping their front wheels over the curb. Doors opened. Uniforms leaped out. Doors slammed. Silent on the screen. But Jake knew what it sounded like.

"Jake? You hearing me over all this?" DeLuca's voice was almost trampled by the sirens, which were still wailing even though the cops had arrived on scene. "Situation here."

"I hear you," Jake said into the mic. He stashed his notebook in his back pocket. Looked at the monitor. "And see you, too. On the sidewalk. What you got?"

Jake watched his partner running toward the hotel.

"University Inn." Jake heard D's voice growing breathless, and the pounding of his footsteps over the radio. "Attempted child abduction, dispatch says."

Catherine Siskel gasped, her hand up to her mouth, and stepped closer to her daughter. Put an arm across her shoulders. Jake now saw four uniforms outside, also running toward the hotel. In two seconds, they were out of sight.

"*Mom,* do we need to—" Tenley began.

"Honey," Catherine whispered, "hush."

Jake could see DeLuca's shape moving closer to the inn.

"DeLuca, stop!" Jake ordered. The black Isuzu was still in place, no lights on that he could make out. What the hell were Hewlitt and that girl doing in there? If she was in there. "You stay on Hewlitt."

"But—" DeLuca had come to a halt, right at the corner of Congress and North. Jake was glad he couldn't see the look on his partner's face. Probably pissed. D loved a good takedown. Some creep trying to abduct a kid from a hotel lobby? All the city needed. But it sounded like they'd already nailed the bad guy. Nobody was dead. And the alleged abduction wasn't their primary case. This was.

"Negative. We can't lose Hewlitt." Jake heard a clatter of commotion behind him. He turned to see a row of bodies, Nancie Alvarez and her crew, hovering in the hall outside the office, eyeing the three of them through the glass door like they were performing animals. It *was* pretty much a circus, Jake had to admit. With him as the juggler.

"Come on in," Catherine Siskel called out, waving a hand. "Our visitor is about to leave."

The door opened and Alvarez came through with her team, owl-eyed and hesitant, trooping behind her.

"Jake." DeLuca's staticky voice cut through the rustle of desk chairs being wheeled into place and the metallic squeaks of the swivels as their occupants reclaimed their desks. Someone coughed. Another sneezed. A phone jangled. "What if our guys need help?"

Three-friggin'-ring circus, Jake thought. He had to extract the info on the Finnerty girl from Tenley. He had to make sure Hewlitt didn't slip away from them. But dammit, he wished he could head to that hotel lobby. If a child had been threatened by a stranger, and that stranger was in custody, Jake would like nothing better than to race down there and handle it. Take the asshole in for questioning. See if he was a sex offender. See if there was more to it than just some pervert scouting for tourist prey. *Disgusting.*

He checked the surveillance screen. D was still on the corner. The Isuzu was still in place. The only puzzle pieces he could reliably control were Catherine Siskel and her daughter.

"Do not move, D," Jake ordered. "I'm on the way down there. One minute. Less." Real police work was about real life, down on the street, not from an ivory tower view of the action. You could know what was going on only if you were in the midst of it, seeing it, hearing it. He'd been so mesmerized by his vantage point he'd forgotten about reality. Where he should be right now.

He saw Catherine Siskel still protecting her daughter, shielding her, one arm clamped over her shoulder. Tenley seemed absorbed by the activity on the street below. Or the black Isuzu, maybe. He pointed his radio at the Siskel women. "And you two. Don't—"

"I understand, Detective." Catherine Siskel sounded ever so slightly sarcastic as she looked him in the eye. "We won't leave town."

"Jake!" DeLuca's voice cut through the moment, his tension blasting unmistakably over the staticky radio. "Shots fired!"

47

"Do it, do it, do it!" the beefy security guard had ordered, grabbing Jane by one arm, essentially dragging her across the floor toward that unmarked metal door, her black flats scuffing when they hit the strip of ugly carpeting that ringed the marble center.

"Hey!" She'd tried again to get his attention, also attempting to untangle her feet. She looked longingly toward the front entrance to the hotel and its revolving door to freedom. "Sir? I don't think you can do this, you know? I'm Jane Ryland, ask anyone, they'll tell you. That girl is my—"

The more she protested, the more they demanded, the beefy guy showing off his muscles by clamping even harder on the top of her right arm. Jane's tote bag banged against her side, the leather strap twisting tighter around her shoulder.

No way. She sure as hell was *not* going to be shoved into some probably windowless office to face these two steroid-guzzling rent-a-guards. She'd done nothing wrong. She understood their concern, sure. She could even imagine how it must have looked on surveillance, with no context, but this was a mistake, a misunderstanding, a misinterpretation. Nothing civilized people couldn't work out in a civilized—*dammit.*

She stiffened her body, resisting. "You can't do this!"

"Watch me!" Beefy was even stronger than he looked. He pulled her arm behind her back, moving her, against her will, across the floor. During all her years of journalism experience, she'd been in tough situations before, even dangerous ones, but this was the most absurd. She couldn't even figure out what her rights were. She heard sirens outside, approaching. They had called the police? About *her*?

"Hey, that hurts!" And it did, it really did, but she had been so angry it almost didn't matter. Could they do this? Take a person into custody? They weren't even cops. She waved her free arm, tried to, at least. "I'm *Jane Ryland*. Ask the desk guy. Ask the manager. Ask anyone."

"Ask me if I care," Beefy said.

She was a few steps away from the front exit, but also a few steps away from captivity. Three steps from that unmarked door. Must be the security office, their private lair. Where they probably tortured people. No windows, no phone. Jerks. Yeah, they were doing their job, but they were doing it *ridiculously*. She wished she could get at the Quik-Shot in her tote bag. She should be taping this. She was either outraged or terrified, and either way, there should be a record of it. This was unfair. Absurd.

"Sir? Sir?" She kept trying to talk, get through to these thugs, but it didn't matter. They were on a mission and she was it. In two seconds they'd be in that back room, and not a person in the lobby was moving to help her. Some jerk had actually *applauded*. Well, yeah, she was the child molester, after all. She'd only been trying to—

"Hey!" She'd tried to twist herself out of this guy's grip. "Hey! I want to make a phone call!"

"Police! Freeze!"

Four Boston cops, uniforms, but guys she didn't recognize, powered though the revolving front door, heading across the expanse of lobby, almost past the fountain and onto the carpeting. Coming right toward her.

Her captors stopped. They backed her against the white stucco wall beside that unmarked door. "Over here!" Beefy yelled. He yanked her, hard, keeping her in place.

"Under control!" The other guard called out. "Got her!"

Got her? Fine. You know what? Bring 'em on, Jane thought. The police might even help her. At least they'd be sane, unlike *these* creeps. The police would know her. If they didn't, she could drop Jake's name. Which would be unfortunate, but holy *crap*. She squirmed, flexed her shoulder, trying to loosen this moron's grip. This was ridiculous. *Ridiculous.*

The first blue uniform got halfway across the room. At least it would be over soon. How had she ever gotten drawn into this?

Then she heard the shot. One. Then another.

Gunshots? Definitely. *Shots.* She ducked, instinctively, even pulled herself closer to the hulking security guard. Who was shooting? At who? The hotel lobby exploded into a chaos of screaming.

"Gunshots!"

"Run!" someone yelled.

And now every scream was contagious, each setting off a cacophony of others, as fear and terror filled the room, echoes clattered off the double-tall windows, amplified and intensified. Four police officers, as one, drew their weapons, held them at their sides, racing toward the sounds of the shots.

Over past the elevator? Jane felt her heart pounding, felt her fear stealing her breath. Gunshots. *From where?* Upstairs? It was hard to tell. *Where was Gracie?*

The guards exchanged looks, then Beefy dropped her arm, swearing, leaving her, and ran toward the cops, his colleague speeding after him. Jane sank to her knees, sliding her back down the nubby wall, trying to figure out what to do. If someone was shooting—which they were, or had been, there didn't seem to be any more shots but who knew what was about to happen—the security guards' unmarked office might be exactly the right place to be. On the other hand, any way she turned, any way she ran, might be exactly the wrong way.

Or—hell no.

She dug into the tote bag, got out the Quik-Shot, flipped up the screen, hit Video, pushed the green button. She was getting this on camera.

Focus, focus, focus, she told herself. She tried to concentrate, on breathing, on thinking, on slowing her galloping heart. Crouching behind the row of fake palm trees, she rolled video, forcing her hands to keep steady.

Protected, she hoped, by serpented plastic trunks and plumes of spiky leaves.

Jane had covered enough stories about snipers, shooters, crazies with guns. But all had been aftermath, reaction. She'd read about them, too. Why didn't she remember what you were supposed to do if you were actually *in* an attack? Run? And maybe get caught in the line of fire? Or hide? And maybe get caught in the line of fire?

But she was a reporter. *That* role she understood. If she'd been assigned to this story—*shots fired at the University Inn!*— racing here in a news car, leaping out with her photographer, she'd do anything to get this vantage point. Now she had it. She checked the red Record light. Yes. Still rolling.

She trained the lens on the cops who'd stampeded toward the sound of the gunfire, which seemed to be—upstairs? Not on the lobby level, she was pretty sure. The camera captured the last glimpse of their uniformed backs as they crashed through a metal fire door, setting off a relentless clamor of clanging alarms.

As the fire door banged shut, Jane panned the Quik-Shot in time to record the concierge huddling underneath his ornate wooden desk. The registration clerk had ducked behind her counter, the top of her curly dark hair still showing. Tourists, a few yelling, one scooping up a wailing toddler, had abandoned their shopping bags and headed for the sheltering wood-and-metal barricade of the broad front desk. No Gracie. No Lewis.

The whirl of the revolving door came from behind her. She kept low behind the row of plants, cowering, wondering how much of her was visible. Maybe she should have run the heck out of here while she had the chance. Now she was trapped by her own decision.

What if more bad guys were on the way in? Would they see her? They would. And where was Gracie? Where was Lewis? What if—*No. Don't create an imaginary problem. Reality is bad enough.*

She held her breath, gritted her teeth, and tried to shoot through the spiky green fronds. Tried to be small. Tried to be invisible. She couldn't turn to look to see who was coming in or she'd be instantly in view.

"Freeze!" An angry voice, commanding, came from behind her. "Come out from behind that thing!"

She turned, hidden behind the pot, back against the wall, still looking through the camera lens.

A gun was pointing straight at her.

And then she saw the gun leave her viewfinder, as the voice slowly pointed the weapon to the floor. "What the hell are you doing here?"

She lowered her camera and looked up.

"Jake," she said.

"Jane?"

What the hell was she doing here? She seemed to be okay enough—rattled, he could tell by the way she was blinking so fast, the way her eyes, wide, clung to his, the way her hand clenched and unclenched. Jane in the middle of some kind of shootout—*shit*. Had she been sent to cover a story? Had she gotten caught in the middle of the child molester case? Had she seen the guy? How had she gotten past the police? How'd she get here—with a camera?—faster than he did?

"You okay?" He tried, almost failing, to keep his voice calm, while scanning the lobby at the same time. "What the hell—did you hear the shots?"

"I'm okay. Yeah, I heard two and—"

"Hang on. *Stay down.*"

He scouted ahead of him, scoping out the situation, taking one assessing step at a time, his mind speeding ahead. At least four cops had been dispatched upstairs. No police presence here in the lobby except for him. Backup was on the way. When he'd run inside the hotel, he saw some people sprinting, yelling, piling into the revolving front door, almost clogging the spin in their panic to get out. So, theoretically, those people were safe. A team was tasked to monitor the perimeter, make sure no one was in danger out there.

But inside. The shots had been fired inside. A guy in a suit huddled under a big desk. Heads, the tops of them, visible behind the registration counter. People were inside, bystanders, and each one of them would be terrified.

"It's okay, I'm police," he called out as he scanned the lobby. Front desk, couch, chairs, palm trees, fountain. Glass-fronted gift shop, empty? Elevators, closed. "Please stay where you are. Stay calm."

Abandoned shopping bags littered the lobby floor, a ladder-back chair had toppled on its side, one little white shoe lay by the fountain.

Who was the shooter? Where was he now? Why? Was he connected to the child molester thing? Was there a child involved? Had they caught that creep? Was the child safe?

There was no traffic on his radio. Why?

"We've got this under control," Jake called out, attempting to reassure the heads behind the registration desk. "We'll have you out of here very soon."

He hoped that was true.

Where were the cops they'd sent in? The damn Muzak seemed incongruous, the sappy synthomusic underscoring an unfolding crime drama. It had been only five minutes, maybe six, since he'd gotten the shots-fired call, raced down the City Hall stairs, across the street, and over to the hotel. DeLuca, on the corner, had given him the finger as he ran by. The black Isuzu, he saw, had not budged.

He finished his sweep of the room. Nothing. Jane was still behind that plant. And she was a witness.

"Jane? What happened? Did you see anything? Anyone?" Jake kept an eye on the room as he questioned her again, his voice low. Weapon at the ready. The lobby, with its bubbling fountain and chandeliers and palm trees, looked like the setting for a giant game of hide-and-seek. With everyone still hiding.

"Why were you here?" he said.

"I was—they were—" Jane, whispering, had edged to her feet, one hand on that big pot, and started to come toward him. Was she holding a camera?

"Gracie and Lewis are supposed to be here, and—"

"Get *down,*" he ordered.

She did. Safer for her to hide behind the plants than risk getting out. The others, too. Best if everyone stayed hidden. He hoped. The cops were here, though, so the shooter would be found. He hoped. Their training had instructed them to play it by ear. Each situation is different. Secure the scene. Protect the victims. Get the bad guy. Christ, what if he'd run out the back?

"Just stay there, Jane, for crap sake, until I tell you it's okay. So Gracie and Lewis? Where are they?" He scanned the room again. Still nothing on the radios. What the hell was everyone doing? "Where'd the shots come from?"

48

Tenley could barely keep up with her mother as she strode down the corridor of City Hall. Her mom could walk really fast, even in those heels. Tenley knew the look on her face, even though she was three steps behind her. Mom was pissed. Why? Something about Brileen, she guessed. But what? How'd she even know her?

"Come with me, right now, Tenley," her mother had ordered. She had steered her out of the surveillance room, all fakey-pleasant, Tenley could tell, fluttering a fakey-nice good-bye wave to those now returned to their desks. But once they'd gotten out into the corridor, the two of them alone, Mom had freaked.

Mom had yanked open the stairway door, almost slung Tenley through. "I've got to check the security desk. If there's something going on across the street . . . But then we're going to my office. *Then* you are going to tell me—how exactly did you meet Brileen Finnerty? And exactly what is your relationship with her?"

The door slammed behind them, their footsteps clattering down the metal stairway.

Tenley couldn't keep up, not with her mother's pace, not with her mother's questions. She didn't understand *anything*.

Mom opened the door to the lobby, strode toward the security guy, then stopped.

"Stay right there, Tenley." Her mother pointed to a tan square on the checkerboard tiles of the hallway floor. "Away from the windows. Do not move. I have to make a call."

Mom had picked up the security guy's desk phone and was pounding the numbers on the keypad. How did Mom know about Brileen? She'd tried to ask on the way down, like about a million times, but her mother had never let her get a word in. Did Brileen have something to do with her father? Or the black car?

Wait a minute. Tenley stared at the tan square on the floor, thinking. The cop upstairs hadn't said anything about her father being killed in Curley Park. He'd asked to see just the same place, *exactly* the same place, but without mentioning Dad.

She did not understand the world. Not at all. She fiddled with the hem of her T-shirt, stretching it out, letting it snap into place. Her mom was still on the phone, hunched over the desk. Ignoring her.

Tenley took one little step off her square. Then another. A long padded bench lined the wall across from her. It was vacant now, but Hall employees often sat there waiting for rides, or sipping the last of their take-out coffees before reporting for work. Someone had left the want ads from the morning paper, sections carelessly refolded, askew on one end. Another step. Another.

And there was the exit. Tenley touched her fingers to the metal handle of the glass door, testing, as if it might be alarmed. Outside was a little alleyway, the covered turn-around the mayor and other big shots used to get into City Hall without getting rained or snowed on. Past that was a strip of decorative cobblestones, then the sidewalk.

And then the street, she thought. *Freedom.*

Where she'd go, she wasn't quite sure. But if she stayed, wasn't she in big trouble? Somehow? Her mother was sure acting like it.

All she had to do was run.

* * *

"Get away from that door!" Catherine Siskel felt like yanking her daughter's fingers from the curved silver handle. "I told you not to move, Tenner. For good reason. If there's danger out there, we need to stay inside."

Tenley looked at her, those dark eyes questioning, her T-shirt all pulled out of shape, just like their lives were. Four flights of stairs had allowed Catherine to mentally regroup. She tried to tamp down her resentment. She wasn't any less angry, or any less hurt, or any less in mourning. But she didn't have to take it out on poor Tenley.

She and Greg had tried to protect their younger daughter from sorrow and grief and loss. Ten long months of bereavement and disbelief. The three of them. Until Greg went off the reservation. Now he was gone. The sorrow welled up in her, so powerfully she almost couldn't see. What if Tenley was in danger, too?

"I'm sorry, honey, I know I sounded angry." Putting her arm across her daughter's shoulders, Catherine felt the girl's muscles freeze, rigid and unyielding. Well, she'd be mad, too, or sad, or confused, or all of the above. "But I'm not angry with *you*."

Silence from Tenley.

"Let's go to my office." Catherine had been so angry when she'd heard the name Brileen, her brain had white-flashed into overdrive. Now they had to deal with it. "We need to talk. In private."

But Tenley had scooted even farther away on the bench. Scowling, she drew her knees to her chest, yanked her skirt over her legs, and wrapped her arms around them. A brick wall.

"We can talk *here*. Who were you calling?" Tenley demanded. "Why were you so mad about Brileen?"

There it was.

The question Catherine tried to avoid, hoped to avoid, hoped never to face anywhere but in her own remorseful memories. Now she'd never be able to sort it out with Greg, either. He'd denied everything, but she hadn't believed him. Why should she? She'd seen too much evidence of his lying. She had always thought, she realized now, she had always thought there would be more time for the truth. And then there wasn't.

"Shhh, honey. I had to check with the guard, then call the mayor about the situation across the street, let him know where I am. And Ward Dahlstrom. I told him you were with me." She stopped as she saw the look on her daughter's face. "I know, he's not the most—anyway. Then this happened." She waved a hand, toward upstairs and outside, encompassing the entire morning. "The mayor says he's been told it's almost all clear, trouble's over. Nothing to fear. But there's a lot of other stuff going on. City Hall stuff."

"Whatever," Tenley said. "Ward Dahlstrom is an asshole."

"Tenley! Language." It was hard not to smile. She had to agree. It was Dahlstrom who'd kept her out of the surveillance video loop. Dahlstrom who had helped put her in the impossible position of having to lie to the police to protect the mayor. So, indeed yes. Dahlstrom was an asshole.

"Be that as it may," Catherine said.

"What about Brileen?" Tenley said.

"Brileen." Catherine looked at her daughter's narrowed eyes, saw the yearning behind them, and the sorrow, and the disappointment. Saw a future ahead of them that no one could have predicted or planned. Lives that had once seemed so promising, so exciting, even *important*. Lives now devolved into sadness and lies and cover-ups and death. Here they were. Mother and daughter, face-to-face on a little bench in the lobby of Boston City Hall.

What they didn't teach at the Kennedy School was how to spin this one:

Telling your teenage daughter about her father's affair.

49

"I heard two shots," Jane told him from behind her barricade of plants. "They sounded muffled, like they came from upstairs."

"Anything else?" Jake checked the bank of elevators. Four doors, all closed. Their call buttons lighted. Floor indicators now all on lobby.

Six minutes since he arrived. Why wasn't he getting radio transmissions? Jake had clicked to the incident frequency, blocking out all traffic except about what unfolded here at the hotel. Unless they'd totally lost the shooter, *impossible,* something was going down. And where the hell was his backup? A squad was supposedly en route to wrangle the people stranded in the lobby.

Christ, they all were probably taking cell phone videos and snapping photos from their hiding places. *OMG, I'm a hostage.* He could just see it on frigging Twitter. Or *TMZ.*

He watched Jane close her eyes for an instant, thinking, then open them.

"Yeah. The shots came from the rear of the building. The cops all ran that way, through the fire door." She pointed, starting to stand up. "That's why those alarms were clanging. There hasn't been anything since."

"Stay down," he told her.

He wanted to get her out of here. But he had to get himself upstairs, too, wherever the team was. As soon as his backup arrived.

"Jake." A voice behind him. He turned. DeLuca?

"I told you to stay on Hewlitt, D," Jake said. "Why the hell are you—?"

"Supe's orders." DeLuca put up a palm, cutting him off. "It's a code one. Hotel security reported attempted child abduction, then shots fired. You kidding me? The supe's going nuts, City Hall's going nuts. The freaking child molester's on the loose. Apparently the hotel security morons let her go when—"

"Her?" Jake said.

Oh, no. *All* she needed. How to explain that she was—or wasn't—the child molester? *There's* a conversation she'd never imagined having with Jake. Jane, still hunkering behind the stupid plants, puffed out a breath.

"Jake?" she said, standing up a little. "There's no child molester. That's what I was trying to tell them."

"Huh?" Jake said. He and D exchanged looks.

"What's she doing here?" DeLuca said.

"I was here to get—nothing. Nothing, never mind." Somehow she'd hoped that whole child molester thing would go away. She should have bolted when she had the chance, although she'd told Tall and Beefy her name—*several times, brilliant*—so they could easily track her down if they decided to. Now, though, that was hardly the point. There was a guy with a gun somewhere. *What if it was Lewis? Where was he? And where was Gracie?*

"All units." The voice came over Jake's radio. "All units. Do you read?"

Jane had heard enough radio calls from cops trying not to sound afraid. They never succeeded. But this was good news, she predicted. If this were a continuing risk, something disastrous, someone dead, a shooter on the loose, their voices would be different. Whatever had happened, it was over.

Maybe no one was even hurt. She'd see Gracie soon. Lewis, too. All would be explained. All would be safe.

"Brogan, I copy," Jake replied.

Jane checked her camera, still on standby, battery fine. Would it be kosher to roll on Jake? Tape him getting this radio call? It felt wrong, but . . . Was she a reporter, or a victim? A reporter, or the police officer's girlfriend?

Why did all of reality have to be recorded? Life never just happened anymore. Memories had to be indelible, every event captured. And shared. And used.

"Brogan, I copy," Jake said again. And to D, "Switch to incident channel."

"Shooter apprehended, repeat, all clear, shooter apprehended," the radio voice began again, calm, solemn, reporting. Unafraid. An alarm, beeps, then an unintelligible voice blared in the background of the transmission, but the sound of that "all clear" filled the lobby.

"One person in custody," the radio voice continued. "Floor three. One victim, calling for transport. Third floor. It appears to be a—stand by, all units."

Appears to be a what? Jane wondered. She stood, pulling herself up with one hand clamped on the huge clay pot as the transmission paused, her thighs creaking, trying to get her balance. She aimed her camera at the registration desk, where heads began to emerge, now a row of hairlines and wide eyes peering over the counter.

She watched DeLuca take one wary step closer to the center of the lobby, then another, then another, his eyes darting to every corner. Maybe not convinced the danger had passed. The sun glinted off the facets of the cut-crystal chandelier, shafts of afternoon light spackling him with patches of shadow. So unnerving, Jane thought, that the fountain still burbled. The elevator doors closed and opened and closed again.

Jane leaned against the wall, letting it support her. Waiting. *Lewis. Gracie.* And nothing she could do.

"Stay down until we give a final all clear, please, people," DeLuca called out. He held up his radio like a baton, his DeLuca-esque sport coat—tweedy, sprung, and seasonless no matter how Kat McMahon tried to make him over—lifting to reveal the weapon still holstered in black leather on his belt. "We will inform you when—"

"All units, all units." The voice came over both radios now, interrupting.

DeLuca and Jake both peered at the black plastic rectangles in their hands, as if they could see who was talking. "We have one victim, stabilizing, floor three, transport is en route. Appears to be a domestic. All units stand by, please."

"Victim? Domestic?" Jane felt the frown returning, stepped away from the wall. *Lewis. Gracie.* "Jake, what do they mean by—" She stopped. There was no other meaning for victim. Or domestic.

Jake put up a hand, stopping her, shaking his head, radio static from the open channel buzzing a fuzzy undercurrent. "You know as much as I do, obviously."

She understood the bitterness in his voice. It wasn't only exhaustion. He still hadn't changed clothes, or shaved, or even combed his hair, she realized, since she saw him at City Hall this morning—how long ago? Almost six hours? No, he hadn't changed since last night at the restaurant. So he was running on empty. Still, she knew he'd want to be up on the third floor in the thick of whatever incident the officers had just conquered, rather than standing in the lobby. She was happy, though she'd never tell him so, that he was down here. Safe, and with her.

"All units? We have a BOLO for a missing girl," the radio announced.

"Shit," Jake hissed. Then into the radio, "This is Brogan. What girl?"

"Jake?" She felt her eyes widen, a shiver of apprehension crawling up her bare arms. She could always imagine the worst possible outcome. Ironically, a personality flaw that made her successful at her job. She knew the worst didn't always happen. She also she knew sometimes it did.

"Jake?" The cop's radio voice had lost its professional timbre.

"Copy," Jake said. He rolled his eyes at her, impatient. "Be on the lookout for *what* girl?"

Jane leaned toward him, aching to hear the answer, wishing away the wrong one.

"Age nine, Caucasian, light hair, curly, yellow dress," the voice said.

That alarm still blared in the background. "We're pretty sure she can't have left the hotel. Gracie Wilhoite. That's spelled—"

But Jane didn't hear the rest of it. "Gracie," she whispered. "Where are you?"

"What's your location?" Jake spoke into the radio. He was trying to keep his eyes on Jane and DeLuca and the people behind the counter and orchestrate a search for a missing little girl all at the same time.

"Floor three," the radio answered.

Gracie Wilhoite. Missing? Or hiding? Kidnapped? The word crossed his mind: *abducted*? Exactly what Jane had been afraid of.

Lewis Wilhoite's preposterous scheme to hand Gracie to Jane. No wonder she looked upset. This is where she must have been told to pick the girl up. *What the hell happened before he got to the hotel?*

Jane had tried to tell him, he remembered. But there had been the more imminently critical matter of the guy with the gun. Was it Lewis? "Who says the girl is missing?" Jake continued on the radio. "You got ID on the shooter? The victim?"

"Confirming ID. Stand by, please." The radio went silent.

"Jake."

Jane had come closer, hovering behind him. She was out of danger, he guessed, and now he could listen to her. And get her to turn off that damn camera.

"They said domestic," Jane said. "That means it has to be either . . ."

"Hang on, Jane," he said. "I hear you."

"Just to make sure, I'm gonna call—" she began. Then stopped.

He saw her grab her tote bag from the floor, paw through it. Looking for her phone? Nothing he could do would prevent her from calling her family. By the time Melissa and what's her name—Robyn—arrived, he bet they'd have found Gracie. How far could a nine-year-old go? Unless someone had taken her. Lewis?

Shit. Maybe Jane was calling the TV station? Even if it was her job, he didn't see why she always had to do it.

"D!" he called out across the lobby. Jake hated this. At least the bad guy was in custody, that was a done deal. Upstairs had indicated the person was not dead. Had the victim reported the missing girl? Was it even connected? He could already hear the wail of the ambulance, on the way to take the victim to MGH.

MGH, where maybe-tattooed guy might have awakened, where his Curley Park case might hang in the balance. Add Kiyoko Naka, still waiting for him to return her call about the ID of Bobby Land.

Gracie Wilhoite was the priority now. He gestured at D with his radio. "Get up there. Get the scoop. Get a team to fan out, look for the girl. She might be with her father, Lewis Wilhoite. He's a white male—"

Jake looked at Jane, questioning.

"Ah, yeah, white male, forty-something." She closed her eyes, as if reciting from a photo. "Brown hair, curly, wire-rimmed glasses, clean-shaven, five ten."

"On it. Back to you ASAP." DeLuca sprinted across the lobby, yanked open the fire doors to head upstairs. The alarms clanged again.

The ambulance sirens grew louder. Maybe the victim would be able to tell them exactly what had happened. Case closed.

Domestic. Shooter. Victim.

"Jane?" A picture of the drama unfolded in Jake's imagination. What might have happened. What must have happened. "Are you calling—"

"Jake?" Jane interrupted, her face full of fear and confusion. She clutched her cell phone. "I told Melissa the situation. And she says Robyn isn't home. She's gone. Do you think—"

"Did Robyn know you're supposed to meet Lewis here?"

"Of course! She's the one who told me to come! She's the one who talked to Lewis. Maybe she couldn't stand it. Maybe she couldn't stay away. Maybe they're *both* here. And if they are—where are they?"

He and Jane stood, shoulders touching, both of them silent for a fraction of a second, alone with their thoughts and the anticipation of what had to come next. Jake could never hear the word "domestic" without fearing the worst. But "the worst" was so often true. The chaos and selfishness that embattled every family on some level, the manipulation and misunderstanding that in too many cases expanded and invaded and destroyed. Parents blinded by their own power struggles. Children trapped in the middle, conflicted and confused, motivated only by love. Or fear.

"This is Brogan," Jake said into the radio. "DeLuca's headed to you. Is the shooter named Wilhoite? Is the victim?"

"Stand by," the voice said.

50

Tenley could not believe what her mother was saying. It was . . . insane. That's what it was, insane. She felt like her brain had been put in a waffle iron, smashed into little squares, toasted and burned, never to be the same.

"Dad? And Brileen?" Tenley could barely look at her mother as the words contaminated her mouth. She turned away, stared through City Hall's thick glass doors onto Congress Street, where Brileen Finnerty had been standing by that black car.

"Did you ever meet her?" Tenley asked.

"Certainly not," Mom answered. "Why would I meet her?"

Brileen? Who'd run into Tenley on the street, like, by chance? And talked to her over coffee at the Purple and invited her to her apartment, and—no. No way.

Plus, how could she talk to her own mother about a thing like that? It verged on gross. But Mom looked so unhappy, hair all scraggly, trying to whisper so the guard guy wouldn't hear.

Tenley put her hands over her face, listening through her fingers as her mother related the story of Dad and Brileen. The voice mail message her mom overheard. The e-mail she *happened* to see. The evasions and denials from her dad and from Lanna.

"*Lanna* knew Brileen?"

"Oh, yes, Brileen befriended Lanna," her mother said. "To get to your father, I expect. She didn't tell you that, I gather. I'm not surprised. And now she's latched on to you. I wonder how she'll feel when she discovers your father is—"

Mom put both hands to her chest, as if the memory had punched her. Dropped her head. Tenley saw her shoulders rise, then fall. This was scary.

"Mom?" What if her mom died, too, had a heart attack or something from stress and all that? She felt like a little kid again, all fear, not knowing what to do with her feet. "Are you okay?"

"I'm okay, honey." Her mother lifted her head, was trying to smile. Mom kept calling her honey, like when she was little. Somehow that made Tenley even sadder. Tenley closed her eyes, covered them with her hands, wishing she could disappear behind that darkness and never face anything again.

Brileen was, like, Lanna's age, right? Okay, a *little* older. No way would her father ever be involved in that. And Brileen never indicated, not in any way, that she'd known Lanna. Or Dad. So what was that whole conversation at the Purple? Tenley tried to replay it in her mind, through the filter of what she now knew was true. Or what her mother *thought* was true. Tenley opened her eyes, remembering. What had Brileen said to her? About *what happened to Lanna*?

Tenley opened her mouth, then stopped as the glass door opened. A couple of middle-aged women, old-lady pants, hideous shoes, and carrying extra-large Dunkin' iced coffees, hurried into the lobby.

"They can't yell at us about being late if the cops wouldn't let us leave," one complained. She slurped on her straw, then rattled the ice in her plastic glass. Displayed her City Hall ID to the security guy.

"Exactly." The other showed her laminated card, then they both fussed with their wallets, putting them away. "We're supposed to help it if there's some maniac on the loose?"

Her mom stood, brushed her skirt. "Excuse me, I'm Catherine Siskel? Mayor's office?"

The two women looked at her, up and down. Like she was going to get them in trouble.

"You said 'on the loose'?" Mom asked. "Police told us—"

One of the women gestured with her sweating plastic cup, dismissive. "Not a *maniac,* really, I guess. Or on the loose, I guess. It's all over now, anyway. The cops let us all leave Dunkin'. Now we're late for work."

"I'm sure your boss will understand." Mom was using her business voice. "Glad you're okay."

"Mom?" Now her mom was madly checking her cell phone. Tenley stood, peering out the glass door again. The black car—was it there? She tried to picture where it had parked, but with the trees and cars, the whole perspective was different from down here. She pushed open the door, leaning out. The sun's sudden glare blinded her for a second. She shielded her eyes with one hand, propping the door open with her hip. Nope. Couldn't see.

Tenley had about two seconds to decide what to do. Was Brileen still out there? Tenley stepped back inside and took out her own cell phone, searching for the number she'd entered. Was it only yesterday? And there it was.

"Mom?" Tenley knew this was it. She felt like she was risking, maybe, her relationship with her mom. She was about to admit where she'd been last night and what she knew. Thing was, if she told, she'd be in trouble. If Tenley kept her secret, her mom wouldn't be mad at her. If she kept quiet, would it all go away?

She pressed her lips together, deciding. Yeah. Maybe it would all go away.

The phone on the guard's desk rang, a clanging buzz. The glass door opened again, so fast Tenley had to jump back to avoid getting slammed by it. People were returning to City Hall again, all briefcases and chatter.

Tenley backed into the corner, feeling the cool marble walls bracketing her shoulders. Was there any way to avoid all this, all the pressure and the fear and the secrets?

Her mom was off the phone. Now or never.

"Tenner?" Her mom took a step closer, reaching out a hand. "What are you doing, honey?"

Her mother was so sad, her face all drawn and tired. She believed so deeply that Dad had betrayed her with Brileen. But gosh, didn't Tenley know enough, from how Brileen treated the guys at the Purple Martin, and how she treated her "roommate" Valerie, didn't Tenley know enough to be sure all that business about her father was—unlikely?

Maybe, finally, finally, finally, she could do something to ease her mother's mind.

"Mom?" she said, "I think you're wrong about Brileen."

"Wrong?" Her mother's eyebrows lifted.

"Yeah." Tenley was sure of this now. It was good and right. Lanna would be proud. Her dad, too. She held up her cell phone. "And I'm going to call her. So you two can talk. Face-to-face."

51

Was there anything she could have done? Should have done? Jane ducked behind the palms again, trying to look invisible, as a swarm of blue-uniformed police banged through the hotel's front doors. Jane thought about that stop for gas and the turkey sandwich. How long it took. Thought about the Twizzlers for Gracie, now burning a hole in her tote bag. Thought about Robyn, who was not, Melissa reported, at home. Robyn, who could easily have gotten to the hotel before Jane did.

The arriving cops ran to Jake, and within seconds, in a clatter of footsteps and bristling radios, they'd trooped into the hotel, reassuring the still-nervous tourists and employees. A line of lobby refugees, some smiling, a few in tears, little kids gawking and clutching their parents' hands, were escorted out to North Street, cops ahead and behind, shepherding. Lewis was not among them.

Through the expanse of the hotel's front windows, Jane saw three news vans, lined up with their numbered logos on the side and precariously balanced satellite-dish uplinks on top. Her colleagues—former colleagues—would be clamoring for info. And here she was, inside. Exclusive. With exclusive video. Pretty soon they'd find out she was in here. Should she call Marsh Tyson?

Was she a reporter? Or a family member? How did she balance the two?

Now two cops were pointing her out to Jake, frowning. She smiled, *nothing to see here.*

"She's fine," Jake told them, waving away their question. "Press."

Which she was and wasn't, but at least the cops ignored her as they listened to Jake's terse orders. Jane stood, no longer needing invisibility. She wasn't the problem. Gracie was. Where was Gracie?

When Jane had approached her, the poor girl, obviously terrified, had called out, "Daddy!" That meant Lewis was here, and she wasn't running away from him. So if Gracie hadn't been waiting for Jane—which she clearly had not been—why had she been in the lobby?

Now four black-uniformed EMTs hustled through the door, then careened around the turn to the elevators, heads down, pushing a clanking metal stretcher. The concierge unfolded himself from beneath his desk and trotted to Jake, his gold-buttoned blazer rumpled and dust streaked, his hair askew.

"What can I do?" He raked his hand through his hair, making it worse, and surveyed his almost deserted lobby. The clanging fire alarm stopped. "You sure upstairs is safe? I can let the guests know? We'd broadcast a message to the guest room floors saying—"

"It's safe," Jake said. "But we're looking for a missing little girl. How many exits in the building?"

"Ah, four," the concierge said. He eyed Jane, concerned. "Hey. This woman's the one who—"

Uh-oh. He'd seen what happened with Gracie. And the guards.

"She's fine," Jake said, cutting him off. "Exits?"

Jake, still glued to his now-constantly sputtering radio, assigned a lobby cop to each exit as the concierge explained. The main entrance went to North Street, the back door down a narrow alley past Dunkin' and a hair salon. The kitchen and side doors opened to the same alley, and all exit routes eventually led to North Street.

"But unless she went out the front," the concierge said, "we'd know."

"How?" Jake said.

"How?" Jane said.

The concierge glared at her, then spoke to Jake. "The back and side doors have special alarms. Not like the fire doors. I'd recognize them. Didn't hear them."

"Good," Jake said. "Thanks. You got an office? Stay there. Got it? Your employees, too. Out of the lobby. Out of the way. You can tell your guests the threat is now over, sir. But please ask them to stay in their rooms for now."

"Gracie didn't go out the front," Jane said as the concierge left. "I'd have seen that."

She had to be here somewhere. Hidden in the hotel.

Gracie had dashed toward the elevators, away from the entrance, Jane remembered. A second later, Jane was corralled by Beefy and friend. Had Gracie gotten on the elevator? Had she gone upstairs?

Gracie. Robyn. Lewis. Shooter. *Domestic.*

Jane could picture, all too well, one chilling possibility of how those words all came together.

What if, when Robyn arrived, maybe demanding Gracie back, Lewis had sent the girl to the lobby so she wouldn't be involved? But then, terrified by Jane, she'd called out for *Daddy* and run back to the safety of her stepfather. Who at that very moment was shooting her mother, who'd come here only to protect her daughter.

What if Lewis had *lured* Robyn to the hotel? Told her not to tell Jane? Would anyone actually do such a thing?

What if Gracie had seen her stepfather shoot her mother?

"Jake," she said. She felt tears well with the rightness of her idea.

"Hang on, Jane," he said. He clicked his radio. "D? What's your status? You got ID on the victim? The shooter?"

"Victim alive, awaiting transport," D's voice came back. "Shooter in custody, cuffed, in the supply room. Headed there now."

"Gracie? Do they have Gracie?" Jane couldn't help it. If something didn't happen soon she would start looking for the girl herself. She was the only one in the building—besides Lewis—who knew exactly what the child looked like. And Gracie wouldn't be afraid of her because—well wait.

Yeah, she would. So maybe Jane wasn't the best person to search. Melissa and Daniel were on the way, though. Maybe if *they* called out to her?

"The girl?" Jake asked.

"Stand by one," DeLuca said.

Jane fiddled with the shiny fake leaves of the palm tree, feeling helpless. Powerless. All her fancy equipment, camera and phone and Internet, all worthless. Was there anything she could do to help find Gracie?

"Jake." Jane touched his arm. She had to interrupt. Of course there was something she could do. "The security guards."

Jake frowned. "What about them?"

"They're upstairs, they followed the cops. But listen, they've got monitors, security monitors. That's how they saw me and—anyway." Jane pointed at the metal door. "The hotel's surveillance equipment is in there. Maybe we could rewind the video. We'd see Gracie, I bet, where she went, or who took her. I mean, if the guards saw *me*—"

"Jake!" DeLuca's voice, tense, on the radio. "Get up here. Floor three. *Now*. We're sending the elevator."

"What?" Jane couldn't stand it. "What is it?"

"I'll tell you the instant I can. I've got to go." He turned, headed across the lobby.

She grabbed his arm, stopping him. "I'm coming with you."

He pivoted. Jabbed a finger at her. "Hell, no. Forget that. You're staying here, Jane. You're not coming upstairs. You go outside, you cannot come back. You move from that plant, you're under arrest. Call me on my cell when you hear from anyone."

"Jake!" She felt like crying, in frustration and fear and bone-chilling dread. She couldn't let go of his arm, clutched it like it might give her strength, or knowledge, or reassurance. "Jake. You don't think someone shot Gracie. Do you? Where *is* she?"

"They're looking, Jane."

"I know."

"We'll find her."

"I know." She hoped, with all her soul and being, he was right. She would never look at a news story the same way again. *Let Gracie be okay.*

Jane watched Jake's back as he dashed across the lobby, watched the elevator doors open and close, taking him away.

She waited two seconds. Three.

Then she headed for the unmarked metal door.

The blaring alarm was the first thing Jake heard, a piercing insistent robovoiced repetition of instructions—*the danger is over, please stay in your room until given the all clear*—followed by earsplitting beeps and a rasping buzz. That's what must have kept interrupting the incident team's transmissions. Before the elevator even shut behind him, he ran past numbered doors, all closed as instructed, toward the open one at the end of the narrow corridor. A triangle of light played on the ugly gray hall carpeting, its apex pointing to whatever was inside.

"D, I'm here." Jake keyed the radio as he ran.

"Room three fifty-four," D's voice came back. "Last door on the right. It's open."

By that time, Jake was there. He stood in the wedge of light, cataloging the scene. Framed photos of Boston statues hung on the walls. Sun pouring through one wide window slashed light and shadow on the furniture. Red-streaked sheets and a flowered spread lay tangled across the unmade oversize bed. Red-streaked once-white towels were piled on the once-gray wall-to-wall. Three toppled water glasses had landed on the floor. Water dripped from a quart-size bottle tipped precariously on the edge of a desk.

Classic struggle, textbook. Who won and who lost?

The loser was clearly on the metal gurney parked awkwardly in the only possible area of the room, a two-yard space between the bed and the mirror-covered wall. A crush of EMTs surrounded it, heads down. One protected the IV drip bag hanging from a thin metal pole, while another leaned close to the patient's face, monitoring the transparent plastic oxygen bag attached to a bright green metal canister next to the motionless body. All the action, mirrored, reflected into twice the disaster.

Two uniformed cops, weapons holstered, stood sentry inside the hotel room door. DeLuca was not in the room. "DeLuca?" Jake keyed his radio again.

"Stand by," D's voice came back.

"Where's D?" Jake asked. "Do we have identification on this victim?"

Taking two steps toward the stretcher, he recognized the graying ponytail of Deb Kratky. Yesterday the veteran EMT had handled the Curley Park victims. Now this. But she was blocking his view. He turned. Checked in the mirror. Still blocked.

Jake touched Deb on one pale-blue shoulder, needing her to move. "Kratky. You make a better door. I gotta get ID."

"We're stabilizing now, Jake." Kratky didn't move, still bent over the victim. She turned her head, raised her eyes from her patient, flipped a palm up, then down. *Fifty-fifty.* She managed a tentative half smile. "One shot, upper right chest. Vitals getting there. We'll transport ASAP, maybe two more minutes."

"Lobby clear?" Another EMT asked him. "Mass General is expecting."

"All clear," Jake said. "Deb, I gotta get ID. And where's DeLuca? Did he get it?"

"With the shooter, he says to tell you." Kratky stepped away from her charge, gesturing Jake to take a look.

A thin white blanket covered the body. Jake didn't need to approach any nearer to get his first bearings. White. Male.

Brown hair, curly, clean-shaven, forty-something, Jake cataloged. But he was hearing Jane's voice saying the words.

Lewis Wilhoite.

52

"Are you still in front of the Purple?" Tenley had dialed Brileen before her mother could stop her. She didn't need to announce who she was. Caller ID would display it.

"How did you know?" Brileen's voice, laughing, came back through the cell. "Hey, are you watching me through your fancy surveillance thing? Whoa, did you see me look at you? I almost waved. I was on my way up to see you!"

Tenley put her hand over the phone mic. "She was coming to see me, that's why she was here," Tenley whispered.

She and her mom stood in the sheltered area outside City Hall. A bunch of cop cars and TV trucks, she could see only the rear ends of them, clustered in front of the U, almost a block away. No sirens or anything.

"Tenley, I'm not sure about this." Her mom was running her hand through her graying hair, then adjusting her blouse.

"I'm right across the street," Tenley said into the phone. "There's someone I want you to meet. We're walking to you now."

"Who?" Brileen asked.

"It's a surprise." Tenley gestured at her mom. *Come on.* "One minute. We'll be there in one minute."

"Tenner," Mom said, "this is a bad idea."

"It isn't. Trust me." Tenley tucked her phone into the back pocket of her skirt, then paused. She draped her arm across her mother's shoulders.

It felt right. "I can't let you be so sad, Mom. You said today, upstairs, it's only me and you now. And it is. And that makes us a team."

"I love you, Tenley."

Tenley felt her mom lean into her, felt her weight against her chest, her hair against Tenley's cheek. She paused, standing that way, thinking about it all.

"I love you too, Mom," Tenley said. And she did. She could picture the ghost of Lanna and the ghost of her father looking down on her. Smiling. The world was only the world. Sometimes it was awful. Sometimes family was all you had. "Now come with me."

Why had Tenley brought her here? The beery din of the Purple Martin, the dingy-noisy hangout Catherine had seen countless times in her years at City Hall. Steps across the street from her office but miles across a generational boundary. No one here probably even knew of the chaos, now reportedly over, just a block away.

She sat in the maroon leatherette booth, hands clasped on the speckled plastic tabletop. The lumpy upholstery was splitting at the seams, poorly repaired with mismatched duct tape, still torn in a couple of places. A ragged edge of the unforgiving fabric poked at Catherine's thigh. She adjusted her skirt underneath her.

Brileen Finnerty. How many times had she said that name to herself? Tasted its toxicity, imagined the reality, her husband with a woman young enough to be his daughter.

And now here they were. Face-to-face. On opposite sides of a table.

"Come meet my mom," Tenley had said. And out on the sidewalk they'd shaken hands, like two civilized people. *Still,* Catherine thought, *I know guilty when I see it.*

Brileen was attractive enough, her coppery hair chopped in a way Tenley probably considered cool. She wore a short flowered skirt, a striped tank top, and an attentively battered jean jacket. A laptop bag slung diagonally across her chest. Not a whiff of femme fatale, Catherine thought, eyeing the bitten-to-the-quick fingernails. *No accounting for tastes.*

She picked up a plastic-covered menu, pretended to read it while she studied Brileen. The girls ordered coffee from a T-shirted waitress while Catherine tried—unsuccessfully—to picture Greg with her. It didn't matter, though. No accounting for tastes, maybe, but there *was* accounting for facts. The voice message instructing Greg to "meet at the usual place." The ridiculously cryptic e-mails she'd read. "I'll be watching for you." Brileen had even signed her name.

Whether Catherine could picture it or not—and she'd never attempt it again—there *had* been something going on between them.

Why on earth had Tenley brought them here? Five more minutes, Catherine decided. Just enough to mollify her daughter. She'd checked her phone, several times. No one had pinged her. The mayor would be waiting for instructions. The cops were wrapping the hotel incident, but she'd been notified there was no more danger. They still had to decide how to handle the Curley Park subpoena.

Her heart twisted again with grief, and with anger, and with grief again. Greg was dead. Brileen couldn't possibly know about that yet, and Catherine certainly would not be the one to tell her. *That* discovery she'd have to make on her own. A reality the girl would have to mourn alone, like all participants in deceit.

"It was so weird to see you from the surveillance room," Tenley was saying. Catherine could tell her daughter was playing something back in her mind. "You looked up at the camera, right? How'd you know where I worked? What room, I mean?"

"You told me." Brileen also seemed to be communicating a private message. "Don't you remember *that*, either?"

"Huh," Tenley said. "So who was the guy in the black car? And why were you coming to see me, anyway?"

Catherine cleared her throat, waved away the hovering waitress. No more chitchat. "Tenley?" She half smiled, tried to, at least, and got the show on the road. "Although your friend and I have never met, she knows very well who I am. I'm not sure why you wanted us to do this, honey, but we're here now. Because you asked us to be. I have five minutes."

"Brileen." Tenley fussed with her water glass, turned it, moved it a fraction of an inch. "Mom thinks you were having an affair with my father."

"What?" Brileen's skin went white under her freckles, the pale brown spots suddenly highlighting her smooth skin.

Catherine saw Brileen's eyes fly open. Those stubby fingernails, deep lavender, went to her lips. She clutched the laptop to her chest.

Yeah, well, that's what happens when the truth finally comes out, Catherine thought. She never considered she'd actually meet this girl. Surely with Greg's death—*Greg's death*—she'd figured this sordid chapter would become part of a history she'd somehow learn to ignore. But there was a grim satisfaction in seeing justice done. *You didn't get away with anything, sister.*

Brileen looked straight at her. And laughed, a pealing, lilting, incongruous laugh. Her head thrown back, her slender throat showing, her hand clamped against her chest.

That's it, Catherine thought. What could possibly be funny? Funny? She gathered her purse, shaking her head, her skin tightening at such a disrespectful and insolent reaction. "Tenley!"

Tenley, looking at Brileen, put up a hand. *Wait.*

Brileen's laughter faded. When she looked toward Catherine again, her eyes were wet with tears.

Had she laughed so hard she was crying? Catherine could not put up with this for one more second. Or maybe the girl was hysterical.

The waitress arrived with two white ceramic mugs, coffee steaming, on a battered circular tray. Instantly silent, the three women flinched back against the upholstery, each side as far away from the other as possible. The waitress placed one, then two mugs on the table, the china clinking against the plastic. She laid out a napkin, then another. Then two spoons. Then the sugar container.

"Anyone need cream?" She paused.

"No," Catherine said, trying to telegraph *go the hell away.* "Thank you."

"Mrs. Siskel." Brileen grabbed a paper napkin, blotted her tears as the waitress finally left them. "I am so sorry. I am so, deeply, deeply sorry."

Catherine narrowed her eyes, trying to parse what she meant. Sorry about being a selfish, beautiful, husband-stealer? Sorry about laughing in her face?

"Lanna must have talked about me, Mrs. Siskel," Brileen said.

"She mentioned you." True enough, but only in passing. They were school chums, right? Which is how Brileen had latched on to Greg. Obviously. If she'd ever been to the Siskel home—*please, no*—it had been while Catherine was at work. Which, sadly for all involved, was often.

"So you know I loved Lanna," Brileen said.

"You did?" Tenley said. She scratched her head, like she was trying to figure this out.

"Oh, Tenley, no. No. I loved her like a sister. Like you did." Brileen touched her arm with one finger. "I'm with Valerie, have been for years. Done deal."

The din and hubbub of the restaurant seemed to wash over Catherine, fried food and burned coffee and the whir of ceiling fans, her brain struggling for equilibrium. So if this girl was . . . *no.* Facts were facts, and what she had seen in e-mails and heard on voice mail was real.

"Then why were you calling my husband?" Catherine leaned forward, accusatory. "Why did you e-mail back and forth? Why did you meet him? Even the day he—"

Catherine stopped. *Even the day he died, there was a message from you,* Catherine was about to say. But she couldn't. She wouldn't say Greg was dead.

"Even yesterday, you e-mailed him," Catherine said. "Yesterday morning."

"I know." Brileen took the laptop bag from over her shoulder and placed it on the seat beside her.

"You did?" Tenley said.

"You admit it?" Catherine felt her back stiffen, her eyebrows go up. That was easy.

"But yesterday morning, you and I hadn't even met," Tenley went on as if she hadn't been cut off. She spun her coffee mug one way, then the other, batting the handle with her forefingers. The ceramic scraped against the table surface. A dark droplet splashed onto the table. "So how would you even—I mean, why—"

Brileen laid her left hand over the top of her own mug, then her right hand over that. She removed them, quickly—the coffee looked hot—and stared at her palms.

"Brileen?" Catherine said. "My daughter is asking the perfect question. Why?"

The girl was clearly stalling. She must be, what, twenty-six? At the most? *Twenty years younger than Greg.* What could she possibly be considering so intently?

The steam from the coffee in front of her rose, dissipated, disappeared.

"I had to protect Valerie. And then Lanna. But now I'm done. *Yes.* This has to end." Brileen laced her fingers together, hands clasped under her chin. She leaned forward. "You have to understand. I—your husband and I—we were trying to protect you," she whispered.

"Protect me?" Catherine said.

"Not only you, Mrs. Siskel," Brileen said. "You and Tenley."

"What?" Catherine could not process this.

Brileen put one hand flat on the table, moved it closer to Catherine, almost touching her. "I'll tell you the whole thing. But first, I am so, so, *so* sorry. And so sorry for your loss."

53

The surveillance room was empty. Jane closed the metal door behind her. Scoped the place out.

How different could all this equipment be from the edit booths and microwave trucks that Jane had worked in for years? The computer console with its array of controls and lights might has well have been edit room 4 at her old TV station. It looked exactly like Marsh Tyson's office. Or Editing 101 at J-school. Which Jane had aced.

She felt watched, even though no one else was in the room. *Probably because you're trespassing,* she thought. But wasn't this where Beefy and Co. had wanted to bring her anyway? She dropped into the ratty swivel chair, its stained upholstery snagged and worn, and rolled herself up to the main console.

Five rows of video monitors spanned the wall, a flickering grid of black-and-white images. Hallways, elevators, vending machines. Stairways, supply rooms. Kitchen, pantry. Closed doors, some with the room numbers showing. Wonder if guests knew their every move was watched and recorded? Some screens were dark, like black holes in the video grid.

The second row of monitors all showed the lobby. Front door, concierge desk. She saw the concierge on the phone for one second, then the screen shots changed and new images swam up. The registration desk. Empty. The palm tree where she'd encountered Gracie. On the lowest row, the five screens were larger, images constantly changing. A pretty expensive setup. She watched, feeling strangely omniscient.

Where was Gracie now? Where would she have gone? Back to Lewis's room on the third floor? The floor where Jake was headed? Or did someone take her?

Wait. All she had to do was find the right screen, and she'd see whatever happened. Police, rescue, shoot-out. Happy ending. Her heart raced with the possibility. She could grab her camera right now, be ready to shoot terrific exclusive video. Would that be legal?

Did it matter?

She stood, hands on hips. *Find Gracie.* And where was Jake? Trying to scan, she leaned forward, squinting. On the highest row, the screens were too small to make out much. Soon as she saw a cop the image would disappear, because the screens kept changing views, rotating every few seconds, like several cameras fed each monitor.

Made sense, she guessed, because you didn't need to look at the same place all the time, so they used fewer monitors and multiple sources. Probably also why they had two guys. Mesmerizing to watch these things all day. Eventually, paralyzingly boring.

Unless, of course, there was a shooting. Or a missing girl.

"Okay," she said out loud. "There's gotta be rhyme and reason."

Five rows of monitors. Ten monitors across. Fifty screens. If this had been her setup, she might have labeled them. But no.

If there were no labels, did Beefy and Co. simply know camera placement by heart? There must be a—*ha*. She yanked a white vinyl binder from between two console banks. The yellowing clear plastic cover was separating at the corners, brittle and peeling away. Someone had made devil horns on the words HEWLITT SECURITY on the cover and added Mickey Mouse ears to their fancy logo of a camera lens. Not-so-happy employees, she thought. With not enough to do.

She flipped open the binder. Bingo. Spreading out a triple-fold piece of paper, she saw a blueprint of what had to be a chart of the monitors. Like a big checkerboard, each square filled in with words. Supply5. Linen5. Vending4. Corridor5A.

Looked like the five rows corresponded to each floor of the hotel. Brilliant. The middle row was the third floor, where Jake and D and a million cops were.

Maybe this was a time suck? Maybe she should run out of here and start going door-to-door. That would be rewarding, because it would feel like she was doing something. It was also inefficient and primitive. And possibly dangerous.

"Find. Gracie," she commanded herself. Was the little girl hiding? Or being hidden? The whole thing was a juggle, because the shots on each screen kept changing.

Still, in this one room, Jane could be everywhere in the hotel at the same time. Most likely, Gracie wouldn't be changing position, right? If she was hiding.

If she was hiding. Which was a big if. Because she might be with—

Oh, my gosh. She was an idiot.

Who had told the police that Gracie Wilhoite was missing? Besides Jane, only one other person in the building knew the girl was here. Or maybe—two?

Now it made sense, Jake thought.

Not good sense, not rational sense, but as much sense as domestic violence ever made. The man on the stretcher was Lewis Wilhoite. Gracie's stepfather, the one who clearly had taken her yesterday.

"Is this the person who told you the girl was missing?" Jake asked Deb Kratky. He repeated the question to the room full of EMTs and cops. "Gracie? His stepdaughter? Did he say any more? Where she might have gone? And why?"

"Negative, Jake," one of the cops said. "By the time we got here, he was down for the count."

"So who—" Jake stopped as a familiar shape filled the hotel room door.

"Come with me," DeLuca said. "Move it."

Jake followed DeLuca, double speed, down the deserted corridor. The amplified warning instructions blared, repeating. All the room doors remained firmly closed. "D, you got people looking for Gracie?"

"Listen, Jake. Of course we do. They'll find her. Lotsa rooms in here, lotsa places to hide. But listen." D stopped in a spotlighted pool of light on the mottled carpeting. A discarded room service tray holding grape stems, ketchup packets, empty breadbasket, and a pile of dirty silverware sat untouched outside the room to his left.

"So, yeah. We have a situation. Got the shooter in there." He pointed to a closed door black-stenciled SUPPLY RM.

"Great work," Jake said. Done and done. Only several million questions left to answer, but at least they knew who to ask. There wouldn't be any more shooting. And then he could get some sleep. All in a day's work. Two days.

"What's his condition? What's his story?" Jake fired questions at DeLuca. "He call for a lawyer yet? What's the plan for HQ transport for questioning? We're the primaries, correct? You recover the weapon? Anything I should know?"

"Shooter's cuffed, seated, basically silent. Got the gun, yeah. Twenty-two. Registered. Hasn't called for a lawyer yet, no."

"Great," Jake said. "Let's get this asshole. Shooting a guy in a hotel. Scaring this little girl to death. Now she's hiding somewhere, I bet. *Shit.* Hope poor Gracie didn't see this go down. Asshole."

"Jake?" DeLuca said. "The shooter's not asking for a lawyer. She's asking for Jane."

54

"I can't look at it," Catherine said.

She put up both palms, blocking the computer screen in front of her. They'd hurried out of the Purple Martin and crossed to City Hall, she and Tenley and Brileen, then closed Catherine's office door behind them. Snoop-faced Siobhan Hult had been sent to tell Ward Dahlstrom that Tenley was still with her. Siobhan had never seen Brileen before, so they would appear, Catherine hoped, to be a typical mom hanging out with her daughter and her daughter's pal. It would all seem peacefully familial. Instead of disgusting and horrific.

Brileen had finished her stomach-turning story, mother and daughter silent, as the din of the Purple faded into white noise around them. "I kept the thumb drive with me, all the time, on my key chain," she'd finally said. "As insurance. It's the only way I could make sure it was safe."

Now Catherine and Tenley were about to see what was on that thumb drive. The video Brileen had protected. The "insurance." Had Greg watched it, too?

"Tell me again." Catherine, sitting in her leather desk chair, her computer humming, was still trying to understand. "*Whose* idea was this?"

"I was only told his name was Hugh." Brileen standing by the desk, hands jammed in her pockets, shook her head. "He said he had surveillance tape of me, with Valerie. From—well, it doesn't matter. He threatened to show her parents, the worst possible situation, if I didn't help him."

"Help him what?" Tenley perched on the edge of the couch.

"With his—I don't understand the whole thing, I don't even want to, but he found me at school. Had me approach Lanna. 'I know all about your little friend,' he said. He told me to tell her he had surveillance video of her, you know." She swallowed. "'With' someone. And that he wanted money. Or he'd make it public."

"Surveillance video? From where?" Catherine couldn't process this. "With who?"

"With who?" Tenley echoed.

"Lanna never told me." Brileen shook her head again. "She asked me— begged me—to go to her father. She couldn't face him. Hugh told me to warn her that it would not only humiliate her." She paused again. "It would *ruin* you."

"*Ruin? Me?* This man knew *me*? How?" After three terms at City Hall, Catherine had met an incalculable number of people. But how many would want to destroy her? Well, plenty, she guessed. It was politics. And all she needed was one. This one. "Do I know *him*?"

"Mrs. Siskel, I simply don't know. I only met him that once, other times it was all by phone. I simply—arranged it. I'm so sorry, but . . ." She paused. Took a deep breath.

"But there was no way out. I had to protect Valerie, you know? Mr. Siskel and I met. Made the exchange. I put the money in the Dumpster, like Hugh told me. But I kept a copy of the video. In case, I don't know, I needed it for evidence." She pulled a chunky rectangular key ring from her pocket, silver with a black suede tassel on the end. She yanked the tassel, and a thumb drive clicked out. She inserted it into the keyboard port of Catherine's computer. "I've never looked at this, though. I couldn't."

"Greg never told me," Catherine murmured. The computer hummed, the screen still black. "Nor did Lanna."

"Me either," Tenley said.

Catherine reached out across the desk, took her daughter's hand.

"Mrs. Siskel?" Brileen's eyes filled with tears. Again. "Do you want to look at the video now? I don't know if your husband ever saw it. Or if he even kept the original thumb drive—he said he'd destroy it. But Lanna was happy, you know? Until this. She had some boyfriend, I guess he was the one on the tape. And her father forgave her. They had pledged never to tell you, decided that it would be their secret. She loved him, your husband, I mean, so much. And you, Mrs. Siskel. And you, too, Tenley. And when she died—"

Catherine's lungs worked to breathe against the weight of the burden suddenly crushing them. "This Hugh. He wouldn't have—do you think he *killed* her? In the woods?"

"I don't," Brileen said. "I mean, I don't know. Didn't the police say it was an accident? I believe them. I have to. It's the only way I can deal with it. It's too horrible, otherwise, thinking that I . . . and now, I'd do *anything* to—"

"We all would." Catherine looked around her office. The same low-bid office where she'd battled the hotel workers' strike and the neighborhood pothole lynch mob and the snow removal budget and the mayor's continuing disconnect with his constituents. Boring, mundane City Hall. Now getting ready to present her daughter on some sex tape from some obviously illegal hidden camera.

"I can't look at it," Catherine said again.

But Brileen had already clicked the silvery mouse. One frame of video now filled Catherine's computer screen. Black and white, that muddy halftone identifying surveillance video. A white triangle violated the middle of the screen. When Brileen clicked the triangle again, the video would start.

"Mom?" Tenley's voice was tiny, the thin, reedy voice of a child. She pointed to the screen, moving the pale pink rounded nail of her right forefinger past the triangle. "Um. I think that's, like, your greenroom."

Catherine stood, slowly, both palms on her desk. The room around her seemed to be off its axis. The floor was moving and the lights were dim, then bright, then dim again. There was no surveillance camera in her greenroom. *That she knew of.* She reached out a hand. It felt almost as if it weren't attached to her arm. Lowered two fingers to the sleek polished surface of the mouse.

And clicked the triangle.

And then clicked it again. To stop it.

"Wait," she said. Catherine had more to think about than the past, more to worry about than what might have been on some contraband video—*in her office! How?*—of her daughter and some asshole who'd taken advantage of Lanna, and Catherine, and practically every other thing in her universe that was honorable and sane. If he had harmed her daughter, in Catherine's own office, it couldn't be any worse on video than it was in her imagination. She would not poison her brain with it.

She needed one more answer. Right now.

"Brileen," she said. "You said you and Greg were trying to protect me *and* Tenley, both of us."

"Yeah. I—" Brileen put her face in both hands. When she took them down, three seconds later, her face was splotchy with tears. "—I *only* did what I thought was best for Lanna. That's what Mr. Siskel was doing, too. We thought it was over. But two days ago, Hugh contacted me again. He told me to tell Greg he had pictures of Tenley."

"What?" Tenley's voice came out a strangled cry. Her hand went to her throat and her face went white. "That could not—I mean—there's no way that—no!"

Catherine clamped her arm around her daughter, holding her tight, so tight that Tenley could never leave. She would never let go.

And now Tenley was sobbing.

"It can't be." Her daughter's anguished words were muffled by Catherine's chest. She could feel her daughter's tears through her blouse, the wetness against her bare skin. "I *never*—"

Catherine steeled herself. If there were pictures of Tenley, how had they been taken? In the greenroom?

"Shhh." She unclenched her daughter, sat her on the couch. Put one hand on Tenley's thin back, trying to offer strength, then sat beside her, their shoulders touching. She reached for the words she knew were always welcome, though not always true. "Everything is going to be all right, honey," she said.

She needed facts. She focused on Brileen.

"I see." Catherine made her voice ice and fire. She forgot about everything but protecting the last living member of her family. "What did Hugh tell you to do?"

"It was like before," Brileen said. "Like with Lanna. He had me tell Mr. Siskel to bring money, in a brown paper bag. But I wasn't the conduit this time. Mr. Siskel was to meet a guy at noon in Curley Park."

"*What?* You know this? And then what?"

"Just like before. Then Hugh or someone would get the money out of the Dumpster. But I was there, hiding. Afterward I even told a cop to look in the Dumpster. Guess they didn't."

"You *knew* this?" Catherine stood, heart pounding, head pounding, trying to understand. If she let it, this would destroy them. But she refused. *Refused.* She jabbed an accusing finger at Brileen. "Hugh killed my husband? You *saw* it?"

Catherine needed the phone. Forget strategy. This was no longer a negotiation, no longer politics. This was family. Their lives. "We have to tell the police. We have to—"

"Not Hugh," Brileen said.

Catherine paused, one hand on the receiver of her black desk phone. She saw her daughter, now silent, face tearstained. Had Greg died protecting Tenley? He'd tried to protect Lanna. And Catherine herself. If only he'd told her, trusted her, confided in her. She wished he had shared this with her instead of taking it all on himself, destroying their marriage and sacrificing his life.

"Five seconds, Brileen," Catherine said. "You have five seconds to explain. Then I'm calling the cops."

"Not Hugh," Brileen whispered, tears spilling down her cheeks. "Yes, I saw it. And I can't stand to think of it. But it wasn't Hugh who killed your husband. The person who did—I've never seen him before."

55

Jake must have ordered a door-to-door search for Gracie. As Jane watched the hotel's surveillance monitors, flickering and changing, they now showed police officers running through all five floors of hallways. Their uniforms turned from blue to black-and-white by the cameras, jump-cutting from monitor to monitor, as if they were electronically leaping through time and space. Even the surveillance guys were involved.

Officers approached door after door, pounding soundlessly. Sometimes they were opened by surprised or frightened hotel guests, panicky tourists who had probably been glued to breaking-news bulletins about the shooting and the missing child. Right in their very hotel. That'd be a story to take home.

A pang of news guilt washed over her. She closed her eyes for a second as it pulled her into its undertow. Should she have called Marsh Tyson about this? Probably. So much for her short-lived career at Channel 2. Without consciously making a decision about her loyalties, she'd chosen family. Good for karma, bad for per diems.

But on the screens, no Gracie appeared. No cop emerged carrying a little girl in his arms. *No.* Jane adjusted her imaginary dénouement. She'd walk out on her own. Gracie was fine. They'd find her.

Keeping her eyes on the screens, Jane dug for her cell phone and hit speed dial. One ring. Two.

"Melissa?" Jane began before her sister even said hello. "Any word from—"

"No," Melissa said. Jane heard cars honking and the murmur of moving air and acceleration. "Any word *there*?"

"No," Jane said. "They're—we're—everyone is looking."

"We're on the way to you, Janey. Daniel and I. I don't understand it—I'd taken a shower, you know? Then Daniel arrived. I went upstairs to get Robyn, to tell her, that's when I discovered she was gone. No note, no nothing. No car in the garage."

Jane kept her eyes on the surveillance monitors. "Are you okay? Daniel? How long until you get to the hotel?" Cameras were everywhere, like electronic windows in this otherwise windowless room. Gracie had to appear.

"It's as okay as it can be. I'm trying to explain it all, to him, and—" Melissa paused. "Fifteen minutes. How can there be rush hour on a Tuesday at three twenty-two?"

"Boston," Jane said. "Hurry."

"Love you," Melissa said. And hung up.

"Love you, too," Jane said. Even though the line was dead.

Okay, she told herself. Start again at screen one. But there was no Gracie. The shots flashed, changed, brought in a new view. No Gracie. No Gracie.

Who knew how many other views there were, maybe cameras she couldn't access. The blueprint was a technomap of squiggly lines and engineering symbols. But there was no symbol for where a little girl might be hiding.

The doorknob rattled. The surveillance guys? If she could talk fast, explain, maybe they'd be convinced she was on the right track. Maybe help her look.

"Jane," Jake said, closing the door behind him.

"How'd you know I'd be here?" It was a relief to see him, okay and safe. Much better than Tall and Beefy. At least Jake wouldn't arrest her. Oh, wait. Maybe he would. He'd ordered her not to move from the fake palm tree. Well, whatever. She wasn't the problem.

"You told me about this room, remember?" Jake smiled, just for an instant. "And I know you never listen to me."

She opened her mouth to make a crack, but no. "Did you find her? I've been looking and looking but didn't see—"

"Jane."

Jake's face had hardened. She knew him well enough to know something bad was coming. She put one hand on the video console, grounding herself. *It isn't Gracie,* her mind reassured her. Lights from the flickering monitors danced in Jane's peripheral vision as she focused on Jake.

"We have the shooter. And I'm so sorry."

"*Sorry?* Who is it?" Jane grabbed his arm. Then the look on Jake's face stopped her.

One shooter. One victim. Domestic. Not Gracie. If she was missing, she wasn't shot, because the medics had said the victim was being transported. If Jake was "sorry," there was only one name to say. The lying, identity-stealing, child-abducting nutcase who'd caused so much misery for his wife and her sister and, *yes*, for herself. *Creep,* she thought.

"Lewis," Jane said.

"No." Jake shook his head. "Robyn."

"Robyn? Is the *shooter*? Of who? Lewis? That's *horr*—"

"Yeah," Jake said. It was breaking protocol to tell Jane like this, but what the hell. "He'll live, though, so—"

She took a step toward him, interrupting. "Does he know where Gracie is? Was she—*there*?"

"Nope. Long story." Jake opened the surveillance room door, checked the lobby, made sure police sentries still kept people out. He knew the cops on the upper floors were keeping people in. The danger had been contained and extinguished. Except for the missing Gracie.

"Short version," Jake continued. "DeLuca found Robyn. Says she was wild, weeping one minute, bitching the next. Self-defense, she swears. Says Lewis had threatened to take Gracie, then he threatened Robyn with a twenty-two. Just how she managed to wrestle a gun from her 'crazed' husband isn't yet clear, but we'll get to that."

Jane had perched on the white counter under the monitors, the shifting video dancing shadows and light around her. "What if it *was* self-defense?"

"Then Lewis will be adding a set of handcuffs to his hospital attire. So look, Jane, Robyn says you'll corroborate her story. She says she doesn't want a lawyer. Just you."

"*Me?*"

Jake watched her trying to process this. "And if she talks to us in front of you, it's admissible."

"What. About. Gracie?"

"She says she has no idea where Gracie is," Jake said. "We're still searching. But there are a hundred seventy-three rooms in this place."

He saw the scenes on the security monitors shift and change as new digital images were transmitted from cameras placed throughout the hotel. Might he see the girl on these cameras? Was Jane right? Jake knew surveillance video was often sent to off-site security companies for archiving and storage.

Little did the hotel guests know. Except when a career-ruining transgression appeared, taped and undeniable, on a trashy news show: celebrities fighting in elevators, coked-up film stars trashing hotel rooms. So much for "security." Those videos, once they went viral—who makes that stuff public, anyway?—could wreck a career.

"You up for it?" Jake asked. "It's unorthodox for you to talk to a suspect. But it wasn't our idea."

"*Robyn?*" Jane said again. He heard the incredulity in her voice. "Is the *shooter?*"

"Yeah. Robyn," Jake said. "I'm all for letting her stew up there for a bit. Let her wonder what's going on, you know? But she claims you'll back her up about Lewis. His problems. His volatility. His threats. Jane? Is that true? Did he threaten her? Or Gracie?"

Jane didn't answer.

"Jane?" It must be tough for her to get dragged into the middle of a family squabble. Hell, more than squabble, this was attempted murder, potentially, and child abduction. Jane was not used to being part of the story, so he'd tread lightly. But he needed to tread semi-fast. Robyn could wait, but not for too long. And Gracie was still missing.

Now Jane's eyes were on the monitors over his shoulder. Not looking at him.

"Jake," Jane said. Still not looking at him.

"I know. It's difficult." Jake tried to sound reassuring and supportive. This would be an emotional tightrope for her. "But is it true?"

"Gracie," Jane said.

"What? Right," Jake said. "Gracie. Or Robyn."

"No, Jake." This time Jane pointed. "Gracie."

56

It's all my fault. *It's all my fault.* The words spun through Tenley's brain, an endless loop of guilt. Finally, she blurted the words out loud, she couldn't help it, and Brileen and her mom turned to her, each face mirroring the other's surprise. The computer on her mom's desk still showed the green square on the black screen, the white triangle protecting the hideous Lanna video. Now Brileen was saying there was also a video of *her*, Tenley, somewhere? And her father had been killed trying to get it?

That couldn't be.

It couldn't. Tenley had never, ever, ever—so why was the Hugh guy saying there was video? Why did her father have to die? There was nothing to protect her from!

"Honey? Honey? I'm right here." Her mom grabbed her by both arms. Her forehead creased, eyebrows pushed together. "Why is it your fault, honey?"

"Because . . ." Tears streamed down her face, her own failure mocking her again. "Because if I had pushed Save on the surveillance computer sooner, like I wanted to, we might have seen this whole thing. On video." The last words came out a wail. That stupid Ward Dahlstrom, if he hadn't hovered, he'd never have known, never have pushed Cancel, and maybe, maybe, maybe they'd be able to see who killed her father.

They'd catch him, and kill him back.

She tried to explain all of this to her mother, who should have understood. And to Brileen, who was clueless about the video save, and the cache, and the twenty seconds, even though Bri had her laptop with her all the time and knew about computer stuff. It didn't matter. It was gone, all of the evidence was gone.

She made it through the whole explanation, finally, her throat clogging. Even though Mom had said she loved her, she wouldn't anymore, not after this. Tenley hadn't told about Lanna's boyfriend. And now her father was dead and they'd never be able to find out who did it.

"Now we'll never know." Tenley's words caught in her sobs. "And I never got to say good-bye. He thought I was mad at him. And I was, because he was always upset, or mad, or gone. And then it turns out he was upset because—"

"He loved you, Tenner," Mom said. "The last thing he told me was how much he did. He knew you loved him, too."

The room went quiet. Mom clicked her computer to solid black, took out the stupid thumb drive, put it in her skirt pocket. Brileen moved to sit in Mom's guest chair, her hands covering her face, only the top of her hair showing.

"Hey, Brileen?" Tenley mentally replayed what happened, *yet again.* "You *knew* me yesterday, out there. In Curley Park. You pretended you didn't, but you did. The whole last night, you were pretending."

Mom looked at her, then Brileen, then her. "What are you talking about? Pretending? Last night?"

Tenley took a deep breath. She talked to the floor, to the familiar tan carpeting, so she wouldn't lose her nerve. "I went to Brileen's last night, Mom. I kind of sneaked out, after you were gone, and Brileen picked me up. I was gonna leave. Because Dad was hating me and you hated me and always blamed me for Lanna."

There. That was it, it was out, and whatever. She felt lighter.

Mom crossed the room and wrapped Tenley up in her arms, so tight Tenley could feel the little round buttons on her blouse, and smell that white soap she used, and her grapefruit perfume, and her mom's metal watchband pressing into her back.

"I'm sorry, Mom," she whispered.

"Shh," her mom's voice went into her hair.

Catherine was never going to let her daughter go. She would never let her out of her sight again. Never let her talk to anyone else, ever again. Never let her come back to City Hall. All her power, all her control. When real life interfered, it proved how little it mattered.

Still. It was all politics. Some people were in power, others weren't. Some people took the power and tried to use it to control the weaker ones.

Catherine refused to be a weak one. She and her daughter would be strong. They had no choice.

If the mayor's secret taping came out, he'd have to take his political lumps. Brileen—arms crossed, now sitting on the windowsill—seemed to have the answers.

"Did 'Hugh' give these so-called pictures of Tenley to my husband?"

She heard her own words muffled by her daughter's hair, the dark strands she'd seen every day for the last eighteen years. Funny how she had stopped looking at her, except to criticize, or demand, or question. As Tenley and Lanna grew older, they'd separated, come into their own. Apparently, each of them kept secrets. Lanna's had died with her, Catherine had always believed. Now, maybe, that wasn't completely true.

"Brileen? Did he?" She settled Tenley into her own desk chair, standing behind her, both hands on her daughter's shoulders as if to keep her from floating away.

Brileen tilted her head back, gazed at the ceiling's swirls of white stucco. "I don't know," she said. "That's why I wanted Tenley out of her house, especially after she said you were gone. I'm sorry, Tenley, but what if Hugh had shown up? Found you alone, and threatened *you*? He called me, *so* angry. I felt I like had to get you away. I—couldn't protect Lanna. I had to at least *try* to protect you."

Catherine blinked at Brileen, imagining. Her Tenley, alone with a blackmailer. What might he have demanded she do to hand over that video?

What video?

There was a way to find out. A fast way. A terrible way, but a way.

She clicked open her purse. Pulled out her wallet. Slipped a finger under the very last credit card slot and pulled out a thin white business card. That detective, Jake Brogan, had printed his cell phone number on the back of it along with the number for Sergeant Kiyoko Naka in the Missing Persons department. She stared at the black felt-tip numbers that meant the end of her career.

She could hear the silence of the room, thick with expectation. She might never work here again. Or anywhere. Would that matter?

"Mom?" Her daughter's voice reached her. Her beautiful daughter, whose life had been trampled by circumstance and politics. Could politics have motivated these attacks on her family? "What are you doing?"

Her intercom buzzed. "Catherine? I'm back at my desk."

Siobhan Hult. Back from her made-up mission to Ward Dahlstrom, a man probably counting his blessings he hadn't been able to oust her from the chief of staff job. *Heavy lies the head,* Catherine thought. And now he'll be happy it's my head that's about to roll. She had to move fast.

"Thank you, Siobhan." Catherine kept her voice chipper, professional. She pulled out her cell.

"Who are you calling?" Tenley asked.

"Everything is going to be all right," Catherine said for the second time that morning.

Again, she hoped it was true.

57

It was almost funny.

"See her?" Jane pointed at the monitor. For reassurance, she snaked her arm through Jake's, her bare skin on his leather jacket. No one could see them, and this was a moment of swirling relief.

Gracie was safe. Not kidnapped. Not missing. Not dead. Jane had found her.

"That's in the—gift shop?" Jake leaned forward toward the screen.

Jane didn't let go, leaning toward the revealing video along with him. "Yup. Poor little thing. Let's go get her."

Jake reached for his radio, extricating her with a final pat. "I'll call off the search. Good work, honey. And I think there's a reward. A personal one."

"Can't wait." She tried not to cry. This was a good thing.

Jane had seen a flicker on the screen first. A movement in row one, monitor three, according to the schematic. When she had looked again, the shot had changed. She'd kept her eye on the screen, listening to Jake at the same time.

"All clear on the BOLO," he said. "Return to base."

When the shot flipped again, Jane saw that unmistakable curly hair. The top of a little face. And then the yellow ruffles, looking gray in the black-and-white. The small figure rose, tentatively, from behind a metal-and-glass display case in the gift shop. Her face looked a little smudged. All the transmissions were fuzzy, but Jane got the picture. Gracie Wilhoite, row one, monitor three, was in the hotel. In the gift shop, where she'd apparently hidden behind the candy counter. And she looked fine.

"I'll go get her right now," Jane said. "Bring her to—*oh*. No."

"What?" Jake said.

Jane envisioned that scene. "I can't go. She's terrified of me. I'm the reason she ran away. That moron Wilhoite apparently never told her—"

"Ah, I get it. You're the child molester. Awesome." Jake shook his head, then turned a switch on his radio again. "Okay, then. At least I can update the troops that the bad guy is in custody. How far away are your sister and Daniel?"

"In traffic," Jane said. "Who knows?"

On the bank of monitors, the screen shots kept changing. Every third time, she calculated, the Gracie view came up.

"We can't leave her there," Jane said. "You have to go. She'll be so frightened. Who knows what she heard or what she saw. The lobby is empty. I can at least keep an eye on her now, thanks to Hewlitt Security."

"What?" Jake said.

"I mean I wonder what she was thinking, all that time. It's been, what, half an hour? Poor child, did some adults just leave her behind? Ran away from the shooter, ignored the little girl? Anyway, go. You have to go get her. Look. There she is."

The third cycle of video came around again. Gracie now appeared in front of the counter, a dark smear of something down her front. She stood, fussing with the ruffles on her dress, as if deciding what to do. She pointed one foot out in front of her, in her white shoe. Then switched to the other foot. Wearing just a white sock. Then the shoe. Then she turned back toward the counter, and—the shot changed again.

"You. Have. To go." Jane didn't take her eyes off the screen. No way were they going to lose Gracie now. "What do you mean, *what*? You're a police officer, you're not stranger danger. She's got to know about police, and badges, right? Or should you call someone in uniform? A woman, maybe?"

"Jane," Jake said. "The security. You said the name of the security company."

"So what?" Jane said. "Hewlitt. It's on the binder. Now go get Gracie."

"Gracie? I'm Jake. I'm a police officer, even though I have on regular clothes."

He stood in the doorway of the hotel gift shop, looking at the candy counter, where he knew the girl was once again hiding. Jane had kept him updated on Gracie's whereabouts over their cell phones. As soon as he'd approached the shop's open door, the child had scuttled behind her protective chrome and glass. He flipped open his wallet, held it up facing the counter. *Hewlitt Security,* he thought. But first, Gracie. "Here's my badge, see? You recognize a police badge?"

No reply.

"Gracie?" Jake started again. "I know what happened. I know you must be scared. A woman came up to you, right? Well, we've talked to her, and everything is just fine. It's all a misunderstanding. Her name is Jane, and she's a good person. A friend of mine. And she really truly is a friend of your—" Jake paused. Who was the good guy here? Lewis? Robyn? "Family," he said.

Nothing.

"Jane came to take you home." This was turning into a disaster. He couldn't go back and pull the girl out from behind her safety shield of candy and souvenirs. She'd freak. There was no reason to put her through that. Surely he could sweet-talk a nine-year-old out of hiding.

"Gracie? Listen, okay? I know you're going to be a flower girl in a wedding, in Illinois. This weekend. Your dad, Daniel, is the groom, and he's marrying Melissa, right? And I think you lost your shoe in the lobby. I know exactly where it is. You could be like Cinderella."

A shift in the silence. Jake could almost feel the little girl considering.

"My daddy told me not to talk to strangers." Her determined voice piped up from behind the cash register.

"Very good advice." Progress. Jake continued to display his badge, took a step forward. "Good for you. But I'm a police officer, and that's different."

"And my parents always told me to yell and run and hide and if I was ever scared by a stranger," Gracie went on. "So I did."

"Very good," Jake said. "And they're right."

She'd appear any minute now. He hoped. Thank God he wasn't out-stubborned by a kid. Jake's phone was buzzing in his pocket, but he'd have to ignore it. He'd get Jane down here, introduce Gracie, smooth out any misunderstandings and make sure all was well, then figure out what to do from there.

"I know you're a policeman," Gracie said.

"Good girl." Jake's phone vibrated again. Gracie could go with Melissa and Daniel. Lewis was already in the hospital. Robyn was in custody. Gracie would have to be protected from that quagmire, at least as much as anyone could protect her. But it seemed like Jake was emerging victorious. One step at a time. He took one more. Closer.

"But Mr. Police?" Gracie said.

"Yes, honey?"

"I need my shoe. And I'm not coming out until you get my daddy."

"Jake, they're here." Jake couldn't answer his phone, so Jane texted, hoping he'd look. Melissa and Daniel had arrived, but the police at the door had stopped them. She'd seen Jake in the gift shop by way of the surveillance camera, seen that Gracie hadn't budged from behind the counter. Whatever he was saying to her, it obviously wasn't very convincing.

"M & D," she continued her text to Jake. *"Tell goons to let them in."*

In seconds the three were running toward the gift shop, Daniel in the lead, Melissa and Jane close behind. She'd filled them in on Lewis and

Robyn—as much as she could—but all they said was "Gracie. Take us to Gracie."

Jake stepped aside to let Daniel through the door.

Gracie was nowhere in sight. And then she was. She leaped from behind the counter, flew across the floor, off balance. She wore only one shoe.

"Daniel! Melissa!"

She called him Daniel, Jane thought. More proof of the weirdness level of this family. None of her business, though. No matter what anyone called anyone, this part of the episode was over.

"Honey bear!" Daniel had met Gracie halfway, scooping her up and twirling her, then plopping her back on the tiled floor. Her dress fluttered into place. He pointed at her, Melissa hovering behind him. "Where's your shoe? You gave us a scare."

"That rhymes," Gracie said. "Bear and scare. And I was the one who was scared, Daniel. Because I didn't know who would find me. And M'lissa? I lost my shoe. Because—"

The front of Gracie's yellow dress was smeared with red. Her mouth, too, that's what Jane had noticed on the video. Then she saw the Twizzler wrappers on the floor. Gracie apparently had a field day at the candy counter. At least the kid is resourceful, Jane thought. And all is well.

Gracie turned and saw Jane. Her face crumbled, the corners of her red-ringed mouth turned down, bottom lip pooching out. And she burst into tears.

"Because of her!" Gracie cried. She leaped into Daniel's arms. Melissa placed a hand on her back, comforting the girl.

"Oh, no, honey bear," Daniel said. "That's Jane. She's—"

All she needed. "Oh, no, Gracie, I—" Jane shook her head, surveying the room, looking for backup. Jake was on his cell phone, shoulders hunched over, facing the wall. *Talking to who?* Jane felt someone touch her on the shoulder.

"It'll be okay." Melissa had tears in her eyes. "We'll explain it to her. And Janey?"

Jane felt her sister's arm link through hers. "Yeah?"

"Thanks, Sis," Melissa whispered. "We'll take Gracie from here."

Jane suddenly felt the entire weight of the day—the stress, the fear, the uncertainty. Her sister's reassurance reminded her of family, and connections, and how they all had to rely on each other, somehow, no matter what. Gracie was unhurt. That's what mattered. At least she'd been in hiding when whatever happened went down. Impossible to imagine how grotesque if this little girl had been faced with—but she wasn't. Now the adults needed to figure out the rest of the story.

"I'm glad that at least—" Jane began. She stopped, watching as Jake brought back the little white shoe from the lobby. Daniel, kneeling, slipped it onto Gracie's foot. Jane had to admit Daniel seemed a reasonable Prince Charming candidate, in a corporate kind of way, jeans and a light sweater, graying dark hair mussed. Not as exotic "man of mystery" as Jane had imagined.

The shoe. *That's what was missing.*

"Liss?" Jane turned to her sister. "Do me a favor? I found Gracie in the lobby earlier, right? Came up to her. But she clearly was not expecting me. Could you ask her—soon as you can—why she was there?"

58

Jake hadn't wanted to miss the happy ending with Gracie and her family, but that phone call he'd ignored in the gift shop was from Catherine Siskel. Her message asked to see him. That was a big deal. He had to call her back. He watched Melissa put her arm around Jane, saw them comfort each other, watched Daniel console his daughter, watched him replace the shoe. He pulled out his phone. Catherine Siskel.

"Jake." His radio rasped his name. If he stopped to think about how tired he was, he'd be tempted to take over Gracie's spot behind the candy counter. Maybe she'd even left him some candy, though from the looks of her face and dress, maybe not. But hey, cops don't need sleep.

"Yeah, D?" D. Upstairs. *Right.* Catherine Siskel would have to wait.

"You bringing the, uh, person requested?"

Jake knew D had to measure his radio transmissions, keeping them legally beyond reproach since they all were taped by dispatch and subject to subpoena. He understood, from years of listening to D's subtext and radio voice, what he was really saying: *Get Jane the hell up here before Robyn Wilhoite decides she needs a lawyer.*

"Copy," Jake said. "Be there in two."

"Jake." Jane had a hand on his arm, stopping him. "Hang on."

He needed to get her up to the third floor to help them solve the puzzle that was Robyn Wilhoite. Was she a frantic mother who'd do anything to rescue her missing child? If not, what the hell was Robyn doing here?

"I didn't tell you what I found out about Lewis Wilhoite." Jane's voice was low, her eyes on Melissa and Gracie. Jane's sister had pulled a pack of tissues from her purse, licked the corner of one, and was wiping Gracie's smudged face. Gracie, fidgeting, grudgingly allowed it. Daniel watched the two, looking exhausted but relieved.

"What about Lewis?" Jake whispered back. Lewis Wilhoite. Victim? Kidnapper? Or both?

"He may not be who he says he is," Jane said.

"Shit, who is?" Jake needed to hear the rest of it, but first things first. He hoped Wilhoite's secrets could wait. "Whoever he is, he's now under guard at Mass General." Where maybe-tattooed guy was still unidentified, still sedated. Was he the Curley Park killer? And who the hell was his victim? That still-unidentified John Doe waited in the morgue.

"We've got to talk to Robyn first," Jake said. "At least, *you* do, Jane. And right now. You up for it?"

The hotel lobby was beginning to come back to life, Jane saw, as she and Jake headed toward the elevators. The concierge at his desk, a phone clamped to each ear. A woman in a blue blazer inched open a door behind the registration counter. Neither could have seen the discovery of Gracie.

Outside the front window, cops in sunglasses and orange-webbed bandoliers still kept the curious away. Hulking TV trucks idled, satellite dishes tilted in place and yellow microwave masts poked into the air, waiting to be given some news to transmit. The reporters and news anchors would have to explain it all soon, Jane thought. As soon as the cops figured out what to say.

And here she was, right in the middle of it. A participant, not an observer. Being an observer was easier. Much, much easier. "Behind the candy counter" now sounded alluring. Gracie's decision to hide was a tempting strategy.

"So, Jake? Where was Lewis, anyway?" She and Jake waited for the elevator to arrive. Jane had assumed she was to meet Lewis and Gracie in the lobby because it was public and crowded. If Lewis had actually checked in to the hotel with Gracie, he would have been easy to find, traceable by credit card, a million ways. If he was trying to cover his trail, that seemed a pretty dumb way to start. Robyn had certainly found him.

Jake punched the elevator button again. "Room five oh three," he said. Again, no light came on. "Damn. They're still switched onto cop mode and I don't have a key. Let me radio, get the damn thing switched off."

Jane scanned the lobby while Jake checked in with his troops. Checked in. *Checked in.*

"Be right back," she said. She hurried past the palms, past the fountain, and across the lobby to the registration desk.

"I'm Jane," she said to the woman behind the counter.

MS. SIEGER, the gold plastic name tag on her fitted jacket read. And underneath, HAPPY TO HELP.

Jane hoped that was true.

"I'm working with Detective Brogan," she said. Which was accurate. Accurate enough. "Can you check on a guest's registration for him? Lewis Wilhoite." Jane spelled it.

Ms. Sieger frowned, looked up from her computer keyboard, a lock of curly auburn falling over one cheek as she tilted her head in thought. Eyed Jake, still by the elevator.

Jane pushed, the tiniest of bits. "Ms. Sieger? The detective is on his radio, as you can see. He just needs to know who made Mr. Wilhoite's reservations. And when." She smiled, oh so reassuring and unthreatening.

"You're Jane Ryland," Julie said. "The reporter. Are you still a reporter? I'm Julie. I'm new."

"Nice to meet you," Jane said. Avoiding the questions.

"I love your work." The clerk scratched an eyebrow. "I guess it's okay for me to show you, if you're working with the police and all. I saw them take out an injured guy. On a stretcher. Oh—is that the guy you're asking about? Your job is so *intense!*"

"Sometimes," Jane said. A man shot and a woman in custody—real life, not a movie—and this girl was making conversation. Maybe life was getting back to normal.

"Got it." Julie turned a computer monitor to face Jane. "Okay, see? The reservation was made, um, four days ago? By . . . let me see. A Robyn Fasullo?"

"Four days ago?" Jane kept an appropriately blank expression on her face as her mind whirled.

"Yes. I remember this especially, because I was on reservations that day." The clerk swiveled the monitor back into place. "The woman wanted a room close to the pool. She said her little girl loved to swim."

59

Elbows on her desk, Catherine Siskel stared at the phone receiver in her hand. The light on her phone console blinked green, the dial tone humming, expectant. Detective Brogan hadn't called her back. He was homicide, she'd discovered. And that's who she needed. But there was one more option. Not a very pleasant one, but pleasant was over for the foreseeable future.

So far she'd lived her life solving problems for others. Now it was time to solve her own problems, and her daughter's. The dial tone changed to the hurry-up signal, harsh and insistent. Catherine hung up. Thinking it through one more time. Making sure.

Even though shafts of late-afternoon sunlight persevered through the barely opened blinds, it felt like the walls of her office were closing in. Tenley sat in the corner of the couch, her legs storked underneath, her dear little eyes still red from her tears, as quiet as Catherine had ever seen her. Brileen, in the guest chair facing the desk, clasped her hands in her lap, staring at nothing.

Catherine needed that damn thumb drive. With the pictures of Tenley.

What if it had been in her dead husband's pocket? If Greg had died to get it, what if he still had it? Which meant the police had it now.

Catherine eyed the white business card again, decided, and dialed.

It didn't even ring once.

"Naka," the voice said.

Catherine paused. This was the moment her job ended and her life changed. She'd lied to the police. On purpose. But at least she *had* her life, and Tenley did, too.

"This is Catherine Siskel," she said. "Detective Brogan told me to call you. It's about my missing husband, Greg Siskel."

Tenley uncurled herself from the corner of the couch, wary, listening.

"I think I know where my husband is," Catherine said.

Catherine heard Naka clearing her throat.

"I see," Naka said. "So he's not missing?"

Tenley stood up, came to the desk.

"He's the victim in the Curley Park incident. So I suppose he's in the"—she looked at Tenley, about to say a word she'd kill to spare her daughter from hearing—"morgue."

Tenley came closer, nestled into her mother's shoulder, her head fitting just under Catherine's chin. Brileen wrapped her arms across her own chest and stared at the floor.

"I see," the voice came back. "Why do you think that, Mrs. Siskel?"

"Because—" Catherine gulped. She actually gulped, she'd never thought that was something people really did. And then she found her words. "Because it's all on tape."

"No, it isn't." Tenley stepped away from her, frowning. "Mom, I *told* you—"

"That's right," Catherine answered Sergeant Naka. She held up a palm to stop Tenley's protest, added a wan smile. *Wait, honey.* "I've seen the tape of it. I've called Detective Brogan to tell him the same thing. Now I need to see my husband."

Catherine heard a long breath on the other end of the line, the sound of a thin spool of air coming through the phone. She imagined this Naka, assimilating it all. Considering protocol. Planning her next move.

"I see," the police officer's voice came back. "In fact, that's where I am right now. At the morgue. We're compiling the missing person dossier, in fact. Getting a photo for identification. Inventorying the possessions.

Someone will have to come do a formal identification, I'm afraid, Mrs. Siskel."

"I can be there in fifteen minutes," Catherine said. She hugged Tenley closer to her. "But you said—possessions. Was there a phone? A wallet? And might I ask, did you find a thumb drive?"

Another pause. Tenley took a step closer. Brileen stood, putting the tips of her fingers on Catherine's desk. The three women waited.

Catherine took a chance. Pushed the button for speakerphone. Heard the staticky buzz that meant the next words could be heard by all in the room. All three had a stake in this. They should all hear it at the same time.

Silence.

"Sergeant Naka?" Catherine leaned toward the speaker. "Did you hear my question?"

"Yes." The voice crackled through the tiny holes of the black metal speaker. "No, there's no phone, and no wallet. But yes, there's a thumb drive. It was hidden in his shoe."

"Jane!" Robyn stood, holding out her arms, sobbing, as Jane opened the door, Jake close behind her. The supply room looked like a padded cell of towels and sheets, identically folded piles of white linens stacked on metal shelves, almost floor to ceiling. The place smelled faintly of bleach and summery fabric softener. A long rectangular table occupied the middle of the room. Robyn had been seated on a beige folding chair, its back against the table. She was flanked by two uniformed cops.

One of them, a surprisingly attractive woman with a French twist under her billed cap, not quite gently returned Robyn to her seat. The other was DeLuca. Though he leaned against one row of shelving, one leg crossed over the other—a study in nonchalance—he seemed to be in charge.

"Clearly you're free to leave, Mrs. Wilhoite," DeLuca said. Jane had never heard his voice like that, saying one thing and clearly meaning the opposite. "At any time. But if you stay, we'd love to have you keep your seat."

"Tell them, Jane." Robyn's voice, entreating, needy, insistent, reached out and encircled Jane, almost pulling her closer. Robyn's lipstick was gone, her hair wild, a single trail of black mascara jagging dramatically down one check. Her pale yellow blouse floated over black capri pants, her toenails painted pale blue. She still looked gorgeous, Jane thought. Even after she'd just shot her husband. And she was a complete liar.

In the elevator on the way up, Jane told Jake what she'd discovered at the front desk. "Which changes things, right?" As the elevator doors opened on the third floor, she added, "Does Robyn think Lewis is dead? Are you going to tell her he's not?"

"Let's see how that plays out," Jake had told her.

Jane felt a pang of hesitation, her reporter instinct balancing both sides of the story even while she was also part of it. "Don't you have to give her the chance to ask for a lawyer?"

"Not as long as she insists she's the victim," Jake had said. "Anyway, Judge Ryland, I *did* give her that option. And she said she wanted you."

Now here they were, face-to-face. Robyn had called Jane to be her lifeline.

"Mrs. Wilhoite? You said you wanted to talk to Ms. Ryland." Jake directed his words to Robyn, using his cop voice. "Here she is."

Uh-oh, Jane thought. We were all at dinner together. Was Robyn savvy enough to use that against them? To wonder why Jake was suddenly calling her "Ms. Ryland"? DeLuca knew about them, of course. But the female cop . . . Exactly why this was a problem. She hoped they didn't have to cross that bridge.

"Tell them, Jane," Robyn gestured, entreating, with both hands. "Tell them how worried I was, that Gracie wasn't home from school, that Lewis had called in sick for her, how I didn't know that. Tell them!"

"So you were shocked when Gracie and Lewis weren't where you thought they'd be," Jane said, nodding, encouraging her to tell the story. Hoping she didn't mention dinner.

"Exactly! Can you imagine? You were there, you heard it all."

"I heard *you*," Jane said. The Rubik's Cube that was Robyn began to change colors, clicking into place a different way. Jane had heard *Robyn*, only Robyn. Never Lewis.

"And tell them how upset and frustrated I was when they had the idiotic flat tire, and they had to stay in the garage, that horrible garage, and—"

"What garage was that?" Jake asked.

"What?"

"Just wondering what garage was open that time of night, which place your husband would have called for a flat tire."

"I don't know! Why would I know? How would I know? He didn't tell me. You heard him, Jane."

"I heard *you*," Jane said. The cube clicked again. "Not Lewis."

Robyn raked both hands through her hair, making her wild curls even wilder. "But tell them, Jane, about what you found in the computer. About who Lewis really was? Or wasn't?"

Click. It had been awfully easy for Jane to find that "fake" identity. Jane had never heard about Wharton from Lewis. Only from Robyn. What if Robyn simply found another Lewis Wilhoite? And facilitated Jane's finding him? To pretend he had stolen an identity? *Click.*

"So you were shocked when they wound up in this hotel?" Jane went on, ignoring Robyn's last question. "Is that what you're saying?"

"Yes, of course!" Robyn leaned forward, beseeching, convincing. "You were there, Jane, when Lewis called! To *finally* say where he was, to tell me to let you come reclaim my darling Gracie—"

She stopped. The white-walled room went still.

"What, Mrs. Wilhoite?" Jake's voice was even, calm, hard as onyx. Jane knew exactly what was coming.

Robyn's eyes searched the room floor to ceiling, then side to side, a frantic sparrow searching for a way out. Then she sat up straight, shoulders squared, back not touching the curved metal of the chair.

"Where is she?" she demanded. "What have you done with her?"

"Yeah, interesting you brought that up." DeLuca looked at his watch, as if he'd been calculating the time. "Wondered when you'd ask about her."

"She's fine," Jake said. "She's with her father. Daniel Fasullo."

Robyn rolled her eyes. "I want to *go*," she said. "So tell them, Jane, tell them—"

"But why did you come here, Robyn?" Jane almost felt like crying. Her voice wasn't quite working. She was tired and stressed, yes, but this story was such a wretched one. "You said Lewis would give Gracie only to me. Why didn't you just let that happen and let it all be over?"

"He called again, while you were gone," Robyn said. "Told me he'd changed his mind, that *I* had to come. He demanded *I* come. He insisted that he and I had to talk it out, face-to-face. He sounded horrible, ugly, I know how he gets. I tried to call you but—"

"But?" Jane said. She felt one eyebrow go up.

"I kept getting the wrong number, I don't know," Robyn said dismissively. "You know phones."

"So it was a surprise to you that Lewis chose this particular hotel?" Jake had pretty much stayed out of it so far. Now he took a step forward, his right arm almost touching Jane's left. Jane didn't move. Letting him play the card. "Mrs. Wilhoite? A surprise?"

"Yes, of course. Tell them, Jane. You were there. You heard the call."

Jane kept her expression even. No wonder Jake closed cases. He was methodically reeling Robyn in. But Jane had thought of asking about the room reservation. He owed her one.

"I heard *you*," Jane said again. She mentally replayed their conversations, the phone calls, one after the other. Remembering. "Not Lewis."

"Well, whatever!" Robyn waved her off. "And then I got here, and went to his room. And he was completely out of it, drunk, I think, and crazy and demanding and—"

"Was Gracie there?" Jake asked.

"Yes. No. When?" Robyn shifted in her chair, then seemed to gather herself. She clasped her hands in her lap, the picture of maternal virtue. "No, when I arrived she was—I don't know. Wherever Lewis hid her!"

"I see," Jane said. Jane thought of Gracie at the palm trees, Gracie not expecting her. Gracie aimless and bored. She'd been sent away. On purpose. By who?

"And then what?" Jake asked.

"And then Lewis, or whatever his name really is, pulled out a gun and tried to shoot me! What do you *think*?" Her voice tightened, rising pitch by pitch as she talked. "So I kicked him and grabbed the gun—he's such a fool—and he came *at* me and I had to shoot him. He would have killed me! What else was I supposed to do? You know it! You know it! I was defending myself and my daughter. Jane, you *know* this! He was going to take her!"

60

"Mom?" Tenley's rear hurt from sitting on the long wooden bench in the waiting room. She was thinking so hard, it seemed like it made her heavier, the weight of everything on her shoulders and in her brain. There could *not* be any secret video of her doing anything wrong or embarrassing. Because she'd never done anything. So what had her father been trying to protect her—and their family—from?

The sign on the wall was a circular seal of Boston, like the one in her mother's office and the one on the wall in her own stupid office, the surveillance room. But underneath this one, the blocky black letters spelled OFFICE OF THE MEDICAL EXAMINER. The police officer, that Sergeant Naka, had asked them to wait here in the little lobby place. "Ten minutes," she said, looking at a round clock on the wall. The kind with big black numbers and big black pointing arrows. It actually gave a little click as each second went by.

Tenley wondered if time could stop, maybe. Just stop. Or rewind, erase, and start over. The video of their lives, take two. But in real life there were no second chances.

Behind the closed blank metal door, Tenley knew, was her father's body. Mom had already identified him. The police had called, saying they'd come talk to her later. Mom was really upset.

Now they had to wait for the "effects." What Dad had in his pockets. She almost couldn't breathe thinking about that, because some of it was supposed to be about *her*, but she couldn't let her mother face this alone. Mom, who was now holding Tenley's hand maybe for the first time in ten years, stared at the space in front of her. Tenley kind of wanted to let go, but when she gave a little tug, her mom held on tighter.

Brileen sat on the other side of her, clutching her laptop bag as always. Why had she even come along? Tenley still couldn't decide if Brileen was good or bad. She'd only tried to help, she'd told them. Everything she did was to try to help. But Brileen had made a bunch of really shitty decisions.

Tenley knew how that felt.

Thing was. What Tenley had been thinking about so hard this whole time and throughout the silent drive from City Hall to the medical examiner's office. The video of Lanna.

"Mom?" Tenley said again. She kept her voice low. It seemed like the thing to do in a place full of dead people.

"Yes, honey?"

Her mom turned, looked over at her, shifted a bit on the bench but still didn't unclasp her hand. Mom was off in some other world, seemed like, and was almost whispering, too. The clock ticked, one hand moved ahead a little space.

"I know you don't want to look at the thumb drive video of Lanna," Tenley said. "Neither do I. But what if it's connected? What if the person on the video is the person who killed her?"

"No one killed Lanna, Ten." Her mother's eyes filled with tears. "It was an accident."

"But why was she in the woods?" Tenley had to make Mom at least think about this. "What if she was meeting—whoever it was? And what if that's who's on the video? You know what I mean. The horrible video and the boyfriend and the money. And Dad." Tenley paused, knowing she was running all her words together. "What happened to Dad. Maybe it's all connected."

Silence. Except for the stupid clock.

Tenley felt Brileen shift in her seat again, probably embarrassed and humiliated by the whole thing. It was Brileen's fault, really, some of it, at least.

"You said she had a boyfriend." Mom interrupted Tenley's thoughts.

"Yes," Brileen said.

"Yes," Tenley said at the same time.

"But you don't know who it is? Was?"

"No." They answered separately this time. Tenley remembered even the police couldn't find him.

Brileen slid farther away, got as close to the end of the bench as possible.

The clock ticked again, so loudly Tenley wondered if it was her imagination. Nothing could be that loud. Six minutes to go.

"Brileen," Mom said, "may I use your laptop?"

Jane felt the vibration of her phone through her tote bag, even heard its insistent buzz in the padded silence of the supply room. All eyes were still on wild-eyed Robyn, who'd paused in her tirade. She was watching Jake and DeLuca and the other cop, watching Jane, obviously gauging their reactions.

Jane didn't believe a word she said. But how to prove she was a liar?

This was Jake's show. She kept silent, waiting for his cue. Probably Marsh Tyson was calling her, wondering why the hell she was in the middle of this huge story and hadn't let him know. She'd have to come up with an answer for that one.

Her phone buzzed again. Jake nodded, giving her permission. "Might be—"

True. She hit the green button. "Yes?"

Melissa.

"Can anyone else hear me?" her sister asked.

"No." Jane checked Jake's expression, to see if Melissa's voice had carried. "No."

"I asked Gracie what you told me to," Melissa said.

"Okay," Jane said. "And?"

"I'm going to put her on the phone so you can hear it, firsthand. I think you'll be interested."

"Okay." Jane heard a rustle and a murmur, Melissa handing the phone to the little girl. "Tell Jane what you told me, sweetheart," she heard Melissa say.

"Hi, Jane," Gracie said. "I'm sorry I was mean to you."

"You did exactly the right thing, honey." The girl sounded so sincere. "I'm proud of you. I didn't mean to scare you."

"Who is that?" Robyn tried to get to her feet. "Who is that?"

"So remember what Melissa asked you?" Jane said, pretending to ignore Robyn's demand. "Why were you waiting in the lobby, Gracie?"

"She doesn't know, for heaven's sake." Robyn's voice, disdainful. Dismissive. "You can't talk to a *child*. You can't expect a child to tell the truth."

Jane smiled at Robyn, a smile of pity and triumph that grew in strength as she heard the truth of what Gracie was saying. The truth of the Rubik's Cube that was Robyn, her fragmented lies snapping into place. Jane put her hand over the mouthpiece so Gracie, now prattling about Twizzlers and grown-ups running, wouldn't be distracted.

"What's wrong with the truth, Robyn?" Jane said. "Perhaps you'd like to hear it for yourself. On speaker." She poised her finger over the red button, saw Jake nod, saw DeLuca's thumbs-up.

"Gracie?" Jane said. "Tell me one more time? Why were you waiting in the lobby?"

"Mommy told me to." Her warble came through the tinny speakers of Jane's phone. "Mommy told me to go wait in the lobby. She said not to talk to anyone. She said Daddy was going to be busy, and going out of town for a long, long time, so I should wait for her, that she would come get me. Add that's what I did."

61

Catherine inserted the thumb drive into the port on the side of Brileen's laptop. Felt the click as the tab slotted into place, heard the whir of the mechanism.

The waiting room at the morgue room was so silent, so expectant, Catherine believed she could actually hear the seconds tick by on the old clock, which had probably hung on the wall since Mayor John Collins or Kevin White ruled the Boston roost. The clock, still here, proved time waited for no one.

The white triangle coalesced into place on the laptop screen.

Whatever was on this video was there whether Catherine watched it or not. And she had to admit her little daughter—not so little, now, but always little to her—was correct. What was on the video Brileen had given her in the Purple Martin might be heartbreakingly horrific to watch, but it might also give them some answers.

In politics, answers were always elusive, changing, linked with the polls or the zeitgeist or the budget. But in the world of her heart, her family, her children, there needed to be some sense of knowing. Of truly knowing.

She sighed, drew on her courage.

Look at the damn video.

Tenley was so close to her left side she could almost feel her daughter's heart beating. She sat quietly, long eyelashes blinking, blinking.

Brileen, too, leaned close.

Catherine clicked the white triangle. The recorded world spun into view.

Her greenroom. Empty. The camera was obviously in the upper left corner, pointed at the door, showing a wide shot of the room, the couch, the big puffy chair, the bathroom door, the coffee table. The rich paisley of the Oriental rug looked twisted, almost distorted, through the surveillance lens.

The door opened, silently, a shaft of light from the hall striping the couch. Catherine had seen exactly that same striping, many times, as she'd escorted pols and performers, supplicants and celebrities to wait there until their meetings or appearances. Lanna had loved visiting City Hall during her college days, exploring the warrens of corridors and secret back stairways. The greenroom had been her study hall, her headquarters. There was even a computer, all hooked up for visitors. In years before, when Catherine couldn't get a babysitter, she'd parked both girls in the greenroom, where they'd played happily, often falling asleep on the couch.

There she was.

Her gorgeous Lanna walked into the room, laughing, almost tossing that mane of hair in an attitude Catherine never remembered seeing. Grown up. Womanly. Promising. She paused, turned on one high-heeled toe. Beckoned with fluttering fingers. Was someone behind her?

Catherine curled her hand through Tenley's. This was awful for her, Catherine realized. Maybe she shouldn't allow her to see it? But Catherine narrowed her eyes as she watched, anger now underscoring her dismay.

Who had put a camera in her office? When? She had never, *ever* known about this. She'd been chief of staff for eight years. Had it been there the whole time? Or could someone have installed it without her knowing? The mayor? Who?

And then a figure, a taller, bigger silhouette, cut through the shaft of light. Whoever it was must have flipped the light switch, not the overheads but the soft glow of the table lamp.

Lanna turned to face whoever it was, her body—was that Catherine's curvy black cashmere sweater?—relaxed and open. Her body language—open arms, canted hip—was welcoming. Familiar. Though the surveillance video was not quite in focus and the muffled sound, barely audible, Catherine imagined she heard the sound of Lanna's soft laughter.

The shadow changed. A foot appeared, then a leg, then a back. A man.

"He's facing her to the camera," Tenley whispered. "He knows it's there. He's staying out of the picture on purpose."

Catherine's blood chilled as she watched a hand caress Lanna's face. Her daughter didn't move. The man, only the edge of his back barely visible, put one hand on each of her shoulders. Her daughter, smiling, flirtatious, didn't move.

He began to lift the black cashmere, teasing the sweater up from the bottom edge, Lanna, full out laughing now, lifted her arms.

"Mom," Tenley said. "Mom."

"Mrs. Siskel?" Sergeant Naka called from across the room. "We're ready for you now."

Catherine slammed the laptop closed.

62

Nothing like a takedown to give you a jolt of adrenaline. Jake watched the collapse of Robyn Wilhoite's charade with some satisfaction, the reality emerging, absurdly, in the ridiculous towel-lined supply room. Apparently Angie Bartoneri had wrapped up her doctor's appointment and returned just in time to work the big event with DeLuca. As always, Jane had asked just the right question. With Gracie's coup de grâce answer, the woman's story began to unravel. And now was pouring out of her.

As Jake had predicted, it was all about the money. The child support that Daniel Fasullo had paid all these years. The money he had sent to support a child who, Robyn had finally admitted, was not his biological daughter.

"You can't understand what it was like. What was I supposed to do? It *might* have been Daniel's, you know? He *believed* it was, and he—did the right thing."

"Even though *you* didn't," Jake said.

"Does Daniel know?" Jane asked. "Does Gracie?"

With the wedding on the way, and Gracie about to be taken from them, Lewis had lost it, Robyn said. Insisted she should tell the truth. Threatened to spill all to Daniel and Melissa in hopes of keeping Gracie at home.

"I told him, I *told* him," Robyn wailed. "Gracie was happy, we were happy, he *wasn't working,* for God's sake. I should never have told him in the first place! We needed the money and—"

"So you just made it all up? A phony abduction?" Jake asked. *What a freaking piece of work.* "So you could pretend to kill him in self-defense?"

He pointed to DeLuca and Angie, motioning them into action. "Robyn Wilhoite, you're under arrest for the attempted murder of Lewis Wilhoite. You have the night to remain silent . . ."

Robyn struggled against D and Angie as they put her in cuffs, talking over Jake as he finished her rights.

"It was all for Gracie," she insisted. "I want a lawyer."

"Good call," Jane said.

"Your husband will live, by the way," Jake said. "So you know."

Lewis would live, Jake had said. Jane thought of the man she'd seen only in photos. Lewis with his sandy hair, his glasses. Just like Gracie's.

Almost afraid to ask, Jane looked at Jake, then back at the woman in custody. Jake couldn't ask any more questions, she knew, since Robyn had demanded a lawyer. But Jane could. "Robyn? Is *Lewis* Gracie's biological father?"

"Lawyer," Robyn said.

"Good one," DeLuca said.

"We're done here," Jake said.

DeLuca and the woman detective cuffed Robyn, who continued to mutter under her breath. Jake opened the supply room door, motioned for the team to take their prisoner away.

"Jake," Jane said.

He turned to her as the others went into the corridor, and she signaled with two thumbs—*text me.* He signaled back—*drink?* She pointed to her chest—*my house.*

Love you, he mouthed the words. And turned away.

"Love you, too," she said, silently, because Jake was already gone.

*   *   *

Back downstairs, Jake saw that the hotel lobby had fully come back to life. Fountain. Muzak. Tourists. Again, Jane had asked the killer question. A DNA test—and Lewis's testimony—would provide the final answers.

With a thank-you and adios to the cops still monitoring the hotel's front door, Jake headed for City Hall.

Now Catherine Siskel wanted "to talk." Well, yeah. He did, too.

Curley Park was in full rush-hour hubbub, as if nothing had happened here—he looked at his watch—about thirty-six hours ago. But he'd gotten past being tired. Closing a case, at least being close to closing, always helped.

He punched the Walk button at the intersection, impatient. In one second, he was going to jaywalk.

Robyn Wilhoite. Piece of freaking work. She'd arranged a prewedding father-daughter outing—leaving father and daughter in the dark about her true motive. She'd found another Lewis Wilhoite and planted the phony identification to set her husband up as a diabolical con artist. Pretended to talk to Lewis on the phone, dramatically and calculatedly escalating her "panic" to Melissa and Jane. If Lewis had died, it might have worked.

Domestic violence. Jake hated that term. It was simply violence. He wished these stories could have happy endings, no kids affected, no one hurt, only adults working out their stupid differences while their kids' lives stayed untouched. But in real life, tragedy damaged everyone involved. After all these years, Jake knew there were more victims than the ones who wound up in hospitals and morgues.

Like every cop who dealt with the aftermath of violence, Jake could do no more than hope that Gracie would be okay.

Jake pushed through the heavy revolving glass door into the first floor of City Hall and flashed his badge at the rent-a-guard.

Now to Catherine Siskel. Who had promised to tell him the truth about *her* husband. When Jake called her back, she'd haltingly admitted Greg Siskel was not missing, but murdered.

That she knew it because she'd seen it on the video that did indeed exist. She'd told him about a girl named Brileen and a mysterious middleman. And about a five-minute clip of unauthorized surveillance. Who was on it and how she'd obtained it.

The Siskels and the Wilhoites. There were no happy families in Jake's line of work.

63

"What can I do for you?"

His voice sounded so superior. Tenley'd always known he was a sleaze. Tried to tell Lanna so, too, every time her sister mentioned him, hadn't understood why Lanna kept talking about the guy. Now she knew. Now, here he was, in Mom's office, acting like nothing horrible had happened.

Her mom stood, waved him to a chair across from her desk. "Hey, Ward."

Tenley had recognized what her boss hadn't disguised in the video. His stupid watch. "Mom," she'd said. And then she'd told her. And Brileen.

Even though Ward Dahlstrom tried to keep himself out of the greenroom camera shot, Tenley knew he must have been Lanna's . . . Tenley couldn't even think about it. Mom had gone crazy. They'd rewound the disgusting tape, twice, confirming. Then Mom made the phone call.

"Sorry our meeting kept getting postponed." Tenley couldn't figure out how Mom, hair in place and even wearing lipstick, could look so pleasant. "Lots going on. Any more on the police subpoena? For the Curley Park video?"

"Nope, nothing. Kelli Riordan says we may have dodged this bullet. The key is to steer clear of the cops, long as we can." Dahlstrom scanned the room, ignored Tenley, gestured to the guest chair. "Mind if I—"

Mom ignored him, which rocked. Ward Dahlstrom, king of creeps, stood there, shifting his stupid feet.

Tenley sat in the corner of her mom's couch. She'd promised she'd keep quiet, just watch and listen. City Hall was pretty empty. Almost six and most employees had bolted, even annoying Siobhan had buttoned her sweater to her chin and scuttled away. Tenley's father had been dead—oh—for a little more than a day. Tenley almost felt like she existed in a different world as half an hour ago they'd taken the thumb drive her father had died for, plugged it into Brileen's laptop, and held their breath. And clicked.

But there were no pictures on it. Nothing. There was video, and it was from Mom's greenroom, but there was no one in the picture. They'd watched until it ran out. No one. Nothing. An empty room.

Her mom had jerked the blank thumb drive from the port, then stood, holding it like a bug, as if she didn't know whether to throw it away or stomp on it. But the police had taken it back.

"Extortion, pure and simple," her mother had said as the three of them drove away from the morgue place.

"That bastard," Brileen said.

"Bastard is right," Mom said. "I bet—dammit. Once your father paid the money, who knew if he'd ever look at the drive? Even if he hadn't watched the video of Lanna, she'd confessed it was real. So when Brileen was told there were pictures of you, honey, maybe he simply believed it was true. And wanted to protect you."

Tenley felt so sad. Had her father not trusted her? But Mom had told her that Dad said he loved her. She'd remember that.

Her mom had sighed, an angry sad frustrated sigh. "Question is, who else knows? And who got that money? And who killed Greg?"

So now here was Ward Dahlstrom, all pin-striped suit and pocket square. Standing in front of Mom's desk like it was an ordinary day. Had he known about the money? He had to, right? She wanted to leap up from the couch and punch the guy, but that wasn't the part she was supposed to play.

Her mom's desk phone rang, as Tenley knew it would. Her mother answered.

"Yes," Mom said. "Give me a minute, please." Mom hung up, flapped open her computer, clicked the mouse. Narrowed her eyes at the screen. Then turned to Ward, still with that smile.

Tenley could hardly keep from smiling too. She felt powerful, for the first time.

"It's the police," Mom whispered to Ward.

"Shit," he muttered. He glanced at Tenley, but she pretended to be looking at her fingernails.

"Yeah." Mom pointed to the side door, conspiratorial. "Why don't you wait in the greenroom? I'll let you know the minute they're gone."

Before Jake could say a word, Catherine Siskel had opened the door and gestured him into her office. She put one finger to her lips, then pointed it to her desktop computer. Signaled him to follow her across the room.

Jake nodded, understanding. They'd stay quiet. Could her plan work?

Tenley uncurled herself from the sofa and joined her mother and Jake behind the desk. On the computer screen, Jake saw an unnaturally blue-tinted view of a flowered couch, two wing chairs, two end tables, an elaborate Oriental rug. A closed door in the back wall. And, pacing in front of the couch, a man in a pin-striped suit. Ward Dahlstrom. The "chief of surveillance." Perfect.

Jake acknowledged Tenley's skills with a thumbs-up. Tenley shrugged, accepting the approval. On the phone, Catherine had explained the girl had rigged up the greenroom laptop as a one-way computer video feed—like Skype or FaceTime. And this time Mr. Surveillance had no idea he was the one being secretly watched. And recorded.

Catherine had flapped a yellow legal pad to a clean page. Uncapped a felt-tip pen.

Tenley says he can hear us, she wrote.

"Hello, Detective," Catherine's voice was louder than normal. She looked at the screen, not at him. "What can I do for you?"

Jake matched her volume, also keeping his eyes on the screen. "We need to talk, ma'am. I need to see your . . ." Jake paused, made something up. ". . . calendar from the past week."

On camera, Dahlstrom took three paces to the left, turned, and paced to the right. The man stopped, hands on hips, and looked up at somewhere on the wall in front and above him.

That's where I found cam, Catherine wrote. *Upper left, in smoke alarm.*

Jake held his hand out for the pen. *You touch it?*

No.

"Let me look for that calendar, Detective," Catherine said. "It'll take a moment."

The camera's microphone made a barely audible buzz thorough the computer speaker. Dahlstrom, fidgeted, looked at his watch.

Jake and Catherine exchanged glances. Tenley stood, pulled out her cell phone, looked at her mom, then at Jake. Held up her phone, inquiring with her eyebrows.

Jake nodded, mouthed the words. "Do it."

Tenley's thumbs moved across the phone's tiny keypad. Jake saw her hit Send, then smile.

On the screen, the light changed in the greenroom, the surveillance blue diffused by a fluorescent glare as, with a click, the door in the back wall opened.

Dahlstrom turned at the first sound, his back now to their clandestine computer. "What?" they heard him say.

And there, on camera, was Brileen.

Moment of truth, Catherine thought. Would Brileen be able to pull this off?

Catherine watched the video feed coming from the greenroom. An opaque wall separated them, but thanks to the laptop's video camera, the layers of wallpaper and plaster and insulation might as well be nonexistent. They could see and hear everything.

"What are *you* doing here?" Brileen said. "I was in the bathroom."

On the way back from the morgue, the three women, Catherine, Brileen, and Tenley, had plotted the trap to catch Ward Dahlstrom. They knew they couldn't simply confront him with the Lanna video. He'd just insist he hadn't known it was being taped.

They needed the police to clinch the trap. Now the three of them—mother, daughter, and cop—would watch the charade unfold.

Brileen had sworn she'd do anything to make up for what she'd done. Now they'd see.

Brileen had positioned herself behind the couch. A barrier. Just in case.

Even with the inferior video quality, Catherine could see Dahlstrom's posture change, his back straighten.

"What are *you* doing here?" Dahlstrom's voice, wary, came through the speaker perfectly. He reached into his pocket. "I have no idea who you are."

He took a step toward Brileen.

"Mom," Tenley whispered.

Catherine saw Brogan move toward the door to the greenroom, hand to his waist. As they'd planned. If Brileen were in danger, he'd have to act.

But Dahlstrom had simply taken out a cell phone.

Catherine signaled the detective to come back to the screen. "Is this the calendar you wanted to see?" she said, keeping up their pretense. She hoped Dahlstrom was too distracted to eavesdrop.

"Let me look," Brogan said. And he *was* looking. At the screen.

"My name is Brileen Finnerty," they heard her say. Brileen planted both hands on the back of the flowered couch. Leaned toward Dahlstrom. "Mean anything to you?"

Dahlstrom didn't budge, his back to the laptop's eye. "Should it?"

"Wish we could see the guy's face," Catherine murmured.

Brileen shook her head, as if impatient. "Look. Don't screw with me. I'm Tenley's 'friend' now. As you well know. But Siskel's got the police out there, I assume you know that, too."

"Does she know you're in here?"

"Are you kidding me? She *sent* me here. Just like she sent you! She'd do anything to protect her reputation. You of all people know that. She's trying to keep us both out of the cop's way because *I* know about the thumb drives, and *you* know about that murder video."

"I don't know what you're talking abou—"

Catherine thought she detected a quaver in Dahlstrom's voice. A hesitation. So frustrating not to be able to see his face.

"But they *don't* know we know each other!" Brileen interrupted, insistent. "And they don't know about Hugh. And that's what makes this perfect."

Who's . . . Detective Brogan wrote.

"Don't you see?" Brileen went on, persuading. "Catherine Siskel has the thumb drives. Both of them. They were in her dead husband's pocket. The cops gave them to her. Both of them."

Both? Not true, Brogan wrote.

Catherine nodded. *Exactly.*

"But here's the thing," Brileen went on. "The cops didn't watch the videos. And Catherine didn't either. But Lanna told me about you, Ward. *All* about you."

"Lanna who?" Dahlstrom said.

"Lanna *who*?" Brileen voice was a mocking echo. She smoothed a hand along the back of the couch, then pointed at Dahlstrom. "Oh. I get it. You think I'm—"

Catherine held up crossed fingers. Brogan nodded.

"—wearing a wire?" Brileen stepped around the side of the couch, came toward him. Arms outstretched. Offering herself. "Are you kidding me? Please. *Fine.* You want to check?"

Dahlstrom turned away. And as he did, his glance flickered to the upper left, exactly where Catherine found the hidden camera.

He knows, Brogan wrote.

Yup. Catherine wrote. "Is there anything else you need, Detective?" she said out loud.

Brileen had grabbed him by the arm. "Don't you see?"

"It's not gonna work," Tenley whispered.

"Shh," Catherine said. Though she agreed. Maybe Dahlstrom was too cagey. But Brileen was giving it all she had.

"When they figure out it's you on the thumb drive video," Brileen said, still holding Dahlstrom's arm, "they're gonna nail you for the murder of Greg Siskel."

Brileen pointed to her chest, then gestured, wide, with both hands. "And then—like you're gonna protect me? I'm in as deep as you. But listen. I can get those thumb drives from Siskel," Brileen said. "I know I can. And I'll destroy them."

Silence. Dahlstrom's back was still to the camera.

Catherine saw the determination on Brileen's face.

"Dahlstrom, hear me," the girl said. "I am your only. Frigging. Way out."

Dahlstrom looked at his cell phone. "I need to make a call."

Catherine looked at the detective, triumphant. She could almost, almost, make out the numbers he was dialing. But she'd be able to look again. Because even though Ward Dahlstrom's back was to the computer's hidden camera, he was holding his phone directly in its view.

Tenley mimed applause. Catherine put her arm around her daughter. They'd won.

Then Brogan's phone rang.

64

Jake flinched at the sound. Catherine Siskel turned to him, questioning. He waved her off. Clearly Dahlstrom wasn't calling *him*. It was DeLuca.

"Hey, D," he kept his voice low. "Hang on."

On the computer screen, Dahlstrom had turned away from Brileen as he talked. Jake saw Brileen touch her ear and shake her head.

"She can't hear what he's saying," Tenley whispered.

"It's okay," Jake reassured her, his voice low. "I can take his phone."

"Whose phone?" DeLuca asked.

"Later," Jake said. "What's up, D?"

"John Doe 2 has the tattoo we saw in the bystander's photo," DeLuca said.

"Awesome." Jake kept his eyes on the screen. Dahlstrom was still on the phone. "Did he tell you what happened? Why he killed Greg Siskel?"

"Killed who?" DeLuca said. "Greg—?"

Right. DeLuca had no idea about any of this yet.

"Later," Jake said. "But that's great." This was all coming together. Though it had only been, what, not yet forty-eight hours? But if tattoo guy was talking, case closed. Jake could almost envision his own apartment. A beer. A pillow. "What'd he say? About what happened?"

"Nothing," DeLuca said. "He's dead."

In an instant, in his mental video, Jake saw Curley Park, Greg Siskel— trying to protect his daughter from humiliation—with a knife in his back. Saw what happened in Franklin Alley. Finally Jake had enough to make his move.

"Get a warrant for Calvin Hewlitt for the murder of . . . call him a John Doe," Jake said. "Bring that asshole in. I've got one more thing to do here."

Jake clicked off, stashed the cell in his pocket.

"Ready?" Jake asked. One more asshole to go.

"Totally." Tenley brandished her cell. "Say when."

Jake turned to the greenroom door. Yanked it open. Before Dahlstrom could react, Jake snatched the phone from the man's hand. Put it to his own ear.

"Hey!" Dahlstrom yelled, waved his arms as he grabbed for his cell. "Hang up!" he called out. "Hang up!"

Jake stood, smiling, holding the now-buzzing phone. Whoever was on the other end had followed directions, leaving only a dial tone.

"You trying to hide something, Mr. Dahlstrom?" Jake said.

Dahlstrom's face reddened, a lock of hair falling over his forehead. A muscle in his neck twitched. "You can't take my phone," he insisted. "Not without a warrant."

Jake tilted his head left, then right, pretended to think about it. "Possibly," he said. "But it won't save you. We've got the whole thing on tape."

"On tape? That girl?" Dahlstrom waved toward the greenroom. "She said she wasn't wired—I could have looked!"

"She wasn't," Jake said. This was almost fun. "The room was."

He signaled Catherine, who reached out and swiveled the monitor, turning it so Dahlstrom could see it.

Brileen, on her cell with Tenley, waved at the camera. "Hi, Ward," her voice came over the speaker.

"You can't record my voice without my knowledge!" Dahlstrom swept his hair from his forehead, then sneered at Jake, hands on hips. "It's illegal, even for the cops, *Detective*. I'd have thought you'd know that."

"Oh, I do," Jake said. "Massachusetts General Laws chapter two seven-two, section ninety-nine requires all parties to know they're being recorded." Jake paused, savoring the moment. Saw Catherine draw a deep breath, take her daughter's hand. Saw Tenley almost smile. "However."

Jake held up the thumb drive.

Dahlstrom flinched, his eyes narrowing. He tried, too late, to hide his reaction.

"Yeah," Jake said. "Because in fact, you *did* know. Right? You set up a taping yourself. Up in the smoke alarm." He tucked the drive back in his jacket pocket. "So it's all legal and admissible. Now, tell us about all this. Or you're going down. Alone."

"I don't know what you're talking about," Dahlstrom said. "I want a lawyer."

"Noted." Jake examined Dahlstrom's cell phone. The keypad was still illuminated, black numbers encircled in black. "But meantime, why don't I just give your partner in crime a call?"

He tapped the button for Recents. Clicked on the top listing. And hit Send.

Jane winced as her phone rang. The sign in the police waiting room said NO CELL PHONES, but she had ignored it. The black-uniformed guard stationed at the metal reception desk glared at her.

"Sorry!" Jane said, trying to look sorry. Robyn Wilhoite had been taken to some interrogation room. Jane was parked here and ordered to wait. For what? she'd asked.

But the cop, an icily chic detective named Bartoneri, had declined to elaborate, saying she'd be back "at the appropriate time." Jane remembered Bartoneri—she'd been in the supply room with DeLuca for Robyn Wilhoite's questioning. Jane especially remembered the eyebrows. The heels on her black boots. And that body. She couldn't wait to ask Jake for the scoop about her.

It had been half an hour now, at least, that Jane had waited on this

lumpy sofa for word on Robyn, distracted only by the local news broadcast on the TV monitor mounted high on the plaster wall. The sound was
muted, but she recognized the story—the exterior of the University Inn,
the blue lights of the ambulance that she knew carried Lewis Wilhoite,
and silent talking heads identified only as "hotel guests." The graphic, a
target superimposed over the University Inn logo, was accompanied by
the headline "Downtown Drama."

What you see on TV is only part of the story, Jane thought. That had
never been clearer, how little of reality could be revealed in the brief snip-
pets of video and supposedly catchy headlines.

When the guard went back to her paperwork, Jane surreptitiously
checked her cell. Melissa had texted that she and Daniel had taken
Gracie for ice cream—and the girl seemed fine. She'd have a difficult
road ahead. But lucky to have Melissa and Daniel.

"Miss Ryland?"

Jane looked up at her name. The desk clerk was now pointing to Detective Bartoneri, who'd just arrived and stood at the waiting room door,
a cell phone to her ear.

Finally. Jane tried to read Bartoneri's expression. Something must be
going on in that phone call, it was obvious from the woman's frown and
her downcast eyes. Jane stood, worrying, yanked her tote bag to her shoulder. Took a step toward the door.

Bartoneri's expression changed again. Surprise? Concern? Fear? The
detective took the phone away from her ear, narrowing her eyes at the
screen.

Then the detective's face paled. She took a step back. And hung up.

"Something wrong?" Jane had to ask. Clearly there was. Maybe—
Lewis? If Robyn had succeeded in killing him, they'd never know the
real story. And poor Gracie . . .

Detective Bartoneri had slipped her cell phone into a pocket of her
black blazer. Jane saw the gold badge clipped to her belt and the edge of a
black leather holster.

"Not at all." Bartoneri squared her shoulders, looked Jane up and down. "I'm here regarding Mrs. Wilhoite," she said. "She's asked for an attorney. We'll be holding her until he arrives. As a result, there's no reason for you to remain, since—"

Bartoneri's phone rang. The three-tone trill came clearly though the detective's jacket. The woman's eyes widened. She yanked out the cell, looked at the screen. Seemed to make a decision.

"Hello?" she said.

65

"Off the record?" Jake leaned back against the pile of pillows on Jane's leather couch, his shoes kicked off, his legs stretched the full length. Coda, as always, had curled herself on his lap, tail wrapped to her pink nose. Jake was not a cat person, but Jane's calico aggressively refused to accept that. "Yeah. It was Angie."

Jane plopped a wooden bowl of twisty pretzels on the coffee table, then handed him an IPA, the icy brown bottle wrapped in a napkin. She took her usual spot, leaning back at the opposite end of the couch. Her legs, in those somehow sexy black sweatpants, paralleled his, her toes against his thigh.

"Everything on the couch is off the record." Jane kneaded her toes into his jeans. "Especially after midnight. But I can't believe I was right there when you called Angela Bartoneri. Rats. Wish I had known what was going on."

Jake tried to calculate how long he'd been awake. It was risky to collapse on Jane's couch, but they were both flying on adrenaline right now. Jane already knew Robyn Wilhoite was under arrest for attempted murder. And Angie Bartoneri was in custody as a co-conspirator in the secret City Hall taping and extortion. "I'll tell you the rest—if you keep it secret."

"Who am I gonna tell?" Jane toasted him with her glass of red wine. "I'm unemployed, and probably without prospects, since I blew off Marsh Tyson to take care of the Gracie thing."

He saw her face fall.

"I know, honey." Jake shifted, pressing the weight of his leg against the length of hers. "We'll all take care of Gracie, right? However it turns out? Lewis will be fine. We know Gracie loves him, and he loves her. She's lucky, you know, to have Melissa and Daniel. And you."

"And you." Jane took a sip of her wine, closed her eyes briefly. "We can't control the universe," she said. "We can only do the best we can."

They sat, silent, for a moment, Coda's purr vibrating against Jake's chest. As peaceful and domestic as a scene could be—for a cop and a reporter after forty straight hours of deception and murder. And two families struggling with a new reality.

"Curley Park," Jane said.

"Just what I was thinking," Jake admitted.

"You're such a romantic." Jane poked him with a toe. "But yeah, off the record. Tell me. You grabbed that Ward Dahlstrom's phone and hit Redial—very cool. Legally iffy, right? But cool. And that's when you reached Angela Bartoneri?"

"Former Detective Angie Bartoneri—who's now in custody for extortion and conspiracy and a shitload of other stuff," Jake said. "Along with her partner in crime, Ward Dahlstrom. Apparently he's hated Catherine Siskel ever since she got named chief of staff instead of him. Decided to use her daughters to get revenge."

Dahlstrom, the weak link, had ratted out Angie the second he'd had the option. Once Jake had heard Bartoneri answer Dahlstrom's phone— he'd recognized her voice instantly this time—their scheme had begun to disintegrate. Angie in turn had ratted out Calvin Hewlitt, who she said used his security systems for an extortion scheme, threatening to leak embarrassing security videos unless victims paid them off. Apparently the University Inn was a prime source. Jake had already subpoenaed every bit of video from Hewlitt Security.

"They couldn't sell the stuff to *TMZ* and places like that," Jake said. "They'd be too easy to trace, you know? Instead, they demanded payoffs from rock stars and pols to keep that stuff under wraps. Private citizens, too. We found they'd taped a girlfriend of Lanna Siskel's in a hotel room with her still-closeted lover. Seems like the University Inn's surveillance system supported a cottage industry in undercover video."

"Disgusting," Jane said. She wondered if Tall and Beefy were involved. Be fun to cover their trial.

"Problem is," Jake said, "Calvin Hewlitt—the guy you saw in the alley?—insists he had nothing to do with anything. No question his company installed the hotel surveillance systems, and his college buddy Dahlstrom hired Hewlitt Security to wire City Hall all on the up-and-up. But he says he had no idea anyone was *using* the videos. He insisted Dahlstrom, on his own, wired the greenroom to his personal computer. And that Dahlstrom also made the Lanna Siskel video and the phony one of Tenley on his own. Well, 'on his own' in cahoots with Angie. I knew she'd hooked up with some computer guy. Dahlstrom and Angie. *Geez.* Both bitter about their careers. Both out for revenge. I bet they were quite the happy couple."

"Easy enough to find out about the hookup." Jane crunched a pretzel, brushed the salty crumbs off her chest. "The computer hookup, I mean. Not Bartoneri and Dahlstrom."

"Yeah." Jake tipped his beer, finishing the last drop. Sleep was about to overtake him, but now his brain was revving. "Wish we could link Hewlitt to Curley Park, you know? He was in Franklin Alley, we know that. But he insists he wasn't anywhere near the stabbing."

"Want another?" Jane drained her wineglass. Uncurled herself from him. He could still feel the heat from her leg against his.

"Sure." If they wound up here on the couch all night, what the hell. Even though tomorrow—*it was already tomorrow*—he and D still had a shitload to solve. "We can't figure out who the dead guy with the tattoo was—but again, it's not like we're a TV show. It hasn't even been forty-eight hours. We've got Dahlstrom and Bartoneri. We'll crack this. I know Hewlitt's the link. I just wish I could put him in Curley Park. He was probably all over those photos Bobby Land took. Obviously that's why he smashed the damn camera. We just can't prove it."

* * *

"Poor Bobby Land," Jane said. She saw three more IPAs in her fridge, but Jake was fading fast. She'd never seen him so tired. Scruffy face, eyes spiked red, his T-shirt sagging. He was still adorable, no question, but exhausted. She kept talking as she came back into the living room. Jake had draped one leg over the top of the couch. Coda hadn't budged. "So Bobby Land—you think Bartoneri and Dahlstrom were in on that, too?"

"We'll find out. Like I told each of them, first to talk is the first to walk," he told her, taking the beer. He took a swig, then tucked the bottle between his arm and the back of the couch, settled into the pillows. Yawned. "Oh, sorry. Anyway. Yeah. They clearly thought Land had witnessed the stabbing. The kid made a big deal of it, remember? My bet's on Angie. She knew the blind spots of the police HQ surveillance cameras. And Angie had left the hospital at the time of the attack. She's got means, motive—and no alibi. And remember, she was alone in the ambulance with the tattoo guy. Who knows what she did to make his condition worse."

Jane pictured it all again, Bobby Land, just a scrawny kid who longed to hit the big time with his photos. He'd clearly latched on to her because . . .

"Jake?" she began, then stopped. He was out cold, the mutterings of his snores competing with Coda's purr. She smiled, not wanting to wake him. She eased herself up from the couch, pausing, one foot on and one foot off, as Jake shifted, cozying into the pillows. She leaned across him, smelled the beer and the Jake scent, pulled the half-full bottle from the crook of his arm. He shifted again, oblivious.

Coda jumped down and followed Jane into the dining room. With Coda curling around her legs, Jane zipped open her tote bag. Dug in. In seconds, she'd rewound the Quik-Shot video to the very first moment she'd arrived at Curley Park, her first shaky wide shots of the scene. Frame by frame, she inched the video forward. She knew just what—well, who— she was looking for. Red hair, blue oxford shirt, khaki pants. She'd seen

Calvin Hewlitt in Franklin Alley, gotten video of him in handcuffs. Had her camera also seen him at Curley Park?

There were all the cops. The crowd. The flashing lights of the ambulance. That brown paper bag that had caught the breeze fluttered by her. And *there*. At the outside of the circle around the body and moving away fast. Calvin Hewlitt. Caught on Jane's little camera. Exactly where he'd insisted he never was.

"Jake!" she called out, then remembered he was asleep. And then she remembered why she'd shot that video: as a reporter for Channel 2. Remembered who Jake was. A cop investigating a crime. And remembered, by all the rules of journalism, she could not show it to him.

Or could she? What was the goal, anyway—to break a big story, or to bring justice? Why couldn't that be the same thing?

"What?" Jake's eyes fluttered as he scooted himself upright. He yawned, dragged his hands across his face. "Yow. Sorry. I'm wiped."

"I have Calvin Hewlitt," Jane said. They'd figure out the ethics later. "At Curley Park. Right here on camera."

"You do?" Jake tumbled from the couch, was at her side in two steps. "Let's see."

Jane rewound the Quik-Shot, held it out to him. "This is before the alley thing. It puts him right here. So funny, though. When I heard De-Luca yelling at you about him, I couldn't figure out what D was saying. *Hyoo*-something. I didn't know it was Hewlitt."

Jake had a funny look on his face. "Hyoo?" he said.

66

Well, this was a first. Jane sat in the front row of Mayor Elihu Holbrooke's news conference, middle seat in the line of dented metal folding chairs set up in the walnut-paneled conference room. She was here without portfolio, except as secret girlfriend of the cute cop now standing cross armed (and freshly shaved, she noted) on the raised carpeted dais and as the secret almost-relative of the woman now charged with the attempted murder of her husband.

Another first: Jane hoped to keep all that knowledge from the swarm of media types now filling the chairs around her. Though Robyn and Lewis Wilhoite's names were irretrievably public, the cops were calling it "a domestic," shorthand for "no one else is in danger so we're done." No reporters knew about the little girl in the middle of it all.

Lewis would recover, and if there were a trial, he'd certainly testify. Melissa and Daniel had whisked Gracie to Chicago, as already planned, and were working out what to tell her. Jane crossed her fingers, and, as almost Aunt Jane, asked the universe to take care of her new niece.

But City Hall was under siege. The secret taping of the chief of staff's greenroom and the alleged extortion plot of Bartoneri, Dahlstrom, and Hewlitt had been revealed in a tersely worded press release. The media had been notified to attend a "brief" news conference.

Now the room buzzed with pinging texts and humming cell phones, still photographers checking light levels and elbowing for floor space, a crowded row of TV guys clicking video cameras onto spiky tripods. All the local TV stations sent their big gun reporters, even Channel 3's Emmy-magnet Charlotte McNally. Jane's colleagues. Ex-colleagues. She could have skipped this, she supposed. But she couldn't resist seeing it firsthand.

"Hey, Jane." Beverly Chorbajian, brandishing her reporters' notebook, arrived in a waft of musky-rose. "What're you doing here? Did Marsh Tyson finally get in touch with you? Are you—"

"Long story. Oh." She pointed, relieved to change the subject from Channel 2. "Here comes Siskel. And Holbrooke."

Catherine Siskel, black skirt, white shirt, hair pageboyed, and chunky gold earrings, strode to the podium. Jane knew her husband had been murdered just two days ago. How had she switched off her grief? Was it strength? Or denial? Or necessity?

"I'm Catherine Siskel, Mayor Elihu Holbrooke's chief of staff," she said. "The mayor will make a short statement. He will take no questions. Bottom line, everything is under investigation. Understood? You ask a question? We're done. Got it?" She scanned the room over the top of Jane's head, assessing. "You rolling?"

"Rolling," a voice from the back.

The silver-haired Brahmin marched to the podium in gray worsted and burgundy tie. Still cameras flashed, their pops of light and clicking motor drives punctuated his movements as he adjusted the microphone, raised his chin, calculated the waiting audience.

He had everything money could buy, his opponents in the mayor's race had sneered. But he couldn't buy away the murder that had taken place right under his window. Or the involvement of his own employee. Or the discovery of a dirty cop.

"Almost exactly forty-eight hours ago . . ." Mayor Holbrooke looked at his watch as if he were actually calculating and not reading from the huge-fonted typed pages Jane could see in front of him. "Our city was hit with a series of terrible crimes. But through the brave and quick-thinking work of our city's homicide division, we can confidently say the danger is over."

"How could your own surveillance chief be involved in extortion and sales of sex tapes?" Charlotte McNally stood—how'd she always manage to get the first question?—pointed a thick ballpoint at the mayor. "Did you know of the greenroom camera?"

Siskel flew to the podium, frowning, edged in front of the mayor, both hands waving McNally off. "No questions! I specifically—"

But now more reporters clamored to their feet, one after the other, pelting Holbrooke with demands, their voices overlapping.

"So a police detective was in on it? What's her status?"

"Can you confirm that your chief of staff's husband was the Curley Park victim?"

"Who killed Greg Siskel?"

Jane couldn't bear it. She stood, not exactly looking at Jake. He'd understand. She was doing it for the public's right to know.

"Does City Hall have surveillance video of the Curley Park stabbing?" she asked.

67

"Who was that on the phone?" Tenley Siskel stood at the entrance to their kitchen, saw her mother standing at the sink, staring out the window, her cell phone on the counter. Tenley knew Mom was looking across their backyard to the lush oaks and maples of Steading Woods. Where Lanna had gone, and never come back.

"Come here, honey." Her mom turned to her, holding out one arm. She was still in her black funeral suit but had kicked off her black heels, like she always did, left them in the middle of the kitchen floor. "Come talk to me."

Funny how, like, a week ago, Tenley would have been mad because her mom was thinking about Lanna. Funny how so much had changed.

"It was Detective Brogan, sweetheart," her mom said. "And . . ."

And then, standing in their kitchen like it was any old day even though it wasn't, Mom told her what the detective learned. They were still in the midst of an "interview" with Hewlitt, he'd said, but he wanted them to know that the cop who'd questioned Tenley about Lanna—that creepy Angela Bartoneri who Tenley had never liked—was part of the whole thing. Detective Brogan said that while investigating Lanna's death, Bartoneri discovered Lanna's connection with Ward Dahlstrom, as well as his secret taping with college crony Hewlitt. Dahlstrom admitted Angie'd convinced him to let her benefit from their scheme in return for covering it up.

"I always wondered why that Detective Bartoneri couldn't find

Lanna's boyfriend. I guess, in fact, she did." Her mom drew Tenley closer. "Now they've reopened the investigation, honey. It's still possible her death really was an accident. But maybe now we'll get some real answers."

Tenley looked out the window, past the greening forsythia and the last of the tulips. Last year, they had put tulips from their garden on Lanna's grave. And earlier this morning on her father's.

Now it was just the two of them. She felt the weight of her mother's arm around her waist, a weight that was good and strong and connecting.

"Why did Dad have to die?" Tenley couldn't believe she was asking that out loud, but Dr. Maddux had told her to always say what was in her heart, and maybe now she knew there was no other way.

"Oh, Tenner." Her mother turned, put one hand on each of Tenley's shoulders. Tenley knew she was trying to smile, but her eyes were still red from the funeral, and Tenley knew her own eyes probably looked exactly the same way. "According to Detective Brogan, your father refused to give that—whoever he was—any money. When that person found out Greg was refusing to pay, and threatening to tell the police, he tried to stop him—and stabbed him. And ran."

"What do we do now?" Tenley asked.

"We wait and see. It's only been three days. Brileen's with the lawyer. We'll see what we can do for her, too." Her mom reached out, cranked open the kitchen window. A waft of early-summer breeze came through the screen, and Tenley saw her mother's chest rise with a deep breath. "When you and Detective Brogan saw her meeting Hewlitt, she was telling him Valerie had come out to her parents, and as a result he had no more hold on her. He bolted when the cops arrived at the U. But Ten? If you hadn't forced me to talk to her, none of this would have been solved. We know what happened to your father, and maybe to Lanna—only because of you."

Tenley tried to figure that out, tried to understand how each little decision anyone made pushed the world in a direction they could never predict, and how even when good people tried to do the right thing, it wasn't always perfect, so how did you even know? But it was too big, and too hard, and her mom was right. They'd wait and see. Together.

"I love you, Mom," Tenley said.

68

Jake stood in the hallway outside the interrogation room, hung up his cell phone, stashed it back in his pocket. Through the one-way window he saw Calvin Hewlitt sitting at the conference table, buzzing with anger and shepherded by the pinch-faced lawyer who'd arrived in a flurry of brief-case and demands. Jake had left them to stew with DeLuca. The Siskels needed to know what he'd discovered.

He still felt the weight of the phone call he'd just made to Catherine Siskel. There would be more to come, especially in the fight over the sub-poena for the City Hall surveillance. But since Jake and the Siskels had nailed Dahlstrom and his co-conspirators Hewlitt and Bartoneri with their greenroom trap, it turned out the forbidden tape wasn't needed to clinch that case.

As he'd told Catherine Siskel, they simply needed Brileen Finnerty. If she'd turn state's evidence, she'd be their star witness. Now, with Finnerty as potential ammunition, Jake was about to fire his final shot. He entered interrogation room C. Endgame.

Hewlitt's attorney stood, as if some "round two" bell had clanged. "Detectives, we're ready to provide certain information," she said, flapping over a page of her yellow pad, "in return for—"

"That's not how it works, Ms. O'Shaughnessy." Jake clanked open a battered folding chair but didn't sit. "Information first, then we go to the DA. As you are well aware. Ready, Mr. Hewlitt?"

Jake had seen this look before, the deflating of arrogance, the collapsing of ego, the cold realization that whatever a suspect had believed about his own invulnerability, it was defeated by the sometimes successful system of justice.

Sometimes, like today, it worked.

"Hewlitt?" Jake said. "Again, this is all being recorded. First. You're Hugh, correct?"

The lawyer gestured a weary hand toward her client.

"Whatever."

"That a yes?" DeLuca sat the end of the table, one ankle on the other knee. He pointed toward a microphone mounted in the corner. "You have to say it out loud, Hewlitt. You know how tape works, don't you?"

"Yes," Hewlitt said to the corner.

And it was yes that Angie Bartoneri was in cahoots with Hewlitt and Dahlstrom. Hewlitt had explained she'd hired a street guy named Rodney Field to do the money-for-thumb-drive exchange.

"All he had to do was take the fricking bag," Hewlitt complained. "It wasn't my fault he went nuts when Siskel refused to pay. He'd put a fricking phone book in the bag to make it look heavy. Field told me he thought it meant *he* wouldn't get paid. Fricking crankhead. I *told* you the truth! I told you he was the bad guy. Remember? You should charge *Field* with murder, not me."

"Mr. Field is dead," Jake reminded him. Angie was, too, professionally and personally.

DeLuca leaned toward Hewlitt, pointing. "After we stopped *you* from trying to kill Rodney Field, you knew Angie Bartoneri would make sure of it."

And then Jake saw the whole thing, how even though relying on surveillance felt reliable, felt unassailable—in reality, it wasn't.

"Think of it, Hewlitt," Jake said. "If you'd succeeded? You'd have been the hero. Catching the Curley Park killer. And the surveillance tapes would have proved you right. Except they'd be wrong."

"Screw you, *Officer*," Hewlitt said.

Jake shot D a look. *Don't.*

"Nice mouth," DeLuca said instead. "Getting ready for lockup?"

"We're done." Hewlitt's lawyer stood, flapped her legal pad closed. "I'll wait for your call, Brogan."

In fifteen minutes, Hewlitt was in custody, DeLuca at his desk with one last assignment, and Jake in his car. He pulled out of the HQ parking lot. Four hours until takeoff. But this damn case still bugged the hell out of him.

The whole crime was caught on camera, Catherine Siskel had admitted it, all on the illicit City Hall video. At least now they knew what it meant. But according to the supe, Mayor Holbrooke and the lawyer Kelli Riordan had already called, strong-arming them to withdraw the subpoena, demanding that the police superintendent, a mayoral appointee, keep the taping confidential. The supe had ordered Jake—"for now"—not to mention it. Jake wouldn't be surprised if the supe had known about it all along. But the cover-up appeared to be under way.

That was way above Jake's pay grade. He wasn't sure how he felt about caving to City Hall, but he'd decided not to think about it. For the next four days, at least.

But he had one more thing on his preflight checklist. One last bit of police work before he turned off his brain.

Angie Bartoneri. What had happened to twist her from ambitious young cop to a jaded manipulative . . . ? Well, greed, he guessed. Power. Ego. A destructive combination. And in a cop, especially dangerous. She'd even leaked information to the media. Unforgivable.

She'd admitted she'd tried to cover up Greg Siskel's identity to give her crew time to get their stories straight. But was she complicit in murder? Though Jake's crime scene guys were on it, there was no real evidence to link her to Bobby Land's death. Jake needed a smoking gun to put her away forever.

He stopped at the light at Beacon Street, pulled out his cell phone, scrolled to D's speed dial.

"Anything?" he said.

"You oughta be a cop," DeLuca said. "Guess our Ms. Bartoneri forgot there was surveillance video in the back of the ambulance. We got her dead to rights, yanking out the poor tattoo guy's oxygen tubes. She put 'em back just as they arrived at Mass General. And Jake? Get this. It also shows her swiping his ID. She probably took Greg Siskel's, too. And his phone. She just couldn't know he'd hidden the thumb drive in his shoe. She was there, right?"

"So . . ." Jake smiled, listening as D explained. "Live by the sword, you know?"

"Yup," DeLuca said. "What you see is what you get."

"What Angie Bartoneri gets is murder one," Jake said.

69

For a moment, the only sounds Jane heard were the roar of the jet engines and the rattle of suitcases, black rectangles on wheels, rolling side by side across the concrete pavement of the short-term lot at Logan Airport.

Her gray chiffon maid of honor dress was safely in Chicago, pre-teen Eli upstairs happy to cat-sit Coda. Wedding of the century in progress as planned, with Daniel telling her "he'd always suspected" about Gracie but that there was "more to love and fatherhood than DNA." Gracie had sent Auntie Jane a selfie, her little arms wrapped around a smiling Melissa. Next to them was Lolly, Gracie's white cat, who everyone agreed should be wherever Gracie was. Today was all about beginnings, not about endings. Which is why they ought to change the name of the parking lot.

"Terminal parking," Jane said. "They should call it something else, you know?"

"Jane." Jake's suitcase wheels came to a halt.

She turned, wondering. "You forget something?"

"Thank you, you know? For showing me that Quik-Shot video?"

A car eased by. Jane stepped away, even though it couldn't be anyone who'd care. But it might be they'd have to start hiding again. Maybe.

"That must have been a tough call for you."

Jane rolled her suitcase to tap his. "Aw," she said.

She paused, stepped back as another car trolled past them. The golden light of the afternoon spilled through the open sides of the parking lot, casting Jake's face in half shadow. She and Jake would be away—together—

for four whole days. They had so much to discuss, but she couldn't do it right now. And who could predict the future? She'd wait. Tread lightly. She didn't have to tell Jake everything. Right now, at least.

She gestured toward the elevator, pulled the handle of her roller bag. The two sets of wheels sounded again as they walked.

"I was at Channel 2 after the news conference, though," she said, skipping the important part of that meeting. The part where Tyson had offered her the job. The part where she said she'd think about it. "I gave the tape back to Marsh Tyson. So if you want it again, you're gonna have to subpoena it. Without mentioning me." She poked his arm to remind him. "I know the station won't give it to you."

"Ow," Jake said. "Turns out it wasn't the tape we needed to clinch it. It was simply you saying 'hyoo.' That's when I remembered what Brileen Finnerty had said in the greenroom. I'd never heard 'Hugh' before."

Jane thought back, remembering when she'd first heard DeLuca yelling the name. When Bobby Land had latched on to her as his ticket to the big time.

"Poor Bobby Land." She pushed the elevator button. "All he wanted was fame."

"Well, you know," Jake said, "if Bobby Land hadn't bragged about what he saw, Hewlitt would have ignored him. If Hewlitt hadn't trashed Land's camera, we might not have been able to take him into custody. If it hadn't been for Bobby Land, they might have gotten away with it."

"So Bobby gets to be famous after all," Jane said. "He'd have loved that. I'll talk to his mother, maybe. Maybe do a story about him."

She winced. Had Jake heard that? The elevator doors opened, and the two of them circled their luggage into the space. The silver doors closed them in, and Jane pushed the button for their floor. They were off, on a journey of family, and change, and reunion, and healing. Families were not always easy.

"So," Jane began. She had one more question. She wasn't sure whether Jake would answer, but she had to ask. Even though she wouldn't be a reporter again until—well, she'd think about that when she got back. "Is there a City Hall surveillance tape of the Curley Park murder? Catherine Siskel cut off the news conference without answering. But did Dahlstrom or Siskel ever admit it existed?"

"So, this," Jake said. He patted his jacket pockets, reached into the inside left.

Was he about to give her a tape? Or a DVD or something? Of what?

"You don't have to give it to me now," she said. They'd arrived. The elevator doors slid open, and they walked side by side into the light-filled expanse of the Logan terminal. "Over there," she said, pointing past a chattering group of backpacking kids and a line of blue-suited flight attendants. "We need to check for the gate."

But Jake wasn't following her. She stopped, pivoted, turned back to him.

"'You don't have to give it to me now,'" he said, imitating her. He reached out, a look on his face she'd never seen before, and offered her a little white box tied with a light blue ribbon. "Jane Elizabeth Ryland? I think I do."

"What—is it?" she asked, although as soon as she saw the box, she knew. Inside was her future. *Their* future. And here they were, surrounded by the hubbub of hundreds of others traveling their own journeys. Some arriving, some departing, some, like them, at the beginning. If they could make it work. Jake apparently thought they could. Did she? Could they?

"What is it?" Was all she could manage.

Jake leaned in close. Kissed her. Barely, briefly. "Well, why don't you open it? What you see is what you get."

ACKNOWLEDGMENTS

Unending gratitude to

Kristin Sevick, my brilliant, hilarious, and gracious editor. Thank you. The remarkable team at Forge Books: the incomparable Linda Quinton, indefatigable Alexis Saarela, and copy editor Cynthia Merman, who noticed everything, thank you. Another wow of a cover—my story fully realized—from Seth Lerner and Vanessa Paolantonio. Desirae Friesen and Bess Cozby, I am so grateful. Brian Heller, my champion. Bob Werner, you are amazing. The inspirational Tom Doherty, leader of us all. What a terrifically smart and unfailingly supportive team. I am so thrilled to be part of it. Thank you.

Lisa Gallagher, a wow of an agent, a true goddess, who changed my life and continues to do so.

Francesca Coltrera, the astonishingly skilled independent editor who lets me believe all the good ideas are mine. Editor Chris Roerden, whose care and skill and commitment made such a difference. Editor Ramona DeFelice Long—your insights are incomparable. You all are incredibly talented. I am lucky to know you—and even luckier to work with you.

The artistry and savvy of Maddee James, Jen Forbus, Charlie Anctil, Erin Mitchell, and Mary Zanor.

The inspiration of John Lescroart, Mary Jane Clark, Linda Fairstein, Tess Gerritsen, Lisa Unger, Mary Higgins Clark, and Reed Farrel Coleman. To Linda Miele, Alice Jacobs, Ed Ansin, and Chris Wayland—thank you for letting it happen, for your vision and your devotion to journalism.

Sue Grafton. And Lisa Scottoline. And Lee Child. Words fail me.

My darling posse at Sisters in Crime, and the dear Guppies. Thank you. Mystery Writers of America, you rock. Facebook pals, thanks for the grammar guidance, character names, and enthusiasm.

My amazing blog partners. At Jungle Red Writers: Julia Spencer-Fleming, Hallie Ephron, Rosemary Harris, Roberta Isleib/Lucy Burdette, Susan Elia MacNeal, Jan Brogan, Deborah Crombie, and Rhys Bowen. At Femmes Fatales: Charlaine Harris, Dana Cameron, Kris Neri, Mary Saums, Toni Kelner, Dean James, Elaine Viets, Donna Andrews, and Catriona McPherson. At Lipstick Chronicles: Nancy Martin and Harley Jane Kozak, who brought us all together.

Law enforcement and surveillance insiders who, as promised, will remain nameless, thanks for the scoop.

My dear friends Amy Isaac, Laura DiSilverio, Mary Schwager, and Katherine Hall Page; and my darling sister, Nancy Landman.

Dad—who loves every moment of this. And Mom. Missing you.

And Jonathan, of course, who never complained about all the pizza.

Do you see your name in this book? Some very generous souls allowed their names to be used in return for an auction donation to charity. To retain the magic, I will let you find yourselves.

Sharp-eyed readers might notice I have tweaked Massachusetts geography a bit. It is only to protect the innocent, so forgive me. And I adore it when people read the acknowledgments.

Keep in touch, okay?

www.hankphillippiryan.com
www.jungleredwriters.com
www.femmesfatales.tyepepad.com